Bound Island

G.D. Roman

Midnight Tide Publishing

Bound Island

Copyright © 2023 by G.D. Roman

Published by Midnight Tide Publishing | https://www.midnighttidepublishing.com

Edited by Shadow Rain Publishing | https://www.instagram.com/shadowrainpublishing

Book Cover by Maria Spada | https://www.mariaspada.com

Map Illustration by Danielle Graves | https://www.instagram.com/designsbydaniellelg

eBook ISBN: 9798988310303
Paperback ISBN: 9798988310310
Original Publication Date: November 22, 2023

Note to Reader

This book has references to: fantasy violence, emotional and physical abuse, burns, mass violence (burning of bodies), coarse language, and the death of a parent.

To all of us bound together.

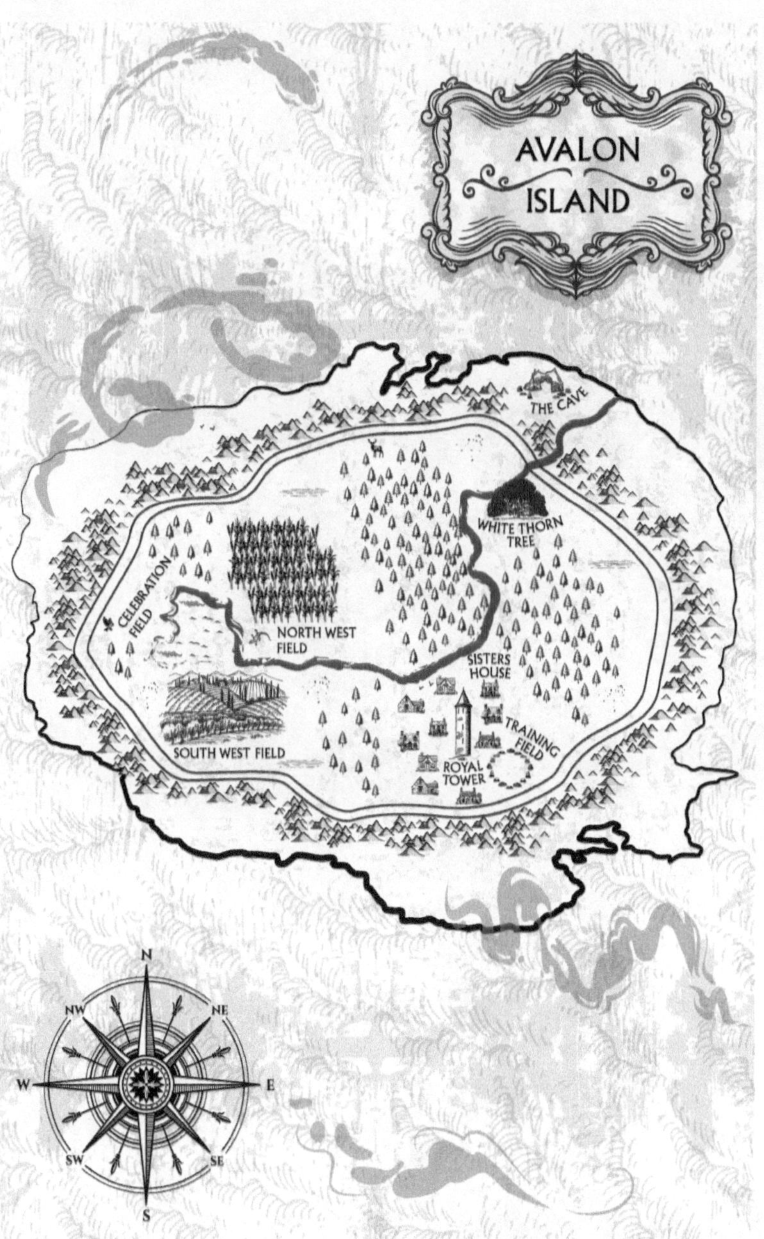

AVALON
ISLAND
THE CAVE
WHITE THORN TREE
CELEBRATION FIELD
NORTH WEST FIELD
SISTERS HOUSE
TRAINING FIELD
SOUTH WEST FIELD
ROYAL TOWER
N
NW
NE
W
E
SW
SE
S

Part I

Bedtime

EVERY PARENT HAS TRUTHS they live by, even in the chaos. A single second can last a lifetime. There are never too many questions. A story can give comfort as much as a hug, a kiss, or a kind word. Children are most cranky when hungry or sick.

As a mother, Elsywth knew all these things, but she asked herself the same question every night. When eyelids grew heavy and the sun had long since set.

Every.

Single.

Night.

Will this be the day they finally get to sleep on time?

"*Maither!*" Tara's deep, russet eyes grew round as she pulled at her dress. "Tell us the story of the Three Founders."

No, it will not.

It was bedtime, and all three girls sat waiting at the worn table. They had finished their chores and now looked expectantly at their mother. Elsywth held back a groan. A cold shiver ran down her spine, and she removed Tara's tight fingers from her sleeve. "You've heard this story a million times."

"It still is a wonderful story, *maither*," her oldest child Brye added to the petition. It was rare for those two to agree on anything, but this was one point they always had.

"What do you say, Lenna?" Elsywth asked. Her middle child sat on the table with her back straight, and her gaze lost.

"If they want to." Lenna shrugged.

"Alright, but no interruptions and the three of you will get in bed."

Chairs immediately scraped back. One chair almost fell over in the girls' haste to get in bed. Elsywth picked up their empty dishes and plates as they padded into the next room.

A large archway connected the sleeping room to the main living quarters. Half of the space was filled with toys and children's clothes. No matter how often the little girls organized their playthings, it only took moments for the room to become a walking hazard. It appeared remarkably more organized this evening, with Tara's toy swords leaning against a small table full of discarded flowers and a basket of threads.

The room's liveliness grew as her daughters battled to get in bed. Day clothes were abandoned in favor of night dresses. Water was splashed, and squeals erupted as Brye scrubbed Tara's face. Lenna stood back with a towel and waited her turn.

Elsywth was about to intervene when they finally headed for the bed they shared. Brye pushed Tara to the side. Tara whined, and Brye made a face at her. Lenna sighed and placed herself between the two before her mother said so. Tara hugged Lenna while she gripped the blanket. Lenna leaned in and played with Tara's curls. Brye sat back, satisfied she got her way.

"We are ready!" Tara announced.

Elsywth's laugh filled the room, and she fought the desire to snuggle and kiss them to death, but she knew they wanted their story.

She walked to their side of the room and sat on the bed, patting Tara's leg over the covers. Elsywth's heart swelled with joy. How many more nights did she have left to enjoy them? Children grew quickly, and her little girls would not be little for long. Isn't that why parents spend so much time retelling stories, repeating snuggles, and watching tiny eyes droop? Wanting to keep them like this forever?

"*Maither?*" Tara impatiently tugged at her sleeve again.

Elsywth shook herself. "A long time ago, there was a vast place we called the Continent," she started. "It was so far-reaching it took weeks, sometimes months, to travel from west to east. Like its rulers, its name has changed over the ages, but it remains a large land divided by race. When societies began to form—"

"What are societies?" Tara asked.

"It is when people get together to create villages like ours. To live and work together, as we do here," Elsywth explained.

"*Maither* already told us this," Brye complained.

"But I forgot."

"Shhh!" Lenna whispered. "Let her tell the story."

"Shifters and Yuansu were at peace in the beginning times," Elsywth began. "The Shifters were strong warriors, skilled when in tune with their animals. The Yuansu were wise, with vast knowledge of the elements and spells. They worked together to build their world, and there were no divisions between them. It was seen as favorable that races mix. Only by working together would both Shifter and Yuansu be stronger."

"Strong like me?" Tara whispered.

Brye groaned.

"Yes, like you and your sisters." Elsywth patted her leg again. "Magic holders were born in almost every generation. The strongest of the Shifters, or the most experienced of Healers, did not belong to one race alone. Magic would choose to whom it was born. There could be powerful Yuansu Shifters like dragons immune to most magic.

"Those born of magic would learn their trade and help their people. Everyone lived in harmony. But, one day, a new Shifter King came to the throne."

"The Mad Shifter King," whispered Tara in awe. Brye shushed her.

"Yes, a Shifter who became mad. Mad with power. He thought Shifters and Yuansu were not alike."

"He knew there were magical beings even more powerful than him, right, *maither*?" Tara interrupted again.

"The Pure Ones," Brye answered. She had stopped shushing Tara, lost in the story. Lenna's eyes grew wide.

"Yes, the Pure Ones. The Mad Shifter King did not trust the Pure Ones, especially when they were his children. He had only three children. Two girls and a boy. They were the most powerful beings of their time: a Shifter, an Elemental, and a Bondmaker."

"Tell us about the Shifter, *maither*. Was she strong?" Tara asked.

Elsywth nodded. "They all were. Helene the Shifter was the strongest and bravest of her kind. She could channel any animal, connecting to living beings and using their abilities as her own. She understood them, spoke their language, and helped them thrive. She could shift with ease and was a powerful fighter. Of course, she was the eldest of the three. She was born screaming and wailing so strongly, many had to cover their ears."

"Like Tara," Brye giggled.

"Not true!" Tara scrambled onto her elbows to whack Brye, but Lenna patted her back down.

"You are more than her, my wild one." Elsywth rubbed her cheek. "The Elemental could manipulate all four elements and channel them into creating more. But she was temperamental and indulgent. She liked to have fun and to be the center of attention. When she was born, lightning struck the tall tower of the library, destroying it."

"Then Tara is more like her." Brye crossed her arms and nodded. Tara opened her mouth to complain.

"What about Clothos, *maither*?" Lenna interrupted.

"The Bondbaker." Tara imitated Brye by crossing her hands and nodding.

"Bond*maker*," Brye corrected, giving her younger sister a knowing look. "Remember, he was a powerful advisor."

"Clothos the Bondmaker was the rarest Pure One of them all. He could see, read and manipulate the threads of life and time.

He was so powerful that even the Mad Shifter King feared him. The Mad King made him the Grand Master, forcing him to use his magic to hunt down others. The Mad Shifter King went to war against all magic holders, using his Pure One children as tools to accomplish his goals."

"I don't like wars," Lenna moaned. Tara hugged her tightly.

"He hunted magical holders, even his own family. It did not matter if they were powerful. Thousands died. Family and friends betrayed each other, fearing what the Shifter King could do."

"But Clothos did not like that." Brye rubbed Lenna's shivering arms.

"Yes, my little ones. Clothos, the Bondmaker, took action. He and his two siblings knew killing the Mad Shifter King was impossible, for he had many followers. Fanatics that—"

"Fanatics?" Tara asked.

"People who believed he was right and did not question him. They did not tell him he was wrong. They were as dangerous as the Shifter King himself."

"They were not good friends then," Lenna spoke softly. "Real friends tell you when you are doing something wrong, even if they are scared."

Elsywth smiled. "They were not his friends. But the Three Founders were not only friends but family. Family loves you, cares for you, and wants the best for you."

"Like us?" Tara asked.

"Exactly like us. One night, the Bondmaker awoke from a dream. He dreamt of an island off the shores of the Continent. He knew the only way for them to find peace was to make a place for themselves. With the help of the Elemental's power, an island rose from the sea, creating our sanctuary."

"Avalon." Brye smiled.

"Our home of Avalon became a refuge for all those magical holders being prosecuted. Only those who choose to sacrifice their greatest treasure would be permitted to enter. Near the Continent but hidden away by thick mists and treacherous rocks. Our hills and stone walls protect us, and we live here isolated but safe."

"What happened to the Mad Shifter King? Did he ever know he was wrong?" Lenna asked.

"No. Sadly, he never stopped being evil. He died believing he was right. Others took his place. The Continent was divided by the Yuansu and the Shifters, each race choosing its rulers. Till this day."

"That is very sad, *maither*," Brye said. "To always be evil is sad."

"Tell us about the magic," Lenna whispered.

"The Bondmaker fortified the island, creating magical knots in the earth so crops could grow out of season and animals could produce healthy offspring."

"What happened to the Founders?" Tara asked.

"You already know that part," Brye groaned.

"But I want *maither* to tell me!" Tara whined. Elsywth soothed her wild child by patting her leg again.

"The Shifter, the eldest, became our ruler. She was wise and strong. Her favorite was the wolf because she felt more in tune with its needs."

"I love wolves." Tara grinned.

Elsywth continued, "The Elemental was the youngest, a powerful woman who invoked our mists and controlled the weather. She was instrumental in helping and guiding the magic of the elements.

"Clothos, the Bondmaker, was wise beyond his years. With the help of his sisters, he created the bindings which help protect our island and give us everything we need."

"Bindings *maither*?" Lenna asked. She sat up straighter. Brye leaned back, lowering herself into the bed. With her favorite part over, Tara yawned and pulled the bed sheets up to her chin.

"Yes, like when you create your tiny tapestries, Lenna. You tie the threads together." Elsywth linked her fingers to show them.

"What happened in the end, *maither*?" Brye asked, even as her eyes dropped. Lenna was the only one left sitting up.

"All three Founders lived for centuries. Until one fateful night, the Shifter Queen of Avalon was killed with a glass dagger by newly arrived Dragon Shifters from the Continent. Clothos, always so wise, feared it would happen again. With his last breath, he bound the walls around the island. Any magic holder born on the island would serve the people, and those who chose to use their gifts to harm would have their magic drained away."

"And the Elemental?"

"She disappeared after Clothos did. No one knows what happened to her."

"But what about Roweena, our royal advisor? Does she not know magic?" Lenna asked.

"She does. She was a Mist Maiden and now the most powerful advisor in the land. She continues the Founders' legacy by protecting our island and village."

Tara was sleeping softly, her head burrowed against Lenna. Brye had turned away from her sisters, the blanket covering most of her head. Only a tiny puff of hair appeared at the top. Lenna was the only one still awake, sandwiched between her sisters. Her brow furrowed.

"What is it, Lenna?"

"What happens if they break?"

"If what breaks, sweetling?"

"The bindings around our island. Our protection. Will something bad happen? Will the Mad Shifter King come?"

Elsywth gripped her daughter's hand and looked deep into her eyes, a mirror of hers. As she did, a voice echoed softly in her head. A voice tied itself around her heart and haunted her dreams. A voice she knew well.

A shiver ran down her spine.

Until the knots of Avalon break.

"Nothing," Elsywth replied slowly. "Nothing will happen, for the bindings are eternal. We are safe here, on our island. From the mad shifter kings and anything that wishes to harm us."

"Promise, *maither*?"

"Of course, sweetling." Elsywth helped her daughter lay down and placed a kiss on her forehead. "I promise.

Societal Expectations

15 years later...

Lenna

"Are you even listening?"

Lenna slowly blinked her deep, green eyes and focused on Enid again.

"No," she responded honestly.

Enid groaned, and Caitlin, who sat beside her, sighed. She must have called more than once. They had been gossiping about something. What was it?

Right, mating season.

Lenna returned the flower rings she was making.

Beltane, the well-anticipated celebration, had arrived, signaling the time between the spring equinox and the summer solstice. It meant the lighting of the Beltane fire at sunset and an all-night festival that ended in the early morning hours.

Decoration and preparations fell to the women while the men were in charge of the ale, boar, and the celebration area next to the lake in the west field. Presently, Caitlin's house was filled with trimmed branches and May flowers used to create flower rings.

The house was like all homes in Avalon—one-floored with an extensive cooking and working area. Usually, the sleeping area was an adjacent room, but long ago, it was divided into two smaller spaces giving their only son, Aiden, privacy.

Today, the main area was packed to the brim with flowers. The two tables were piled with buttercups, daisies, fairy foxglove, sceach gheal, lavender, and roses. The small fire in the hearth intensified their scent, confusing the insects that entered through the open windows and door.

Work was not limited to the day of the event. The day before, the women—with neighbors' help—had created various branched rings for the crowns. This morning, they'd begun weaving flowers and ribbons into the rings, a tedious task that would take them most of the day.

Enid, the Healer with a round figure, pleasant face, and demeanor, was the eldest of the group. She passed the finished decorations to Caitlin beside her.

Aiden's mother, Caitlin, was the same age as Enid, with a medium build and shoulder-length curly brown hair. Her eyes were bright, and her smile was easy. Both women were old friends of Lenna's mother. Since Elsywth's disappearance, they felt it was their duty to give an opinion on Lenna's future and well-being.

Well, not just her. They would also impart their wisdom to Brye and Tara when they could. Except for today, when her sisters were elsewhere. Brye was tending to patients while Enid was here. Tara was probably working with Aiden in the fields or preparing the celebration area. She avoided gossip like the plague.

Lenna was not as lucky, which was why she attempted to ignore them. Gossip was a great deal of nonsense. She had more exciting things to consider, like imagining a new tapestry work or clothing design.

Lenna's mind wandered to those more pleasurable activities until Enid brought her back to the tedious task with one short phrase.

"Have you heard?" Enid said before she took a sip of tea.

"No," Lenna replied, pretending to show interest in the conversation. Since she'd awoken that morning with a persistent heaviness in her head and stomach, she kept losing her focus, her mind distracted. She rubbed her temples as the discussion continued around her.

"The queen is looking for a mate for the prince," Enid shared.

Lenna lowered her hands from her temples and raised her eyebrows. Enid gave her a worried look, but she dismissed it with a shake. "And how does that work?"

Caitlin continued, "The queen decides on a list of qualities important in a future princess. Then, she makes a list of candidates. Those candidates are given to the prince to select a mate."

"From what I heard," Enid poked a rose into the crown, "he has been dragging his heels. It is the second list he has rejected."

"It must be tough to find a maiden with the proper qualities," Caitlin said. "If you give it some thought, she must be regal, intelligent, and diplomatic. I wonder if we know of someone that might own such qualities."

Lenna bit her lip and turned away to roll her eyes. She drummed her fingers on the table before choosing another flower. "Clearly, he's looking for someone of high standing." Keeping her eyes on her work. "I wonder if there are any women with those characteristics. The list must be very, very short."

"Lenna, maybe it's an opportunity, ' Enid pointed out.

"Oh, I am definitely not on that list."

"Do you think so lowly of yourself? You have many fine qualities worthy of a prince."

"Perhaps," Lenna responded. "But fine qualities don't predict compatibility."

"You never know."

Lenna was uninterested in the prince's prospects, and so were her sisters. In fact, the few times they had crossed paths, he ignored them. It wasn't as if the island was big enough never to cross paths. It was more as if he was always busy or interested in his duties than socializing.

"What about love?" Lenna said, standing and moving to place her completed crown in the full crates by the door. Messengers would soon take the crates to the celebration area for decoration. "I believe finding a mate must also mean falling in love. Does the queen not wish that for her son?"

"I think when you are part of the royal family, you have to consider the village's well-being," Caitlin explained, placing another finished crown on the table. "You need to choose wisely."

Lenna nodded. It made sense, but it seemed a bit disheartening.

The island boasted of having a royal family and a magical advisor who governed and supervised the village's well-being. A little over eight thousand lived on the island, and the population did not grow as quickly as expected. Lenna suspected that the need for mating was based on a diminishing population.

"It's not as if Avalon is a big kingdom. We are more like a large village. The titles they hold are only nominal at best," Lenna muttered. She picked up a buttercup, twirling it with her fingers before sticking it through the ring. "I think the only thing that would compel me, or any of my sisters, to accept a mate would be love."

"Be hopeful if there is one available when you feel ready. Don't be surprised if you end up alone," Enid said with her brow furrowed.

"Don't say that, Enid," Caitlin sighed.

Lenna pinched her lips and shrugged. She rubbed her temples to release the tightness around her head and returned to her work without further comment.

The room grew silent, with each woman lost in her thoughts. Lenna focused on other things, trying to find some interest in the flower crowns, but she couldn't. The branches and thorns pricked her fingers, and the sap made her hands sticky. It was detailed and monotonous work made even more unbearable by the expected topics of conversation.

"Hello!" called a voice from the open door. Lenna looked up sharply and smiled. Warmth spread down her chest, and her heart sped up when Aiden walked in carrying crates with more flowers.

Aiden was tall, like most Avalonean men, broad-shouldered and long-limbed. His most striking features were his ice-blue eyes, decorated with slight wrinkles and surrounded by thick eyebrows and eyelashes. If not for the beard, one would think him older than his twenty-five years.

"I come bearing gifts!" He set the crate by the flower mountain and leaned in to give his mother, Caitlin, a kiss. Then, he turned and gazed around the room, hands on his hips. "You have a very productive workforce, mother." When his eyes fell on Lenna, he bit back a smile. "I also see the birthday girl is hard at work."

"Yes, some of us want to be productive even when it is our birthday," Lenna stated, working a daisy into the crown.

"Will you be dancing, my dearest son?" Caitlin chuckled.

"Wouldn't miss it." He grinned.

"Aiden, stop mingling. We have things to do," hailed a thick voice from the door. A contrast of oranges and gold, Tara's lean frame entered the room with the same power as the sun.

Almost as tall as Aiden, Tara's skin was a warm, deep tan, covered in freckles around her nose, cheeks, and shoulders. These only multiplied due to her unquenchable need to be outdoors.

"I hope you dance with the available girls," Caitlin continued. "I know of a few that will be waiting anxiously. Take this night seriously. You are not getting any younger."

"I take duty very seriously," he responded. "When it's convenient." He gave Lenna a wink. She rolled her eyes and went back to work.

"Aiden," Tara said. "We've got to go."

Aiden stood straight and uncrossed his arms. "See you all later, ladies."

He knocked his knuckles on the table in front of Lenna. She raised her gaze, mouthing *flirt*. He chuckled.

"See you later, Lenna?" Tara called from the door, her scowl back in place. Aiden waved goodbye to his mother, and they disappeared as swiftly as they arrived.

"Your son is getting more handsome by the day." Enid chuckled. "He will be a wonderful mate for any girl."

"Yes," Caitlin spoke slowly, releasing a sigh. "My son is well aware of that." She smiled.

"Does he have someone?" Enid asked in a whispered tone.

"Oh, I am sure he has more than one," Caitlin said sternly. "If they are serious, it is yet to be decided."

"Do you think Tara is interested in him?" Enid asked Lenna as she passed a completed crown.

Aiden and Tara. It was more than a possibility. They spent a lot of time together.

And Tara was a bit territorial of him.

One of them may make a move.

But it wasn't up to Lenna to say anything, especially to Enid and Caitlin.

"I don't know. My sisters don't tell me everything." Lenna answered. It was increasingly more difficult to follow the conversation. Her stomach and head grew heavier, while a tingling along her spine only increased her discomfort. She ignored it and picked up the reddest rose on the table.

"Well," Caitlin said in whispered tones. "It would be nice for him to settle with a decent woman finally."

"Good and decent?" Lenna asked.

"Someone who makes him happy. It is all a mother ever wants."

All a mother ever wants.

Lenna didn't have that privilege. Her mother had been gone for fifteen years, and her memories were non-existent.

How would Lenna know what her mother would have wanted? Would she have wanted Brye to be twenty-four and unmated? Or Tara running around at eighteen, climbing trees, and waiting for her chance to change the world?

And for me?

Would her mother have wanted Lenna to sit and wait for life to happen to her or take some initiative? What was the right path for an unmated twenty-one-year-old on an enchanted island?

One with secrets so heavy that every birthday was more exhausting than the last.

Lenna leaned back, clenching her jaw and gripping the rose tighter. The thorns pricked her skin, but the pain was only secondary to the cold shivers that ran up her spine. The sensation around her intensified. She was so tired of wondering what her life should be.

A snap rang inside her chest as if a thread had been pulled taut, only to break under pressure.

The crowns on the table burst into flames. Enid and Caitlin thrust their chairs backward, screaming as the flowers in their hand crawled with angry fire. They tossed them into the enormous mountain of blooms by the door, and the room erupted.

Lenna leaped out of her chair. It toppled, hitting the back of her legs.

What have I done?

"Out!" yelled Caitlin and pushed Enid out the door. Lenna backed against the wall. Her hands were stiff at her sides, her mouth agape.

No, no, no...

The smoke grew, and she coughed. Lenna's eyes burned, and she gripped the wall, terrified to move. A tall shadow came into the room and lifted her effortlessly over the flames. Just as quickly as it started, the fire was put out.

"Are you alright?" Prince Gareth materialized out of the smoke. His chiseled stone face was close, framed by a thick beard and prominent ears. For a moment, his stiffness softened and concern filtered into his dark eyes.

He repeated his question, and Lenna nodded. He let go of her arm.

Lenna bit down hard on her lip and took slow breaths to recover. Her eyes pricked from unshed tears. She raised her hand to pinch her nose, only to realize her fingers were covered in blood from the thorny rose.

"Well, that was unfortunate," stated Roweena, the royal advisor. She must have been with the prince because she came out of the house moments later. She raised her hand and turned it in a circle. The smoke from the windows rose, and the fire died.

"What happened here?" Gareth asked, his eyes falling on all of them. Enid stood close to Lenna, her hand on her shoulder.

"The flowers suddenly caught fire," Caitlin explained. Lenna stared at the floor, gripping her arms against her queasy stomach. Enid rubbed her back. The intense unease only increased when Roweena narrowed her gray-streaked eyes at her.

"Were you close to the hearth? Perhaps a spark jumped onto the flowers?" Gareth continued questioning."

"And you?" Roweena approached Lenna. Their eyes locked.

"I'm going to be sick." Lenna turned away, and vomited all over the path. Enid quickly pulled her hair back.

"I see," Roweena spoke slowly. She tapped her lower lip with her fingers. "I think you should come with me."

"She isn't well," Enid snapped. Caitlin had gone inside the house and returned with a cup of water that she handed Lenna. She gargled some in her mouth before spitting it out.

"She'll feel better now." Roweena motioned for Lenna to follow. "Right, Lenna?"

It was over.

Oh, how she wanted to turn back time. She could start her birthday again, working on tapestries or mending Tara's torn dresses.

Anything but this.

But she couldn't. There was no way to ignore the truth.

She was caught doing magic, and her fate was sealed.

Her few dreams faded one by one as her eyes settled on Roweena's expectant face. The Lenna that moments ago was irritated by gossip and bored by flower crowns and thoughts of mating ceremonies was packed up inside with the rest of her disappointments.

"I feel better now." She gave Enid a forced smile, recovering her self-control. The woman's eyes betrayed her concern.

"Maybe you should rest."

"I will be fine." Lenna squeezed Enid's hand. "I'll see you later at Beltane." She leaned in to kiss her and whispered in her ear. "Please don't tell Brye or Tara. I will tell them later."

Enid nodded, and Lenna turned to follow Roweena back to the Royal Tower. The older woman walked before her and only looked back momentarily to ensure she followed. Lenna gripped her hands tighter and held her head high.

Happy Birthday to me.

New Roles

Tara

Aiden and Tara left the crates of flowers in the celebration area by the lake. Warriors, farmers, and women from the village set up the tables and the woodpile for the fire. The sun had borne down on them all day, and Tara couldn't help but complain about the heat.

Repeatedly.

Aiden came up with the usual solution for hot days.

"I'm going for a swim in the small pond in the eastern woods," he said, leaving the celebration area with long strides. "You can join me if you want, or stay here and continue to waste away."

"What about the northern river?" Tara called to him.

"Too far away!" he yelled back, leaving her behind.

Tara growled but quickly followed. They avoided the village by following the southern part of the wall. Once the wall curved and headed north, they would meet the eastern woods. Aiden attempted to engage Tara in conversation, but she mumbled back short responses. Her pace equaled his stride, but she'd often kick anything found in her way.

Since they had left Aiden's house, she couldn't escape the burning in her chest and stomach.

"Are you really looking for a mate this year?" Tara finally asked when they reached the woods. The tall, robust trees were visible in the distance, and the sun was high. She squinted in Aiden's direction.

"So that's what has been bothering you?" Aiden raised an eyebrow as he picked up the pace to get to the coolness of the trees. The woods provided the much-wanted shade while invading their senses with the scent of fern and wildflowers. Tara sprinted to catch up. The woods opened up as they reached the pond, and Aiden let out a long sigh.

The pond was large and deep in some areas. It was empty, except for the buzzing insects and the sound of water that circulated underneath. The underwater stream that connected the pond to the main river kept the water clear and fresh.

Aiden removed his boots, keeping his back to Tara. "It's Beltane. Choosing a mate is part of the celebration. Dancing as well. If I recall, I dance with you every year." He continued to undress, removing his over-tunic, then his undershirt.

Tara turned around, disgruntled. "Can't you give me a warning?"

"It's hot, Tara," he complained. "I am not in the mood to slop around with wet clothes. They are already sticking to my skin." He dropped his pants near her feet. Tara kept her eyes downcast, her face flushing, as red as her hair.

"It's not like I have anything you haven't seen before."

"Really?" Tara crossed her arms. There was a splash as he entered the pond. She cleared her throat a few times and rolled her shoulders to relax. "Going back to Beltane..."

Get a grip on yourself! It's not like it's the first time you have come to the pond. Or the first time you've gone for a swim.

But Aiden was not usually naked.

"I am not having this conversation with you right now," Aiden said.

Tara turned around and placed her hand on her hips. He was kneeling in the deepest part of the pond, scrubbing water over his face. Except for his chiseled chest, and muscled arms, the water obscured her view.

It is still a view.

"Why?"

"Because I don't want to." He leaned back and gave her an assessing look. "I know how your mind works."

"Do you?"

Aiden rolled his eyes. "Are you getting in or not?"

Tara motioned him to turn with her fingers. She took off her boots, belt, pants, and overtunic. She removed her stays last—a laced shirt with boning—but kept her thin, short tunic and under-clothes. Tara shuffled in carefully, feeling the soft, mushy bottom of the pond.

Aiden kept his back to her, and Tara took long strides until she was at the deepest part of the pond. There, she knelt and dunked herself. The cold prickled her overheated skin and scalp. She rose from the water, clearing the excess off her face. A long-satisfied sigh escaped from her lips. Aiden turned back to face her.

"It's just that some girls are awful and desperate. You hate those types of girls." Tara insisted.

"It's just dancing, Tara."

"But it's Beltane, and dancing takes on a new meaning during the celebration."

Aiden walked back a few steps and cocked his head to one side. "You and Brye dance during Beltane as well. Are you desperate for a mate?"

"Us? No! Of course not. Brye is, well... Brye and I... I don't know..." her voice trailed off.

"What don't you know?"

"About that role," Tara spoke slowly. She looked down at the water, her hands balling at her sides. "Being someone's mate. There are so many expectations for a woman. I don't know if it is what

I want. Most Avalonean men want women who will bear them children and tend a home. I can barely cook, and we know how organized I am."

Aiden waded closer until they were a few feet apart. "So, you don't want a mate."

"That is not what I said," she sputtered.

He was getting too close, and it was against their rules. It made her uncomfortable, and she did not know why. Naked men were no big deal. She had seen a few of them. But Aiden was different. He was like a brother to her.

But he wasn't her brother. He wasn't any other man. She took a step back. He stayed where he was.

"Then you do?" He raised an eyebrow and smiled back.

He was teasing her! The nerve!

Tara scowled, and Aiden released his smile. "See? That is why I did not want to continue this conversation. You don't even know what you want."

"I know exactly what I want."

"Oh?" Aiden waved a hand in the air. "Enlighten me, please. What does Tara want?"

"You are being an ass!"

"I know, but so are you." He pointed a finger. She slapped it away, splashing water in his direction.

He was right. She insisted on the conversation, and it was no surprise he was using it for amusement. Tara should have shut her mouth, but imagining Aiden with other girls or looking for a mate. That rubbed Tara even worse.

"Fine!" she said. "What I want is to train to be a warrior."

Aiden froze. "What does this have to do with a mate?"

"What do you think?" she continued. "Men want mates at home. They don't want one who can wield a sword or work the fields like them. They want someone like Brye or Lenna: a homemaker. It's just not me."

Aiden looked away. "Have you asked permission to train?"

"No," she sighed. "But I am considering it."

"What will happen if they deny your request?" His tone was uncharacteristically serious.

"I won't know until I ask." She crossed her hands over her chest under the water. "So, you see, it isn't about wanting a mate. Who will truly have me as I am?"

Aiden took a long breath and made his way out of the pond. Tara turned around. He splashed out and moved along the shore. She wasn't comfortable with his silence.

"You can come out now," he called. Tara got out while Aiden stood with his back to her, his hands on his lips, looking out into the woods.

"Riddle me this," his tone back to its humorous self, "when such a man appears—"

"If," Tara corrected as she removed her wet underthings and tossed them on the grass. Naked, she pulled on her pants and clothes over her damp skin. She was reaching for her shirt when Aiden continued.

"When he appears," he persisted, "what would this man have to do to gain your affection?"

Tara tightened her belt and touched his shoulder. He turned back to her, raising an eyebrow. She picked up her wet things, wringing them as she spoke. "Well, that is a difficult question because I find it hard to believe such a man exists."

"Pretend he does." Aiden crossed his arms over his chest.

"All right." Tara flung her wet clothes over her shoulder. "If such a man did exist, the biggest challenge would be to get along with me. We both know that is a trial by fire on its own."

Tara walked back into the woods toward the village. Aiden kept pace with his hands in his pockets. "Second, he would have to get along with my sisters. Brye would make it hard for him. Lenna will probably like him right off."

"No, she wouldn't," Aiden said. "Lenna would give him a chance. But if she didn't like him, she'd ignore him."

"I keep forgetting how close you and Lenna are," she muttered. He bumped his hip against hers. "Is that all?"

"No." She stopped short. His face was drawn and serious, but his eyes were bright. "It isn't. The hardest point would be to get along with you."

"Me?" Aiden pointed to himself. "What do I have to do with it?"

"I can't imagine my life without you. If that man did not get along with you." She resumed walking. "He isn't worth my time."

Aiden was silent for a long moment, keeping his gaze ahead. Tara glanced at him just before he bumped her with his hip again.

"I am sure someone out there fits that impossible criterion. He would be one poor, lucky bastard."

"To be worthy of me, you mean?" She bit back a smile.

"No, to be worthy of my friendship! With you, he would be in hell." He chuckled. Tara rolled her eyes and elbowed him against the ribs. He groaned.

"Are you going to dance with me?" Tara's face grew warm.

"Of course, Tara. I will always dance with you."

They made their way back to the village side by side. Tara stretched as she walked, in a much better mood than when they arrived.

Old Roles

Lenna

LENNA FOLLOWED ROWEENA BACK to the Royal Tower in silence. Along the path, people were going back and forth, talking and taking food and decorations to the shores of the west lake. Lenna dodged running children, while the smell of flowers and baked goods reminded her of the breakfast she had thrown up in front of Caitlin's house.

Once they arrived at the tower, Lenna's heart sped up in her chest. It was the only tall structure in Avalon. Built in the Founders' time, the tower was made of white stone and clear glass windows, with a massive wooden door for an entrance. The door was open on this special day, welcoming every villager who wanted an audience with the king or queen.

Roweena led her into the tower and the receiving hall. Lenna did not have time to examine her surroundings. She sprinted up the stairs to the second-floor apartments, where the royal family had private audiences.

The small receiving rooms were bright, with windows looking out at the tower's entrance and the long path leading to the village. There was an unlit fireplace, furnished benches, and tall chairs. A small table was paired with two tall chairs, and another was against the wall near an open window. Lenna wrung her hands and bit down hard on her lower lip until Roweena motioned her to sit.

"I will be right back. Please wait here." Roweena lit the fire with a flick of her hand before exiting, leaving Lenna with one of the most dangerous things imaginable—her thoughts.

What had happened? How could she have done it? She should have recognized the signs, the tiredness, and the nauseating sensation. But wasn't that how she always felt? With each passing year, it had grown worse. How was she to know today was going to be any different?

Because it was her birthday.

In previous years, it had been minor. A table turned over when she was upset—a slight drizzle when she was sad. Or pottery would break when she was angry. It never drew the attention of others. Only her sisters knew about her budding magical abilities.

But today, everything changed. Lenna pinched her nose and exhaled a shaky breath. She almost burned Caitlin's house down. They could have been seriously hurt, all because of her untamed magic.

The doors opened again and Roweena entered, placing a gray bag on the table. Lenna released her swollen lip and took her time to assess the woman.

Roweena wore her long black tunic with a silver belt for a touch of elegance. Her face was heart-shaped, with creamy alabaster skin and lips so red they looked unnatural. Soft ebony curls flowed down her back.

But it was her eyes that gave Lenna shivers. Cold dark pools with gray-stricken irises. Like frozen steel, like a prison, trapping Lenna in her stare.

"Are you done examining me?" Roweena crossed her arms over her chest and cocked a brow.

Lenna flushed and looked down at her toes. Roweena sat in the chair opposite and observed her with equal curiosity.

"So, you made the flower crowns burst into flames?" she asked.

"I do not know, madam." Lenna wet her lips, gripping her hands tighter in her lap. A violent nausea swept over her, churning her stomach. Just as fast as it had arrived, the feeling dissipated. She swept her hair off her forehead in a casual gesture, discovering that her face was damp with sweat.

"Oh, come now. No need to evade the question."

Lenna swallowed. "You can't prove I did anything. A spark could have jumped onto the flower crowns."

"I am wondering," Roweena continued the conversation as if Lenna had not participated. "How could you have hidden your magic so well?"

"Perhaps because I do not have any?" Lenna dug her nails into her palm until she left crescent marks. She needed air. The room was suffocating, the fire blazing heat, the open windows doing nothing.

"You can pretend it does not exist, but you have some elemental magic. We need to identify which one and train it."

"If what you said was possible, then it must be very little magic. So little that it isn't worth training."

Roweena scoffed and motioned her hand in dismissal. "All magic, no matter how little, must be trained. And in regards to secrets, Lenna, all secrets come to light eventually. Especially in Avalon."

"I was hoping this one wouldn't be," she whispered.

"Then, you must be very disappointed. Do you know what will happen?"

"No, I do not."

"You have been the first Avalonean to show elemental magic in decades. It is a blessing! It would be best if you became a Mist Maiden, and my future successor." Rowena smiled attentively as she explained. "This means you will practice and perfect your magic in order to protect our island and call the mists. I will teach you everything you must know to accomplish it. However, this also brings sacrifices."

Lenna's heart plummeted in her chest. This couldn't be happening.

"Mist Maidens do not mate and therefore do not have families. They are devoted to the well-being of Avalon and dedicate their lives and magic to its protection and safety."

"And if I refuse? If I do not want to be a Mist Maiden," Lenna attempted to keep her voice stern, although inside, she was breaking.

"What makes you believe you have a choice?" Roweena placed the bag on Lenna's lap. "Inside, you will find a dove gray cloak. It will help you fade into the mists. Training will begin after Beltane. I will have you informed about the specific day."

Lenna sat, her body paralyzed by the sudden weight of responsibility. Tears threatened to fall, but she kept them unshed. She only nodded in response to Roweena's instructions. She had a life. A predictable life focused on her sisters and her tapestries. Now, what will she have? A life devoted to the island, with nothing in return.

"Go, and I will see you tonight."

Lenna carefully gripped the cloth bag with her hands as if it were dangerous and stiffly exited the room.

Once in the hall, she leaned her back against the door. Her body lost its battle with her control. She pinched her nose and headed down the stairs, her steps gaining momentum until she was nearly fleeing. Air, she needed air. And a moment alone—

She crashed into a large body standing on the landing. "I'm so—"

"That's all right," said the prince as he gently steadied her. "Are you feeling better?"

The pressure around her eyes increased, and the pinching did not help. Lenna sniffled, and he led her through one of the oversized doors of the receiving area on the first floor.

Gareth closed the door behind them. Lenna hated him for it. She covered her face with her hands and turned away. He guided her to a bench by the wall and helped her sit.

The kindness was too much.

She burst into tears.

Gareth did not speak, only sat on the bench with his back against the wall. Once her sobs turned to sniffles, he softly kicked the gray satchel. He leaned back and rubbed his face.

"Did you start the fire?"

"Yes." Lenna let out a shaky breath. "And it is the beginning of a new unwanted path for me."

"How so?" He handed her a handkerchief. His features were hard but not unpleasant. Unlike his parents, who seemed to be born regal, the prince was framed like a muscled brawler. He was tall with tanned skin, dirty blond hair, and a scar that ran from his forehead to his left eyebrow, increasing his menacing demeanor.

She tried to remember when they had crossed paths, but her memory ran short. She had met the king and queen upon occasion, but the prince was elusive. Lenna and her sisters always believed he had avoided them. Brye thought he was too full of himself, but that was because he was the only male who ignored her.

But, this prince sitting by her side, talking and asking her questions, was far from that. He seemed attentive and sincere.

It was unexpected.

Why did she feel a kinship? It was there, poking the edge of her memory, but she couldn't grasp it.

"I am to become a Mist Maiden," she explained.

Gareth nodded slowly. "A rare gift, to be born with magic. No one is born with magic in Avalon."

"Apparently, I am an exception."

"You do not want to be a Mist Maiden."

Lenna nodded and leaned her back against the cold wall. It was then she noticed the room. It was a large hall with a tall ceiling, benches against the wall, and two thrones on a dais. The room was covered in dirt and dust. It must have been the old royal audience hall.

The present king and queen preferred to spend their time directly with their people or have small meetings in the upper rooms. For as long as she could remember, the celebrations were held outdoors, even in winter.

The prince was speaking to her again. Lenna shook herself. "Sorry. What did you say?"

Gareth smiled. "If you were not found out, what would you have liked to do?"

"I hadn't decided yet. I do tapestry work, as well as read and write." Things that brought her pleasure, but she hadn't considered what she would do with her life, really.

"Have you considered finding a mate?"

Lenna shrugged. "If there was ever the right person, perhaps."

The prince gazed around the hall, and when he spoke, his words were slow and even, as if he were choosing each one carefully.

"Sometimes," he rubbed his hands against his thick thighs, "we are set on paths we did not choose to walk. We are placed on them and forced to walk them. We might think we don't have control, but we do."

"How?"

"We see where it takes us and, along the way, use it to our advantage. We might not have chosen the path, but we control what we do on it."

Gareth seemed to be attempting to not only convince her, but himself. She remembered the horrid gossip. The queen wanted him to find a mate. Was he trying to find the best option by refusing the lists?

The prince was not who he appeared to be.

She stood, and he did the same.

"Thank you, your highness. You have given me something to think about."

"I always wish to serve my people," he responded with a stiff nod. He motioned to the door, and she led the way. He followed and accompanied her outside. The sun had begun to set, and people headed toward the celebration field.

"I hope you enjoy Beltane this year, your highness." Lenna gave him one of her warmest smiles. His lips twitched somewhat, even if his face remained serious.

"I hope you do so as well, Lenna," he said. "And please have Brye tend to your hand. The punctures look painful."

He bowed before closing the large wooden door. She had forgotten entirely about her hand. The handkerchief was covered in tears and dried blood from the puncture wounds left by the rose. She did not even remember when or where she dropped it.

Lenna took one step, then stopped, her gaze falling to her hand once more.

Brye? How does he know my sister?

Well, she was a Healer. Everyone knew Brye.

But the way he said her name. As if he was unused to it. Lenna looked back at the closed door. It was more than a passing comment. Biting down on her lip, she headed home.

I can't put my finger on it. Why do I feel there is more there?

Mist Maiden

Lenna

Lenna made her way down the bustling paths. They were filled with people who walked merrily toward the east lake, a good ten-minute walk from the town center.

The site of the Beltane fire was one of many places decorated during the celebrations. The entire village took the whole event to heart. Flowers were placed along the doors and windows of the houses. Some even hung ropes of them in between homes. The decorations created a path leading to the lake. The air was imbued with their scents, and many found themselves sneezing their way to the celebration. Lenna was one of the few who was walking in the opposite direction.

Beltane was more than an event. The preparations took days, and every available man and woman looked for a future mate. Today's conversation only proved how much pressure they all were under.

It was as if an invisible presence pushed everyone into motion, and tonight, as the Beltane fire burned, everyone would bow to it continuously. Pressuring them to mate, to start families and increase population. Girls would prepare themselves for hours so that men would ogle and choose. All girls were chosen at one time or another and were given the right to choose.

Lenna rubbed her face trying to erase her thoughts.

It wasn't that she wasn't interested in finding a mate, because she was. It wasn't that she disagreed with drinking, dancing, kissing, sex, or even relationships, because she didn't. Even her sisters danced and drank, kissed and had sex. They had to be desirable activities if everyone engaged in them.

They just didn't happen to her.

Because I never had a chance to begin with. And now?

Who was going to be interested in the new Mist Maiden? Who would even want to be her mate? And she did want one. It only made everything worse.

Lenna paused against a wall to catch her breath. Sweat moistened her forehead, and dizziness came over her. She took deep breaths, and the feeling subsided. Licking her lips, she walked to the village's northern edge at a much slower pace. Here the paths were sparse of people; most had already left.

Her home was a small stone structure with a thatched roof and a carved wooden door. On either side, two windows with wooden shutters squeaked on their hinges. Lenna had decorated the entrance with flower crowns, and Brye added dried blooms and herbs to ward off insects. Apart from these small details, it looked like every other home from the outside. Like many things in her life, what mattered was what was inside.

And she loved her home.

After such a difficult day, she sighed and reached for the handle. She could hear avid conversations coming from within. One loud voice, in particular, made her smile.

Lenna stepped into the main room. It was made up of two rooms connected by an empty doorway. The main room had a cooking area next to an open stone fireplace. Half of the room was full of drying herbs Brye collected for her tonics and mixtures. Her older sister dominated that side and was meticulous in her workspace. Large square hangers contained drying herbs for medicines or teas. A tall bookcase with carefully labeled ceramic jars was beside a long work table by the wall.

Lenna inhaled deeply, pulling in the welcoming scent of lavender deep into her lungs. The sweet and distinct scent was Lenna's favorite part of their home. Brye hung the flower from almost every corner to cover the more potent stench of the other herbs.

Opposite the saturated working area was another long table with chairs where they cooked and shared meals. It was a mix of decorated chaos, with many herbs, sewing materials, and tools lying around the fire and over chairs.

All the furniture was old and tarnished with age and stories. Three small stools from when they were children were placed near the fireplace. A small door led to the washroom, where they would bathe and wash their clothes. Someone must have just exited because the mirror was covered in steam, and toiletries were littered over the sink. The fire was low, and the windows were slightly open.

Home. This chaos is home.

Lenna hardly had time to put down the gray satchel and flowers when Tara jumped from her chair by the fireplace and skipped toward her. She was half-dressed, in her undergarments, her fiery curls untamed. She inspected Lenna from head to toe.

"Finally!" Tara threw her hands in the air. "The birthday girl blesses us with her presence!"

"I wasn't gone that long." Lenna patted Tara's arm.

"Well, long enough for us to need your help."

"Speak for yourself!" called a hoarse, deep voice from the other room. "I didn't need assistance!"

Tara winced. "Traitor!"

Lenna chuckled. "And here I thought I was the birthday girl. What is the tragedy?"

"I already told you. My dress is torn."

"Yes, you mentioned that." Lenna laughed and rolled her eyes as she picked up the green dress hanging on the back of a chair.

Indeed, the hem was torn. She fingered the ragged edges before she placed the dress back on the chair. "Tara," she groaned. "I mended this only yesterday when you gave it to me. What were you up to now?" She moved toward the sink to wash her hands, her skin still stained with blood in places, and she winced as the soapy water touched the wounds.

Tara wiggled her eyebrows, dropping a comb on the table and drumming her fingers. "Besides the hem, you have no evidence I was doing something I was not supposed to."

The owner of the hoarse voice appeared from the bedroom, raising a perfect eyebrow. "We don't need any more evidence. The hem is more than sufficient." Brye gave one of Tara's curls a pull.

Tara scowled, whipping her head to the side to free the curl from Brye's fingers.

If Tara was like the sunrise, Brye was akin to the woods on a sunny day. She was slightly taller than Tara, with a curvy, full figure and elegant beauty accentuated by creamy skin covered in freckles. Brye was the center of attention wherever she went, and she knew it. There was more than one proposal each year, but she still hadn't accepted one.

It did not stop the men from asking.

Brye sat in her underclothes at the table. "I heard about the fire at Caitlin's." Her deep-set dark eyes narrowed with suspicion.

Tara gasped. "Right! I left you there!"

"Thank you for remembering," Lenna said.

"What happened?" Brye leaned in, placing her elbows on the table. One of the straps of the underclothes fell over her shoulder, revealing even more freckles.

"How did you even find out?" Lenna stalled, carefully threading a needle from the sewing kit, using the tedious task as an excuse not to look at her sisters.

"I went to get you and ended up tending to Caitlin and Enid."

"Were they hurt?" Tara asked.

"No, just in shock. Enid acted brave but she was concerned. Caitlin was trembling, but I gave her a mild sedative."

"I am glad they were otherwise unharmed." Lenna kept her gaze on her work.

"So?" Brye insisted.

"Are you going to wear the red dress?" Lenna attempted to change the subject. "I finished adjusting it this morning."

Brye poked Lenna's arm. "What happened?"

"What have you heard?" Lenna laid Tara's dress on the table and checked the stitches. Brye gasped, noticing her cut hand.

Tara hissed at her carelessness while Brye retrieved a small basket by the door. She removed a ceramic bowl and a small bottle of liquid and sat back down. Tara handed her a clean cloth.

"Are you going to tell us how Caitlin's house caught fire and why your hand is covered in puncture wounds? Or do I have to bring Caitlin or Aiden here so they can talk some sense in you?" Tara asked.

That was an unpleasant situation she wanted to avoid. Most of her family and friends badgering her was enough to make her nauseous.

Brye cleaned the wounds with a thick, foul-smelling liquid. Her sister's fingers tingled along her skin.

When did that start to happen?

"Lenna?" Tara prompted.

"Alright." Lenna's shoulders slumped. "Tara, could you get the satchel by the door?"

While Brye wrapped her hand in a long, clean bandage, Tara emptied the bag's contents on the table. The gray cloak slithered across the wooden surface.

Brye's eyes widened, touching the soft edge of the fabric. "They found out?"

"It was an accident." Lenna pressed her free hand over her stomach. She told them everything that happened up to the fire, including the prince's arrival. "He didn't come alone. The royal advisor was with him. Roweena put out the fire even faster than how it started. When she walked out of the house, she knew. I do not know how, but she did. I met with her, and she gave me the cloak."

"Oh, Lenna." Brye reached for her unbandaged hand. Tara sat close and rubbed her back. Lenna exhaled a shaky breath, remembering Roweena's words.

"Secrets always come out. Magic is too difficult to hide."

"What will happen now?" Tara asked.

Lenna walked into their shared bedroom and took out her deep indigo dress, decorated with an embroidery design of tiny silver stars on the bust and cuffs. She had been proud of the fit and low cut. Now, she had to hide it under a drabby gray cloak.

"Tonight, a royal family member will make the announcement, and I will begin training after Beltane."

Brye took her thin hand. As she rubbed her knuckles, the tingling sensation increased. "Lenna, does she know about your condition? If she pushes you too far, it might... I mean...."

Lenna shrugged. She knew her nature, which contrasted with her lively and colorful sisters. Physically, she was the smallest of the three.

She never understood why she had such a weak constitution. It made every task a challenge. She'd tire easily, and sometimes get dizzy spells. No matter how much she ate, her weight would fluctuate. It took them years to consider that perhaps it had to do with her magical abilities.

Between the three, they tried to hide Lenna's magic, fearing the consequences if someone found out. Their caution was for naught. Lenna had no control over what was happening.

"I couldn't tell her anything. She didn't want to hear me." Then, with a heavy sigh, she removed Brye's hand. "There is no point in dwelling on this much longer. We knew; eventually, it was going to happen. Such a shame it had to happen on my birthday!"

Lenna cut off Brye and Tara's attempt to continue the conversation with a wave of her hand. "Where is the red dress?"

Brye stood and removed the garment from where it hung on the back of a chair. She held the dress over her body, swaying it back and forth.

"Thank you for the alterations, dearest." Brye pulled it over her head. "It's not like anyone will comment. Men seemed to be a bit tongue-tied around me."

Lenna smiled as her sister attempted to continue as if nothing had happened. She knew it was a slight respite, but normality was what she wanted more than anything. And complaining about it was part of their everyday life. Especially if it was Tara, she was the expert.

"I thought men stopped asking you to dance because you did not indulge them in lifting your skirts?" Lenna grinned, her eyes alight.

"No!" Tara laughed, giving Brye a knowing look. "I think it was when you kneed Dagonet in the balls when he tried to kiss you."

Brye scowled while adjusting the waist of the dress.

"No, that was Marcus. He danced with me and then attempted to put his hands down my dress. He pinched one of my breasts so hard it left a bruise! The nerve!"

"Then who got kneed for kissing you drunk?" Lenna asked as she helped adjust the ribbons on the back of Tara's dress.

"Malcolm," Brye responded as she tied a pink ribbon around her waist. "He slobbered all over my face. It was highly unsatisfactory and disgusting. Thank the Founders, Dagonet came after. He at least had some finesse."

"Your expectations are exceedingly high," Lenna remarked.

"And yours are excessively low." Brye sat down to do her hair. Lenna motioned Tara to do the same so she could attack her curls.

"Not as low as before." Lenna glanced at her sister. "The prince has risen in that respect."

"Prince Gareth?" Tara tried to turn her head.

"Stand still," Lenna ordered before she continued working. "Yes, he got me out of the fire. The queen is looking for a mate for him."

"You, investing in gossip?" Brye raised an eyebrow. "That, I find hard to believe."

"It was all anyone would talk about today, at least before the flower combustion." Lenna continued. "I couldn't avoid it."

"You never can." Brye rolled her eyes.

"So?" Lenna persisted.

"So what?"

"In your opinion." Lenna attempted not to grin. "What kind of candidate is he? Too high? Too low?"

"Why are you only interested in her opinion?" Tara asked.

"I already know yours," Lenna answered, pulling one of the braids she made for the coronet. Tara winced. "You don't even consider him."

"That is true," Tara said. "I still don't like him."

"How come?" Lenna asked.

"The way he trains. He shows no mercy and seems to be full of himself. He has sparred against everyone and has no equal. I think it is wrong for anyone to be so high on the instep."

"That seems more like envy on your part," Lenna said.

"Perhaps." Tara drummed her fingers over her thighs, then gave a secret smile. "I know if I had a chance, I could set him on his ass. Take him down a notch."

"Oh. Now, who is full of herself?" Brye asked.

"And you? Sister, why do you dislike him so?"

Brye placed flowers in her braided hair; the colors she chose contrasted with her chestnut tones. "Like Tara, I don't or didn't, like him on principle. He completely ignores me the few times we have been in the same vicinity."

"Why do you care if he sees you or not if you think so little of him," Lenna said.

Brye sighed. "I don't know. He just seems odd."

"Odd?" Lenna finished taming Tara's braid and reached for the other flowers. "How so?"

"We crossed paths today at Caitlin's house." Brye stood and went to the small mirror. "He acted very strangely toward me."

"Really?" Tara asked. "Was he disrespectful?"

"No," Brye responded slowly. "He barely spoke to me, which is how he usually is. I could be next to him, and he doesn't even acknowledge I exist."

"That sounds more like your wounded vanity than his actions toward you, big sister." Lenna waved a pin before sticking it into Tara's curls.

Brye narrowed her eyes before patting her dress and sitting once more.

Lenna bit back a laugh. Brye was beautiful and accustomed to having attention, even if she tended to shy away from it.

"So?" Tara asked. "What has you so confused now? You don't have to like him."

Lenna continued listening as she stripped into her underclothes and went to wash in the bathing room quickly. Her sisters continued the conversation, raising their voices so she could participate.

"As I mentioned, I went to see Lenna at Caitlin's and was outside. Enid told me what had happened when Badar came out with the prince."

"And what was so strange?" Tara asked.

"He came out, gave me one look, and froze in place like a statue. Pale as if he had seen a ghost."

"No!" Tara handed Lenna a drying cloth. "I would have loved to see that!"

Lenna chuckled as she dried herself, her back to the fireplace.

"He stood there rubbing his face and looking at me strangely. Badar even had to touch him twice and speak to him directly. He looked like a fish out of water." Brye opened and closed her mouth to demonstrate. "When I realized he was staring at me, I did what everyone should do."

"Gave him an obscene gesture and walked away?" Tara asked.

"No. I asked if he was alright. He gave me a curt nod without uttering one word. He turned and told Badar to let him know if he needed help getting the house to rights. Then, he bowed and left."

"Are you sure he was even looking at you?" Lenna asked.

"I am sure," Brye answered. "It was the first time I felt him look at me. He looked confused."

"Wow." Tara helped Lenna dress. "That is strange."

"Indeed." Brye motioned for Lenna to sit on the chair, taking up the comb. "So, to answer your first question, I don't know what candidate he is. He has always seemed so very uninterested in me, now this bizarre behavior."

"Perhaps he was so interested; he was struck dumb," Lenna replied with a smile.

"Of course." Brye combed her sister's hair before braiding it. "And pigs will fly."

"You never know," Lenna said slowly, remembering how the prince said Brye's name. Brye may think otherwise, but Lenna knew differently.

The prince was very aware of who her sister was.

Beltane

Lenna

AVALON'S MIST WOULD MOVE its way over the valley after sunset every night. It would make the paths unnavigable without the aid of a magical mist candle.

Except during Beltane.

For the celebration, the royal advisor would limit the mists to the outer perimeter of the village. Once the sun had set, the villagers could move wherever they chose.

The girls were late arriving at the west fields, the sun already sinking low over the lake and casting long shadows tinted orange.

"That's strange," Tara pointed out as they reached the refreshment stand. "No sign of the royal family yet." She handed a glass of ale to each of them.

The celebration area near the lake had tall poles and dangling ropes with flowers. Decorated benches surrounded the giant bonfire, and tables ladened with honeyed fruit, cheese, and slices of bread were placed farther away from the heat of the bright blaze.

The smell of burning wood and roasting meat filled the air. The latter was the product of two wild boars being turned on spits. The repast was more extensive and more extravagant than any regular fare, punctuating the importance of the evening.

Lenna sipped her ale and turned to see the crowd around her.

Musicians played harps, flutes, and a small drum. Their music was inviting, and couples and small groups danced around the fire. Children old enough to attend played farther away, skipping stones in the lake or tossing balls. They were watched by some of the women and girls too young to for mating. Villagers who were not dancing stood or sat on the benches talking, drinking, and eating from platters.

The environment was lively, and the conversation animated, with yells from friends and the squeals of the children. People stood in clusters, and Lenna noticed that the conversations and twittering seemed particularly elevated. She glanced around, searching for something out of the ordinary. But other than the fact that the royal family wasn't present yet, this Beltane celebration looked like all the others she'd attended.

"What do you suppose is going on?" Lenna asked.

Brye handed her cup of ale to Lenna. "I shall find out." She left them momentarily, strolling toward a group of unmated females lingering near another food table. When she came back, she brought the news.

A visitor had come to Avalon from the Continent.

A mage.

He had bridged the gap in the northern wall and went straight to present himself to the royal family.

"What?" Tara sputtered. "How?"

"Perhaps that is why they're late." Lenna munched on an apple slice, covering her mouth with her hand. "It must have come as a surprise. There hasn't been a visitor in years."

"They say he is a young man," Brye said. "Handsome."

"Gossip, fantastic," Tara groaned. Brye rolled her eyes.

"Does he bring news from the Continent?" Lenna asked.

"Yes." Brye's foot started tapping to the music. "It seems the Shifter King has made peace with the Zuanshi Empress. After almost two millennia of wars, they recently signed a peace treaty."

"Does it affect us in any way?" Lenna picked up another fruit. "We have been isolated for a long time. Maybe Avalon can make peace with the Continent, and we can reintegrate with the other world?"

"Since when have you been so interested in the Continent?" Brye raised an eyebrow.

"It is a new development, I assure you. I question if being isolated is such a good thing."

"The Founders thought about that for a reason," Brye pointed out.

"Yes, but they are long gone. The reasons they had might no longer seem relevant."

Tara scoffed and searched the crowd. "I hope the peace lasts. A thousand years of war is more of a habit than peace."

"Tara, why do you have to be so pessimistic?" Brye moaned.

"Habit?" Tara bounced on her toes when her eyes landed on Aiden, who was with a group on the other side of the fire. She winked and waved at her sisters. "Got to go!"

"Really." Brye sipped her ale. "Tara might say she doesn't like gossip, but I am sure the group is enjoying it just as much."

"She only chooses whom she wants to hear it from," Lenna said before popping another slice in her mouth.

The music began to pick up its pace. A tall, muscular man with white-blond hair nervously approached them. Lenna recognized him and gave Brye a knowing look.

"Round two?" she whispered.

Brye turned around to see Dagonet standing with his hand extended. "Uhm, Brye, would you like to dance?"

Lenna pushed her sister in his direction, smiling. "Of course, she would!" Brye turned back and scowled as he led her away, forcing Lenna to laugh

Soon both her sisters were dancing around the fire, hand in hand with handsome men. Lenna stood back from the crowd and watched. The gray cloak around her shoulders was hot, but it gave her social protection. No one approached her. She took one final look at her sister's joyful face and walked toward the edge of the field.

Trees surrounded the lake and celebration area. They provided enough shadow for privacy and couples took advantage of it.

Lenna did so as well. She hid herself enough that she could see the light of the fire but not the dancers or the crowds of people.

She sat down with her back against the trunk, wrapping her arms around her bent knees. With a long sigh, Lenna closed her eyes and emptied her mind.

It had been a long day, and the revelry was just beginning. The music filtered through the trees, as well as conversations. She recognized the laughter and giggling of the children. It warmed her heart to listen to it all, but it gave her peace not to participate.

Lost in her thoughts, it took her a moment to become aware of the sound of crushed grass as someone approached.

"There you are."

The voice rolled over her like soft, warm waves, and she smiled before opening her eyes.

Aiden's dirty blonde hair was combed back from his face, and his beard was trimmed. He wore an indigo tunic, open at his neck by loose cords, and rolled up the sleeves that revealed tanned arms sprinkled with blond hair. His pants were a shade darker than his tunic and boots.

"Here I am," Lenna replied.

"Hiding." Aiden gulped down the drink he was holding. He then wiped a hand to clean his sweaty brow.

"Observing," Lenna corrected.

"Where you can't see anyone?" He raised an eyebrow.

"I see what I want to see." She extended her legs in front of her, leaning back against the trunk. Her shoes touched Aiden's booted feet.

"I heard about the fire." He set his empty cup beside Lenna and placed his hands in his pockets. "I wanted to know if you were alright."

"I am fine." She played with the cord of her gray cloak. "Grateful no one was hurt." Lenna looked away toward the glow of the fire hidden by the trees. Another round of music started. "Seriously, fire is dangerous. We were lucky the prince and the royal advisor came along."

He nodded, but his eyes became serious. "You were discovered."

Not a question. A statement. Lenna stopped playing with the cord. "Yes."

Aiden carefully sat down and pressed against her. The heat from his body made her shudder. He wrapped an arm around her shoulders. Lenna had to remind herself once again they were childhood friends. His family had been theirs even before their mother disappeared. She regarded him only as a brother, right?

Feelings are so complicated.

Lenna sighed and leaned her head on his shoulder. "I thought if I pretended it was not there and ignored it, I could be like everyone else."

"Lenna, you are not like everyone else. It would be best if you learned to accept it. Maybe it is a good thing you were discovered."

"I don't—"

"You're afraid because you don't know how your magic works."

"You know what happened today."

"I do, but no one got hurt."

"Not this time Aiden."

"By learning, you can prevent events like that from happening again. We need to accept we have roles to play. Just like I must become intimately acquainted with a long piece of steel."

She sat up, eyes wide. "A warrior?"

"Or a double-bladed ax. Neither seems like warm comfort." He gave her a wide smile. His humor was an ill attempt to lighten the mood.

It didn't work.

"You are to train? I thought you had already been assigned to the fields like your father. Since when?"

Aiden sighed and turned toward her; his eyes were devoid of emotion. "I was called yesterday evening to the Royal Tower. I was not the only one. It seems some roles are to be readjusted. Some young farmers, such as myself, will also train as warriors. We will be fulfilling both roles."

"But you do not want to become a warrior."

"What I want doesn't seem to be taken into account. I have been assigned."

"I guess it makes two of us."

It was useless. They were trapped. Besides, Tara would fight with him regarding the subject. The last thought brought a wicked smile to her features.

Aiden narrowed his gaze. "What?"

"Have you spoken to Tara about this?"

"I tried this afternoon," he spoke slowly.

"And?"

"The conversation turned in another direction."

Lenna's smile deepened. "Better prepare yourself for when you finally tell her. She has wanted to train as a warrior longer than she can walk. This will make her even more determined."

He winced and looked back in the direction of the celebration. The music had changed tempo, and a group of rowdy villagers had begun to sing.

"Don't remind me. She is determined to at least petition. I will try to talk her out of it, and so should you."

They sat momentarily before a voice rang out, and the music stopped abruptly. A sense of dread settled in the pit of her stomach.

The royal family had arrived.

Royal Insights

Lenna

LENNA AND AIDEN RETURNED to the celebration, where people stood around expectantly. A minstrel announced the entrance of King Manus and Queen Celine.

The king was a large man with long arms and build. His hair and beard had gone completely white from a young age. His most striking feature was his smile, completely transforming his serious face. He supervised the fields and livestock, taking an interest in the goings-on. Those few times Lenna had crossed paths with him, he would stare at her. The one time she had spoken to him, he looked hurt and uncomfortable. She has avoided him ever since.

Now we know where the prince got his social graces with women.
This evening he stood tall with the queen at his side. He gave her warm glances that seemed to communicate more than words. Tall, graceful, with fair hair and clear eyes, Queen Celine was as fine as her partner. She wore a long blue dress with a plaid underskirt decorated with metal and silver jewelry. She waved behind for the next figure to follow.

The murmers intensified when Prince Gareth's muscled presence came into the circle. Lenna raised herself on her tiptoes to get a better look as Gareth walked into the space around the Beltane

Fire. He scowled and glanced around the crowd as if searching for someone. Lenna's eyes widened when his gaze settled on Brye.

Her sister stood at the crowd's edge, sandwiched between Dagonet and Tara. A slight change came over the prince's cold features. His mouth softened with a pinched smile. It was quickly suppressed when the queen touched his shoulder.

"What are you staring at?" Aiden whispered in her ear. His breath tingled the hairs that fell out of her coronet.

She flinched away, unnerved. "I don't know yet."

Roweena, the royal advisor, was last. Lenna forced her feet to stay put.

The woman was a stark contrast to the bright queen. Even at night, she was dressed in black, with her dark raven hair braided around her head. Lenna's stomach tightened when the royal advisor's eyes made contact with her. There was no escape from the cold depths.

"My fellow subjects," the king's voice resonated across the field, "it is Beltane, the beginning of spring. We are united by the fire to celebrate the future bounty of the land, as well as the union of the Sun with his mate, the Earth. With that in mind, we have two important announcements to make."

King Manus turned toward the prince, who stepped forward. "The first one is long overdue. We will soon have a mate for our prince! One who will continue in our traditions and ensure our hidden sanctuary is cared for."

The applause went out with hoots and whistles. Lenna met Tara's gaze across the fire, and her sister rolled her eyes. Lenna chuckled.

"What's so funny?" Aiden asked.

"Tara is overwhelmed with joy." Lenna motioned in her sister's direction. They exchanged glances and Aiden chuckled.

"And for our second announcement," the king continued. His gaze fell on her. "We must drink... to our new Mist Maiden!"

Lenna's heart dropped to her stomach as all eyes fell on her. The king motioned her to join them, and Lenna forced her lead-filled legs to obey. Gareth made space beside him and the royal advisor.

Head high, she smiled expectantly at the crowd of surprised onlookers. Lenna found her sisters in the group and used them as an anchor. Aiden made his way to stand beside Tara, who scowled at the prince. Brye's eyes were pinched with concern.

But they were there, holding her steady when she only wanted to collapse under the nerves. She kept her hands together to keep from trembling.

The king came beside Lenna and placed a steady hand on her shoulder. "We have been blessed with a new protector. Another woman, like our royal advisor, who will dedicate her life to the safety of Avalon and its future. A blessing after so many generations without magic holders. We have much to rejoice in Avalon. Music, please! Ale, please!"

He waved his hand toward the musicians, who bowed and began to play. A yell alerted the crowd that a new keg of ale had been opened on the refreshment table. People regrouped, and the celebration resumed instantly.

Aiden took Tara back out onto the dance floor. Beside Lenna, Gareth stiffened slightly when Brye spoke in whispered tones with Dagonet. She looked up at him, but he turned to the table, leaving her beside the king.

"Let us eat," the king invited.

Lenna bit hard on her lip, unsure if she was to be included. She took a step toward the table.

"Oh Lenna, you'll never guess!" Brye appeared beside her, smiling. "I wanted to talk to you about something." She linked her arms with Lenna and led her away from the table before anyone said a word.

Lenna's body relaxed the farther they drifted into the crowd. She exhaled a long breath. "Thank you."

"No problem." Brye squeezed her arm. "I think it went well."

"I assume you are referring to the dance with Dagonet." Lenna chuckled, giving her sister a side glance.

"Of course." Brye's voice filled with sarcasm. "What else did you think I wanted to discuss?"

Lenna laughed and patted her sister's arm. A tingling sensation crept down her neck. She turned to see the prince staring darts in their direction, only to continue talking to the queen.

"What?" Brye asked. "You have that look."

"What look?" Lenna blinked slowly.

"The one you have when trying to figure out a difficult puzzle."

They made their way to the refreshment table. Brye reached for one and handed another to Lenna. "I hope I am not one of them."

Lenna wet her dry mouth, observing her sister over the glass. Brye's hair was still in place, but her cheeks flushed and lips pink. She looked beautiful and healthy. It was never a surprise that eyes would fall on her sister.

Lenna looked back to the royal table. The prince stood, watching the crowd, pretending not to watch them. He failed. His eyes would skip in their direction, and his scowl would deepen.

I wonder...

"Why do you dislike the prince so much, Brye?"

"I thought we already talked about this."

"No." Lenna played with her glass. "You said you found him odd and did not dislike him, but you did not truly explain your reasons."

Brye squinted a moment. "I already told you this story."

"Remind me again."

Brye sighed, picked up some dried fruit on the table, and nibbled a moment before speaking. "Do you remember the Beltane you turned eighteen? The night you left early."

Lenna remembered every moment of that night. It was scarred into her memory, and she buried it along with all her other disappointments. "Yes. But I did not see you interact with the prince."

"It was after you left. I stayed behind. It was the second year Dagonet asked to be my mate. I refused him, of course."

"I am aware." Lenna chuckled. Brye continued to play with the dried fruit. Lenna took it from her hand and ate it. "What is the point, Brye?"

"The prince asked everyone from my group to dance. Every single girl from my group, except me."

"So, your vanity and pride have been bruised."

"No, if only." Brye grimaced. "I then went to his group of friends and returned the favor. Asking every man to dance, except him."

"You did what?" Lenna almost choked on the food. Brye patted her back.

"It was easy." Brye waved. "A few batted lashes and a smile were more than sufficient. But someone let slip that the prince did not ask me to dance because he found me *too tempting to be sincere.*"

Lenna's eyes widened.

"Me?" Brye scoffed and lowered her glass. "Tempting to be sincere indeed. I can't help it if others find me appealing. Since then," she glanced toward the royal table, "I have had no patience for him."

Lenna followed her sister's gaze. The prince was seated at the royal table with his arms crossed, leaning next to another man Lenna had never seen before. Their faces were grim, and the prince motioned to the crowd.

Brye finished her glass and plunked it on the table. "So that is it."

"If you are too tempting to be sincere, what is he?"

"Easy. He is too serious to be entertaining."

Lenna's laugh exploded out of her, and Brye's followed.

"Now." Brye gripped her arm. "Stop whatever you are thinking, and let's discuss more interesting matters."

"You don't know what I am thinking." Lenna blinked slowly, her eyes twinkling.

"I don't want to know." Brye wrapped her arm around Lenna's. "Now, about Dagonet."

Cross Stitch

Lenna

Brye and Lenna walked around the Beltane fire holding hands, lost in conversation. The tingling sensation appeared again, and Lenna turned around to find a man watching them. He was the same stranger who had been conversing with the prince.

The visiting mage.

His features were dark, with tanned skin, ebony hair, and eyes. His face seemed set in stone, only softened by a well-kept beard and an easy smile. He wore black from head to toe, which was not a wise choice in the oppressive heat. The only color in his wardrobe was a leather belt and sheath.

"He looks interesting and younger than I expected," Brye whispered before they came upon him. She cocked her head to one side. "Are you looking for someone?" she asked, addressing the stranger.

"No, I am not," he replied shyly. He spoke their language with a deeper accent that sounded odd to Lenna's ears. "I was asking myself, who are those two beautiful young women? Why are they not dancing?"

Lenna suppressed a scoff by pinching her lips.

Beautiful? Me? Next to Brye?

"Well," Brye replied smoothly. "We were wondering about you as well." She gave him a bright smile. "What is your name, sir? We haven't received emissaries from the Continent in a long time."

The man laughed, and his eyes twinkled. "I am always willing to please. My name is Beltran, and my family is from the southern borders." He leaned in and lowered his voice. The smile never left his face. "The air is dense due to the heat and the humidity, and you can smell the spices. It is no surprise people choose to rest during the day. The temperature drains your strength."

"This humid weather must be difficult for you," Brye said.

"A bit," he replied, standing taller. "I was born in the south and trained there. Only until recently have I moved to the north. I am still becoming accustomed to this misty weather."

The musicians, who had been playing softer music, changed the pace. Instantly the sounds of percussion and flutes surrounded them.

"You still have not answered my question." Beltran placed his arms behind his back. "Why are you not dancing?"

"Oh, the answer is easy." Brye drummed her fingers on her lips. "No one has asked us."

I know what happens next.

Lenna laughed and let go of her sister's arm, pushing her toward Beltran. He tilted his head curiously.

"I believe you are right." He extended his hand toward Lenna. She looked down at it, eyes wide. "Shall I have this dance?"

Brye held back her smile. "You can't dance with that." She quickly removed Lenna's gray cloak from her shoulders.

Before she could even react, Lenna was being pulled toward the dancers. The first turn had begun. With his hand warm in hers, he set her in place.

"Don't tell me you can't dance?" Beltran grinned as he clapped twice and stomped.

Lenna laughed, her face bright as she let the music guide her.

They stood in a line facing each other, and when the music increased tempo they would cross, stomp and dance close together. Lenna focused on the steps, excited her body was cooperating. After the first pass, she relaxed. She could not stop laughing and smiling.

I should have done this years ago!

After the second pass, they would cross and do two circles with his hand on her waist.

"I take it back," Beltran said, lifting her effortlessly for the second twirl. "You are an exceptional dancer."

"Miraculously so! Your feet are still intact!" Lenna called to him as they passed. His teasing was contagious, and Lenna couldn't help but join him.

I'm flirting! And he is flirting back!

They crossed a third time, and the music ended before she realized it. They stood facing each other in the line.

"Thank you." She grinned up at him.

"It was a pleasure," Beltran responded, placing a hand on the small of her back and leading to the crowd's edge.

Brye and Tara stood side by side, smiling so much that Lenna was surprised they could stay in their skins. Aiden was equally amused, with his hands behind his back, rocking on the balls of his feet.

"Don't make it a big deal," Lenna whispered. She then regarded Beltran warmly. "Thank you, once again."

"Have a wonderful evening, ladies." Beltran bowed and left them.

"Wow," Tara remarked in awe.

"Yeah," Brye added.

"Interesting." Aiden raised an eyebrow.

"Oh, shut up!" Lenna crossed her arms, but her voice lacked conviction.

Another piece was announced a few moments later. Aiden gripped her hand.

"Time for another dance, Lenna. Don't insult me by saying no."

She barely had time to catch her breath before he escorted her back to the Beltane fire.

They stood facing each other moments before the music started. She looked up into his ice-blue eyes, and her heart lifted higher. For the rest of the dance, she couldn't erase the smile from her face.

It was well past midnight when Lenna walked back alone through the clear, empty streets. She crossed paths with some villagers and young mothers with their children.

Once home, she sat at the table and removed what was left of the flowers in her hair. Lenna placed the wilted blooms in front of her, recollections of her evening swirling through her mind.

After her dance with Aiden, she had not danced again. She had sat near the refreshment table, watching the couples. Her sisters and Aiden would come and sit with her for a while before leaving to dance and mingle. They always had partners. Aiden had even danced with his mother and Enid. Beltran spent most of the night at the royal table, whispering with the prince. Lenna was grateful not to have been called back there.

Two highlights of the evening were difficult to forget. The first was watching the prince dance. He had sat at the table most of the night, but sometime after Lenna's last dance with Aiden, he had walked around, hands clasped behind his back, searching. All the single girls around the fire had perked up, preening and smiling coyly. They bowed and spoke to them but did not ask any to dance.

That is, until he had reached Brye's group, where her sister had been standing, facing the prince, her arm around Tara. When they realized he was close, the group opened up and bowed.

He had opened his mouth to speak in Brye's direction, but at the last moment, he had turned and invited another girl. Lenna had smiled, happy that the prince was giving the girl some attention.

He had kept his face stern but danced at a quick pace. Afterward, he led the girl back to her group and proceeded to ask everyone near Brye to dance.

Everyone except her sister.

He might have pretended to ignore Brye, but his eyes had always seemed to find her in the crowd.

And Brye had noticed this time. She was not immune to the prince's *apparent* lack of interest. In retaliation, she had asked everyone near the prince to dance. Even Beltran was plucked from the table. The prince had only responded with a soft lift of his lip.

The interaction, if it could be called that, between Brye and Prince Gareth had not been the only curious revelation.

It started as Lenna watched Tara and Aiden dance together. They often danced at a small, intimate event or past Beltane celebrations. But this time, something was different. The looks had been warmer, hotter. Tara had searched for him in the crowd, her face lighting up. He had pretended not to be affected, but his eyes had done the same.

When she realized what she was seeing, Lenna's stomach hardened, and her eyes prickled. She had pinched the bridge of her nose and decided it was time to go home. She gave Brye a signal and headed back before anyone noticed her departure.

By now, Lenna was freed from the coronet and in her underclothes. Thanks to the absence of mist in the village, the night was hotter than usual. Lenna pulled a chair near the open window and let the air cool her sweaty neck and brow. Lifting her knees to her chest, she let out a long sigh.

"Tara, I know this is what you want to do. But have you thought it through? You only mentioned it this morning."

Lenna jumped. She could make out two forms walking toward the house from her seat at the window. The tallest figure held a lantern.

"So, you believe I can't do it?" Tara asked, her voice strained.

"It isn't that, and you know it," Aiden said sternly.

"All I need is a chance to prove myself, and you must help me." She gripped his arm.

"Oh no! You do not involve me, Tara." Aiden moved away, placing his free hand on his hip.

"Aiden." Tara snatched his hand. "I have to do this, and you are my dearest—"

Aiden sighed audibly.

"—and truest friend. My only support in this matter."

Aiden let go of her hand and rubbed the back of his neck. "Tara, have you ever considered the position you place your sisters in?"

"What do my sisters have to do with it?" She crossed her arms over her chest.

"Lenna has become a Mist Maiden. She is supposed to set an example in traditional roles. What will it look like if her younger sister becomes a warrior? Your actions reflect on both your sisters."

"Did you even listen to what was said after the king announced? As soon as King Manus finished talking, betting started on how much time she would live," Tara lowered her voice at the end, a nasty edge to her tone.

Lenna's heart sank.

Does no one honestly believe in me?

Lenna ground her teeth.

"Tara," Aiden hissed. "And you did nothing to stop it? That wasn't kind."

"Lenna doesn't want to be a Mist Maiden any more than you want to be a warrior. She was forced into it. I will not wait for my life to be decided. I will take my future into my own hands."

"Oh? Then why do you even ask if you already have decided?" His voice lost all humor.

"I was not asking anything. I was letting you know that I made my decision." Tara's voice rose. "And I will prove to you that I can make him accept. You'll see."

She walked toward the front door. Aiden rubbed the back of his head and cursed under his breath. He watched the door for a moment longer before turning and heading down the path, the lantern light receding into the dark.

Lenna waited quietly until Tara walked in. "Did you have a nice time?"

Tara jumped, biting back a curse. "You're awake."

"Evidently." Lenna waited a moment before jumping right in. "So, there are bets to see if I will survive my training?" She actively kept the emotion out of her voice.

Tara stopped beside the bed, her body visible from Lenna's place at the window. Her sister took her time undressing before whispering, "Yes. But they are wrong. They do not know your strength."

Lenna wanted to believe her, but the lack of conviction in Tara's voice was disappointing.

How could my sister lie to my face?

Biting back a painful retort, Lenna carefully asked, "Do you know yours, sister?"

"I will find out soon." Tara sat on the bed, her back against the wall. Her long exhale filled the silence.

Sometime later, Lenna stared at the ceiling as her sisters slept. Her mind was clouded with dread and a sense of finality.

Change was creeping up on them. What happened on her birthday was only the beginning.

There was no going back from this path. We are meant to walk it and see where it takes us.

The Eldest

Brye

BRYE AWOKE AFTER A long night, the sun gleaming into the room, bright and airy. She rubbed her tired eyes and focused on the messy mass of curls visible from under the blanket on the opposite cot. Tara was still asleep, the blankets rising and falling with each breath.

Lenna, however, was gone.

Brye exhaled sharply. Lenna had started her training after Beltane. Every day she would leave early in the morning and appear late in the evening, too weary for conversation. She would mumble responses and sometimes fall asleep with her clothes on. With each passing day, the bags under her eyes grew more pronounced. No amount of tea and herbal remedies seemed to work.

It had only been a week, and Brye worried what the long months of training would do to her delicate sister.

Tara, on the other hand, was too edgy to have a decent conversation. Brye had tried to get to the bottom of her persistent lousy mood, but Tara would only hiss and walk away. It did not help that Aiden was absent. He was the only one capable of getting to Tara, but he had started training in the mornings and was missing from the fields. Brye had made the mistake of asking Tara how his training was going. She snapped and growled at Brye, saying, *"everything was fine."*

No, things were not fine. Everything was far from it.

Concern gnawed through Brye's bones. She wanted to help or talk to her sisters, but neither made an effort. Tara would eventually explode and reveal what was eating her up, but Lenna would hold out longer than most.

Debating whether she should wake up Tara or not, Brye got out of bed. She stretched her hands overhead, exhaling as her joints cracked. Lenna's section of the room was organized, with her bedside made up and her trunk closed. She was fussy about keeping her things in order, especially since she shared her side of the room with Tara.

Like her untamed curls, Tara's side of the room was a mess. Clothes were scattered around, some coming out of her trunks or hanging over chairs.

As the eldest, Brye became accustomed to picking up and tending to her siblings. As a Healer, her workplace needed to be spotless. Organizing, cleaning, and working with her herbs was one of her many daily steps to keep herself balanced. Cleaning up after Tara was another.

Once the room was in better shape, Brye prepared for the day. She bathed and dressed in socks, garters, underclothes, and a dress. Finally, she lifted the apron over her head and tied the strings around her trim waist.

Brye smiled as she rubbed her hands over Lenna's tiny flower and leaf embroidery over the pocket. She finished a slice of sweet bread when a yelp came from the bedroom.

"Why didn't you wake me?" Tara groaned loudly.

"I care for my sanity," Brye called back, chuckling.

The splash of water came seconds before a screech. "So darn cold! Why did you have to finish the hot water?"

When Tara emerged from the room, she was fully dressed in her work clothes, consisting of a pair of pants and a shirt tied to her waist by a belt. Her left cheek was covered with pillow marks, and her hair was a wild nest. She handed Brye a comb before sitting in the chair next to the table. Brye, in protest, gave Tara's curls a slight yank with the comb.

"Ouch!"

"Not sorry," Brye smirked.

Tara stuffed her face with sweet bread and cheese while Brye braided her hair.

"Lenna left early again," Brye remarked.

"Yes," Tara grunted.

"She came back late last night."

"Stating the obvious."

"Aren't you concerned?"

"Do you want me to be?" Tara drank some fresh milk.

"What do you think, Tara?" Brye's voice edged as she tied a string at the bottom of Tara's braid. She gave it a pull.

"I think if Lenna couldn't handle it, she would have said something."

"Do you honestly think she would?"

Tara shrugged. "I'd hope. Brye, training for a new skill isn't easy. It takes a toil. If you don't believe me, ask Aiden. He looks as bad as Lenna and has to work in the fields every day before training."

Brye nodded and patted her sister's shoulder. Tara used that as her cue to clean up, grab her satchel and leave, banging the door in her wake. She didn't glance back once at Brye.

Brye sighed. Maybe she was being overly cautious.

Then again, Tara can be self-centered.

They had lost their mother young, and Tara was the smallest, almost a baby at four. She grew up pampered and spoiled. It didn't help that she was vibrant and strong-willed, getting away with anything.

Brye and Lenna were not immune to Tara's faults. They loved her despite it. But in times like these, Brye sometimes wished Tara was more in tune with what was happening around her.

With another long sigh, Brye collected the basket of dried herbs and tinctures she had prepared the day before. With it in hand, she set out for Enid's.

The paths were full of people going about their days. Some worked in the fields, tending to the new harvest. Others were on their way to prepare for the market. Children ran for lessons near the base of the Royal Tower. Their squeals and complaints followed their steps.

Trade was the currency of Avalon, and everyone worked for the well-being of its people in different ways. The Founders magically knotted the fields with spells to produce varied crops faster than expected. Animals were tended to and reproduced regularly. The island inhabitants worked year-round to provide services.

The paths cleared as Brye reached the end of the road. Enid's home was more extensive than most, and it was the last in the southern part of the village. It comprised two connected central buildings, a walled garden, and a workshop. The main building faced the front of the paths and was the blacksmith shop. It was a semi-open structure with two walls on either side and a large stone hearth in the back.

Brye skipped that entrance and stepped to the side of the house, where a large stone wall engulfed the herb garden. The garden door was always open, and once inside, Brye let out a long-awaited breath. The sun was going over the wall, and the light hit the dew-covered herbs and flowers.

The medicinal herbs grew close to the ground, and Enid made small paths between the batches to keep order. The walls were covered in ivy, and trim bushes of elderberries were placed at its base. Lemongrass, bergamot, and meadowsweet were mixed with chamomile and calendula. Weeds were pruned and welcomed among the plants and the helpful insects.

Walking down the path, Brye left her basket at the table outside a small building. It was Enid's workshop and where she tended to patients. Deciding it was a good time to harvest some herbs, Brye retrieved her tools and knelt to work in the moist soil.

This is what she needed. Her knees pressed into the dirt, the moistness of the soil in her fingertips. She trimmed the plants carefully, tending to their needs and her own. It gave her peace to think. Usually, she would happily work side by side with Enid as they updated each other on patients or gossip.

But lately, Brye needed the time by herself. Her abilities had changed, and the adjustment was causing her discomfort. From a young age, Brye had shown superior knowledge of plants and their properties. After her mother's disappearance, she was apprenticed to Enid and since then, she has grown in experience and knowledge.

However, recently, the growth in those abilities has been exponential. Before she could touch herbs and plants, intuitively sensing what they could do. Now, with her hands, she could intensify the plants' abilities. With proper direction, her tinctures could heal faster and better than before.

This was not the only new skill she had discovered. Her hands had begun to tingle and grow warm when she was healing others. They had always tingled, and her sisters had constantly complained about it. But now, she could feel health, sickness, and death.

Her sisters were not the only ones with worries on their minds. Brye always suspected her abilities were uncommon, but since Beltane, she wondered if Lenna wasn't the only one with magic.

Brye was kneeling by a stubborn bush of weeds when Enid appeared trudging along the path.

Since inheriting her position, Enid has never stopped working hard and providing services to everyone in the village, including the royal family. She had mated young and had five healthy children and three grandchildren. Not only was she blessed with healthy offspring, but also with good looks that hid her age well. Her dark, black hair held some gray, but the soft wrinkles around her eyes only accentuated her face.

"I thought you would be here." She picked up the basket Brye had set aside to place the harvested flowers. "I'll make us some tea. We need to talk."

"Should I be concerned?" Brye stood, wiping her dirty hands on her apron. She placed the sheers in the basket.

"No," Enid answered, "at least not for us."

The workshop was a small, one-roomed building similarly organized to Brye's workroom at home. A large bookcase was filled with marked bottles and herbs that dried overhead on hooks or the walls. A worktable was placed on the right, and two chairs were in front of the tiny little fireplace. Like her house, Enid kept dried lavender to hide strong smells and provide a relaxing atmosphere.

The older woman placed the basket on the work table while Brye sat. She knew Enid would talk when she was ready, usually in bits and pieces as she worked. Enid filled the kettle with water and hung it over the fireplace. Only then did she sit with her hands clasped as they waited for it to boil.

This must be serious.

"What I am about to say is in the strictest of confidences." Enid handed Brye her journal with marked points on some pages. Brye followed the notes as Enid started to recount her observations.

"The queen is unwell and has been for some time. Initially, I thought she was going from her fertile to the infertile stage. She is almost 50, and her menses have become irregular, with some erratic bleeding. Intercourse with the king has been painful."

"Do you have any suspicions?"

"I do." Enid stood and retrieved the kettle. She placed a scoop of chamomile and rosemary in the teapot and poured hot water over the herbs. She sat back down while it steeped. "My diagnosis is cancer of the womb."

Brye looked down at the journal to hide her face. A heavy feeling filled her chest, and she rubbed her eyes.

Cancer was rare in Avalon. The knots on the island did not only affect the land. People were supposed to be born healthy and terminal sickness was odd besides some seasonal chills. Or they used to.

Since Brye has been apprenticed out to Enid, they have registered the health of each member of their small society. Many changes have occurred since then. This suspicion of the queen's condition was another piece of evidence. It did not hide the fact that it was sad. Brye remembered the queen's face during Beltane, her smiles and laughter. How the king doted on her, and the prince showed every attention.

At least the few times I looked his way. ... Alright, maybe I looked at him more than once.

Brye let out a long sigh. "Have you spoken to her?"

"No. That is why I wanted to talk to you. I need a second opinion on the matter. You are an extraordinary Healer. The only one close to your ability was your mother."

Brye doubted she was as good as her mother, but she didn't correct Enid. She placed her elbows on the table and her chin in her hands. "What do you wish for me to do?"

"I have mentioned to the queen that I wanted my apprentice to examine her and give me another perspective. I made an appointment for you to see her this afternoon. I left her resting."

Enid poured the tea into each cup, offering one to Brye. She then placed her hands around her mug.

"I am starting to wonder," Enid began.

"Wonder what?" Brye lifted her tea to sip while she examined the journal.

"When are you planning on finding a mate?"

Brye burned her tongue, nearly spitting the tea out.

Enid raised an eyebrow, ignoring her evident pain. "My two daughters were mated by your age. One was already with child."

"I remember. I helped with the birth." Her words were slurred due to the burn.

"Yes, and it was beautiful." Enid tapped a finger on the table. "Be that as it may, it is long past you had a mate: a good man and some babies. You have taken care of your sisters long enough. Lenna has become a Mist Maiden. I feel bad that the girl won't find a decent young man, but perhaps it is better for her." Enid waved a finger. "And don't get me started on Tara. We all know Aiden follows her around like a pup. Won't be long before he does something about it. Hopefully, she will come to her senses before that!"

"Is that what everyone is gossiping about now? Lenna's lack of prospects and Tara and Aiden?"

"Don't change the subject. Being the oldest, you should open your eyes and see Aiden has had feelings for Tara for a while now. It won't be long before she knows what's good for her and gives him a chance."

Brye went to open her mouth, but Enid continued without taking a breath.

"But Brye, you will be left alone if you don't take some action in finding a mate for yourself. I've seen you dance, flirt, and sometimes even go for a walk with a few. But you scare them away. Especially after you kneed that one young man; what was his name?"

"Which one?" Brye sat back, crossing her legs.

"There was more than one?" Enid sighed, and Brye caught a hint of a smile before the woman's face hardened once again. "Brye, listen to reason. Unmated men are rare now. There are fewer births, and you have to think for yourself. I am sure some good young men will be honored to have a mate with your healing skills. Mayhap this Dagonet who you danced with during Beltane? Or perhaps the sage would stay here if you drew his eye, or he yours."

Brye flushed. Enid had made some comments over the past years at Beltane but had yet to be as direct as now.

She didn't want to lie to herself. There was a time she wanted a mate. She had considered Dagonet once, and even Malcolm if only he kept his hands to himself. Since she came out, there had been passion and interest but no spark. Something was always missing, and kissing them was exciting but bland.

"I will take it into account, Enid," Brye answered, ending the conversation. "I promise."

"Good." Enid sat back with a knowing grin. Brye's stomach sank, and she narrowed her eyes.

"What is it?"

"You must know the queen is looking for a mate for—"

"Don't start."

Healer

Brye

THE MORNING WENT QUICKER than Brye had expected. They had concentrated on replenishing their supplies from the gardens. A few patients arrived, and Enid tended to their needs while Brye took notes. She tried to forget her meeting with the queen later that afternoon but found her attention wandering. She'd grip the quill tighter when taking down the information of a small child, and she had to repeat one of her ointments from scratch.

She wasn't typically a nervous woman, which agitated her further. In fact, Brye prided herself on her ability to focus in times of crisis. Even if it was a rare occurrence, she had tended to patients on her own before. But she couldn't escape the jumpy, tight feeling in the pit of her stomach.

Shortly after lunch, Brye changed her apron and made herself presentable for her visit with the queen. Checking her reflection once more in the mirror, Brye picked up her basket.

"I'm off!"

"Don't be so nervous," Enid called back.

The walk to the Tower took longer than expected because villagers would stop Brye every other step. They would call her, asking about her sisters or a remedy she might recommend. Brye would smile and listen to their needs, taking notes of those she wanted to remember for later. By the time she reached the massive door, they had appointments for most of the week.

Brye had only been inside the Royal Tower once, the night after her mother disappeared. Since then, she'd had no reason to visit.

It was the tallest building in Avalon, four stories high and made of stone. The doors were of thick carved wood. When she opened them, she found a spiraling stone staircase covered in red carpet. To the right were the audience rooms, where King Manus held morning attendance twice a week. To the left was the Great Hall, a space used for parties and dances at one time long ago. Now it was locked up, with the royal family preferring parties outdoors.

Brye stood in the entrance hall, attempting to catch the eye of a retainer, when a figure came down the steps.

"It's you."

Prince Gareth arrived at the bottom of the stairs with a bewildered look.

Brye turned to see if he was referring to someone else. They were alone.

She raised an eyebrow. "I guess so. I am here to see the queen. Enid, the Healer, sent me."

Prince Gareth cleared his throat, and his face became unreadable once more.

"She is resting."

"I am aware, but—"

"Finally!"

A short older man came rushing in from a back room, holding his arms up. He wore a dark blue tunic with a plaid undershirt, symbolizing his role as a retainer of the royal family. "The queen has been expecting you for the last thirty minutes, Brye the Healer."

"I apologize." Brye smiled, but the man only paled when he realized who was in the hall.

"Sorry, your highness, I did not see you." The older man's chin wobbled.

"That is alright, Edgar." Gareth nodded.

Edgar coughed to clear his throat, then motioned Brye toward the stairs. "Come with me."

Edgar took one step, but Gareth blocked his way. The older man fumbled back. Brye moved to catch him, but the prince was quicker. He reached out and steadied the poor man before he fell.

"I'll escort her, Edgar."

"Yes, well," Edgar bumbled, darting his eyes from an annoyed Brye to a bored Gareth. "I was instructed to take her."

Gareth gave Edgar a firm look.

The retainer faltered momentarily, then gave the prince a slight bow and scurried off. Brye watched him go, a furrow between her brows.

"That was rude," she pointed out, her hands tight on the handles of her basket.

"Oh?" Gareth shrugged.

"He was only doing his duty."

"So am I." Gareth turned to climb up the stairs. "Come with me."

A bit full of himself.

Brye cursed under her breath and followed. The stairs were carpeted to prevent slips and wide enough for two people to climb side by side. A wooden rail was inserted on the side of the wall for aid. However, if a person weren't careful, they'd fall four flights of stairs onto a stone floor with one slip. Brye paled at the thought.

The second floor was the private social room assigned to the family. There, they held meetings and smaller audiences than required by the main hall. Brye slowed, trying to look inside, but the prince kept walking. He chuckled when she picked up her skirts and climbed stairs two at a time to reach him on the third-floor landing.

The landing opened up to a hallway with four doors, two on each side. The prince led her to the room closest to the hall. He knocked and waited.

"Enter."

Gareth poked his head in and then opened the door. Brye followed behind.

The room was larger than expected, with another adjacent area that appeared to be a connecting bedroom. The tall windows helped keep the room light and airy. Even though it was stifling outside, a fire burned low.

Queen Celine sat on the bed with massive pillows behind her back and a deep burgundy blanket covering her legs. As she regarded the woman, regal was the only word that came to Brye's mind. Her light blond hair was braided down her side, and she wore a white shirt with colored embroidery of red roses with thorns around the bodice and sleeves. Brye recognized Lenna's handiwork.

"Who have you brought me, son?" she asked, raising a perfectly designed eyebrow. She extended a hand in their direction. Gareth exhaled, and his shoulders lost their tightness. He took her hand gently and kissed her palm.

"Brye is here, on behalf of the Healer."

He let go of her hand and softly kissed her head.

She cleared her throat, undone by the sudden display of tenderness from the prince. "A pleasure to see you, your majesty."

"Oh, please don't give me that," Queen Celine cringed. "Even after almost 30 years holding the title, I can't get used to it. Address me as ma'am or my lady."

"Yes, ma'am," Brye answered, testing the words on her tongue.

"I will leave you two." The prince gave his mother a soft smile before bowing toward Brye. She attempted to curtsy, but it became a clumsy affair. The prince's mouth twitched.

Brye flushed and he left the room.

"My son is a good man," the queen said.

"To all mothers, their sons are good men," Brye replied as she approached the bed. She placed her kit on the small table, taking out only the journal and pencil.

"A very diplomatic answer," Queen Celine sighed, "but by the look on your face when you walked in, your teeth must be ground to dust at the remark. My son is a good man, but it does not take away that he can be stubborn and irritating like all men in the world."

"Perhaps," Brye chuckled, pulling a chair closer to the woman.

"Enid has been tending to me for some time now, but I am not getting any better for reasons we both are not honest about."

Brye swallowed her anxiety at the tart remark. "Enid has given me information about your case. She wants my point of view on the matter."

"And what skills do you possess that Enid does not? How can you give a new perspective on my condition?" The queen narrowed her eyes at her.

Brye was not intimidated by the older woman. "I learned everything I know from Enid," Brye said carefully. "But I have a different method of approach."

"Another diplomatic answer. You could have said you are better than Enid, but you did not. I respect that." The queen cupped her hands in her lap. "Well, how shall we proceed?"

"If you will let me," Brye leaned in the chair, "I would like to examine you carefully, but it would help if you were sedated."

The woman paled, her mouth gaping open. "You want to put me to sleep?"

"No." Brye waved her hands from side to side. "It is only a sedative. You will feel so relaxed you might fall asleep. This way, I can examine and probe the areas causing you pain. All I want is for you to be comfortable."

The queen gripped her hands tighter in her lap but nodded. "All right, let's get this over with."

Brye retrieved from the kit a small bottle with a tonic. She poured two fingers into a glass and gave it to the woman, who sniffed cautiously. "It smells sweet."

"Not all medicines need to taste unpleasant," Brye replied.

"You mean like cat piss or cow dung?"

Brye covered her laugh with her hand. The women's humor was refreshing and unexpected.

The queen chuckled before drinking the liquid in one gulp. She smacked her lips, "That was wonderful!"

While they waited for the tonic to work, Brye assisted the queen in lying back and raising her shift. She ensured not to touch the woman's skin until the medicine took effect. Sedating the queen was not entirely necessary. She could have examined without it, but Brye was still adjusting to her growing skill. For her well-being, she preferred the woman to be calm.

As her healing skills expanded, Brye had discovered an increasing connection to the suffering of her patients.

In the beginning, it had been gradual. If Brye wasn't paying attention, she might have confused the sudden connection as part of her imagination. A sting when she held a patient's hand in a delicate procedure. A burning sensation when aiding a child who played too close to the fire.

It was confusing and terrifying to experience. She did not yet understand the depth to which her abilities could manifest, and frankly, she was a little afraid to try.

Once the medicine took effect, Brye rubbed her hands together. The tingling sensation intensified until her hands burned. She then placed them on the queen's swollen abdomen and closed her eyes.

Knowing where to check, she started by probing the area of the swelling. She could sense and picture the internal organs of the different systems that made up the area. Brye's hands went lower toward her womb. She could see it and found a large lump in her uterus. Judging from her notes from Enid, the lump had grown in size and was probably causing her discomfort.

The queen moaned when Brye pressed down harder on the area. She soothed her with words. Taking a small jar of green ointment, she layered some on her hands and rubbed until the burning sensation increased again. The heat from her hands and the medical properties of the balm helped lower the swelling in the queen's abdomen.

Brye could heal the queen if she concentrated hard enough. But it was a risk. One she was not willing to take. Instead, she decided to help decrease the lump size and lower the inflammation. It would offer the queen some relief until they agreed on a treatment plan.

As Brye massaged the area, images appeared in her mind. Shocked, she pulled back, and they disappeared.

Should she continue? It was not the first time she would be able to see memories or thoughts, but the clarity of these were unsettling.

But she had to.

It was her responsibility. Carefully, Brye placed her hands again on the woman, and memories took shape like a fog being lifted. They were not her own.

Oh, but they were so painful.

❧

She was screaming, biting hard on her lower lip to take the pain as the unexpected contraction overcame her.

A miscarriage.

Another one.

The third one in three years since she became queen.

Her arms were wrapped around a young woman with wild copper hair.

"Oh, Elsywth, not again." She sobbed in the woman's arms. "How can I face him after another loss like this one."

"You can and you will." Elsywth rocked and soothed her with tingling fingers on her back.

Celine looked at Elsywth's plump face, with tears in her eyes as another contraction came over her. She felt the gush of blood in the swaddle between her legs. The metallic scent filled the room, a screaming reminder of her failure. Her loss.

I am a failure if I don't produce a child."

"That is untrue." Elsywth's nostrils flared, and she forced Celine to look at her. "You are the queen. Your sole purpose is to rule and do it wisely. A child will come when it is time, but your purpose in this world is not linked to only that role. If anyone makes you believe it, then you look down on them! They are the narrow-minded, ignorant beings below you. A woman will be whomever she chooses to be!"

Celine held her tighter as her words enfolded her like a blanket.

"The next child will be a boy, and he will be strong and brave," Elsywth whispered. "You will be so proud of him. You will see. I promise."

The Prince

Brye

Brye shuddered awake as a hand was placed on her shoulder. She abruptly sat, biting down a scream. The queen was sleeping, thankfully covered by the blanket.

Gareth removed his hand from her shoulder and stood back.

"I apologize," she whispered.

"That's all right. You seemed tired."

Brye stood up and stretched, rubbing her eyes, attempting to erase the images burned into her mind.

"I came to bring you refreshments. You were taking some time, and the king was asking questions. Once he knew you were here, he wanted news. I found both of you resting."

"That was unprofessional of me." Brye exhaled.

Gareth shrugged. "How is she?"

"She is in less pain," Brye informed in a low tone. "I need to discuss the result of my examination with Enid. She will be back tomorrow to speak to the queen."

"You won't be joining her?"

Brye glanced sideways, regarding him carefully. He stood with his arms crossed over his chest. His posture said disinterest, but his tone seemed genuinely concerned. Brye caught an earthy scent as he leaned in to speak in low tones, not to wake his mother.

"Only if required," she answered.

"I am sure it will be."

"Is that so?"

His twitching mouth drew her attention, and she quickly looked away, crossing her arms.

"My mother would prefer it." He coughed into his hand. "I believe."

"We shall see," she responded, emphasizing each word. Brye quickly put away her ointments. She placed a small bottle on the table. "If she is in pain, give her a spoonful of this."

Gareth uncrossed his arms and placed his hands in his pockets. "Noted. I'll accompany you out."

"I can find my way." She picked up the basket.

"I insist." He opened the door, gesturing for her to lead the way. She breezed by him, aware of him at her back the entire way down to the entrance hall. Brye expected him to leave her at the main entrance, but he continued beside her down the paths.

"You don't have to escort me all the way," she said, aware of his presence and the attention it drew.

"I don't have to do anything," he replied. "Are you heading back to your home?"

"Yes," she sighed. "I will meet Enid tomorrow."

For a while, they walked in silence. It was awkward in the beginning, neither exchanging words with each other. The only conversations were with the villagers who crossed their paths. The distance from the Royal Tower to her home was quite long, and Brye half expected him to get bored, especially as villagers continued to stop her for questions and concerns. Yet he waited patiently each time someone stopped her. She also found herself waiting for him when people sought his attention.

Once they reached her house, she turned. "Well, thank you—"

"I have a—"

"I'm sorry," Brye gave a tired smile. "You were saying?"

"I have a question." Gareth bit the inside of his mouth as he balanced on the balls of his feet.

She huffed out a breath. "Will it ever be asked?" She moved her kit from one arm to another, emotionally tired of the day. She needed to wake up early to meet with Enid.

"Do you know how to swim? I mean…" He rubbed the back of his neck. "Have you ever swam in the river or the lake?"

Brye's jaw dropped. "That is your question?"

"Yes."

"Well, not since I was a little girl. I was told my mother took us to the northern field by the river to swim." Her tone wobbled.

"Told?"

"Well," Brye eyed him carefully. His line of questioning was odd. She hadn't been asked that in a long time. "I don't remember much of my life before my mother died. I only have what others have told me or what I might think happened."

He looked away, nodding. "So, no one has told you who taught you to swim?"

"I assume my mother. How is this relevant to my healing abilities?"

Why is he so curious about such a vague piece of information?

Who cares how she learned to swim when what was important was the memories of her mother? Or the lack of. Her response must have put him on edge. Gareth took a step back and placed his hands in his pockets. His face became a mask of boredom once more.

"Nothing. You are right. It isn't relevant." He exhaled. "Goodbye."

"Goodbye," Brye said to his retreating figure.

Brye watched as he reached the end of the path. He stopped and looked back at her for a moment, shaking his head and mumbling.

Why was he so steamed up about it?

One thing was for sure. The prince was more than odd. He was something else entirely.

But what?

"Brye!" her mother called from the river's bank. "Be careful!"

"Oh, maither!" Brye yelled. The water was cool on her skin as she waddled through. She could see Tara running along the banks, splashing around and kicking the water angrily because she was still too small to swim out. Lenna attempted to calm her, only to be covered in water from head to toe.

"Here," said a voice behind Brye. "Let me teach you how to swim."

Brye turned, but the light was too strong, and she couldn't make out her teacher's face.

But she knew his voice.

His voice sounded as if he was a boy. He extended his hand and guided her further into the river. The water was calm, and slowly it rose to her chin. Brye lost her footing and dog paddled. She tried to stay above until the nerves took over. She thrashed about, trying to reach the shore.

The boy grabbed her by the waist and raised her head above water. "It's okay. Don't be scared."

Brye sobbed, wrapping her arms around his neck.

"It's okay. I've got you, and guess what? You swam!"

"I didn't," Brye whimpered into his shoulder.

"You did, too." He rubbed her back. "And next time, you will do it even better."

His fingers on her back were warm, and she could read his thoughts and emotions so clearly. He was happy. So very happy to be there with them. To be with her.

"Brye!" Her mother's voice came from the banks. "No reading others without their permission!"

"How does maither know these things?" Brye whispered in awe.

"Mothers know many things," the boy replied. "Want to try again?"

Brye pulled back and looked into the powerful features of her friend. He was grinning from ear to ear.
"Yes. Please."

Wild One

Tara

TARA SLOWED HER PACE as she reached the edge of the training fields. They were lush and green, with tall stones and trees to prevent the people from being hit by stray weapons. Most stones were on higher land, and the training circle was on the lower side of the incline. The massive stone wall and mountains protecting the village and valley from the outside could be seen in the distance.

Tara surveyed the surrounding trees. While the men's backs to her, she climbed the closest one and sat, her legs stretched on the branch and her back to the trunk. It was not the first time she had hidden away to watch training.

Training as a warrior was one of the villagers' many roles. There has never been a need for a war to fight, but being prepared was important. The fear of invasion from the Continent was at the back of their minds. Usually, only a few young men were assigned to warrior training. They would train for up to five years before retiring. The older men were required to continue training, but the younger did so more vigorously. In addition to those duties, active members kept the peace, especially when cups overflowed and tempers ran hot.

But the number of trainees had increased in the last two years, and even more so in the previous couple of months. More and more young men were assigned to warrior training, fulfilling two roles, like Aiden, who trained every morning and then worked in the fields helping his father. It was a current trend in the gossip mill. Everyone wondered why the increase in duties, yet no one decided to pose the question.

Except for Tara, who wondered continuously, and wanted to be an active participant in the training.

From her vantage point, Tara saw the head trainer Duncan come into the circle of trainees. He was a large man with bulging muscles, skin covered in scars, and a bald head. He had to be about the same age as the king, but his face was weathered by the elements, giving him an older appearance. But Tara was not deceived by his old man's looks. He could flatten any new trainee with one of his massive hands.

He called out to them to take out their weapons and shields.

"We will practice the coordination sets that I showed yesterday. But this time, you will do it right, unlike some weak girls." He spat on the ground.

That comment was rude and unnecessary. And untrue.

"Now, line up!" he barked, and the men scrambled to take their places.

Training started, and Tara was distracted from her thoughts of injustice by the activity in the field. She took mental notes of their mistakes in movement to recreate at home. Aiden had provided her with an older sword and ax to practice with. He might be against the idea of her training, but he never stopped providing her with the tools to do so.

Tara's attention shifted from watching the men in general to watching the prince, and she hummed under her breath. She had to admit, the prince was skilled. Not a single movement was wasted. She gave each warrior some time, but then her eyes fell upon Aiden. He lowered his left shoulder, which unbalanced him as he worked with the ax.

He could do it better. All of them could do better.

Tara understood that training took time and dedication. Most trainees had never used weapons before, and those with the experience needed more patience than those without. It only made Duncan seem more agitated.

A new figure entered the field from the south. Dressed in black and wielding a short sword, the young man strode in and went directly to the prince's small group. He was a stark contrast with his exotic looks and self-assured attitude.

That's odd. Beltran the mage is still here?

He decided to stay on, even though no registered visitors existed for centuries. Why? Did he find us a curiosity? Maybe his arrival reaffirmed the need for warriors?

As he entered, his presence on the field drew attention, even though he spoke with familiarity to Duncan and the prince. It was not his first time in the training field. He demonstrated superior experience in comparison with the new members.

Did they train sages for battle on the Continent? Do they need to learn to use weapons if they could use magic instead?

Then again, Tara had yet to see the mage use any magic.

She took note of his fighting style. He used his short sword as a weapon and part of his defense strategy. It differed from the crazed moves the new trainees brought or the prince's style with the long sword. Each movement was thought out and used to undermine the opponent's weakness. Fascinated, Tara leaned farther down the branch to get a closer look.

Duncan and the prince took turns sparring with the sage, stopping to discuss. The prince improved, if it was possible, with the techniques. Even at this distance, Tara could see they were evenly matched.

Gareth exchanged words with Duncan before leaving the field. Beltran stayed for further training. He stood to the side, arms crossed over his chest as Duncan made his displeasure known to the warriors. He repeated instructions and demonstrations repeatedly until the trainees had them down.

Tara watched, her heart beating rapidly in her chest. She was a warrior to the bone. From a young age, she dreamt of strategy and technique and awoke to put them into practice. She tested herself with every weapon she could lay her hands on, even the bow and arrow that were not widely used. Most men were trained in close combat, using shields, swords, and axes.

Yet, she was born a woman. She had to sit on the sidelines and watch with frustrating exasperation while the men were allowed weapons and training.

Especially when I could do it better.

For Tara, men and women were no different in battle. It was about potential and skill. Women might not be as physically strong as men, but they had more pain tolerance and agility.

Oh, the potential! We should have more opportunities than what has been set for us.

To be mated off and have babies.

To take care of animals.

To assist in the harvest.

There were all important roles, but there should be much more.

Lost in her thoughts, she did not notice when Duncan called for a rest. The men were coming toward her to sit under the shade of her tree.

No! Shit...

If they came closer, they would see her. But there was nowhere to go. Taking an uncalculated risk, she jumped down as the men arrived.

"What the—" Aiden jumped back as she landed behind him. "Tara, are you crazy?"

"Not at the moment," she answered.

"You are not supposed to be here," Aiden groaned. "You are supposed to be in the field."

"I should be doing a lot of things, but this–" she waved a hand in the direction of the training field. "is much more interesting."

"Yes," Aiden's gaze jumped around him as the crowd grew. "I am aware that it is, especially for you. However–"

"By the way, you lower your left shoulder too much in the first movements. It makes your aim lopsided when you trust your sword. You should—"

"I think she is all talk and no show," a man interrupted. Aiden narrowed his eyes at them, then at her. Tara waited with bated breath as more trainees joined the group around them. It was only a matter of time before they drew too much attention.

"Are you sure about this?" he whispered close.

"Deadly," she muttered.

It felt like an eternity before he removed his sword from the scabbard and held it out.

"Show us."

Tara shifted her stance. Aiden crossed his arms, keeping his face serious. The only betrayal of his true intentions was the twinkle in his eye. He was giving her the opening she needed.

"Yes, all mighty one," someone mocked.

Tara reached for the sword, feeling the weight, trying to hide her smile by biting the inside of her cheek. It was an extension of her arm, a part of her. She took one deep breath and completed both sets of movements perfectly.

"Something like that, right?"

Silence followed, and Aiden's grin vanished instantly.

"What are you doing here?"

Duncan.

"I was just—" Her explanation was cut short by Duncan's grip on her arm as he violently dragged her across the field toward the village.

"Hey, Duncan! She wasn't doing anything wrong," Aiden called out. He attempted to pull Tara away from Duncan. The older man backhanded Aiden across the face with one swipe, and continued to drag Tara away.

"Get your hands off me!" She struggled against him.

Duncan stopped. He held a deathly grip on Tara's arm, staring her down.

"Don't think I don't know. This is not the first time you have been to the training fields."

Tara looked away, scowling.

"You have been a thorn in our side for years, Tara. Sneaking about and trying to do what you are not supposed to."

Tara ground her teeth almost to dust. Duncan leaned down at her, spit falling on her face with the force of his words. "Know your place, Tara."

Aiden pushed Duncan aside and got in between them.

"She'll leave, Duncan," Aiden said. He gave Tara a pleading look. "Go! I don't want you to get hurt."

Her? Hurt? She could take anyone on, if she wanted. But Aiden would probably get hurt as well, bringing a sour taste to her mouth. Her hesitation must have been read for stubbornness, because Duncan stood taller, took out his sword and motioned toward Aiden. "Ready yourself."

Beltran held Tara back as a circle of onlookers formed around them.

Aiden held his sword at the ready. His stance was tense, while Duncan appeared relaxed. He circled Aiden, sword extended, examining. In a blink of an eye, Duncan charged. The younger man blocked, but the force of the blow pushed him back.

It was painful to watch. Aiden was quick in his movements, but experience superseded youth. Duncan was barely winded. He disarmed Aiden with a quick flick of his sword. Then he took the opportunity to give the younger man an uppercut to the chin. He fell back to the ground.

"This is an important lesson to learn," Duncan instructed the crowd of onlookers. He pointed his sword at the sprawling body on the ground. "The head leads the body. If the head goes down, the body goes as well. Here is another example."

Duncan grabbed Tara by the hair, pulling her across the field. She yelped as unwanted tears of pain and anger ran down her cheeks.

"Never, ever..." Duncan's voice was cold and low. "Humiliate me again. Rules are there for a reason, and one must obey them. If you truly want to train with me, as you have made public, you must first learn to obey and respect the ranks. If you can't show respect to authority, you have no place here. Do you understand?"

He released her hair but gripped her arm, shaking her.

"Understand?"

Tara opened her mouth, but nothing came out.

Duncan brought his face closer to her. "You only get others hurt when you think of only yourself."

He let her go where she had started, underneath the tall tree.

Stupid. How can I be so stupid?

The warriors returned to their activities. Tara crossed her arms over her chest, digging her nails into her skin.

Lenna appeared, her eyebrows furrowed and her bottom lip swollen from her teeth. "What happened?"

"I could have taken him if I had a sword," Tara mumbled.

Beltran separated from his group and came in their direction. He gave each of them an assessing look before speaking.

"I think you both should go," Beltran warned.

Lenna placed a hand on Tara's back and led her away.

Before leaving, Tara saw Aiden stand and spit on the ground. Duncan snapped an order to the trainees but held Aiden to the side. He spoke in low tones. Duncan's face flushed, and whatever he said made the younger man tense. After he was done, Aiden locked eyes with her. He gave her a short nod and an uneasy smile.

Unfamiliar shivers ran down her spine. She bit down on her lip and ran home, leaving Lenna alone at the edge of the field.

An Impulsive Decision

Tara

THE RUN HOME DID nothing to calm Tara's nerves or her anger. It only made her realize what a fool she had been to expose herself. She had always been forthcoming in her desire to become a warrior. Like Duncan had said, it wasn't the first time she watched. But she had never participated. She had never shown what she could do.

And that made it worse. She'd shown her hand before she needed to play it.

It only made what she was about to do even more important.

Tara reached home before Lenna and found Brye working. Her older sister dropped the herbs she collected on the table, eyes wide.

"What on earth happened to you?"

Tara quickly looked in the mirror. Her face was flushed to the top of her head and covered in dirt. Ignoring Brye's questioning gaze, she went into the bathing room and slammed the door.

She came out just as Lenna entered the house. "What is your plan?"

"What plan?" Brye looked at both of her sisters.

"Nothing." Tara snapped, scrubbing her face hard.

"I don't believe you," Lenna said sternly. "I know you. You won't let this go. If you are going to do something stupid, we need to know beforehand."

"Will someone please tell me what's going on!" Brye shouted, placing her hands on her hips.

"Nothing!" Tara sat down. "I'm going to petition to train as a warrior."

Tara kept her voice conversational. She grabbed a brush and worked on her hair with fury, pulling at her scalp until it ached.

"A warrior?" Lenna sank into a chair. Her eyes were twice as big on her face.

Brye momentarily paled but recovered her color quickly, and her voice grew with each breath. "Are you out of your *mind*, Tara?"

"To be honest, I am surprised you waited this long." Lenna rubbed her face.

"You knew about this?" Brye gaped.

"She hasn't made it a secret." Lenna looked at the ceiling before waving her hands. "I wouldn't be surprised if all of Avalon knows by now how badly she wants to be a warrior."

"It's evident that you haven't thought this through." Brye massaged her forehead before giving Tara a pleading look. "For once, have you considered the consequences of your actions?"

"I thought maybe you, of all people, would understand." Tara dropped the brush with a clatter on the table. "Brye, you are a renowned Healer. Your tonics are extremely effective. You, dear Lenna, have magical powers. Each of us has a gift. It's what makes us special. Since Beltane, I have had this energy and impatience to do something, to be someone. I'm even stronger and more agile than before. I was not put on this world to be a spectator."

"That's all well and good until you realize there is more to being a warrior than using a weapon or hitting a target," Brye explained.

"Tara." Lenna took her hand and forced her to look at her. "I know how you feel. The constant need to prove yourself. But you should not compare yourself to either of us."

"You're not going to go along with this?" Brye sat appalled at both of them.

"Do you honestly think anything I would say will hold weight by now? She has made up her mind."

"I'm right here." Tara pointed to herself.

"For all the sense you seem to show," Brye grumbled.

"Do you get my point or not?" Tara said. "It doesn't matter. I know what I am good at."

Lenna placed both her hands on the table and released a long breath. "Make your petition, Tara. I hope you know what you're doing."

Brye sat back and turned away, crossing her arms over her chest. "Just go."

Tara had never been to the Royal Tower by herself. It was still relatively early, and she did not know if the king would be in the audience room. Determined to be heard, she knocked on the door, tapping her foot as she waited. She avoided biting her nails by crossing her arms over her chest.

I will not lose my temper. I will state my case. I will plead and, if necessary, beg, but I will only leave once he says yes.

The small attendant opened the door and raised an eyebrow.

"Three sisters in less than a month!"

Tara narrowed her eyes at him.

"I wish for an audience with King Manus. It is of grave importance."

Edgar blinked, confused, but he let her in and escorted her to the second-floor receiving rooms. He knocked and waited. The door opened, and Tara came face-to-face with Roweena. The royal advisor assessed her before she opened the door further.

"Please do come in."

The royal advisor made Tara's skin crawl. She seemed too beautiful to be real, except for her deep black, gray-streaked eyes. They bore into a person, seeing right through the skin.

She is like a poisonous snake, beautiful but deadly.

"I requested to see the king," Tara said cautiously.

"I know, but the king is indisposed. He has asked me to field all his audiences for the day." She gestured to the bench. "Come, please be seated."

Tara carefully sat on the bench, her back straight, while she drummed her fingers on her thighs. Her eyes wandered around the room. It was large, shaped in a semicircle, with a carpet covering most of the stone floor and luxurious cushions on the chairs and seats. The fireplace burned with low embers; faded tapestries surrounded the mantle. The room was cozy and surprisingly warm.

Except for the woman sitting opposite her.

Cold. Deadly cold.

"Now, tell me what has brought you here."

Tara cleared her throat. "I would like to petition the king to train as a warrior."

"Oh?" Roweena raised a curious brow.

"Yes, and I want to start training soon."

"You know it is forbidden for women to train."

"It is forbidden now but doesn't have to be forever. Avalon can evolve and change to benefit the whole community," Tara explained, her arms gripping the bench until her fingers ached.

"What skills do you possess that would make you a satisfactory warrior?"

"None." Tara leaned forward. "I have skills that would make me exceptional. I am strong and agile. I'm a fast learner. I have already taught myself a great deal, but it is not enough."

Roweena tapped a finger on her plump lips, deep in thought. She was about to say something when the massive doors opened, and Gareth walked in. He was filthy from the training field. Behind him followed Beltran, equally as dirty. The prince's eyes fell on

Tara rather than the advisor. His brow furrowed. "Is my father not attending court today?"

The royal advisor stood and bowed upon his entrance. Tara was slower to follow.

"I hope your training went well, your royal highness," Roweena spoke, ignoring the question.

"Very." Beltran turned to Tara and grinned. "We had some interesting entertainment today."

Tara looked down at her feet, ignoring the bait.

The prince insisted, "My father?"

"He is with the queen," Roweena answered crisply. "She feels better, but he wished to attend to her. He instructed me to receive the daily requests."

"Did he?" Gareth circled them slowly, one hand on the hilt of his sword. "Well, I am here. I'll attend to her request."

"I am sure your highness has more pressing matters," Roweena continued.

"I will be the judge of that." He turned toward Tara. It was hard to distinguish his intentions when he looked continuously bored. Her heart and stomach sank. It was one thing to ask the king, who in all appearances looked like someone easy to convince, but the royal advisor and the prince were a different matter entirely.

Don't lose your temper. State your case. You have come this far.

If only she could believe in her bravado.

"Well?" Gareth snapped impatiently.

Tara stiffened her arms and raised her chin. "I would like to petition to train as a warrior."

The prince smirked and rubbed his bearded chin. "Really?"

Tara gripped her hands harder. "Yes. As I have stated to the royal advisor, women might not be encouraged to train as warriors, but they should not be forbidden. We should be given a choice."

An idea came to Tara, and she ran with it. Turning toward Beltran, she asked, "I am sure women and men train side by side on the Continent. Is it not so, Beltran?"

"Yes," Beltran's voice trailed off as he darted looks between Gareth and Tara.

Yes! It worked.

Roweena sat silently, watching the exchange with open curiosity. The prince gave Beltran a nod to continue.

"On the Continent, most women can train or do as they wish. It would depend on where they were born."

"Avalon is not the Continent. The Founders made us different. There has been no need for women to train," Gareth said. "There are currently more men than women. It is wise to protect the population we have."

He had a point. Damn it!

She needed a new tactic.

"Be that as it may," Tara said, her voice edged. "If the men fight as I saw today, I do not see the point of training so many. Quantity cannot be better than quality. Having 100 skilled warriors of both genders is better than twice that of inferior men."

"Is that so?" Gareth repeated. "Do you think you could do it better?"

He had a death wish.

The blood pounded in her head as she attempted to keep her temper in check. "I know I can," Tara said, enunciating every word.

Gareth crossed his hands behind his back and balanced on the balls of his feet. He motioned Beltran to the window, and they both spoke in hushed tones.

What was with those two? They seemed to have grown close in such a short period of time. It didn't sit right with her. Tara sat back down stiffly, rubbing her temples. Did she stay? Did she go? She couldn't leave without an answer.

She jumped when the prince next spoke.

"Then, it will be settled that way." He crossed his massive arms.

"Sorry." Tara looked around the room. "What way?"

Roweena was still quiet and observing. She had not participated in the exchange nor engaged Tara in conversation. The sage stood with his back against a wall.

"If you wish to train, then like the warriors, you must prove your worth," Gareth explained. "Tomorrow at dawn, you will spar with an opponent of my choosing. You will be permitted to train if you win by disarming or dropping your opponent."

A current of electricity ran through Tara's body. Her dream was within her grasp.

There has to be a catch.

"If you lose, you will never set foot on the field again on pain of banishment," he finished.

Ah. The catch.

"I would consider carefully before answering."

"How do I know I will be given a fair chance?" She narrowed her eyes.

"According to your own words, you have observed the warriors on the field. It would insult your intelligence if I selected an opponent who is not your equal."

"I must agree with the opponent."

He nodded.

Tara bit her lip and thought. The cost was high, but so would be the gain. It was what she always wanted, to prove she could train with the best of them. Neither her sisters nor Aiden understood. Tara had no intention of losing this first challenge. There was no room for failure.

"I agree with your terms," she said firmly.

Gareth smiled with genuine amusement. "See you tomorrow at dawn."

Warrior

Tara

Dawn came faster than Tara had anticipated. None of them got much sleep waiting for the tell-tale dwindling light to reach the window.

"Tara, have you thought what would happen if you lost?" Brye asked her head in her hands. "You would have to stay away from the training field. Something you will not do. Banishment means exile to the Continent by yourself. Death might be easier."

"I did consider it," Tara answered, rubbing her face and taking a deep breath.

"Then, why?" Brye insisted. Lenna was slowly pacing the room, arms over her stomach. Her sister stayed behind instead of going to her training.

Tara looked away, silent for a few breaths. "I am not like you."

"We already know that, but—" Brye said, but Tara waved a hand in her direction, silencing her.

"I need to do this. I can't rest. Every night I dream of a battle I can't win. My mind has become a place where memories and fears are all jumbled together. However, when I awaken, I know only one clear thing. I need to be stronger. I need to learn to fight and be a warrior, for my sake and others.

"It's only a nightmare," Brye whispered, but her voice held no conviction.

"Is it, Brye?" Tara asked.

"I dream about the strangest things," Lenna said. "Since Beltane, I dream of big tapestries with no beginning or end." Lenna's eyes were hollow as she spoke. "I remember bits and pieces. I always wake up drenched in sweat and so cold. They feel like broken glass, as if they got mixed up and need to be sorted and reconstructed. I feel that if I concentrate hard enough, I can sew them all together again, and they make sense."

"I dream of *maither*," Brye confessed slowly. "Or at least, I think it's her. I forget easily during the day. It's frustrating to wake up and not know if it is a memory or a dream. To know if, for once, I have something I remember about my past and not what I have been told. It never made sense. I was the oldest. I should remember more of it."

"But you don't, Brye," Lenna gently touched her arm. She rubbed it carefully. "And you shouldn't blame yourself for it."

"Isn't it odd?" Brye continued. "All our memories start the day after she disappeared?"

They stayed silent for a few breaths; each lost in their thoughts.

"What could all this mean?" Tara asked. Brye shrugged. Lenna sat down and placed her hands on the table.

"It means things around us are changing. We are changing, and we need to adapt. If you need to train as a warrior, then you must."

Brye sat back in her chair, rubbing her hands together for comfort. "I guess so, but I can't shake the feeling we are on some cliff, and soon we will fall."

"Leave it to you to be lyrical about it," Tara chuckled softly. Lenna took each of her sisters' hands and squeezed.

A large crowd had arrived to see the fight. Tara stood with her sisters when Aiden came running toward their small group, his gait a bit forced.

"Is it true?" His face was black and blue from training the day before. Tara would insist Brye heal him after the bout.

"Is what true? Be specific." Tara said. She winced when she saw him up close. It was worse than at a distance.

"You are to prove yourself to train to be a warrior?" he asked apprehensively.

"That is true," she responded, her eyes leveled. "If you are going to start giving me the same old—"

"No." He raised both his hands in a sign of peace. "I know when I have lost a battle."

"But not the war," Lenna mumbled.

Tara overheard her, but Aiden seemed to be focused on something else. He took her hand in his. She winced. They were swollen, with his knuckles wrapped with bloody bandages.

Oh, Aiden. I got you in trouble, didn't I?

Tara looked into his eyes, and the warmth there shocked her system. He was always there, being kind and holding her hand. Despite all the pain and his terrible appearance, he came to support her dream. Even if he didn't wholly agree with it.

"I will be fine, Aiden," she reassured him.

"No, Tara, I—"

"Shall we get this started?"

She hadn't noticed Gareth's approach, and she and Aiden quickly stepped apart. Tara curled her fingers, still feeling the heat of his hand in hers.

"Yes." She nodded to the prince. "Let's get this over with."

The prince motioned Duncan forward with another warrior. The man was shirtless, covered in scars, with muscled arms and legs. He wore a breastplate, and his dark hair was braided back away from his face. Tara knew this was not an unskilled trainee. This was the prince's equal.

"Wynn will be your opponent," Gareth said. He gave Tara a pointed look. "Do you approve?"

She assessed the warrior, then nodded. Once.

"Choose your weapons."

Tara chose a small shield that was easy to maneuver. She tested the weight by moving it in a defensive strike. She had brought the old sword she used in training and a small dagger tied to her hips as a secondary weapon. Wynn chose a giant shield and a small, single-handed double-bladed ax. Both approached the center of the sparing circle and stood ready.

"Remember," Gareth shouted for everyone around the center circle to hear. "The first to incapacitate their opponent in any way will be the winner."

Tara held her stance, shield up and sword hand ready. Her stomach tightened with nerves, and blood rushed with every beat of her heart. Breathing deeply, she concentrated on the shield's weight, the blade's tension, and the ground's firmness beneath her. It was not the time to see or hear the crowd, only her opponent. As if by magic or instinct, time slowed. Duncan gave the go, and Wynn approached with steady quick strides.

He wanted the fast kill—the easy win.

But Tara was ready.

She widened her stance and prepared for the first blow of the ax as it hit the shield. The impact vibrated through her arm and pushed her back a step. Tara evaded and deflected, pacing around in a circle as she studied Wynn's actions for the next moments. She did not expect him to slow his advances. Instead, he would try to tire her out with a quick succession of attacks. He was an offensive fighter, clearly, using his size and superior strength to his advantage, the type of fighter who liked to barrel through opponents. He would wear down her shield until her arm gave out, either too sore or too broken to lift.

But Tara would not play his game.

He swung the ax in a wide backswing and she leaned back, letting the ax miss her chin by a mere handwidth. He came around again, lifting the ax. Tara raised her sword arm and blocked his weapon, timing it so she caught him at the peak of the downswing. And she shoved. He stumbled, momentum interrupted, and he took a step back.

Time to put him in his place.

Her sword scraped against the ax, metal on metal creating sparks. Before he could recover, she used the shield to redirect the ax to the side. She opened her hand and let the shield fly. It skittered across the ground like a rock skipped over water. Wynn watched it go, then spat at her.

"Stupid girl," he hissed gleefully.

Good. Make him believe she lost the shield on purpose.

Tara regained her stance and forced him back with a solid kick to his shield. Her boot cracked with the blow. Gripping the sword with both hands, she circled him once more. He growled at her and dumped his own shield as well.

"No one can say I didn't give you a fair shot now, little girl." He gestured with his free hand. "C'mon. I don't even have a shield now."

Tara smirked, breath heaving in and out of her lungs.

Now, I've got you.

Sweat had worked into her eyes, but she did not stop to wipe it away. He lunged forward, and she blocked with her sword again, sliding in close and under his arm, using her small size to her advantage. The ax tangled with her blade's hilt. It was a move she had seen Beltran use the day before. The crowd made a noise, but Tara ignored them, her arms shaking with the force to push his ax away from her. Determination and pride burned through her.

She caught movement out of her peripheral vision, his meaty hand swinging up to grab her. It was bold and risky, but she released one hand off her sword, wrapped her fingers around the leather strap of his breastplate, and yanked his body forward at the same time as she brought her knee up, connecting with his groin.

Hard.

Wynn yelled, and his force on her lessened. Hand still wrapped in the strap, she banged her forehead against his nose, feeling the soft cartilage crush under her skull. With her own yell, she brought her foot up and planted him solidly in the chest, kicking him backward. Tara bit her lip bloody, holding back the pain as he fell to the ground

She gave him no quarter, closing the distance between them and pressing a foot to his thick throat. The tip of her sword touched his groin threateningly; one slice and the damage would be fatal.

"Do you yield?" she demanded. Blood dripped from her cracked lip, and the roar in her ears made it difficult to hear anything but her own heartbeat. She pressed down harder. "Do you yield?"

"He yields," answered Gareth.

Tara blinked and glanced up, the world rushing back to her again as the adrenaline faded from her mind. She took her foot off Wynn's throat and retreated a step, letting her sword hang limp at her side.

She gazed around the circle of spectators, finding her sisters and Aiden. With the high of the fight fading, she became more aware of her arm throbbing from splinters, her broken boot, and her wrist was turning an alarming shade of blue and purple. But the pain was inconsequential to the satisfaction of finally proving to others that she was born to do this. Determined, she turned to the prince, who crossed his arms in the circle's center. His face was set, and his jaw worked as if he was trying not to say anything.

"I will train," Tara said to him, raising her sword to point at him.

Not a question or a plea.

A command.

She dared him to say no.

The prince's eyes assessed her from head to toe, and Tara held her breath, not wavering as she waited for his verdict.

He nodded. "You will train." Gareth's mouth twitched slightly as if holding back a smile. It was one of the few times it seemed genuine. "And the Founders help us."

Choices

Brye

WHEN THEY RETURNED HOME, Brye shooed Tara off for a bath and some rest, despite it being only early afternoon. Her sister needed the respite after her fight. Brye shook her head with a sigh.

She was torn between feeling fiercely proud of Tara and concerned about what training would look like for her, but Brye supposed that was just her sisterly worry getting the best of her. If anything, Tara had proven to be strong, resilient, and resourceful. She would be fine in the training ring with the men.

A soft knock sounded on the door interrupted her thoughts. She was surprised to find Edgar, the royal retainer, outside, cap in hand.

"Good evening, Miss Brye."

"Evening, Edgar." She wrapped her blanket tighter around her shoulders. The mists were dense, dropping the temperature and chilling her bones. "Is there something wrong with the queen?"

"No, miss." His head bobbled. "But your presence has been requested to the Royal Tower."

Brye narrowed her eyes. "Is it important? Can't it wait until tomorrow?"

"I don't know, miss. You would have to ask."

"One moment."

Brye closed the door and swiftly got ready. She braided her hair, grabbed her cloak, and headed out. The mists settled on the ground, and Brye could see very little. Edgar was waiting outside the door with a mist candle which provided an efficient way of navigating the path. As they walked, conversations bounced off each other, indistinguishable. Brye pulled her cloak tighter around herself.

"Please keep up, miss."

They reached the Royal Tower some moments later. Edgar helped remove her cloak and led her to the royal family's private apartments on the second floor. He motioned to a chair outside one of the rooms.

"Please wait here." He hung the cloak on a peg in the hall and knocked on the door. He went inside, leaving the door somewhat ajar.

Why did they call her in late in the evening? Was there another issue with the queen? No, they would have called Enid. Was it something to do with Tara? The king did not seem angry or upset after the bout that morning. If anything, he seemed surprised and entertained with the idea.

Brye's mind wondered when the door opened again and Edgar motioned her forward. She smoothed her skirts and made sure her hair was still in place. Her stomach turned in knots as she entered the chamber. King Manus, Queen Celine, and Roweena stood like a receiving party. It did nothing to help her nerves.

Many candles, including the fireplace, lit the room. It would have been stifling without the open shutters that let in the cool, sultry night air. Queen Celine stepped forward, gripping Brye's hands, and led her closer to the fire.

"Thank you for coming on such short notice," the queen said, excitement filtering through her touch. Her color looked better than when she saw her last. Her smile illuminated the room. "We know it is late."

The king stood back with both his arms behind his back. "We hope we have not inconvenienced you."

Brye let go of the queen's hands and curtseyed. "Not at all, Your Majesties. As long as I can be of service."

The queen motioned for her to sit. She was about to do so when the door opened again, and the prince strolled in. He stopped in his tracks, only to narrow his eyes at each person.

"Son! You have arrived just in time!" the king greeted Gareth with a thump on the back.

Gareth cleared his throat, and his eyes met Brye's. "What is going on?"

Brye gave a slight shrug. He looked at his mother and raised an eyebrow. Queen Celine sat, rubbing her hands and fixing her hair. Brye and the royal advisor followed.

"I will leave it to you, my dear." The king kissed his mate on the cheek and left the room. The queen looked visibly uncomfortable with the prince's arrival and Brye's curious gaze. Roweena sat back in her chair with her legs crossed, waiting.

"Would you like me to inform them?"

"Inform us of what?" Gareth demanded.

The queen shook her head, then straighter. "We have important news. The king and I have spoken to the royal advisor about the future. Your future, my son. And yours too, Brye." Queen Celine's voice became more animated with each word.

Roweena looked entertained.

Gareth glared with his hands on his hips, evidently not as much.

Brye's stomach filled with dread. "My future?" she interrupted. "I am training to be a Healer, Your Majesty."

"Well, it seems your future has changed. Expanded! Gaining even more potential! Considering your lineage, abilities, and presence, the king and I have decided to sanctify a union with our heir."

Brye tried to speak but couldn't form coherent words.

Sanctify... a union?

Mate the prince? Her? Of all people. Enid's words slowly filtered into her mind. Her mouth went dry. It would have been comical if it was not her future being discussed.

Have they all lost their minds?

Gareth cursed.

"There must be someone else." Brye attempted to regain some part of the sanity of the conversation. "I mean, I am honored to be considered, but perhaps the prince can decide for himself?" She turned around in the chair to pin Gareth with a look, panic rising in her throat. "Don't you want to? Decide for yourself, I mean."

His jaw was set, and his hands were fisted at his side. Brye had never seen him so disjointed.

"It is custom for the king and queen to choose the mate of the prince or princess," Roweena explained. "The queen was wisely selected for our king. A lot must be taken into consideration. The well-being of the entire kingdom depends on it."

"We have been discussing it for days." Queen Celine smiled nervously at them. "Your family has been blessed with magical abilities. We considered all three of you. Tara was a top choice—"

"What?" Gareth hissed out.

Horror filtered through the panic until both wrestled for dominance in Brye's mind. Tara? Her wild, chaotic, fierce baby sister?

She glanced at Gareth. Brye had dried herbs in her house with more personality. Tara and Gareth? Not on her watch.

And Lenna? Sweet, quiet, delicate Lenna—

"However," Queen Celine continued. "With all that has occurred in the last few days, we realized a match with Tara would not suit. Lenna is a Mist Maiden, and she cannot be mated. We considered you but at the time we believed that you might have had a previous engagement. Only until recently were we informed that you did not."

Previous engagement? Who? *Enid.* She must have told the queen that she was available. She was going to murder the woman after today. How dare her?

The queen continued speaking, even as Brye's mind whirled. "You are the best choice of all the women in Avalon. You do not need to stop training in the healing arts or attending to others. It was a quality we considered to be valuable!"

Brye shook her head very slowly.

This can't be happening. Someone, help!

Gareth recovered from his shock and took command of the situation. "I would like a word with Brye."

The queen regarded Gareth cautiously.

Roweena smirked. "Where there is hate—"

"Now!" the prince growled, cutting Roweena off. He went and opened the door to the room. Edgar jumped to his feet in the hall, knocking off a candle. He fumbled on the ground before it could cause more damage.

"You are right, son." Queen Celine stood. She gave Brye an encouraging smile and patted the prince's arm as she left.

"Interesting." Rowenna took her leave as well, clasping her hands behind her back.

The door closed, and silence screamed through the room. Gareth let out a long breath and rubbed the back of his neck. Brye didn't move, her eyes wide as she tried to gain some sense of this information.

Gareth dropped his long body into the chair opposite her. "This was not what I planned."

"Did you know about this?" Brye whirled on him.

"My mother mentioned something to my father about it being time I mated, but I did not give it another thought."

"I think one would take such a comment seriously."

"It wasn't the first time they mentioned it. I had other important business on my mind." He pointed at her. "They only started taking it seriously after Beltane. Even more so after you visited my mother. You are all she ever talks about."

Brye blushed, then cleared her throat. "I'm flattered."

"It's the highest compliment."

"I will take it as such." She gripped her hands tighter in her lap.

Gareth sat back, arms over his stomach and legs crossed at the ankle. He must have been outdoors because he wore the same black pants and a loose tunic from that morning. His hair, curly on the top, was a mess from his hands continuously running through it. He wasn't conventionally attractive, but there was something she couldn't place about him.

Gareth raised an eyebrow, and his mouth twitched.

Caught staring, Brye looked away. She wet her lips before speaking. "They have faith you will convince me to accept."

"They believe we might agree."

"I find it unlikely. We have nothing in common. Nothing can be used to negotiate what the other wants. You don't even like me enough, and I certainly don't like you."

"Is that so?" Gareth pinched his lips. "What evidence do you have that I dislike you?"

"Isn't it obvious? You make an effort to ignore me. What was it your friend said?" Brye's face hardened. "That I was '*too tempting to be sincere.*'"

Gareth's head fell back, and he laughed. The loud, full sound surprised Brye and made her stomach flip.

"Sounds like something a jealous man would say." Gareth smiled. "I am sure Dagonet happily spread the rumor along."

"Why in all of Avalon would he do that?"

"Come now, Brye. We both know the answer."

Brye flushed and crossed her arms over her chest. Dagonet had been insistent that year, and every year since, for her to accept his suit. Her eyes returned to Gareth, whose intense gaze made her squirm. "Don't you want to have an opportunity to find love? We barely know each other."

He leaned in her direction. "Is there someone you already love?"

"No. And if there were, it would be none of your business."

"Then my love life is none of yours."

"Be that as it may," her voice cracked. She cleared it. "My answer stays the same. I do not accept your proposal."

Brye stood and headed for the door. Gareth reached it faster, blocking the exit with his arm. She rolled her eyes. "Let me pass."

"Can we at least discuss this?"

"There is nothing in this for me." Brye pushed at his chest.

"Just hear me out." He gave her some space, and lifted his hands as a peace offering. "Please."

Brye crossed her arms. "Alright, what will I gain?"

"To be a princess and then the queen would help you gain access to resources not only from Avalon, but we can start a way to get them from the Continent. More importantly, you can have access to something you would protect more than your life, your sisters."

A short awareness ran through her. It was as if he said exactly what she needed to hear even to consider this ridiculous proposal. "Now, you do have my attention."

"I'm glad that I am speaking a language you find appealing."

"My patience, not so much."

Gareth sighed and rubbed the back of his neck. "Okay. If you consider my proposal, you can be closer to Lenna, ensuring that Roweena is training her respectfully."

Brye froze, her gaze narrowing. Lenna had been haggard the last few weeks. She avoided discussing her training and Brye's concern grew with each passing day. It was clear that Roweena was not interested in keeping her sister healthy.

"For my part, I will ensure that Tara is treated fairly. She will not be harassed and trained to her full capacity."

Brye knew Tara could hold her own, but an extra pair of eyes would be more than helpful.

"You and I have the potential of working together to change Avalon for good. You will not achieve that by standing on the sidelines."

"And if I like the sidelines?"

"Brye." His eyes twinkled as he spoke. "We both know you are not made to stand on the sidelines. Every Beltane ceremony proves it."

He had been watching her. Gareth had been aware of her the entire time, as much as she was of him. Of course, she will never admit it.

Ever.

Gareth cut through her thoughts, closing the distance between them. "I know it is overwhelming, and you have much to consider but, maybe we can agree to at least get to know each other. It would make my mother unbelievably happy."

His hands were soft on her arms, still projecting an insistent warmth and strange emotion. Brye should have been insulted and irritated, but the heat radiated from her was the opposite. Her body wanted to lean into him. It was unexpected, and at that moment unhelpful. She forced herself to stand her ground.

Brye lowered her gaze to the line of tattoos on his neck. "And her happiness is that important to you?"

"Wouldn't you do anything for those you love?"

She would. Brye would break herself apart for her sisters. They would never ask, but she would.

"Then, you gain nothing."

"I gain more than you know." He let go of her arms, placed his hands on each side of her head against the wall. "I get what I truly want, Brye. What I have wanted for a long time," he whispered a second before his lips reached for hers.

It was unexpected and completely different than what she thought kissing the prince would be. Brye thought a kiss from him would be hard, brutal, and painful. Cold. It was what he showed the world.

This kiss was everything but.

It was soft and warm. He played with her lips, tasting her. One of his hands caressed her cheek and moved to her neck.

It was sweet and gentle.

A warmth spread from her chest, and the fleeting emotion grew until she caught it, savored it, and identified what it was.

Longing.

A sear, unbearable longing for more. So much more. Her hands went to his chest, gripping his shirt and urging him to change the kiss. To quench the thirst that invaded her. But Gareth drew back, scorched by her touch.

Brye repeatedly blinked to regain focus.

What was that?

The feeling of longing disappeared as soon as the kiss ended.

Was it his feelings?

It had been intense.

"What do you say?" His thick voice was the only clue he was affected.

Brye had to take a moment to remember what they were agreeing on. The conversation and the entire evening had thrown her in a loop. This couldn't be happening to her.

"Could you be more specific?"

Is that my voice? So breathy?

"Will you, in all appearances, be my mate, Brye?"

Brye was of two minds. He had made strong points. Ones that would bring her closer to what she wanted. To help her island, and her sisters. But there was more to all this, right? What did he truly gain? Was he so selfless that he would mate with someone he apparently dislikes all to make his mother happy? To make the kingdom happy?

She could say no, and push him away. Damn the consequences. But, something about his proposal rang true. And if the prince was hiding something, she needed to be closer to him to find out. The only question left was if she would survive the entire debacle emotionally.

"Yes," she responded, touching swollen lips. He stared at her mouth. Brye removed her fingers and frowned at him. "I will accept your proposal, on one condition."

His lips twitched. "And that is?"

"We are honest with each other."

"To the best of my abilities, I will be honest with you, Brye."

Clearly, that was misleading, but it would have to do. For now.

"May I be dismissed?"

"Of course." Gareth nodded. "I hope we can spend time together. It would be nice to get to know each other a bit. My mother would also love to spend time with you. I think she might take up more of your time than me."

Brye didn't trust her words. She nodded, pushing away from the door, her hands tense.

"Anything else that needs to be considered?"

"Not for now."

Gareth helped her with her cloak, and accompanied her to the door of the Royal Tower.

Before the open door, he took her hand softly, rubbing her knuckles with his thumb. He gazed at it for a moment before raising it to his lips. The fleeting feeling was there again, wanting to be caught, and examined right there at the edge of her fingertips.

I could try to read him. I could do it right now.

But she didn't. Not like this. Besides, the warmth of his hand and lips were distracting. He released her and opened the door behind her. "Thank you for your time, Brye."

She sensed his gaze on her as she disappeared down the path, rubbing her hand the entire time.

Splitting

Tara

"Everything hurts." Tara trudged back from the fields, Aiden trailing along beside her. The sun dusted the skies in purples and indigoes, and in the distance, she could see the mists creeping in.

Tara gave a satisfied sigh that ended in a wince. It had been her first day of training. Duncan had a fit when he was told, but Gareth remained firm. He did not go back on their agreement and forced Duncan into compliance. King Manus aided matters by supporting Gareth's decision. They were adamant Tara would train, and there was no argument.

They had gone through a grueling schedule. Her wrist was not nearly healed enough, making every movement painful. Most of the men had been dismissive of her, hardly paying attention, but she'd kept pace with them just fine.

They would see, in time, that she had a right to be there.

After training, they were told to go help in the fields with the crops. A few hours of toiling in the soil, and either of them was fit for more than their beds. Tara had attempted to motivate conversation or continuously complain to see if Aiden reacted.

"At least tomorrow we don't train," Tara pointed out. "We could help your father at the field."

Aiden nodded again in response, walking with his gaze lost.

They reached her house. There was a light at the window alerting them that someone was home.

"Say something." Tara stopped outside the door.

"What do you want me to say?"

"Anything." She looked up at him, trying to figure out what was wrong. Still silent, Tara took his hand. Since Brye's tending, it was no longer swollen and showed his strong, calloused fingers.

His hands were farmers' hands, evidenced by the dirt underneath his fingernails. She wiggled her eyebrows, attempting to lighten his mood. Aiden bit back a smile, but his gaze remained intense.

A different type of feeling invaded Tara's chest. One she recognized but did not want to explore. He kept looking at her as if he wanted something.

Would I even want to know?

"Well?" she asked, her voice low.

Aiden's jaw worked, trying to form the words.

"Are you just getting home?" Lenna's voice called.

Tara pulled her gaze away from Aiden and down the path. Lenna wobbled along, dragging her feet. Her face was ashen, and dark circles curved under her eyes. Tara's expression narrowed. Lenna always returned from the Royal Tower looking like she had one foot in her grave.

"It was a long day," Aiden sighed, letting go of Tara's hand. He turned toward Lenna and ran the back of his index finger along her cheek. "Are you alright?"

"Yes." Lenna flinched away. "I'm only tired."

"You have been training pretty hard lately," he said, placing his hands behind his back.

"So have you." She raised an eyebrow and pointed at his black eye.

Tara's chest burned, and her stomach knotted at the exchange. The intensity of her reaction made her take a step back.

Jealous? Of Lenna and Aiden?

She shook her head.

What is wrong with me?

"Both of you, get some rest," Aiden said. "I'll see you in the fields tomorrow, Tara."

Tara nodded, and Lenna waved before heading inside. Brye rose from her chair to greet them.

"You're home early," Lenna said, removing her cloak and placing it on a chair. Tara began shedding her armor and weapons, leaving all her gear by the door.

"I should say the same to you." Brye cocked her head to the side.

"There seems to be an event. Roweena gave me the evening and tomorrow off." Lenna looked away as she spoke. "Did you find the food I left out?"

"Yes, but I wasn't hungry." Brye placed a hand on her forehead as if remembering something. "You both look tired. I'll prepare some special tea. I have something important to tell you."

"All right. Let me clean up." Tara went into the bathing room and stripped down, cringing at the smell of her clothes. She attempted to control her thoughts as the cold water hit her skin. Her sudden feelings of jealousy took her by surprise. Aiden and she were friends. They had been all their lives, right? Ignoring the weight in the pit of her stomach, she quickly finished cleaning and wrapped herself in a thick, dry towel.

Outside in the main room, Brye played with the bottles on the table. Lenna came out from the bedroom only in her underclothes. Lenna helped pull her long red hair into a plait on her head.

"Ugh, this will never get easy." Tara hissed, wrapping the towel tighter around her chest. "The amount of grim was impressive."

"You wanted to train like a man. Now, you get to smell like one," Lenna answered, waiting for her turn to take a bath.

"I find that offensive as a woman and for men. Not all men smell disgusting." Tara chuckled.

Lenna headed for the bathing room door, but Brye stopped her. "What happened to your back?"

Tara paled at the sight of the burn marks that ran down her sister's spine. They were circular and covered in painful blisters.

"Training was dreadful tonight," Lenna said softly

Brye retrieved a cooling balm from her kit. Tara quickly put on some clean underclothes. When she returned, she scrutinized Lenna's back. It wasn't only the puckered skin that drew attention but also the jutting of Lenna's spine and ribs. Her sister was thin. Too thin.

Tara exchanged a look with Brye.

"Ouch," Lenna hissed as Brye applied the balm. Tears ran down her face, but she wiped them away.

"Is the training going as you expected?" Brye asked, closing the small ceramic bowl.

"No. I am bloody horrible at it." Lenna kept her gaze averted, her hand going to her eyes every so often. "But, then again, I wasn't any good initially. Can't get any worse." Lenna pulled down her underclothes and forced a smile.

"Give it some time. Everything improves with practice. It also would help if you'd eat more. Get some meat on your bones." Tara rubbed Lenna's arm.

"You eat at least three times as more as anyone in the house." Lenna gave a shaky laugh.

"Then use me as an example." Tara sat at the table, bringing the cheese and bread. She made sure to place a serving in front of her sister.

Brye placed a cup of tea on the table. "Lenna, if you think it is too much—"

Lenna cut her off. "What is so urgent?"

In one breath, Brye placed her hands on the table and said, "I am engaged to the prince."

The bread Tara was about to eat stayed suspended in the air. A wave of shock forced her to place the bread slowly back on the plate and her hand trembled with the effort. "What did you just say?"

"Last night, I was invited to the Tower by the royal family. They informed me I was selected to be the future queen, and I accepted."

"Are you out of your mind?" Tara stood, and the chair fell back with force. "How could you agree to something so foolish, so unthinkable! I forbid you to do it."

"You don't even know the prince," Lenna said, dropping her thin frame into another chair at the table.

"I have already accepted. I won't go back on my word," Brye said, her voice edged.

Tara pointed the finger at the door. "You get your ass back there and tell them you changed your mind!"

"I can't, and I won't. You are not looking at this the right way." Brye sat taller and her voice turned to steal. "You always complain about how Avalon is and should it be?"

"What I was trying —"

"That there is so much we could do to improve our lives. That the role of women is too narrow. Did you not say so? Is this scheme of your training as a warrior, not another way to push for change?"

"Yes, but—"

"Did you not also continuously comment about how the crops are not as bountiful? That the animals do not reproduce with such regularity? Do you think you are the only one who sees problems that must be addressed?"

"Like what?" Lenna asked.

"We register everything as Healers; for every live birth, a woman has at least two losses. Population growth has not been continuous. It has only worsened since we stopped receiving people from the Continent centuries ago."

"That's beside the point—" Tara huffed.

"Avalon has changed since its foundation. As part of the royal family and a Healer, I will be able to strengthen the community. I can work to make the changes that would benefit us all."

"What makes you believe Gareth or the royal advisor will let you accomplish this goal? Where do you get this certainty?" Tara asked.

"You are one to talk." Brye pointed her finger. Tara flicked it away. "Did he not let you train?"

"He allowed me to prove myself."

"Tara," Brye exhaled, deflated. "Of all people, I thought you would understand. You wanted things to change for women. Why can't I do my part?"

Tara shook her head. "This isn't changing for women. This is you falling into what society or the gossiping mothers want you to do." Tara's face flushed. "Can you honestly tell me this is what you want?"

"I will not go back on my word."

"So, this is it." Tara sat back, crossing her arms. "You will renounce it all to become a queen and bear children?"

"Don't say that, Tara," Brye pleaded, her voice cracking at the end. "We can both find ways to do what we think is right. For you, it is clearly being a warrior, for me, it is serving my community. Besides, I may not express it clearly, but I have always wanted family and children."

Tara rubbed her face while Lenna sat dazed and confused, eyes flitting back and forth between them.

"It is a great honor bestowed upon me. Before the challenge, we discussed how things would change the other night. We are changing, and the island is as well. If I can get closer to finding the true problem behind everything by being Gareth's mate, then so be it. You said it yourself. We must each do our part."

"There has to be another way." Tara turned to Lenna and scowled. "Well? Aren't you going to say anything else?"

Lenna looked at each of them, biting down hard on her lower lip.

"I don't want this for you, Brye," she finally said, her voice gaining conviction. She grabbed Brye's hand, looking into her dark brown eyes.

"Have you considered another alternative? Any other way you can do your part without having to mate the prince? I mean, you would be mated without an ounce of affection. Is this what you want for yourself?"

Tara waited as emotions crossed her sister's features, only to settle on a superficial calm appearance. She knew that look. Brye had already decided, and nothing was going to change her stubborn sister's mind. Not Lenna, and definitely not Tara.

Brye sat straighter in her chair and placed her arms carefully on the table. "I have, but this course of action seems the best. Perhaps on better acquaintance, the prince might grow on me."

"Not likely," Tara muttered.

Brye pinched her lips. "And some of us might not know what we have until it is too late."

Tara's stomach sank, and her mind drifted back to Aiden and the thoughts she had pushed aside. She did so again. It was not the time to be persuaded by her sister.

Lenna gripped Brye's hand harder. "The last thing I want is for you to make a regretful decision. You deserve happiness."

"Do you even know what the consequences of your actions will be?" Tara waved a hand.

"You're one to talk, little sister," Brye enunciated each word. *Okay, maybe she went too far with that comment.*

"On yourself, Brye. This is your life." Tara didn't let it go. She gave Lenna a pleading look when she got up to clear the table.

Lenna shook her head, then asked, "Do you know when it will happen?"

"It will be soon."

"You still have time to find a way out of this, to run," Tara pleaded.

Brye snorted almost derisively. "Run where? Leave the both of you? Where would I go? The Continent? The In-Between? The Unknown? There is no place to run because this is not something I need to escape. I have made my decision, and I will stick to it. Do you understand?" Brye stood and rolled her shoulders. "I am going to bed. Good night."

"Fine, be that way! Good night to you too!" Tara shouted back. "And you are no help at all, Lenna." She slammed the chair back into its place, rattling the table.

Fringe Stitch

Lenna

LENNA SAT ON A cot by the fire, with her legs pulled to her chest and her head on her knees. It took her sisters forever to go to bed. They cried themselves to sleep. Neither sought comfort in the other. It was heartbreaking to hear her sisters cry and not be able to help. Then again, she too wanted to cry herself to sleep.

Oh, why did they have to be so persistent about my training?

How could she let her sisters know the truth?

They would only worry, and what was even the point?

Tara was not the only one who wanted to rebel. Lenna fought every day with her desire to run away. She wanted to escape the torturous role as a Mist Maiden, training under the watchful eyes of the royal advisor. Lenna spent every moment wondering if she would ever accomplish her task.

And she suffered the consequences when she did not.

But Brye was right. Where would she go? How could she even escape such a fate? Could she leave her sisters behind?

No. I could never leave them.

No matter where she went, she would miss them. They were all she had.

But her sisters were so busy with their own lives. The burns on her spine and the protruding bones were only the beginning.

If they looked closely, they could see painful ring marks on her ankles, and wrists and bruises on her hip. Lenna's entire body was a colorful display of abuse. If only they knew half of what training with Roweena was really like.

What would they do?

If they looked closely, they could see painful ring marks on her

"I want you to move the mists. Is it so hard?"

Roweena paced around the Royal Tower's roof, her dark dress billowing in the calm wind, her face strained and tense. She had been like this every terrible, tormented day since Lenna had started training.

Lenna would come to the Royal Tower, up five flights of stairs, and through a wooden door, only to be met with a scowl and crossed words.

The excitement and hope of finally understanding her magical abilities were tucked away with all her dreams. It took only a few minutes on that first day for reality to settle in. Lenna was not here to train her magic, to learn how to control it and use it wisely.

No, Lenna was to have her magic beaten into submission.

To be poked and provoked.

To be reminded how inferior she was.

To the best of her abilities, Lenna would follow Roweena's direction to visualize and materialize matter around her. She would do it until her head wanted to explode, her arms would be weighed down, or her spirit would be crushed. The training was sucking the life out of her.

It was a never-ending nightmare.

"Lenna, this would have been easier if you had told me much sooner. Magic takes time. You're such a disappointment."

Lenna pinched her nose and sniffed.

Roweena pinched Lenna's arm. "Stop crying. Try again."

Lenna closed her eyes and stood with her arms outstretched. She concentrated, centering her energy on a specific point in front of her. She visualized how the hot air moistened her face mixed with the cool air at her feet.

A slight breeze stirred the plastered hair on her forehead. A blissful second of relief before her hands and arms burned. She pushed through it, trying to get her magic through whatever held it back.

The slap on the back of her head cut off her concentration.

"That was pathetic." Roweena pushed Lenna against the tower's edge. The back of her head hit the stones with a soft crack. The shock vibrated in her skull, and the older woman's voice intensified the pain. "We have been training for weeks and have been here for hours, yet you can't even move the mists? You can't call fire and let alone convert mists into water. The simplest of tasks."

Lenna's stomach turned knots, and she bit the inside of her mouth to keep the bile down.

"How often must I tell you that raw Elemental Magic is worthless? A clear understanding of the elements is needed to manipulate water, fire, earth, and air. Here is what I can conclude." Roweena raised her fingers with each point. "You have no fire magic, little to no air magic, definitely no water magic, and we haven't even gotten to earth. Nothing you do causes a ripple."

"You have made abundantly clear," Lenna said, her hands at her sides. "How inferior my magic is, but I don't believe it is all my fault. My magic doesn't flow with ease. It is as if it's trapped, bound up inside me with no way out."

Roweena narrowed her eyes at her. The irises appeared darker in the setting sun.

"Bound?"

"Yes, or something like that.

Roweena looked at her carefully. "Explain."

Lenna wet her dried lips. "I don't know how to describe it, only what it feels like. I know I have magic abilities. I have always been able to sense it under my skin, crawling and tingling to be released, but I can't completely access it. Like when you wrap a thread over the spool, but I am the spool. I have to get my magic out from layers of threads."

Roweena paced silently, her fingers tapping her plump lips. Lenna waited on bated breath, attempting to decipher what the woman was up to. She stopped her pacing, and her eyes brightened. Lenna's skin crawled. This was not good. There was something on Roweena's mind that was intensifying her unease.

"It is clear that training with me has produced no effect."

"Then who will train me?"

"You will."

Lenna's jaw dropped.

"Your mother was a Healer, but she sometimes went off on her own and trained herself. Perhaps that is what you need to do."

Lenna's emotions conflicted with a sense of relief. After all the supposed training that left her sick and drained, the woman decided to leave her alone. "Is there a condition for this training?"

Roweena's eyes glowed. "Of course, there is!"

Lenna fell over in shock as fire ran down her spine. The stones under her hands were barely in focus as she attempted not to pass out. As quickly as it started, it stopped.

"When you completely control your powers, you will be a true magic holder. The symbols I have burned into you will appear. Now go, start training and come back when you become interesting."

Roweena dismissed her by leaving.

Lenna tried to stand on her trembling legs but ended up sitting against the ramparts. She wanted to leave, to go home, but she couldn't. Her back was raw, and so were her emotions. They were spilling out of her in starts and stops. She brought her knees to her chest and hid her face.

No matter what I do with my magic, I never want to be trained by her again. Malicious, vile woman.

The tears came shortly after, and Lenna sobbed into her dress. The sky rumbled in tune with her emotions. It threatened to rain but remained dry. No tears would empty Lenna of the disappointment or the fear of failure.

The shuffle of steps outside the door of the house roused Lenna from her thoughts. She must have fallen asleep on the blanket by the fire, and it was down to embers now. The mists were particularly thick, making the night humid despite the chill. She reached for more wood and peat to reheat the fire when the steps outside grew closer. Someone scratched at the door.

That's odd. Who would be here at this hour?

Lenna opened the door and jumped back, her hand over her mouth. Outside was a male wolf with dark, patched fur and tawny eyes. He was one of the wolves from her dreams. He was larger than she expected, with his head reaching her shoulders. He stood in the path in front of the house, staring.

Lenna stared at him for several long moments, frozen. She wouldn't say she was afraid of the wolf, but she was certainly unnerved, and she wasn't quite sure what the purpose of his visit was.

He finally snorted at her, making a deep whining in his throat. He twisted in a circle and turned his head over his shoulder to look back at her.

"Are you waiting for me?" she whispered. "Am I to follow you somewhere?"

The wolf nodded.

Before losing her nerve, Lenna grabbed a dress and pulled it on. She gripped her gray coat and satchel before leaving through the door.

While the wolf seemed to know where he was going, Lenna did not. She bit down on her lip, keeping close and gripping her sack tighter. Her mind filled with never-ending questions while it reprimanded her for mindlessly following an unknown creature.

They walked for some time. Once the dirt path turned into thick grass, Lenna became uneasy. She leaned closer to the wolf, bumping into him when she tripped over uneven ground.

"I'm sorry." She pulled back only to have a small branch smack her in the face.

The wolf made a noise that she could only interpret as a groan. He put his nose under her hand and flicked it over his neck.

"You want me to hold on to you?" Lenna rubbed her face, feeling the sting where the branch hit her cheekbone. He slowly nodded, and she gripped his thick hair.

She managed to get her bearings and realized they must be on the island's northern edge, where the wall and mountains meet with the river. It was forbidden to go this far north. The closest she ever got was the White Thorn Tree which stood sentry by the river.

The wolf continued its path near the edge of the wall. They reached the river, and he jumped over, his body floating over the air. Gasping, she came out and touched where he was standing with her hands. The air under his paws was condensed and hard, with the smoothness of polished metal but the softness of grass.

An invisible bridge.

The wolf didn't wait, only continued his path over the bridge. Lenna wasted no time; she grabbed her skirt and carefully placed her foot on the soft air. She put more pressure, expecting the air to give way, but it remained firm.

"Magic, real solid magic," she whispered. For one moment, Lenna's chest was weightless. She jumped up and down on the invisible bride with too much nervous energy to stay in one place. Noticing the wolf had already crossed, she quickly followed.

Even on the other side of the bridge, the mists stayed thick, and Lenna grabbed onto the wolf's fur. He led her up the river until they reached the rocky ground. In the distance, a constant roar grew stronger as they walked.

"What is that?"

The wolf didn't answer.

But Lenna's curiosity and excitement did not dissipate. The roar was consistent, bringing the smell of salt and water.

Could it be the sea?

Avalon was an island. It made sense that it would be surrounded by water.

The wolf led her to a small cave hidden close to the river's outlet. The cave was dry, and someone had placed a cot near a fire.

"Rest," said the echoing voice of the wolf. "We will begin training before sunrise."

Lenna plopped herself face down on the cot. Her body relaxed with the scent of fire, fur, and sea. For once, the nightmares let her sleep.

Dancing Magic

Lenna

THE PATHS WERE FILLED with people going about in the cold. Even with the weather, the market was bustling. Lenna paused at stalls with goods. There were so many. She especially liked the flowers that grew in the hothouse during winter. They brought a spot of color to the landscape.

Aiden's house was on the opposite side of the village, to the west, near the fields. His father, Badar, was one of the best farmers. As she approached, she saw Badar leaving with the king at his side.

Badar saw her and gave her the warmest smile she had ever seen, like the sun on a chilly day. Its warmth reached her bones. She smiled back tentatively.

"Now look who has come to visit." Badar's blue eyes crinkled. The king cocked his head to the side. "And who is this?" His voice was gruff, like a bear.

"I am Lenna." She curtsied, wobbling only a little.

"Our sweet, Lenna." Badar patted her shoulder softly. "She is one of Elsywth the Healer's children."

A soft change came over the king's features, and the smile didn't reach his eyes. "You have your mother's eyes."

"People tell me that. But they are mine. I didn't steal them."

The men laughed, and the king's tension broke.

"You came to see Aiden?" Badar asked.

Lenna nodded, raising her basket. "Maither *sent medicine for his cough.*"

"Go right in. Caitlin had to go to the market. Perhaps you can keep him company until she gets back?"

Lenna nodded and went inside. From the door, she saw dirty blond curls peeking from under a blanket in one of the bedrooms.

"Aiden! You have a visitor," Badar called. "A new Healer."

"I don't want another Healer," he groaned, letting out a cough, but when he saw Lenna, he sat up straight.

Her hands grew warm inside her mittens.

"I will leave you to it," Badar whispered and left.

Lenna stood, biting her lip. "Maither *sent me. Brye and Tara wanted to come, but they had to stay home.*"

"Lenna." He sat back and coughed. "Come in. I'm a lot better than I look. I'm so glad to see you."

Lenna placed the basket on the cot and pulled the small stool beside him.

Aiden sat on the bed. His face was flushed, but his blue eyes were clear. He was tall and thin for his age. Maither *said Aiden would soon grow like a weed.* She hoped she did too.

"Aren't you warm?" Aiden asked. Lenna looked down at her hands.

"Oh." She blinked, removing her mittens and scarf. She kept her cloak on. "How are you feeling?"

"Better," Aiden whispered hoarsely. "But the cough is driving me crazy. And not being able to go out and play is the worst. It snowed."

"Yes, it did."

"I wish I could play in the snow. All my friends are playing, and I am stuck in here."

"Would playing with snow make you very happy?"

"The happiest." He grinned. "It might have melted by tomorrow, and Mother says I can go outside the day after if my cough improves."

Lenna rubbed her hands. "If I show you something. Will you promise to keep it a secret?"

His eyes widened. "Is it a dangerous secret?"

"I don't know," Lenna whispered, "but it is mine. Will you keep it?"

Aiden stuck out his hand, reaching for Lenna's grasped one. He twisted his index finger in hers, his eyes wide. "I swear to keep this secret. If I ever betray it, may lightning strike me!"

Those were solemn words. Lenna's cheeks turned pink, and she smiled.

"Okay, show me." He leaned back, his hands in his lap.

Lenna placed the stool under the window to open the latch. Outside there was snow on the ground and in the bushes. Lenna stuck her hand out and concentrated. Slowly, the delicate snowflakes took form and floated toward her.

Lenna turned on the stool carefully, with the snow dancing over her hand. Aiden's jaw fell. She lowered herself to the ground and brought the dancing snow to him.

"Your hand," Lenna whispered. Her stomach tightened, and nausea crept its way up her throat. She bit the inside of her mouth to control the sensation. She wanted to show him a bit more.

Aiden held out his hand, and the snow danced over his palm, then his face. It made figure eights over his head until it melted into water.

The drops floated, forming a small ball that moved up and down. It then spun and collided with Aiden's face with a splash.

Lenna giggled. Aiden blinked and wiped his eyes before he burst out laughing.

"That was amazing," he marveled. "How did you do it?"

"I have been practicing, but I am not very good."

Magic made her sick. It gave her stomach pains and headaches. Like the one she had right now.

But Aiden laughed, and he was happy. It was enough of a risk for her.

"You are amazing!" He grinned. "I can't wait to see what you can do."

Something wet nudged Lenna's shoulder. The dream, or memory, blurred, and she couldn't recall much of it. She groaned and slowly opened her eyes to find herself face-to-face with the dark wolf.

The fire had died down to embers and it was still dark outside. It must be close to sunrise. She pushed herself into a sitting position and rubbed her face. Lenna expected to feel drained after the day but was surprised to find herself energized. It was as if the weight she carried was lifted from her body.

That's odd.

The wolf nudged her again.

"Alright." Lenna pulled herself up, dusting off her cloak and dress. "What would you like me to do?

The wolf motioned to the embers and then proceeded to sit.

"I have nothing to light the fire with." Lenna waved in the ember's direction. "It's not a type of magic I have accomplished."

"Try," an echoing voice said.

Lenna wrinkled her nose. The voice sounded familiar, but she couldn't place it.

Refocusing her attention, she walked around the dwindling embers and considered. It was supposed to be the first magic learned and the last lost, but she still couldn't do it. On one occasion, the royal advisor had pinched, slapped, and placed her hand in an open flame. None had succeeded in provoking her to create fire out of nothing.

Well, not nothing. All elements must come from what is already there.

Lenna turned to the wolf, whose deep gaze didn't falter. For a magic teacher, he was pretty silent.

Or perhaps this is all in my head, and I am dreaming.

She pinched herself and felt the pain.

"I am real," the wolf pointed out.

"It seems that way."

"What stops you?"

"I am afraid," Lenna whispered, gripping her skirt tighter. "Terrified of failure."

"You are afraid because you have been taught to fear magic. But as you gain knowledge, you will be less afraid. Give it a try."

Lenna took a deep breath and nodded. Closing her eyes, she extended her hand, palm open, toward the dying embers. She imagined how the sparks would grow and flick, gaining energy as they tried to find something else to consume. She narrowed her mind's eye and focused, visualizing the spark coming back to life.

Then, there it was—the familiar snap in her chest.

Lenna opened her eyes and found the flames alive, softly eating away the new wood. Her heart pounded, and a smile of relief came to her face. It was replaced with a satisfied laugh. It surprised her once it left her mouth.

"I did it!" she squealed, jumping up and down, then twirling in circles.

"First lesson taught."

"Last lesson lost," Lenna said, stretching her hands to the top of the cave. A bluish light came from the entrance, announcing the dawn. "Time for me to go back."

The wolf nodded.

"Will there be other lessons?"

"Many more."

As he led her back in the dim light of dawn, Lenna bit back a gasp.

The wolf had an accent.

Awareness

Tara

Tara arrived late at the eastern field. It was fast becoming a habit. She awoke alone with a cold hearth; the only food was a slice of bread and an apple.

They could have woken me up!

They probably tried but failed. She wasn't surprised. Tara was a terrible grumpy morning person. They were training in groups, and today Tara was assigned to fieldwork.

She banged the door on the way out and ran, dodging people with ease. Many villagers had gone to the west fields to harvest the wheat. She found Aiden there with his father.

"I thought you weren't coming." He smiled and handed her a tool. He was shirtless, with a cloth on the waist of his pants. Tara grabbed the sickle and scowled back at him.

"I overslept." She rubbed her face before working the wheat, giving Aiden a side look. "Someone could have woken me up to come to work."

"And wake the sleeping beast?" He leaned in, eyes sparkling. Tara caught the scent of sweat and fresh-cut grass. A fluttery sensation filled her stomach. She bit the inside of her mouth, narrowing her eyes at him.

He continued speaking, grinning widely. "Never! I still have a sense of self-preservation."

Tara bit back a scowl.

What is wrong with me?

They worked side by side in silence, each focused on their tasks. But Tara was having difficulty concentrating, her gaze wandering back to Aiden. It was not the first time she had seen him without a shirt. How often had she seen his tall build, lean shoulders, and chiseled chest?

Too many to count.

He bent and picked up a stack of wheat, his muscles flexing with the strain. She bit her lower lip and turned away.

Why did he have to be so attractive? He had always been attractive. And, if she was going to be honest, she looked up to him when she was younger.

No, that is not true. She fantasized about him.

But he always treated her like a little sister.

At least until lately.

Maybe it was time for her to find a partner. Not a mate! That was out of the question! Mates were trouble on every level. But someone to take the edge off. A tumble or grind on the soft grass in one of the woods. Anywhere private and quick. One of Brye's castoffs might be up to the task.

And she has a long line of those.

Tara knew she wasn't entirely without appeal. She could flirt and seduce any willing male if she set her mind to it. It couldn't be so hard. And what is Aiden but a willing male? Perhaps she could consider sex with him? They were friends, after all. If they chose not to complicate the matter, their friendship might not suffer.

A familiar warmth spread from her chest down her belly. She blinked, realizing the train of her thoughts and inner monologue. She was going crazy. Did she really want to complicate her life further?

A hand passed in front of her face.

"What?" Tara snapped.

"You seem distracted," Aiden said as he moved the sickle. "Did you sleep well after training?

"It was a long night," she answered vaguely, keeping her eyes away. "I didn't get much sleep."

Aiden, seeming to sense her mood, shrugged and went back to the task in silence. Tara was glad he did, then she wasn't. She didn't want to be left alone with her thoughts. Thoughts of the shirtless man before her. Thoughts of Brye's news. None of them were helpful.

Tara didn't understand. How could her sister let it happen? Brye disliked Gareth. They all did! Didn't they? What does the prince gain by marrying Brye? The whole "for the good of the kingdom" was bullshit.

Tara's mood had only darkened when Lenna did not take her side. How could Lenna not make Brye see the colossal mistake she was making by even considering the prince's proposal, let alone accept it?

As if reading her troubled mind, Gareth and the king appeared in the fields to speak to Badar.

"I wonder what they are doing here?" Tara cleaned the sweat from her brow with a cloth. They were too far away to hear the conversation, but it seemed serious.

"My father says they come by every couple of days," Aiden answered.

"Why?"

"He has a theory. He has been discussing it with the king and prince for some time, but there is no way of proving it."

He sat, stretching his long legs in front of him. He reached for the horn of water and drank before handing it to Tara, who sat close to his side.

"The crops are not faring well. You have noticed that they are growing smaller," he began. Tara nodded.

"He believes that if it continues, in about two or three years, we might have to consider learning to take care of them yearly and not depend on the magic infused in the land."

"What do you mean?"

"The Founders made the land bountiful by magic. We can grow crops out of season. According to historical records, the fruit, vegetables, and grains were initially great in size." He picked up her hand and opened the palm. "Imagine a tomato the size of your hand but now reduced to only half the size. The crops did not suffer the effects of fungus, bad weather, among other things."

"Yes, but it hasn't been that way in a while. We had the fungus on the tomatoes at the beginning of the year."

"Exactly," Aiden said emphatically. "Father thinks something might be wrong with the magic knots that protect the crops."

"How?"

Aiden shrugged.

"The royal advisor is in charge of the magic on the island. Has she come? Has she said anything?"

"That's the point," Aiden said, picking up a blade of wheat and playing with it. He crossed it over until it became a knot. "She has come and doesn't say much. It seems she has no explanation for the waning magic. She mentioned testing out a few theories the last time she was here. But nothing has happened since then."

Tara rubbed her hands on the thighs, drumming her fingers. "Maybe Brye will find out more."

"Brye?" Aiden raised his eyebrows. "I'd think Lenna would be the one to ask."

"You'd think, but no. My older sister will be the prince's future mate."

Aiden's jaw fell. Tara would have found it humorous if it was a joke. Considering it was true, she couldn't enjoy his discomfort as much as she wanted.

He recovered enough to blurt out, "Brye engaged to the prince?"

Tara let out a deep sigh and nodded. She hadn't realized how much she wanted to tell him until it came out. Part of her was relieved.

"Didn't she say no?"

"You'd think her of all people, but she agreed. She only thought about all the good she could accomplish in the role. I'm finding it difficult to believe my wise sister can be so self-sacrificing. I keep going back to an idea I had."

"About?" Aiden sat back down, recovering from the shock.

"Isn't it odd that since Beltane we can't escape the royal family and the royal advisor?"

"Lenna is a Mist Maiden, Tara," Aiden pointed out. "She can't avoid the royal family. And let us not forget how you recklessly placed yourself in their path as well. While Lenna might have been assigned the role, you chose yours. I think avoiding the royal family was highly unlikely."

Tara sighed, rubbing a hand over her sweaty face.

Damn his logic.

"Brye was the last candidate to marry the prince. Doesn't the candidate need to show some interest? When Brye and Gareth are at the same gathering, they ignore each other or point daggers."

"More on her part—"

Tara raised her hand to hold his comments.

"Even so. Now, they are engaged? Then there is Lenna." Tara waved a hand in the air. "There hasn't been a Mist Maiden in decades. Now all of a sudden, we need one? Roweena has been an advisor for the longest time. I doubt she would want a successor."

"What you say makes sense. However, have you considered that Lenna being a Mist Maiden and you being a warrior might have brought Brye's value out in the open?"

"How so?"

"Brye is a known Healer. She has trained with Enid for years, and her tonics and care are superior to her trainer. She has value on her own. Perhaps that is why she has been chosen."

Tara nodded reluctantly. "Maybe you are right."

"You will find I am right on many occasions. This will be one of them." Aiden stood and extended his hand. "Time to get back to work."

Tara frowned as she reached for the sickle and let him pull her up. He let her go and went back to work. Tara rubbed her clammy hand on her pants, still trying to ignore the warmth in her belly.

Training

Brye

BRYE CAME HOME AFTER sunset to find Tara sitting alone by the fire on the floor.

"Have you seen Lenna today?" Brye asked. "I thought she had the day off from training. I want to see the imprint on her back."

Brye emptied her kit to take inventory. Tara had been rude and selfish, and there was no way she was going to forget that immediately. Besides, another concern was pressing on her mind.

Lenna's deep burns made her uneasy. Her sister was keeping secrets, but her emotions were on the surface of her skin. The sense of disappointment and failure tangled up with a sense of fear that gave Brye nausea. That, coupled with her growing thinness, was enough for Brye to wonder.

What was Lenna's training like?

"She was leaving when I arrived, before the mists settled." Tara looked up from her place on the floor. They stared at each other for some time, neither speaking. Brye sighed.

"I have only one thing to say," Tara's voice grew serious. "I disagree with your decision. But I am tired of fighting with you, Brye. I don't enjoy fighting with my sisters. At least not fights I can't win." Tara's voice cracked. She turned her head away, sniffling. Brye looked down at the table, feeling her eyes water.

"I don't enjoy it either," Brye's voice hitched.

"Let's accept what is and do what we can with it."

"Yes," Brye smiled, even if it didn't reach her eyes.

"So, what should we have for dinner? I am starving!" Tara stood up and brushed the tears from her face and the dust from her pants.

"I think we can make some eggs with bread and cheese?"

"Sounds good. I might steal some extra food from Aiden's house."

"Why? We have enough."

"But Caitlin is a better cook."

"That is true. Should we wait for Lenna?" Brye asked, picking up a small skillet while Tara fanned the fire.

"She said not to wait up. She was training tonight."

"She says that a lot lately." Brye handed Tara a skillet to place over the grill on the fire. A sinking feeling settled in her stomach. "I hope it goes better this time."

Lenna

Lenna waited for the sun to set before heading north. She wanted to arrive near the river bend before the mist thickened around her. She brought a mist candle and some extra food to her satchel.

That morning, the wolf and she had parted ways at the wall and headed back to the village alone. For the rest of the day, Lenna wondered if the wolf was part of her imagination.

But I can't make up an accent.

It gave her a clue to the wolf's real identity. Only one person with an accent was on the island: Beltran the sage.

But why doesn't he reveal himself?

She pulled her cloak closed and warmed her hands underneath. Even though it was high summer, the mists dropped the temperature, cooling the air around her.

"Why didn't I think about it before?" Lenna reached for some branches from the nearby tree. Keeping her back to the river, she placed the small sticks in a pile and opened her hands over them. Like before, she focused on the sticks, imagining them heating up slowly, igniting.

Lenna focused until her brow was covered in sweat. She even smelled burnt wood, but the sticks did not catch fire. The only result was an upset stomach and a pounding headache. Looking down at her hands, she wondered why it was so difficult. Why did it take so much effort here, inside the wall?

Was it contained?

A dark form came out of the mists. Lenna bit back a scream. "You scared me!"

The wolf chuckled and pushed her hand over his neck with his muzzle. Lenna held on to his fur as they walked down the river to the edge of the wall. As she passed the gap in the wall, the sluggish exhaustion was lifted away.

Lenna kept her grip on the wolf as they descended the bridge and reached the grass and rocky path. The salty, briny air filled her nostrils, making her more determined to enjoy the moment.

Yet, there was so much she wanted to know. Not only about magic but the world outside. Were there threats as the stories have portrayed? Beltran had shared very little about the Continent. Was it such a terrible place?

It has been thousands of years living apart. Perhaps it was time to move on, to explore and discover.

They reached the cave. The fire was unlit, and the pyre was ready with fresh logs and peat. She circled it and rubbed her hands together.

"Light the fire," said the wolf as he came closer.

"I tried, but it didn't work," Lenna answered. The wolf narrowed his eyes at her and motioned again to the fire with his nose. Using the same method as the night before; she extended her hand over the wood. The now familiar snap echoed in her chest, and the logs instantly caught flames.

"That's strange."

She walked around the lit fire, examining it from every angle. A different type of magic must be involved and not only elemental magic. Another kind that prevents magic from working inside the island effectively.

Was this type of magic connected to the magical knots in the fields or Roweena's abilities? How did this magic work?

"Move the fire," the wolf instructed, interrupting her thoughts.

"Is that today's lesson? Move fire?"

He nodded.

Lenna shrugged and extended her hands in front of the flames. First, she pushed the flames higher and taller, growing in strength. They were almost as tall as her. Lenna smiled, satisfied. Deciding to be bolder, she moved the fire in an arc. It hopped slightly from one side of the pyre to another to finally settle back.

"How can it seem so easy?"

"Magic should feel easy."

But it wasn't. Inside the wall, magic was hard, brutal, and painful. Lenna's eyes glazed over momentarily, and her heart rate increased. Images of agony and burns filtered into her mind, clawing their way into her memory, searing themselves and erasing any happiness. Lenna placed a cold, clammy hand over her face.

I am doing well. Magic should be easy.

A wet nose nuzzled her hand, drawing her back from memories best left unvisited.

"Do you have a name?" she croaked out.

"Yes."

Lenna continued to give him sidelong glances. Whatever the wolf was hiding or thinking, he would not elaborate. He was looking at the entrance, then back at her, waiting.

She could do one of two things. She could insist he answer her questions or wait until he did in his own time.

If it were me, I'd want my wishes respected.

Lenna rubbed her hands together. "What is next?"

"Time to play with fire," the wolf answered.

They spent hours working. Lenna would move the fire around, grow it, and extinguish it only to relight it. At one point, she could draw it close to her fingers. She placed it back, afraid of burning herself. After the experiences with Roweena, she preferred to keep the fire under control.

This time they didn't stay until morning. Near midnight, the wolf motioned Lenna to follow him, and they headed back to the wall.

Lenna did not know what motivated her to start talking. Whatever the reason, she couldn't help herself.

When she was younger, Aiden would listen. He would keep her secrets and fill the void after her mother disappeared. But then it changed. He and Tara started spending more and more time together. He would still listen, but his mind was elsewhere.

Brye was constantly training with Enid, distracted by cases that needed attention. And Tara was goal-oriented and only listened to what she desired. For the last few years, she found herself increasingly with ideas and no one to share.

Lenna loved her sisters but knew they had their own lives and problems. Tara's new role and Brye's engagement only made it more evident—Lenna was left to herself.

So, she talked without expecting any answers. All she wanted was to have someone to listen. Although some details were lost,

Lenna told him the story of Avalon and the Three Founders. She avoided speaking about her mother, mostly because she couldn't remember. He chuckled once and growled another time. It was the only response she received, but it was enough.

They reached the river, and Lenna followed behind the wolf over the bridge. As they passed the break in the wall, a heavy weight collapsed over her body. The exhaustion of the entire day smothered her until she could barely breathe. She motioned for the wolf to stop once they reached the bridge's end. Lenna touched her forehead with the back of her cold hand.

"One moment." She sat on the ground, black dots around her vision.

Lenna breathed deeply and closed her eyes, regaining her strength. It did not return entirely, but she stood with the wolf's help and headed south.

"I was feeling fine before," she spoke after some time. "I don't know what has come over me."

After a while, the wolf said with reluctance. "It is the island."

"The island?"

"The island binds its magic."

"How does an island bind its magic?" she asked, confused.

"The island did not bind its magic. Someone else did."

"Who can do that?"

The wolf did not respond but guided her further south. Biting down on her lip, she refrained from asking more questions. Not because she had none, she had plenty, but placing one foot in front of the other took every effort.

An island that binds its magic.

An island bound *by* magic.

The thought hit her, making her stumble.

The Bondmaker!

A Bondmaker Founder helped protect and bind the island's magic so it could thrive. Could he have done more than preserve the island and knot the fields? Did he create other bonds that affect the magic inside the walls?

As they approached her home, she let go of his fur.

"I will see you tomorrow evening?" Lenna asked hopefully.

The wolf nodded before quickly disappearing into the mists.

Lenna pushed back the door to find her sisters still awake by the fire.

"Where have you been?" Tara asked.

"I told you not to wait up for me." Lenna exhaled.

"When you said not to wait, did you mean arriving this late? Sunrise is a few hours away," Brye said.

Weary, Lenna ignored their stares. She dropped the bag and undressed, leaving only her underclothes. She was on the floor by the hearth, unbraiding her hair, attempting to recover warmth into her cold body. Brye pulled the chair closer to her and took up the task.

"I was training," Lenna admitted reluctantly.

"Where?" Tara asked. "Aiden and I went to fetch you at the Royal Tower. We discovered you haven't been training with the royal advisor for some time."

"Roweena instructed me to train by myself. After I have completed some tasks independently, I will resume training with her. One of those tasks is creating and moving the island's mists."

At least, that is one of the tasks she has set.

Her sisters did not need to know the extent of what she had to do.

"If you haven't moved the mists, why are you training at night?" Tara asked as she got ready for bed by changing her clothes and brushing her curls into submission.

"Because I need to move the mists, I train at night. It helps me concentrate when there are fewer distractions." Lenna stood and took the comb from Brye's hands.

Tara was about to open her mouth when Brye pinched her. Tara slapped her hand away, and they did not insist on the topic.

Lenna fed the fire some more to warm the house. Then she got into the bed she shared with Tara. She closed her eyes and dreamt of hopping fire and dancing snowflakes.

Shifting Impressions

Brye

"THERE'S NEWS."

Tara's crazed curls tickled Brye's face. Brye pushed them away and sat up in her bed, rubbing her eyes. What time was it? The room was filled with morning light. Had she overslept? "What is it?"

Lenna sat on the foot of the bed, wrapped in a blanket. "Edgar came. You've been summoned to the Royal Tower."

"Is it the queen?"

"No," Tara answered, crossing her arms over her chest. "It's the prince."

"He wants an audience with you." Lenna patted Brye's leg over the blanket.

"It must be about the announcement." Brye's stomach sank. Gareth and she hadn't spent any time together since that night. She was starting to think he was avoiding her. Again. It was as great a time as any to find out.

"Let's get you ready to see the prince," Lenna said.

"And we will take you to the Royal Tower, together," Tara said, leaving no room for argument. Brye got up and took a quick wash in the bathing room.

Upon coming out Brye discovered that Lenna had picked out one of her best dresses, a burgundy with embroidered trim over the bodice. She ran her fingers over her work and took a deep breath.

They were so focused on their tasks that they did not even glance at each other unless necessary. But Brye's magic threaded out, seeking out her sister's emotions.

Tara's underline anger sizzled with each pass of her fingers, while Lenna's deep concern made her heart ache. It took great effort to tune out those unwanted emotions and focus on her own. But when she did, they all came up jumbled together, causing a heavy sensation in the pit of her stomach.

Once dressed, Brye stood before the mirror hanging on the wall, placing the herbs and flowers into the braid. They were a nuisance to remove in the evenings, but they gave her hair a pleasant scent.

Brye knew she was beautiful; at least, that was what she'd been told her life. And the constant proposals only confirmed she was attractive.

Is that why he chose me? Because I am pretty to look at?

But appearances fade—a poor reason to be mated only for looks. Sighing, Brye pinched her cheeks and reached for one of her aprons. She found one cream-colored, decorated around the edges with vines and soft flowers.

"Those vines reminded me of you," Lenna said as she wrapped a sash twice around her waist to adjust the dress. Although Lenna had been eating better, deep purple smudges stained her emerald eyes, and her skin was so translucent that her veins looked like tattoos along her arms.

I need to make sure to give her more tonics.

Brye rubbed the apron carefully. "Oh, does it?"

"Yes." Lenna quickly worked her hair in a messy braid. "You are beautiful and resilient. You can grow anywhere."

Tara muffled a laugh with her hand. "What a load of crap."

Brye raised an eyebrow. "And you being the expert, perhaps?" She laughed and hugged Lenna, willingly absorbing all the concern infused with goodwill. "Thank you."

"That is what I am here for." Lenna pulled away. "To share my happy crap."

Edgar received them. "Good morning, miss. Please follow me."

They were led to the door outside the private royal chambers on the second floor.

"I'll wait for you here." Lenna sat on the bench outside. Tara had left them at the door of the tower. The older man knocked on the heavy doors.

"Enter," called a gruff voice from inside.

Brye gave one last look at her sister before going inside.

All the wooden shutters were open, letting in the morning light. There was no fire, and the room was empty except for Gareth, who stood up from the wooden table. He wore a deep blue tunic and cream pants with high boots. She was surprised to see him well-kept and dressed, with his dirty blond hair pushed back from his face and beard trimmed.

Her heart gave an unexpected jolt, and she gripped her hands in front of her. "You summoned me?"

"Good morning." Gareth came from behind the table and motioned to one of the chairs beside the empty fireplace. "Please be seated."

Brye nodded stiffly and sat on the chair. She clasped her hands in her lap. Gareth cleared his throat and sat opposite, his posture rigid.

He looks as uncomfortable as I do. What a pair we make.

"You look stunning," he said, clearing his throat again.

"Thank you." She looked down at her hands.

"I apologize for the early hour. I wanted to be the one to inform you that we will be announcing the mating ceremony this evening."

"I gathered as much." Brye's stomach filled with knots, and her hands grew stiff from wringing them so tightly. "When will the mating ceremony be?"

"In five days."

"So soon?" Brye's voice cracked, forcing her to clear her throat as well.

"I'd hoped we would have more time, but my mother has been insistent. The royal advisor has been egging her on." He rolled his eyes at the last part. "I attempted to make her see reason, but it wasn't possible."

"They do seem a bit adamant."

"Which is strange because they rarely agree on anything. Would you like something to drink?"

Brye nodded, not because she was particularly thirsty but because it gave her time to think. His face was stoic, but his manners were polite. Except for those moments when he let his guard down, it was hard to know what he was thinking.

Gareth went to a table and brought two cups of cider, handing her one and taking the other. He was careful not to touch her. She sipped, clearing her dry mouth.

"I had thought we would have an opportunity to get acquainted," she confessed. "Being mated is a big decision. We hardly know each other."

"We can get acquainted as we go." He crossed his legs and leaned back in the chair. "My mother wants your opinions about the preparations. She will be here soon."

Brye sipped the ale, and an idea came into her mind. "Why don't we take some time now? Even briefly?"

Gareth sat forward and ran his hands through his hair, destroying his well-combed locks.

"How about one question each? And you promised to be honest." Brye's lips twitched at his unease, making her relax ever so slightly.

"That seems fair," he replied. "I will try to be truthful, but if there is something I cannot answer, I will say so. You may go first."

Brye nodded. She looked past him to the open window, considering her question. There was only one that plagued her mind. She took a deep breath before asking.

"Their Majesties have made it clear why they considered me. The royal advisor had her reasons, superficial as they may be. But what arc yours?"

"Can't they simply be the pleasure of your company?"

Brye laughed and sat back. "Please, besides that," – she waved a hand between them, "moment of intimacy. You don't even like me."

"There you go again, making assumptions." Gareth sighed.

"Am I wrong?"

"I will confess, when my mother proposed the list of candidates with only three names, I was confused. Then Lenna became a Mist Maiden, and Tara made her odd request. There was only one name left—yours."

He looked away, past her shoulder, as if collecting his thoughts. "When my mother and Roweena presented their arguments in your favor. I agreed with them. I was sure we would make a good match. I wanted more time to think about it. I wanted..." he paused and exhaled, rubbing the back of his neck, "I wanted an opportunity to get to know you. To get to know each other. To properly court you."

"Court me?"

"Yes."

"But," Brye blinked and waved her hand, "You had every opportunity during previous Beltane celebrations and chose to ignore me."

"Ignore you?" Gareth's eyes widened.

"Yes, and deliberately."

"Please tell me how I accomplished that."

He cannot be serious. Gareth sat with his legs crossed, and a hand slightly covering his face.

"Are you unaware that in every Beltane ceremony for the past years, you have chosen to dance with everyone but me?"

A grin decorated his features. "Oh, is that ignoring you?"

"Is it not?"

"No one can ignore you, Brye. You outshine every other person in the room. You only need to..." Gareth gestured to her. "Do what you always do."

"Which is?"

Gareth huffed and ran a hand over his face. "You have no idea the effect you have on others. With your smile, your laugh. It's your vibrancy that makes the invisible visible."

Brye sat back, gaping. Nothing of what he said made any sense. She was about to speak when he raised a finger. "One question each, and so you are aware, I answered more than one."

She looked away, pinching her lips. "Fair, your turn."

He was silent again, contemplating his question. Brye continued to twiddle her thumbs.

"Do you remember your mother? I mean, what was life like when she was alive? What did you do, and whom did you play with?"

His question caught her off guard. It wasn't the first time he had asked something about her past. Didn't he ask her if she knew how to swim?

No, who taught her.

Brye wet her lips and exhaled slowly. Her smile didn't reach her eyes.

"I remember bits and pieces of when I was younger. I am the eldest, I should have had more memories of my mother, but strangely, it seems I don't. The most vivid memory is of the night she disappeared and everything since. But my mother she... she faded away," her voice trailed off. "I genuinely don't remember my life before she disappeared.

Gareth's eyes looked pained. "If you could—"

Brye cut him off, raising her index finger. "One question, for now."

His mouth twitched as he leaned back in his chair. "I thought I would get more than one, considering. But I will let it pass. We both have to prepare for tonight's announcement."

"How do we prepare?" Brye placed the half-full cup on the table. Her thirst was now lost.

"The queen will be here soon. She is more than excited to help." His mouth twitched once more, fighting back a smile. Brye's heart fluttered in her chest. She wondered what a genuine smile would look like on his features. Would they distort or grow more handsome?

When did I start to consider him handsome?

Brye looked into the deep eyes of her future mate, her tone mirroring his own.

"Let's begin."

Growing Acquaintances

Brye

Brye waited with Gareth for Queen Celine to arrive. Upon entering, the older woman surprised her by reaching for her hands.

"Thank you for accepting my stubborn son's proposal." Her face lit up with a smile. "I am delighted to have you in the family, my dear."

"I am honored, your majesty." Brye sincerely smiled back, even though it was too soon to see if it would be delightful.

"Finding a mate for my son has been no easy task." Queen Celine raised an eyebrow at him. "He does have a difficult personality."

"Only difficult?" Brye humored.

The prince was saved from answering by Beltran's arrival. He walked in, bowed to the queen, kissed her hand, then Brye's out of respect.

"Congratulations, my lady," he beamed.

Brye blushed and held back a smile.

"I think the honor is all his," the queen said.

Gareth, who stood behind Beltran, groaned before he said, "I am sorry to go, Mother, but we have business." He kissed the queen on the cheek, gave Brye a half-smile, and left. Beltran bowed at the door and closed it behind them.

"He was quite in a hurry to leave the room," Brye pointed out.

"He and my husband have a lot on their minds now."

"It must be a challenge... running our small kingdom."

"More than it used to." She patted Brye's hand. "Now, let us see how we prepare for this evening."

Queen Celine clapped her hands, and an older woman with a young girl entered carrying a tray of baubles. There were pins for cloaks, necklaces, belts, and bracelets. Another tray held sashes, decorated clips, and swatches of cloths.

"I couldn't help myself. There were so many beautiful things. I had most of them brought here so we could choose them together."

The queen removed a bracelet from the tray and placed it on Brye's wrist. She was immediately intrigued by it. The metal was cool and decorated as woven thread, and she could distinguish small engraved symbols. The metal was thicker in some places.

"These knots are for fertility and harmony," the queen pointed to the designs on the bracelet. "The royal advisor created these for the queens of Avalon with her magic. Or so she says." Doubt edged her voice, while she extended her wrist. "I received this bracelet when I was chosen to marry the king."

"Has it aided in your union?"

"It has, although we were only blessed with one living child."

Brye could sense feelings of pain and loss. She blinked them away and carefully removed her hand from the woman's grasp.

To give her time to recover from the influx of thoughts and images, Brye pretended to examine the bracelet. These new growing abilities were challenging to manage and control. They would hit Brye at the oddest moments, and it took great concentration to tune them out.

"Perhaps, in this case, one strong son was enough," Brye said.

"In my case, it was." The queen smiled thoughtfully. "One good, strong, stubborn son is more than enough."

Roweena entered the room wearing her customary dark tunic and silver belt, with her long dark curls braided around her head like a crown. Brye was about to stand when the queen gently held her in place. The change in the room was evident. The air thickened with underlying tension. Whatever harmony there was the night they spoke to Brye had disappeared.

Brye placed her hands in her lap and kept her eyes on Roweena while the woman curtsied like a proud cat.

"Your majesty."

"Roweena." The queen's tone was icy as she waved toward the opposite chair.

"I was told we had a visitor and that you were sharing the prized jewelry. I wanted to make sure the bracelets were to your satisfaction."

"I was giving it to Brye," The queen pointed out.

"I see." Roweena looked at Brye curiously.

Like an insect to be dissected.

Roweena extended her hand to examine the bracelet. Brye hesitated, terrified of what she might encounter. Bracing herself, she extended her wrist and waited. A deep, empty coldness ran its way up her arm. She forced herself not to jolt.

No emotions.

No memories or thoughts.

Nothing.

A shiver ran down her spine.

Brye pulled her hand away and rubbed her wrist.

"It suits you. The metal will not tarnish, nor will the details fade over time. I added one to aid communication." Roweena smirked.

She stayed only a moment before standing back up. "I leave you, my queen. My attention and skill are needed in the fields." Roweena bowed and exited. Once the door closed, the queen let out an extended breath, and her shoulders dropped ever so slightly.

"You will soon find out, my dear, that there are kings and queens, and there are puppets to be played."

Brye wondered who the kings, queens, and puppets were.

Tara

"I don't like it," Tara scowled.

Aiden exhaled and rubbed his brow. "Yes, you keep saying that. Over and over."

"It doesn't change the fact that I don't like this engagement. It makes no sense," she continued as they carried and piled wheat.

The afternoon work had been postponed because of the announcement. The entire kingdom was meeting near the west lake late in the afternoon. The king had promised a celebration and wanted the whole kingdom to come and bring to share. In order to participate, everyone had to be done with their chores.

"It won't make sense to you no matter how much you repeat it," Aiden pointed out.

"I told her I disagreed, but now I can't say anything else. It seems to be happening so fast."

Tara was prepping for a fight. But no one would oblige her, least of all Aiden. Instead of humoring her foul mood, he would get up and leave before he lost his temper.

"Tara." He pushed the wheat into a pile in the center of the field. It would stay there all night, and tomorrow they would bring carts to pull it to be separated. "I know this is difficult for you to understand, but the way I see it, you have two options."

He raised a finger. "Option number one. You slowly accept that your older sister is an adult and can make her own decisions, as you have made yours, might I remind you."

She gave him a look that could curdle milk. "And my second option?"

"You can fight this every step of the way, make your sisters miserable, make me miserable, make everyone miserable until you pick the fight you want. Someone will cave, but it won't make you feel better."

Damn him.

Tara let out a long breath. "You're right." She removed a cloth from her belt and cleaned her sweat before handing it to Aiden.

"You are going to have to trust Brye."

Trust her? How could she when she was proving herself incapable of a rational decision? She was giving her future away in a mating ceremony with a man she didn't even like, let alone trust.

Tara's gaze drifted over Aiden, and her thoughts slipped away for a second as she watched him wipe the sweat from his brow and neck. He dragged it down and across his collarbone, and something about the gesture caused heat to pool in her stomach... and lower....

This is so unhelpful.

"Is there something you find interesting?" he asked when he caught her staring.

She blinked rapidly. "You have a lot of muscles," she blurted out. She blushed, cheeks heating almost to the color of her hair.

"So do you." He pinched her bicep and laughed. Tara moved her arm away.

"If I didn't know you better, I'd think you find me attractive." He smirked, flexing his arms.

"You already know you're attractive. Don't let it go to your head." She poked him in the chest.

"I will attempt to keep myself humble."

For a moment, Tara lost herself in the intensity of those blue depths. Aiden leaned back and winked, increasing her discomfort.

"Time to go." He took her hand and pulled her along. Tara kept quiet, her mind focusing on two equally confusing things.

Against her judgment, Tara reluctantly admitted that Aiden was right. She was prepping for a fight. Her muscles were always tense, and her mind was on edge. There was a consistent sense of stretching along her skin. An ache for something she couldn't identify but grew worse with all the changes.

If only it were the only change.

The new, intense feelings for Aiden burned under her skin.

Who wouldn't be attracted to him? He was handsome in a flirtatious sort of way. He was entertaining and kind. He knew what to say and when to say it. He tolerated her temper.

But liking Aiden and wanting him up were very different things. Tara wanted to eat him by devouring his lips and branding him. That was dangerous, and it was precisely what she was feeling.

Even now, her heart ached from the warmth of his hand. Tara felt needy, distracted, and alarmed whenever he looked at her.

If Aiden noticed her distraction, he didn't mention it. Before long, they arrived at her door, and he released her hand.

"I'll see you tonight."

He turned to go.

"Aiden, wait!"

He came with hands behind his back and a playful smile. "Yes, Tara?"

Tara moved her jaw and fidgeted by playing with the buckle on her belt. Aiden raised an eyebrow.

"Nothing..." she groaned out.

"Of course." He laughed and left. There Tara stood, confused and unsure why she had called him back in the first place.

Announcements

Brye

ONCE HER MEETING WITH Queen Celine was over, Brye headed home to prepare for the evening. The queen insisted on sending gifts for all of them. There was a new tunic for Brye and two almost identical emerald-colored dresses for Tara and Lenna. Lenna examined the embroidery work on the neckline, rubbing her fingers over the floral details.

"The colors will suit you so well, Tara," Lenna said as she continued to play with the material. "It's a shame I must hide mine under my gray cloak."

"That can be easily solved," Brye said, tossing the cloak on a chair. "You won't wear it. I am sure I can give some orders as the future princess." She winked.

Lenna rubbed her hands together. "I like the sound of that."

"And you." Tara held out the dress sent for her older sister. It was a dark blue, with a plaid underskirt and belt. The material and pattern were worn only by the royal family. "This will certainly make a statement. I might not even recognize you."

"And we will make your hair even nicer than us." Lenna twirled a lock of Brye's hair.

"Your energy is infectious, Lenna," Brye said.

"I damn hope so."

Tara gripped Brye's wrist. "Was this also a gift?"

Brye had forgotten about the bracelet. The light, thin metal was warm against her skin, almost like it was part of her wrist. "Yes, supposedly, it has magical knots and will aid my relationship."

"Sounds splendid." Lenna ran her fingers over the metal. "They look like threads."

"It looks like a shackle," Tara mumbled.

"Tara!" Brye and Lenna said in unison.

"What? Worried I might be right?"

Brye sighed, and they dropped the subject in silent agreement and prepared for the evening's event.

As a peace offering, Tara decided to maintain the appearance of an optimistic attitude. Lenna's good mood did not waver. The morning's tension was erased, and a light, playful atmosphere replaced it. Soon, it was time to head out, and there was a knock at their door.

"Here to escort the most beautiful women of Avalon to the royal gathering!" Aiden announced. He was dressed impeccably in a cream overtunic, with dark pants. The tunic had been decorated with embroidered vines along the sleeves. His golden curls were combed back and his beard trimmed.

Lenna was the first to walk out, her hair half plaited on her head with curls running down her back. Her waned features lit up with an excited smile.

Tara followed in the green tunic tied with a belt, her lengthy hair down to her waist. A ribbon tamed the fiery curls briefly, revealing her tanned, freckled face.

It was almost impossible not to notice Aiden's slight intake of breath when he saw Tara. Feelings around them were changing, bringing a secret smile to Brye's lips. How long before Tara realized she was in love with Aiden?

Aiden turned to Brye and gave her his biggest coy smile. "You look stunning. Like a queen."

Brye looked down and surveyed herself. The dress was tight around her breasts and waist, drawing attention to her figure. Her hair was mostly down with a braided coronet with small, decorated pins. She supposed she did look beautiful, didn't she?

Suddenly self-conscious, Brye ran her clammy hands over her skirt. "Everyone will know before the official announcement."

"A lot of young girls will be disappointed," Aiden managed to say before Tara elbowed him.

Lenna gripped her hand. "Let them see you, Brye. What they think is their problem."

"When did you become so wise?" Brye raised an eyebrow.

"I learned from the best."

"Me, of course." Tara grinned as she placed her arm in the crook of Brye's elbow. Laughter erupted, and Brye set out to the lake with a sister in each of her arms, with Aiden trailing behind. The paths were mostly empty, with only stragglers heading to the area.

Torches were placed in the center and around the field. Tables of food were set, with a boar roasting on a pit, and barrels of ale lay waiting to be opened. People drank and chatted. There was still some time before sunset, and the sky was clear and bright.

Not trying to draw attention to themselves, the four held back near the edge of the fields and waited. A few moments later, the drums announced the royal family's arrival.

The first to enter was the royal advisor, who wore her costumery black and gray tunic, her dark hair braided. The king, queen, and prince made their way to the dais. All were dressed in dark blue tunics with plaid underclothes.

Brye played with the bracelet to keep from fidgeting. Around them, people whispered, and some even motioned in their direction. Brye lifted her head higher, although she was drowning in nerves.

Lenna squeezed her hand, and a sharp sense of anxiety ran up her arm and tightened along her stomach. Brye looked down at her sister briefly, but her face was calm.

"Everything will be fine, Brye," Lenna whispered. Brye nodded but released her hand. The feeling in the pit of her stomach disappeared instantly.

Was it even hers?

"That's odd," Tara said, examining the crowd. "Beltran seems to be absent."

"He might be busy," Lenna said cryptically.

"Do you know something we don't?" Tara asked.

Brye didn't hear the answer. Gareth's dark eyes found her in the crowd, and unexpected shivers ran down her spine. He stood next to the king, arms behind his back. His face seemed calm and collected, except for his traitorous mouth, which suddenly decided to twitch. Brye bit down on her lip. His twitching mouth drove her to distraction. How can one slight muscle movement, almost undetectable at this distance, cause Brye to flounder in her resolve? All she could think about was what he could do with that mouth.

I dislike him. Of course, I dislike him. It's just his mouth.

Gareth must know how he affected her. If not, why would he move his mouth that way? Threatening a smile but never truly revealing one.

Brye looked away and attempted to control her emotions. King Manus stood on the wooden stage erected for the evening.

"Good evening to all our subjects," he began, his voice loud and firm. "We have invited you to announce a great event. A great blessing for our family and our people. Prince Gareth has found a mate, and they will commit to each other and the kingdom in five days."

He paused as the crowd hushed in expectation.

Brye held Lenna's hand tightly once more, her heart thumping wildly in her chest. For a moment, Brye was revisited by the nagging sensation in the pit of her stomach until Gareth motioned her forward.

Lenna let go, and Brye's body tensed up, with the new, unfamiliar shivers making their way over her skin. In the background, gasps and whispers came from the shocked crowd. Were they surprised? Were they insulted?

Oh, what must they all think?

Brye kept her eyes on Gareth. His deep, sober features were the lifeline that kept her feet moving in one direction. Before she realized it, she stood beside him in front of the entire village. His face warmed, if ever so slightly, and he reached for her hand. The touch was gentle and reassuring. He rubbed the knuckles and then lifted her clasped hand to his lips, kissing it with almost reverence.

A potent shock of electricity ran up Brye's arm, wrapping around her heart, speeding it up until it hammered into her chest.

Around them, gasps and awes echoed; some even applauded. Gareth lowered her hand but did not release it. "Brye, daughter of Elsywth, has accepted to become my mate. She does me a great honor."

The applause grew around them, and Brye couldn't control the smile on her face. Gareth's mouth twitched once more.

Smile. Come on, smile.

Gareth's mouth grew to one side as if he heard her plea, but he tipped his head away. Brye was left wanting more, needing more than what he was offering.

Noises caught her attention in the back of the crowd. A group of rowdy warriors were screaming graphic innuendos. Brye's cheeks burned. Gareth's face grew cold, and he gave the group a menacing stare. Painful groans followed as Tara cuffed the most vocal of the group. They quieted instantly.

"Let us celebrate this announcement with ale and food," ordered the king as he signaled the servants to open the barrels. Claps turned to cheers as lines formed around the drinks and food table.

Brye let out a long breath. Gareth leaned in. "Was it as bad as you thought?" His breath warmed her ear.

"I do not know what to think," Brye's voice cracked, and she coughed to clear it.

Her neck prickled, and she turned to discover a group of angry young girls watching them.

"Some are not as happy," Brye pointed out.

"Some are not capable of true happiness unless it is their own," Gareth whispered in a playful tone. Brye coughed to hide a laugh, and his mouth twitched again. It was slowly driving her crazy. She went back to observing the crowd.

"I know of a few that did have an audience with my mother," Gareth continued.

"You did mention the list was short." She gave him a side glance. "Not much to choose from."

"In my opinion, I made the best choice."

"How can it be the best when it was the only one?" she asked.

"I am sure we will find out." He placed a hand on the small of her back. The heat from his palm penetrated the fabric, and the tiny electric jolts returned. "Let us join the feast."

"Of course," she said breathlessly.

Gareth led her to the bench at the table, placing her next to Queen Celine. Instead of sitting by the king, he chose to sit beside her. His face was still humorless, but Brye was rewarded by the favored twitch and an unexpected wink.

❧

Tara

"Well, it went better than I thought," Aiden said.

The heavy drinking started, and music played in the background. Couples danced in the field while men and women drank and ate amidst varied conversations. The sun was still in the sky, at least for another couple of hours. The mists would settle an hour after sunset, which meant there was still time for Tara to be continuously irritated with the affair.

"He ignores her." Tara motioned to the royal table with her glass.

"I was talking about you. You only managed to hit one warrior, not attack the entire group. No one has been killed." Aiden grinned before lifting his glass to drink. "I think he likes her."

"They deserved more than a cuff." Tara placed a hand on her hip and popped it to the side. "Likes her? What?"

"Were you the only one who did not see the kiss on her hand?"

"Oh, that was only for show." Tara waved around. "To please the crowd."

Aiden laughed into his glass. "I assure you, Gareth does nothing of the sort."

"See there?" Tara motioned to the royal table with the cup. "He doesn't even look at her."

"He doesn't have to look at her to be aware of her. It's the little things."

"For example?"

Aiden leaned in and his hot breath sent goosebumps down her neck as he whispered, "You see how his arm is behind her chair? And how his hand sometimes touches her back?"

"I can't see his hand," she breathed, distracted by Aiden's proximity.

"You don't have to, but it is happening. He is very interested in her and Brye in him."

"I don't believe you."

"Oh, but it is so evident," Aiden continued. "Tara, she hasn't moved away."

"I mean—that doesn't—" Tara started, trying to find the words, but damn it, she was tongue-tied between Aiden's breath in her ear and the sense that she was losing this argument.

Whatever scrambled response she could gather was immediately shattered as she spotted Lenna moving across the field toward them, returning from the royal table. Tara stepped away from Aiden. He chuckled.

Her sister stood behind Roweena, attending to her until the annoying woman sent her off. Lenna's face relaxed with each step away from the royal advisor. Her features softened a moment, then tensed with resolve.

"Lenna." Tara pulled her sister to her side. "Aiden thinks the prince likes Brye."

"I should hope so," Lenna said as she turned back to see Brye in deep discussion with Queen Celine. She bit her bottom lip. "They will be mated soon. It will be easier if they come to care for each other."

"But she doesn't even like him," Tara persisted.

"Affection changes, Tara," Lenna said, flustered. "People change. He practically is wrapping his arm around her shoulders. She hasn't moved away. She seems very comfortable."

Tara shared a look with Aiden, who gave her a knowing smile. "So, I have been told."

"I must go." Lenna gave her sister a pull on her sleeve. "I have to train."

"Lenna, tonight no one trains." Tara rolled her eyes. "It is a night of celebration."

"Well, I must. Do not wait up, and I mean it this time." She kissed Tara and made a quick exit.

The Cave

Lenna

LENNA RELAXED ONCE THE voices and music faded. She wanted to reach the break in the wall before sundown and the mists settled. Hopefully, the wolf would be there so she could share what had happened.

The training was a source of joy, no matter how tired Lenna had been lately. It was becoming natural and easy. It was all she could think about.

The sun was setting, and the mists fell when Lenna reached the wall. She could attempt crossing the invisible bridge by herself but preferred to wait. She sat at the river bank on a log, holding her body close to ward off the perpetual chill.

She rubbed her nose, her mind blissfully blank until the smell of wet fur filled her nostrils, and a familiar presence arrived.

"I am so glad you came."

A deep, almost human-type chuckle escaped, and Lenna's smile grew. He motioned to follow, and they set out. Once they passed the invisible bridge, Lenna exhaled as the heavy feeling over her body lifted. The salty scent covered her like a blanket, reminding her of the unseen ocean beyond them.

"There is so much I wish to share with you," she said, following the dark form along the path to the cave. "Some you might already know. Brye will be the prince's mate."

By now, they had reached the cave. Lenna easily lit the fire and removed her gray cloak, setting it on a protruding rock. "Tara is displeased with it. Then again, it would be odd if she wasn't."

This time there was a small bowl with water in the cave. She waited for instructions, eager to begin.

"How do you feel about it?" the wolf asked as he gazed at her with tawny eyes. He rarely participated in the conversation unless it was to give direction or encouragement.

Until now.

Lenna paused to consider her answer. "I don't know." She sighed and sat beside the fire, playing with the ceramic bowl. "Aiden believes the prince must like her."

"Aiden's opinion seems to hold weight with you."

"With all of us." She looked around the cave.

"Do you care for him?" The wolf sounded intrigued.

"The prince? I don't know him."

"Aiden."

Lenna blushed, dipping her fingers in the bowl of water. "Are we going to train?" She didn't want to talk about Aiden or anything close to him. He belonged to Tara. End of story. Lenna wanted to focus on her growing magical skills, not her unnecessary feelings.

The wolf cocked his head to one side as though expecting her to continue. When she didn't, he spoke. "We will make water from the air."

Lenna regained her good humor, rubbing her hands together. This was something she could do. This was something she could excel at.

"Sounds like fun!"

The wolf taught her to take water from the misty air to fill the basin, only to move it from side to side. Once she had some control, she floated the water in the air and made it dance. It took some hours until he was satisfied with her skill.

Near midnight, she used the water from the basin to dampen the fire, and the cave fell into darkness. Opening her palm, she called a small flame to light their way back to the river. Lost in her thoughts, she hadn't realized the wolf was talking.

"Beg your pardon?"

The wolf sighed. "I complimented your growth in skill and experience in this short time."

"It's meaningless if my magic is nonexistent inside the wall." She sighed.

"As you gain more strength, it might be possible to push against the bindings."

Lenna stopped at the river bend, her brow furrowed. "Why does the island bind?"

The wolf did not respond, only continued on his way. Lenna grabbed his coat, stopping him. He turned and growled, baring his teeth. She stubbornly kept her grip.

"Stop that!" she ordered. "You said the island binds. The only possible way is if the Bondmaker Founder put a specific bonding spell on the wall."

The wolf continued to bar its teeth and try to shake her off. "Am I right?" She let go of his fur.

The wolf shook his body before responding. "Bondmagic is rare and we don't know how it works. We know the wall restricts magic and that the spell has been slowly wearing off."

If what the wolf was saying was true, then how could Roweena use her magic? Could she be an exception? If so, why? Lenna did not want to go back to train with the temperamental woman. The answer to that question would have to wait.

Lenna examined the tall wall, with the river cutting through and jagged stones from the structure protruding around them. "The break in the wall."

The wolf nodded. "The break was not always here. It has gotten wider with time. The break is at least 50 years, if not older. Before, it was only a passage."

"Are you affected by the binding?"

"All magic is affected differently by the binding." The wolf motioned for her to walk toward the river. Once they passed, Lenna staggered and fell to the ground, her breath uneven. The wolf's wet nose appeared near her side, and she wrapped her arms around him.

"Each... time... I... cross...the... recovery... is..."

"As you get stronger," the deep echoing voice rumbled near her ear. "It will be harder for you to adapt to the bindings."

Lenna nodded against his neck, concentrating on the smell of his fur and steady heartbeat. Her chest ached for a moment on the contact. He smelled of misty woods and a peat fire. After some time, she recovered and removed her hands.

"Do you think I should stop learning?" she asked, her eyes finding his.

"Do you want to stop?"

"No." She stood taller with effort. He leaned into her, and she patted him carefully. "I do not."

Stopping was not an option. Lenna needed to see this through, wherever it took her.

Part II

Changes

Brye

FOR THE FIVE FOLLOWING days, Brye and her sisters barely saw each other, each lost in their routines. When they managed to be together, they would exchange words and maintain good humor.

Until a delivery at their door ended their fantasy and brought reality crashing through.

Queen Celine sent more gifts for Brye and her sisters the day before the ceremony. The sight of the deep red tunics, belts, and pins made Tara pace the room with a sneer. "Is she trying to buy your affection?"

"She is only trying to make Brye comfortable," Lenna said, shaking out the tunics and setting them on the chairs to prevent wrinkles. Brye was working on her herbs on the table. She ground the spices to keep her hands from shaking, but the rolling inside her stomach grew worse.

"By sending her clothes and trinkets?" Tara lifted a belt decorated with small designs. It was beautifully made and probably took more than a few days to prepare. She tossed it on the table and crossed her arms.

"By showing respect to us, she shows respect to me," Brye stated. She placed an empty bowl with more force than intended, making the rest of the objects jump.

"It still feels like too much," Tara persisted.

"That's enough, Tara," Brye snapped.

Tara growled and left the house, slamming the door behind her.

Lenna sighed, staring at the door. "She doesn't know what to do with herself."

"I know, Lenna." Brye attempted to go back to work with her herbs but failed. She slammed the tools on the table and rubbed her face with her hands.

"She wants you to be happy."

"*I know, Lenna!*" Brye roared. Lenna winced. "I know! Do you think I don't want to be happy? It isn't me you should be concerned about."

Brye pushed away from the table, reaching for a bucket of fresh water. "Worry about yourself."

"You and Tara are woven from the same cloth," Lenna pointed out. "You both use anger as a way to hide your feelings."

"And you ignore them." Brye stared her sister down. "Or deflect or belittle them."

"That's not fair." Lenna gripped the back of the chair.

"Is it? Why don't you stand up for yourself?"

Lenna stepped back, eyes wide. "I—"

"You are pushed and humiliated by the royal advisor and do nothing." Brye's voice trembled with every word. "You sit back and take all the pain as if you deserve it."

Lenna's eyes moistened, but she turned away, pinching her nose tightly.

Brye should stop at her sister's discomfort. She should do many things, but Brye was exhausted from pretending. Everyone's feelings and her own overwhelmed her until she wanted to break everything.

And Lenna was the only thing around to break.

"Do you feel anything at all? Are you going to sit there and let life happen to you? Is truly being a Mist Maiden and training what you want? Is this where your story ends?"

The silence extended until it became uncomfortable.

"Answer me!"

Lenna still said nothing, jaw tight, the furrow between her brows. Her barely contained anger and hurt crashed in Brye like stormy waves over rocks. The moments ticked by. Slow. So slow...

Brye brought her hand to her mouth as the swell of her own emotion ebbed away, bringing her back to her senses.

Oh no. What have I done?

Brye's stomach knotted. "Lenna..."

Lenna snatched her gray cloak and satchel. She did not turn around, holding her head high. "Please don't wait up for me. I will see you in the morning."

"Lenna, please—"

"You've said enough, Brye." The room trembled with the force of Lenna's contained feelings. Outside, thunder rumbled in the distance, and the room lit up with the unexpected flash of lightning. Bottles threatened to topple over, and Brye jumped to secure them.

"Please get some rest. Tomorrow is an important day."

The door closed with a snap, and Brye sank to the floor, her body affected by Lenna's emotions. They ran deeper and darker than she had ever experienced. A wave of anger and desolation that could destroy, barely contained by Lenna's sense of loyalty and love.

What have I done?

Brye's hand reached her face, and she broke out in uncontained sobs.

What have I done?

Tara

Tara escaped to the abandoned training field. The warriors were now clearing the wheat and tending to the fields. Aiden would be there expecting her, but she couldn't go.

Thunder roared for a moment, followed by a crash of lighting. She jumped, blinking, as she tried to find the storm in the clear sky. The hairs on her arms rose, and the sense of doom escalated for a moment, but it quickly was replaced with anger and helplessness that did not want to go away.

Things change.

Then why did this change feel like the end? Why did it feel as if she was going to lose her sister? To lose them both? Imagining her life alone was a dismal prospect.

Picking up an ax, Tara went to the target field. She aimed and tossed. It would hit the target off-center, but retrieving, aiming, and tossing made her move.

She was so angry at everything, but deep inside, it was not because Brye was mating the prince or Lenna was a Mist Maiden. She was terrified of the shifting sense inside her.

Tara was stronger, faster, and fitter than ever. Her instincts were sharper, and sometimes her skin itched like a snake that needed to remove a layer. As if even her very skin desired to be something else. Something more.

It was familiar yet unknown, and it terrified her.

Who was she supposed to be? Would she even like herself?

Aiden approached the field, and Tara kept him in her sight.

Her future was one of many problems.

He made her uneasy as well. He mixed up her feelings until she did not know what she wanted. That change scared her most of all. She hadn't imagined finding a mate or even a partner.

No, that's not true.

When she was in her teens, she once believed that if she ever had a mate, he would need to be like Aiden. But there was no one like him.

She glanced at the ax in her right hand, testing the weight. How could she handle these emotions? How could she handle him? This friendship was killing her.

Pulling the ax behind her shoulder to aim, she released a breath, and it hit the target closer to the mark.

"You're working with both hands, I see." Aiden stood back, his hands on his hips. His tone was calm, not flirtatious nor humorous.

"You never know what skills you will need in battle." Tara went to retrieve the weapon.

"You talk as if there will be one."

"We train as if there will be more than a battle." She stood back to him, aiming with her left hand this time. The ax hit dead center. "We train as if we are going to war."

He studied her for a painfully long moment. "There is a war inside you, Tara," he stated, "and you are losing."

Her first reaction was to reach for her temper. But she knew that her anger was hiding her fear. The fear of change, around and most importantly, inside her. Lenna became a Mist Maiden, and now she is wasting away. Brye decided, out of the blue, to mate the prince. A man she disliked.

And what about Tara's feelings? They were so contradictory and uncomfortable.

Yes, anger was better. Moving was what she needed to do.

She took the ax, changed hands, aimed, and tossed.

Dead center.

She retrieved the ax again. Threw it again. Dead center again. And again.

And again.

And again.

Tears ran down her cheeks. She wiped them away as she fetched the ax again.

"Tara, talk to me, please."

"Talk to you?"

"Yes." Aiden took the weapon from her hand, dropping it away from them. He was no longer playful. Alarmed, she wanted to pull away.

His nostrils flared, and he gripped her hand tighter.

"I'm done with these games." He started dragging her across the weapons field toward the northern wall. Tara thought for a second about breaking free. She knew how and could easily escape. But she didn't want to. He had something to say, and so did she.

The fields faded into woods. The tall trees came into view, with the cool shade and the crinkle of fallen twigs and leaves underfoot. Aiden loosened his hold and guided them farther ahead. The smell of moist moss and herbs soothed Tara's nerves. The call of birds and small animals distracted her from the brooding man in front. If only temporarily.

They walked until they reached the pond they had bathed in during Beltane.

"Look at me, Tara," Aiden said gruffly. He turned her toward him, still keeping hold of her. Reluctantly she raised her gaze, and her heart melted at her feet.

"Things change," she whispered, her mouth going dry.

"Yes," he agreed. "Everything has to change, Tara. The world can't stay the same."

"But I need it too. I need everything to stay the same. It's the only way I won't be so afraid of losing my sisters. Of losing you."

Aiden pulled her gently closer as if she were a skittish animal. Maybe she was. Part of her wanted to run, while another wanted so much to stay. He did not say a word, only held her to his chest as she sobbed.

Tara wrapped her arms around him tightly, wanting to absorb him with her touch. Make him part of her. Aiden did the same, with his head resting on her neck.

Tara's tears dwindled as his body encircled her with warmth. She gripped harder, needing his heat to remove the sense of impending doom in the pit of her stomach.

"I cried all over you," she spoke into his tunic.

"I didn't notice," he chuckled, moving the tiny hairs at the nape of her head. "I spent all morning working the fields and dipped in a barrel to get myself clean.

Tara gave a short laugh. He was sweaty and sticky, but so was she. His smell comforted her as much as the warmth of his arms. The ache in her chest expanded.

Aiden loosened his grip, but she held on.

"Not yet." She pressed her face into his smelly tunic, closing her eyes. His chest rumbled with his laugh.

"You don't cry often." He rubbed her back softly. "But when you do, you always become a bit needy."

"You know me so well." Tara listened to his heartbeat. The steady rhythm soothed as much as everything else about him.

"Yes, almost as much as I know myself," he said gravely. Tara leaned back and looked into his sky-blue eyes. He rubbed her arms while she kept her grip on his waist.

And if I risk it?

Her feelings were not going to go away. They were getting worse.

"Things change," Tara repeated.

His hands slowly moved up, with a light caress up her arms. "People also change."

"Affection changes as well." Tara's gaze fell to his lips. Aiden took a breath, and his hand stiffened at her arms.

"Tara, what has changed?"

Everything and nothing at all.

She removed her hands from his waist and placed them on his shoulders. At first, her mouth hovered over his, begging him to take the next step.

Please, don't let this be only me.

"Tara," he sighed.

His lips met hers.

He played with her lips, teasing them open, and then someone moaned and lit them both on fire. Tara's hands moved from his shoulders to wrap around his neck. She needed to imprint him on her skin. Aiden gripped the back of her shirt. She changed the kiss, tangling her tongue with his until his taste was scorched into her memory. She pushed the limits of their control.

Aiden groaned when her hands ran through his hair, and his teeth tugged at her lower lip. He pulled back, taking a ragged breath after another. He attempted to put some space between them, but Tara kept her grip by linking her hands behind his neck.

"How long?" she asked, her voice hoarse.

How long have you felt this way?

She didn't need to clarify. After all, he knew her as well as he knew himself.

"I don't know. Before I knew it, you were already there, wrapped around my heart like you are now."

Tara's breath quickened. Her feelings jumbled together—excitement, thrill, and underneath panic.

Oh, what happens if I mess this up?

"I'm sorry. I didn't want to risk it. I was, am, so confused about it all. Or perhaps very, very stubborn." She gave a nervous chuckle.

"Yes, very." He grinned before a laugh escaped. His rich laugh fanned the heat in Tara's stomach. "I was beginning to think I would have to wait forever."

"You could have told me."

"Was I not obvious enough when I found opportunities to be half-naked with you?"

It wasn't enough.

She bit back a grin. "Still, it would have saved us much trouble. I thought you only saw me as an annoying little sister."

"Little sister? Not for a while." He raised an eyebrow. "I thought perhaps that was how you saw me, as an older brother."

"Oh, no! I turned sixteen, and the fantasies hit. You stopped being an older brother then."

"You will have to tell me about those fantasies one day." He cocked a wicked smile. The heat in Tara's body expanded, pooling itself lower.

"One day." She bit her lip, holding back a coy smile.

"But for now, I think you need to apologize." Aiden took a deep breath. He reluctantly released her, only to keep her hand. "I am sure you did something to someone somewhere, and they deserve an apology."

"You always think the worst of me." She swatted his arm.

"No, never," he laughed.

Before the Storm

Lenna

THE SUN WAS HIDDEN behind dense rain clouds when Lenna passed the break in the wall. The walk had cooled her down, but the underlying tension did not leave her. She set out to meet the ocean. The rustling sound of the water over the pebbles soothed her while the salty, humid air whipped her messy braid.

Lenna rubbed the crusted, dried tears away and exhaled a wobbly sigh. Even though she had trained for weeks, it was the first time she stood on the beach. The ocean was intense and eerie with dense clouds decorating the horizon. Lenna tried to see the Continent's mainland beyond the mists and jagged shore, but nothing was there.

She stood, alone on the shore breathing in the salty air, attempting not to get lost in the massive overwhelming feeling that washed over her with each wave. Alone, and adrift on the waves. The vast ocean could swallow her whole, drawing her into its depths.

She wondered if she would ever tire of it. Was the Continent just as vast and undiscovered? Was there peace between Shifters and Yuansu? What were they even like?

Until her 21st birthday, Lenna had little curiosity about the world outside the island. She spent her days working with Caitlin and the other women tending to different tasks, managing her home, or creating tapestries. Life for Lenna seemed constant and predictable.

But everything changed on the day of Beltane.

Home was no longer a refuge but a place of constant conflict. Little by little, the relationship between her and her sisters was splitting at the seams, and she did not know how to mend it. The threat of going back to train with Roweena. The thought of enduring the consistent abuse that depleted her energy, left her with a persistent hollow feeling.

Avalon was no longer a haven.

Avalon had become a cage where she lived an unexceptional half-life. Perpetually tired and hiding what she felt and thought.

Not even my sisters know who I am.

Do I even know who I am?

Brye had been right. Since becoming a Mist Maiden, Lenna had devoted all her time to training, but for what? Did she truly want to become the next royal advisor? Lenna sincerely doubted Roweena would relinquish her power, stepping aside for a younger, more inexperienced replacement.

Then why train me? Why even pretend to do so?

Thunder came with the dark, heavy clouds. Lenna's cloak billowed around her body as she waited for the rain to arrive. The storm exploded over the sea, the sound echoing over the crash of the waves.

Soon, the clouds made their way to the shore, soaking her instantly to the bone. The cold chilled her, but she did not mind. She was accustomed to it.

Wishing to escape her dismal thoughts, Lenna extended her hand, watching the raindrops pool in her open palm. Concentrating, she transformed the water into a ball the size of her head. She played with it from one hand to another. A pleased smile spread over her features.

"What are you doing here?" a voice growled.

The ball fell at her feet with a splash, soaking her stockings and shoes. The wolf panted behind her, his fur drenched and his paws covered in mud.

"I didn't expect you." Lenna raised her voice above the rain and the crashing waves.

"I gathered as much. Come." He turned, and she warily followed. He was taking her back to the cave. She stepped to the side at the tension that radiated from his furry body.

It was dry inside, and the storm looked worse than it felt, or maybe Lenna no longer knew what was worse. A fire started as the wolf entered, splattering water around as he shook himself off. Lenna stood near the entrance, a growing puddle at her feet.

"It is not safe to be out here alone."

"I don't think anything will come to it," she said through chattering teeth.

"If anything, you will get sick and fall behind in your training."

Lenna, shivering, gave a clumsy shrug. Getting sick was the least of her worries. What she truly wanted was to be left alone. Perhaps not alone with her thoughts, but at least with her magic.

The wolf grunted and moved farther down the dark cave. He returned with a drying cloth and an oversized dark tunic in his jaws. He handed them to her before walking away.

"Thank you."

He growled in response.

This is nice. Now both of us are irritated.

Every piece of clothing was stuck to her skin, and she shivered earnestly as she undressed. The wolf laid down near the fire facing away from her to give her some privacy.

Naked, she dried herself off with the cloth and slipped on the tunic. It was made of surprisingly soft fabric, with small details around the neckline. Lenna ran her fingers over the embroidery, marveling at the silver thread in swirled designs. They seemed familiar, but she could not recall where. She placed her wet clothes over protruding rocks to dry.

Lenna laid a blanket next to the fire in front of the wolf. With a flick of her hand, she made the fire grow. The cave slowly warmed. She then gave him a side glance.

"Whose clothing is this?"

The wolf turned around and sat by the fire.

"Someone who does not need them. You can leave them once you head back."

"Oh?" Lenna unwound her braid and combed her hair out with her stiff fingers. "Yours?"

The wolf concentrated on the fire, ignoring the question.

"Is your voice the same one you use in human form?" she asked hesitantly.

"Why so many questions?"

"Well, you have been asking a few, and I have answered. I only thought you would reciprocate." She stopped combing her hair and sighed.

The silence stretched even longer.

Should I confront him?

Let him keep his mystery. She didn't need it. Lenna got what she wanted—a decent trainer. The rest was unimportant.

For now.

"How did you know I was here?" She brought her knees to her chest and covered them with the oversized tunic. Slowly, the cocoon brought warmth to her tired body.

"I saw you were walking across the field going north," the wolf admitted. "It looked like rain, and I felt you were not coming back."

"I needed time to think. I couldn't stay at home."

Lenna's thoughts returned to Brye's harsh opinion.

Was that thought what everyone thought of me?

She pressed her eyes against her knees, tightening her arms.

"What worries you?" the wolf asked cautiously. He raised his head from his crossed front paws. Lenna gave him a knowing look.

"See what I mean about the questions?" She played with a lock of her hair. "My sister will be mated tomorrow, and they have been pretending it would never happen. Tara attempted to be civil and supportive. Brye seemed content, at least on the surface. Today the queen sent gifts, and it all became too real for them. They lashed out. I was in the way."

"Is he a bad match for your sister?"

A bad match? Gareth was many things, but not in any way unequal to Brye. And no matter how much her sister denied it, they were attracted to each other.

Some feelings can't be hidden.

Lenna shrugged. "I don't believe so. It's just all happening so fast. I don't think we have had time to process it."

"Lenna."

Her head snapped up. It was the first time he had said her name.

"What did your sister say that upset you?"

"What makes you believe she said anything?"

The wolf gave her a knowing look.

Lenna exhaled. "She believes I let others walk over me and do not take action over my life." She stuck out her hand and played with the flames, strengthening and weakening them. The play soothed her, as the water did before. Magic flowed out of her fingers easily, bringing a welcomed tingling sensation. "My sisters know nothing about this."

"And why don't you tell them? You have extraordinary gifts. They should be celebrated."

"I thought about it." She split the fire, creating two separate flames. "I tell myself they will worry."

"I think they worry more because you are not honest."

"It isn't that." She gave him a side glance. "I'm not ready. Contrary to what you might believe, sisters don't tell each other everything." The two flames twirled around each other in a dance. She loved making the magic dance. "Magic has been my curse and my discovery. When I am ready, I will tell them. Besides, my sisters already have a lot to deal with."

With care, Lenna made the flames change their appearance. Two humanlike figures swayed to tune with the rain. The wolf watched from a distance, and the fire created shadows on the wall. It was a playful type of magic, one that Lenna sensed was the tip of what she could do.

"I have so much I wish to learn. About my magic, Avalon, and the bindings. For example, this binding magic that keeps me from my abilities has to be connected to the fading knot magic in the fields or the weakened mists."

"What would you do if it was?" the wolf asked.

Lenna stopped the dancing figures and shot the flames back into the fire. For a moment, the wood crackled, and a log split. "I don't know, but like my magic, the more I know, the less I fear it."

The wolf did not say more. Lenna's eyes grew heavy. With a yawn, she laid down beside the fire, curled up like a ball with an arm under her head.

The storm continued outside the cave. She shivered in her sleep. No matter how much she tried, she couldn't stop being cold—a warm body nestled behind her, furry and dry. The heat seeped into her like a gift, and she drifted off.

Sharing Confidences

Brye

THE MOMENT LENNA LEFT, Brye cried uncontrollably at the table with her head hung in her hands.

Why did I say that?

Tara's tense emotions and Lenna's growing weakness were too much for her to handle. Their feelings penetrated through her pores, disrupting her balance.

There had to be a way to avoid all this conflict.

There was.

That was why she now found herself sitting on a bench inside the tower, waiting.

Brye leaned back, rubbing her hands together in her lap. She and Gareth had not had time together since the night of the announcement, and even then, he spoke very little, letting the queen direct her attention. She had attempted to engage him in conversation, but Queen Celine drew her back.

They had spoken little that night, but she had learned a great deal by observation. For one, Brye became aware of the evident affection between the prince and his parents. He'd doted on his mother, ensuring she was comfortable, with a full plate and glass. Even King Manus would pat his son on the back and whisper a comment in his ear that'd had the prince smiling.

But it had been Brye's reaction to him that disturbed her. Her skin had shivered every time his fingers grazed her shoulders and back. The act had been gentle yet reassuring. With so much uncertainty around her, his caress had grounded her.

And she wanted his smile. The one hidden by the twitch of his lips.

Brye sat straighter when voices came from the third floor. One was Edgar, and the other the prince. They had a short conversation before a door closed. The royal retainer came down with his shuffling footsteps.

"Sorry, miss. The prince is unwell. He begs to see you tomorrow for the ceremony."

Brye kept her face impassive, even when her hands were grasped rigidly in front of her.

"Thank you, Edgar. I will let myself out."

He hesitated a moment, and Brye pretended to leave. She waited a few steps down until he went up the stairs again. The sound of a door closing on the last level was enough for her to sprint up to the next floor.

Brye carefully pressed her ear to one of the doors on the right and heard the faint voice of the king and queen. The voices grew closer. Brye jumped back, fumbling with the door on the other side of the hall. She barely managed to enter before the door opened and the king and queen came out. She heard them softly say something to Gareth, then the door clicked shut. Brye listened intently as their footfalls descended the stairs.

She cautiously opened the door she'd hid behind, peering around the hall. Declaring herself alone, she hastened to shut it softly behind her before she darted across the hall to Gareth's room. Gingerly, she twisted the knob and pushed open the door, peering around the jamb. She could just make out a figure by the window.

What was she doing? She should just leave—

"Brye?" A rough voice whispered from the room. Her mouth went dry as she pushed the door open the rest of the way. Gareth sat in a chair by the open window, a furrow of surprise across his brow. Brye rubbed her clammy hands on her skirt.

Caught. Too late to leave now.

"I wanted to speak to you," she said firmly. "It is about the ceremony tomorrow."

"Now?" Gareth recovered from her abrupt entrance and leaned back in the chair. "Was my order to be left alone only a suggestion?"

"There is no good time as the present," she said.

His gaze stayed on her face. He seemed briefly to examine her features. He must have seen her red-rimmed eyes and nose. "Something has upset you, and you want to cancel it."

"Yes... No..." Brye approached, trying to find another place to sit. The room was not as large as she suspected for a prince. He sat on a chair by a small table against one of the open windows. A simple chest was against the opposite side, with a jar of water on top. A door leading to the bathing room was closed to her left. The only other place to sit was the bed.

Gareth did not move from his chair.

She stayed standing.

"So, you are undecided." He sat forward and ran a hand through his hair. The chair creaked from the movement.

"No... I mean, yes. I mean..." Her arms crossed over her uncomfortable stomach. "I don't know what I mean."

Why was it so difficult to talk to him? She came here with clear intentions, and now? Brye paused at the change in his features. He sat with his shoulders hunched and his drawn face decorated with purple smudges under his eyes. Gareth was not his usual controlled self, and she couldn't ignore him. "Are you alright?"

"Yes." He rubbed his temples. "Just a headache. I have a lot on my mind."

Brye rubbed her tingling fingers together and sighed. Gareth leaned forward with his elbows on his knees and his head down.

Perhaps they both needed a distraction. Or someone to talk to. Brye raised a finger. "One question."

His head snapped up, and he winced. "I beg your pardon."

"We each get to ask one question. This time, you go first."

"So we are clear, you owe me more than one."

"We shall see how the conversation evolves."

Gareth let out a long breath and sat back in his chair. "Why are you upset, Brye? Besides the mating ceremony. Something else is bothering you."

Brye looked everywhere but his face. How much should she tell a stranger? However, was he a stranger? She couldn't shake this feeling of familiarity. The feeling only grew with each passing day.

It makes little sense. We have avoided each other. Until recently, we have never spoken.

"Let me guess. Your sisters have been very opinionated about this whole idea."

She narrowed her gaze at him, but said nothing, unsure how much she wanted to reveal about her sisters. Despite the familiarity, these were her sisters. Her flesh and blood.

"To be more specific," he continued. "Tara has been irritatingly forceful, and I am sure Lenna has been everything but."

There it was again, a nagging sensation in the back of her mind—a sense of having lived a moment like this before.

"It would be unusual if Tara were not vocal." Her lips trembled when she thought of Lenna. She bit hard on them to stop.

"Lenna," Gareth sighed.

Brye nodded.

"Since I answered my own question, I can safely ask this one. What happened with Lenna?" There was no going back from this. From sharing about her life willingly. But she wanted to talk to someone. Someone who would listen and give her perspective.

She wanted to talk to him.

He didn't insist on the question, and the silence prolonged. Gareth rubbed the nape of his neck, and his eyes filled with a soulful expression. "Let's leave it at that. You may ask your question."

"It doesn't seem fair. I didn't answer yours."

"We said at the beginning, if there was something we could not answer, we wouldn't."

Brye tapped her fingers on her legs. Slowly, as if the words came out from the deepest, darkest well, she told Gareth everything on her mind. She talked about Tara's reaction, distrust, and Lenna's support. And that hurt Brye the most because she treated her kind sister cruelly. Before she could stop them, the dreaded tears ran down her cheeks and she wiped them away.

Gareth listened, only moving to hand her a handkerchief from his pocket. His eyes never left her face.

"So... I don't know how to feel about my mating ceremony when it is causing so much discomfort to my family," she finished in a near-whisper.

"Our," he punctuated. "Our mating ceremony."

Her smile was hesitant. "Yes, ours."

Gareth rubbed his hands on his thighs. "I'm sorry about Lenna, but I am sure she will understand once you apologize. And Tara, well...." He rolled his eyes. "Tara is her own master. She doesn't take change well unless she is the one causing it."

Brye chuckled. "That is true."

"Do you feel better?"

Brye's chest was lighter, and she nodded. Gareth's comments were unbiased and thoughtful—qualities needed in a prince and future king. Brye had to admit to herself that he was raised for this role.

"Now." Brye sat forward. "Why are you so upset?"

Gareth hesitated and looked around the room. Brye laughed.

I am not the only one with trust issues.

His deep, dark eyes returned to her face, unsettling her with the intensity of his gaze.

"Many things. The first is the fields. For the last two years, the crops have been affected by uncommon issues due to the magic-infused land." As he explained, his voice became graver. "According to our records, this started around 40 years ago. Not only the crops are affected. We have also seen a decrease in the health of animal and plant life."

This was serious. Brye knew how important it was for Avalon to be self-sufficient. A dependency on the island's magic came at a price.

Brye wet her lips and scooted nearer to Gareth. "I have also observed anomalies regarding health conditions and live births."

His eyes widened as he leaned in closer. "What have you seen?"

"Enid and I keep very detailed records of child health and conditions. This includes the mother's health with the child and after. We have seen more and more complications during and after the child's birth."

"With your records, can you pinpoint when this started to happen?"

"The records only started when I became an apprentice. Enid does remember that these issues were uncommon when she was an apprentice with my mother."

She sat carefully at the edge of the bed leaning forward. Their faces close together, tones hushed. Brye suddenly became aware of their intimacy, as his chair creaked from him moving closer.

Two co-conspirators.

"But it isn't your only concern?"

"No." Gareth went back to massaging his temples. "That could be a minor problem compared to the bigger issue."

Brye gave Gareth's thigh a small pat. He froze at the contact and blinked slowly. Surprise floated up her hand, and she squeezed his thigh.

"Tell me."

He looked down at her hand on his thigh, studying it as he spoke. "The mists are not as thick. The island has been visible for some moments during the day."

"That would mean—"

"Yes," he sighed. "Even though, according to Beltran, the island is located off tall cliffs and on an unexplored beach, it would be only a matter of time before someone might get curious."

"Invaders?"

"We don't know what will happen. Or if we are prepared for it."

"It explains the increase in trainees and training time."

"Very perceptive of you." Gareth's mouth twitched.

"Oh no." Brye smiled. "That was Tara's observation. Has the royal advisor said anything? About the field or mists?"

A creak on the landing outside made Brye sit back. Gareth stilled and paled as he looked past her.

"I think it is time for you to go." He stood and waited for her at the door. Brye blinked. The sudden change in his demeanor once again gave her whiplash.

Brye stopped beside him, keeping her hands clasped. "Do you want me to take care of your headache?" He shook his head, gritting his teeth from the pain. "Thank you, but I'll be fine. Goodbye, Brye." He briefly looked down at her mouth before guiding her through the door with his hand on her waist.

A figure appeared from the top landing. Roweena paused as she studied them with her arms behind her back. One of Gareth's arms wrapped around Brye's waist, his tall body pressed into her. A sensation of unease settled in the pit of her stomach.

"Roweena." Gareth's breath heated her neck, sending shivers down her spine.

"Your Highness." She smiled, bringing her eyes up to his face. "Eager, are we?"

Gareth took a deep breath but did not respond. Roweena then went up the steps to her chambers.

He exhaled, relaxing his grip. "I'll escort you out."

The unease disappeared.

What was that?

Brye was about to ask, but he growled in her ear. "Not now."

Gareth took her hand and guided her downstairs. Not losing a chance, Brye instantly read him. There was controlled anger, concern, and acute pain centered around his temples.

Brye pushed harder, but a mental door was shut, cutting her off.

He blocked me! How?

He gave her a stern look, and Brye flushed. Did he know? There was no possible way that he could know she was reading him. How could he know? She never did it on purpose, until today.

Gareth's self-control must be above the norm for him to block her magical abilities. Then again, Brye was just getting used to them.

Once outside the tower, Gareth regarded her thoughtfully. "There is something you need to know, about secrets and open doors."

Brye looked confused. He leaned in and whispered. His breath raised the hairs on her neck and warmth invaded her chest. "Be careful what you say. You never know what you will hear or who wants you to listen to it."

Roweena might have overheard them. Why was she so interested in their conversation? They said nothing she did not already know. Unless, of course, she was less involved in these events than she let on.

Brye lifted her hand towards Gareth's temple.

He leaned back. "What are you doing?"

"Your head." Brye licked her lips, and her hands tingled once more. "It pains you. Please, Gareth. Let me help."

He exhaled and closed his eyes. Brye touched his temples and massaged. The pain was intense and pressing. Some thoughts moved around his head, but he blocked her out. She managed to get glimpses of fields covered in frost and splashing in water.

Slowly, the pain receded. A minor, nagging sensation was left on her temples, but it lasted little.

"Thank you." He pressed his palms to his eyes.

"I will see you tomorrow."

He eyed her wearily. "What did you say?"

"Tomorrow." Brye smiled hesitantly. "I will see you for our mating ceremony, Gareth."

She came here to end the engagement, only to find herself still entangled and even more confused. But one thing she was sure of, she did not want to back down.

Gareth bowed and went back inside, closing the door behind him. Brye pressed one hand on her nervous stomach.

One more day. In one more day, life will be so different.

Warm Feelings

Tara

R ain pelted down when Tara and Aiden arrived at the house, trailing mud and water in their wake. They found Brye working at the table, grounding herbs with her pestle.

Aiden looked around. "Where's Lenna?"

Brye's face crumbled at the mention of Lenna's name. Tara and Aiden rushed toward her, pulling her to the chair.

"It's all my fault," she covered her face with her hands. Aiden squeezed Tara's shoulder and motioned to the door.

"I'll go look for her."

Tara's body grew warm as he gave her a coy smile. Her heart danced and she could lose herself in his sky-blue eyes. Aiden tapped her chin with his finger and went out into the rain. Tara stared at the door momentarily, waiting for the flush to leave her face. The entire time she felt Brye's questioning gaze on her.

"He finally told you?" she whispered.

"Yes." Tara bit her lip, holding back a smile. She sat down on the chair opposite Brye at the table. It seemed wrong to be excited while Brye was upset, but she had no control over her emotions. She was blissfully happy and she would not be embarrassed. With Aiden at her side, she could take on the world. Or in this case, her distraught sister.

"I'm so happy." Brye gave a garbled laugh.

"I'm sure underneath all that mess you are, but why are you so upset?"

In disjointed stops, Brye told her what she had said to Lenna.

Tara groaned, rubbing Brye's hand. "This is all my fault. You were angry with me and took it out on her."

"No." Brye took both her hands. The tingling sensation under her fingertips sent a small electric current up her arms. "It was always mine for not screaming at you when you were insufferable."

"Yeah." Tara let go of Brye and drummed her fingers on the table. "It would have made things worse, but in the end, we would have both laid it all out in the open."

"I hurt her." Brye gave an uneven sigh. "I cut her down when all she wanted was to help."

Tara nodded. "I think we both did, in our way."

While she usually exploded, Brye would give a warning snap before biting. Each would try their patience until both of them would lash out.

In contrast, Lenna's rare anger had devastating consequences. The house would shake, and ceramics would break. Only after the destruction would Lenna disappear to lick her emotional wounds, leaving her sisters to clean up the aftermath.

If Lenna had not left the moment she had, Brye's workshop would be in ruins.

"We will talk to her." Tara smiled softly, patting Brye's hand. "Lenna loves you too much to hold a grudge, and so do I."

Standing, Tara gave a long stretch, her hands extending toward the ceiling. Her stiff joints gave a familiar pop. Water droplets hit her face, reminding her of her wet clothes.

"I got drenched in only a few minutes in the rain. Aiden and Lenna will be worse when they get back." She looked around the room. The hearth was cold, and the table was full of trinkets and folded tunics.

"I will change, and we will prepare everything for tomorrow."

Brye took a deep breath and nodded. Dressed in dry clothes and keeping her back to her sister, Tara asked, "Do you think Lenna will be happy for Aiden and me?"

Brye took a moment to answer. "As you told me. She loves you both very much. I am sure she will be beyond happy, especially considering how long he had to wait."

Tara laughed, her body relaxing.

"I think he loves me." Tara hesitantly said, testing the words on her tongue. The thought filled her chest again, and she beamed.

"Oh, Tara." Brye mirrored her smile. "He always has."

Lenna

Lenna awoke slowly as her body became aware of her surroundings. She was dry and warm, covered with a thick blanket. The fire still burned, but the rain had stopped, and the sky had darkened outside.

"Did you rest well?" the wolf called from where he was near the fire.

"Yes." Lenna rapidly sat, rubbing her eyes and face. "Better than I expected. How late is it?"

"A bit before midnight."

"Are we going to train tonight?"

"No, it would be wise for you to go home. Your sisters will be concerned."

Lenna nodded, bringing the blanket closer to her face. It was thick and full of fur, with an earthy scent underneath the canine smell. A musty, male odor tickled her nose and reminded her of a rainy afternoon.

The wolf yawned, and she stood, folding the blanket and returning her somewhat dry clothes. Keeping her back to the wolf, she quickly dressed, only to shiver as the humid fabrics touched her skin.

"You and your sisters seem very close. A lot closer than most sisters I have encountered."

She paused for a moment, deciding what to say. "Yes, as close as we can be."

"I was wondering, where are your parents?"

Sneaking glances in his direction, she exhaled. Of course, he would ask. It was an obvious question.

Then why am I reluctant?

"I don't know," she responded, pulling her long hair from where it got caught in the clothing. "We believe our father died before Tara was born. I don't think we ever met him."

Lenna finished getting dressed and approached the fire, sitting close to the heat. She pulled out a comb and string from her bag. Her hair frizzed to waves when not properly taken care of.

It was not soft like Brye's or untamed like Tara's. Lenna did not strive for beauty or strength. She left that to her sisters. Lenna desired to have a purpose for others and her community. But lately, it weighed on her. The wolf brought her out of her thoughts. She realized he'd spoken to her.

"I beg your pardon?" she asked.

"What happened to your mother?" His eyes became deep amber pools as he focused on her.

"Oh!" Lenna nodded. "She... she disappeared." Lenna's voice cracked, and she coughed to clear it.

Initially, Tara cried to sleep every night because she couldn't remember her. She was not the only one. None of them remembered. All the memories of their mother were gone.

But now, more than ever, Lenna missed her mother. With all the changes around them, *maither* would know what to do.

"*Maither* was radiant," Lenna began, her face alight. "Most of my memories are stories told to us. But she was like the sun, especially when she laughed, which was all the time. She was tall or seemed that way because we were so small. Her hair was like fire to her waist, her eyes forest green, and she had freckles on the bridge of her nose. They say I have her eyes, but we all have her freckles. She was the center of attention wherever she went, like Brye. She moved as if dancing instead of walking, like Tara."

Lenna's voice grew with confidence and affection as she continued. "We lived in the home we are now. *Maither* was a healer and worked with herbs. She and Enid were friends, but *maither* was special because she had magic hands."

"Was she skilled in making potions and tonics?"

"I believe so, but I think it was more than that. I was told an interesting story. One evening, a man who fell from a tree was brought to our house. Enid was there with us, but *maither* placed her hands over the man's twisted leg like this." She gripped the flesh of her forearm, moving as if trying to mold clay.

"The man cursed so much it took *maither* a week to erase the creative words from Tara's vocabulary. He recovered."

The wolf gave a throaty chuckle. "I can imagine. Did your mother have other gifts?"

"She was unnaturally strong, like Tara. She could lift objects that doubled her weight but never did it in front of others."

Lenna gave him a sidelong glance as she finished combing her hair. "If you are wondering if my mother was a Mist Maiden, she wasn't."

"It would explain your abilities."

"They would, but *maither* never did magic in front of us, only what I have told you." Her voice faded slowly, some of the memories becoming fuzzy in her mind. She shook her head to clear it.

Lenna braided her hair with her gaze on the fire. "After Tara was born, *maither* would disappear from time to time. She would leave us with Enid or Aiden's family. She would come back for weeks only to leave again. We never knew where or why. She was the same, only more distracted."

Lenna rubbed her hands together, pressing them on her stomach.

"The night she disappeared; we woke up alone. None of us remember our life before that day. Everything I told you were stories Enid or Caitlin would tell. *Maither* left with her satchel of herbs and never came back. We stayed in the dark all night, waiting, but she never returned."

The waiting was the worst. There would be no night like that one. Past midnight, Brye arrived crying holding Enid's hand. She found the two little girls wrapped in each other's arms, hungry and alone. They have been alone ever since.

Lenna grew quiet, lost in her memories. She was startled when the wolf sat beside her, leaning into her. Blinking a few tears away, she smiled sadly.

"That same day, we had an audience with the royal family. *Maither* was well-known and loved. Her disappearance caused an uproar. Many villagers searched for her, but there was nothing. I don't recall the audience. Enid told us later that the king and queen were present, but the prince was absent. He was sick.

"Enid and Caitlin were assigned to help raise us. Brye was given to Enid to train and assist her, and I helped in the field with Badar. He was the kindest man. An older woman raised Tara until she was old enough to work. By then, both of us were in the field, and Tara was running behind the boys. I was too weak to continue. In the end, Tara replaced me in the field, and I stayed helping at home." Lenna let out a breath she might have been holding for years. "Well, you can guess how it turned out."

She patted the wolf's head, then rubbed her hands against her skirt. She motioned the wolf to the cave entrance.

"I am sincerely sorry about your mother." The wolf's tone turned sad as he gave her a long look.

"Thank you," Lenna whispered. "I guess it explains why all this is so hard. Brye mating. My role as a Mist Maiden, and Tara, well... being her. We have been together for so long, only dependent on each other."

They arrived at the river, and Lenna dreaded the next part. The wolf walked by her side, giving her glances from time to time until they reached the wall. As expected, a staggering weight fell on Lenna. She leaned on the wolf's back as they reached the edge of the bridge.

"I... wonder..." she punctuated each word with a breath, "what... would... the... bindings... look... like?" Unable to continue, Lenna sat and waited until she regained some strength.

"Look like?"

"Yes." Lenna put a hand on her chest, checking her heartbeat. "Bindings must appear as something, right? I wonder what the spell would look like."

He didn't answer, nor did she expect one. They set out along the misty paths, partially cleared by Lenna's mist candle.

"I can find my way back by myself. I will see you tomorrow."

The wolf paused as if considering before nodding and returning north.

Playing with Fire

Lenna

LENNA WATCHED AS THE mists swallowed him, leaving her in the dark holding her lantern. It gave off a soft glow as it pushed the fog away. The grass was still wet from the downpour.

If it wasn't misty in Avalon, it rained, drizzled, and it might be slightly sunny if they were lucky. Lenna was surprised they all hadn't grown gills from perpetually living underwater. She chuckled at her thoughts before they turned serious.

I can't believe I told him about maither.

Her mother's ghost had been part of their lives since she had disappeared. But after speaking about her, Lenna's heart was lighter. She was no longer hurt or angry by Brye's words. Her sister was lashing out. All would be resolved once she got home and talked to Brye and Tara.

She had just passed the White Thorn Tree, lost in thought, when a voice called her. Lenna jumped out of her skin, dropping the mist candle.

The mists reformed, blinding her. Wet footsteps approached, and a curse echoed. She gripped her satchel tightly to her chest, reaching for the candle. The footsteps grew closer, and Lenna fumbled with the candle when a body bumped her back, throwing her into the wet grass.

"Lenna, for Founders' sake!"

She recognized the voice immediately. She would know it in her sleep.

"Aiden," she groaned as he helped her up. He was soaked, with his tunic and pants plastered to his skin. His face was tight and drawn, jaw twitching. Lenna's brows rose slightly. Rarely did she experience Angry Aiden. "Do you know how long I have been looking for you?" he hissed, his hand still on her arm.

"Oh, not very long. You are not that soaked."

It was a poor attempt at a joke. His jaw tensed.

"The first time I left to search high and low for you, I was drenched. Then I went home to change, to avoid drowning in the rain. On this second excursion, I am grateful for the drizzle. We've been worried out of our minds!" His voice got progressively louder.

That was never a good sign.

"For no reason!" She pulled her arm away. "I said not to wait up. It is not the first time I have trained until late, and it won't be the last. I don't need someone to take care of me."

Aiden looked down at her, hands on his hips. "Be that as it may, your sisters are worried. It seems after your argument, both are repentant. It would be about time for you to gloat and accept forgiveness."

Great. Just great. He can't decide if he is angry with me or trying to cure me with his wit.

Lenna rubbed her face. "I was unaware such a momentous occasion had arrived. Do you know that siblings fight? It would be strange if we didn't."

"This time, it's different." He relaxed. "And you know it."

Aiden extended his hand as an apparent peace offering. Lenna regarded it as a forbidden object. He gazed up to the heavens and sighed. Without saying a word, he reignited the mist candle and led her away at a moderate pace.

But Lenna was all too aware of the warmth of his large hand as her smaller one disappeared from his grasp. A heavy sensation settled in her chest, a reminder of what she couldn't have.

Did he not realize the effect he had on her?

Of course not. How could he when Tara was right there beside her?

How can a person see the stars when the sun shines so brightly? And Tara was like the sun. She was a vibrant force that illuminated everything around her. The night sky was completely invisible when she was out.

And that was what Lenna was, invisible. Invisible to all men.

Invisible to him.

They were near the harvested west field, and the mists unexpectedly dwindled. A bright source of light was right ahead. Her heart pounded, and her ears roared as a sense of foreboding settled in the pit of her stomach.

Something was not right.

"Aiden?" she asked as they approached the wheat field. The light became brighter and hotter. Aiden gripped her hand so tight her knuckles cracked.

A snap, clear and sharp, exploded inside Lenna's chest, followed by expanding dizziness. A strange, indiscernible feeling was left in its place.

The magic knot broke.

"What the— "Aiden cursed.

An all-consuming fire shaped like a lizard as tall as the Royal Tower came into view. A giant lizard hissed flames and lashed out with its tail. The being was pure fire, with magma falling from its chest and mouth. Its body was decorated with scales of bright crimson and blue undertones where it burned hottest.

The field scorched wherever it walked. Smoke and ash drifted up with each step, followed by crackles of burning wheat. The beast ran in circles, and the fire grew in size. It was only a matter of time before the field and forest beyond would erupt in flames. They needed help and fast. Lenna was not fast enough to return to the village, but Aiden could. He stood frozen by her side. She turned and screamed. "Aiden, get—!"

The lizard expelled a shot of flame in their general direction. Aiden toppled her to the ground, covering her body. The fire singed his hair, but his wet clothes protected him from the worst of it.

Lenna pushed against his chest, smothered by his weight. "Get off me! Get help! You're faster!"

Aiden cursed again before helping her up and guiding her farther away from the rampant animal. The swelling heat from the creature and the burning grass dangerously raised the temperature to roasting levels.

"How can wet wheat catch fire? Doesn't water drown fire?" Lenna asked. She covered her face with her sleeve as the light grew along with the smell of smoke.

"Wet wheat can catch fire quicker than dry," Aiden pointed out, his hand on Lenna's shoulders. He squeezed them, and his brilliant, hard blue eyes filled her vision.

"Lenna, go home," he ordered. "I'm going to alert the village."

Lenna's eyes darted to Aiden, then the fire lizard. Her jaw dropped, and she pointed behind him. "Look!"

The creature moved and set fire to a nearby tree.

"Lenna, go home!" He did not wait for her to respond before sprinting away.

By now, the fire had consumed the entire field. Wheat that had been carefully stacked and selected by hardworking field hands went up in flames. The tree the fire lizard hit ignited. Lenna's mouth dried, and her hand went to her stomach at the sound of screeching birds and screaming animals.

The mists were gone. Tall clouds of dark smoke made her eyes water and her throat ache. Hadn't she been training with fire? But how could she get her magic through? She remembered that fire dies if you stop feeding or suffocating it with water. But everything was covered in water, and the lizard was still here. There was only one option left.

Lenna pulled up the sleeves of her dress and walked back toward the beast on trembling legs. She raised her hands with her palms out and closed her eyes. Concentrating her magic, she willed the beast to become smaller. She visualized the air around the fire dissipating.

Like a kitchen fire. No more air, no more flame.

Sweat coated her brow, and her head pounded from the effort. But it became increasingly more difficult, like walking in a bog. Every step was more challenging than the last. Her magic was too tightly bound inside her. No matter how much she tried to free it, nothing budged.

The fire lizard was the same size and was setting fire to another mound of tied wheat. It instantly went up in flames, adding the smell of herbs to the ash around her. Lenna coughed, her hands covering her face as the smoke grew. By now, the fire in the field was untamed, and the searing heat made her step back.

I won't be able to do this if I don't understand how the binding works! Why didn't I ask more questions?

Cursing, she tried a new tactic. Lenna couldn't do magic easily inside the wall, but she might recognize the bindings. Instead of focusing on freeing her magic, she visualized what magic would feel like along her skin.

A breath later, it was there.

A twitch.

A caress of ropes over her arms and fingers.

With her eyes still closed, Lenna gasped. Her fingers made out the tiny grooves of the threads as they were wound over her skin.

She opened her eyes, only to have them almost bulge out of her head. Tiny threads and thin strips of dark-colored lines were wrapped around her hands and body.

This can't be possible. Only an expert could have made this detailed magic.

Lenna inspected her hands, rubbing the threads with her fingers. They appeared as crisscrossed knotted tattoos. She examined the texture and passed her finger over the one on her inner wrist. It came alive, brightening and jumping at her touch.

It was one of the most intricate works she had ever seen—art all over her skin, invisible to others, even herself.

Until now.

Lenna did not have time to study them further when the creature rammed itself against the tree. It snapped and crackled, collapsing between others. The cries of the terrified animals shocked Lenna back into the present.

Concentrate!

Her magic was tied underneath the bindings, but like every embroidery, there were small patches between the threads.

If I push my magic through the gaps, I can use it to control the fire lizard.

Bracing her legs apart and taking a deep breath, she did that.

Nothing happened.

Her magic seemed to ooze and push against the entire binding. She changed its direction. It was like placing a thread through the eye of a needle.

Now, this I can do.

Slowly, the magic spilled out of her. She groaned as the bindings tightened on her body. Her mind became fuzzy and bile rose in her throat. She was going to be sick, but she couldn't stop now. She needed to succeed.

Realizing it was no longer alone in the havoc, the lizard turned, infuriated, standing on its back legs. Its wail screeched over the field in a piercing, ear-splitting call.

But it was too late. It had already started to diminish in size.

Screams from arriving villagers echoed for her to escape, but Lenna ignored them.

More and more magic flowed from her body. An amount she never knew existed. The tightening sensation grew, sending shivers down her arms and legs. Spots appeared around her vision, but Lenna was winning.

The beast twisted and howled as its body changed from a blinding red to a bright blue. Desperate now, the animal shrieked. With a cry of rage, it hurled a fireball and Lenna's hands were engulfed in flames.

Before losing focus, she screamed and released all the magic she could from her body. With an excruciating clap of her hands, the fire lizard disappeared, leaving only dark smoke in its wake.

Lenna wobbled, repeatedly blinking to make the tiny black dots disappear. The field was covered in ash, smoke, and cinders. The voices she had ignored grew louder and more garbled as they approached.

I'm so, so tired. And it hurts so much.

Her eyes rolled back into her head. She was unconscious before she collapsed into a heap of burned flesh.

Burn Test

Brye

Brye prepared her tonics, and Tara sharpened her sword while they waited for Lenna to return. They would glance at each other and then at the door ever so often, willing it to open.

"She said not to wait, but..." Brye sat, rubbing her stomach. "I can't shake this terrible feeling."

Tara placed the sword beside the door. "Let's try to get some sleep. Aiden will wake us if—"

In the distance, a panicked yell rang through the silent night.

"What?" Tara went to the door. The paths slowly filled with people in different stages of undress, coming out of their doors, whispering, and searching for the source of the unease.

Another yell, but this time, the word was distinct. "Fire! Fire in the northwest fields!"

"What? A fire?" Tara asked.

Brye wrapped a shawl over her shoulders and joined Tara at the door. She gasped. "Tara... The mists," she said, raising her hand to her mouth.

"What about them?" Tara asked, returning inside, putting on her boots, and grabbing her sword.

"They're gone."

Tara's sword echoed as it fell to the floor.

Brye gripped her shawl tighter as the paths came to life with villagers scrambling into action.

But no mists.

The yells and hollers about the fire and the lack of mist spread, growing into a roaring cacophony of senseless sound as people held torches and ran to the field. Women and children stayed, while some joined the mass of moving bodies.

Tara grabbed Brye's hand and set out with the growing crowd. Tara's underlining tension ran through Brye's arm, increasing her unease. People moved in one direction, jostling each other, their steps sounding like a stampede over the dirt path. They reached the Royal Tower and stood paralyzed as an orange glow illuminated the dark sky.

"Oh no," Tara said.

A screech pierced the night, and the smell of ash, burning wood, and soot came with the breeze. It took only moments for alarm and confusion to fill the air, causing the rush of people to become a frantic mob.

"I don't like this," Brye murmured. Tara cursed and let go of Brye, sprinting toward the danger.

"Tara! Wait!"

Villagers pushed past Brye without thought or reason in a frenzy. She lost Tara instantly as the crowd surged. A large arm lashed out against her. She screamed as the back of her head hit the wall. Her teeth chattered in her skull.

Gareth flattened her against the building, shielding her from the chaos. He was disheveled, with clothes roughly put on and a face tense with worry. His calloused fingers came to her face.

"Are you alright?"

She gripped his wrists, nodding. "I'm well."

Gareth opened his mouth as if to say more, but Aiden appeared, his face drawn and covered in ash. Brye stiffened.

"What's happening?" Gareth asked.

"The fields are on fire. I went to alert my father, and he went to get the king." Another cry made him turn back, and his face blanched. "Is Lenna back? I told her to come home."

"No," Brye shook his arm. "Where is she?"

Glassy-eyed, he answered, "If she isn't here, then she stayed. I told her to—" The beast's wail rose over the sound of footfall, and the sky glowed orange and hot. "I think the knot magic broke."

Oh, by the Founder, Lenna.

Brye shoved her palms against Gareth's shoulders. "My sister—"

"Brye, wait—" Gareth attempted to calm her.

"Where is Tara?" she demanded.

Aiden cursed. "I'll find Tara."

"I need to get to Lenna!" Brye shoved at Gareth again as Aiden sprinted off through the crowd, thrusting people aside as he shouted for Tara. Once a large group passed, Gareth took Brye's hand and set out to the field. The urgency in his touch was enough to increase her sense of foreboding.

Brye gasped as the fields came into view. The fire had engulfed the wheat, and two trees were already up in flames. The smell of burning wood and grass was suffocating. Brye coughed, covering her face with her sleeve.

They stood back from what could only be described as a colossal fiery lizard. The body, the size of a house, paced in circles around a small figure. It let out an ear-splitting scream. Brye covered her ears, but her eyes stayed focused on the person. Whomever it was had their arms extended, as though trying to calm the animal.

Lenna.

"No," her voice trembled.

"What is she doing?" Gareth asked.

"I don't know."

He pulled her into the group of onlookers at the edge of the field. Tara stood beside Aiden as she screamed Lenna's name, trying to get her to move back.

Brye screamed until her throat ached.

"Look!" Tara pointed.

The beast's once bright body slowly dimmed into a pale blue. But the creature did not want to be defeated. In one swift motion, Lenna's hands were on fire.

Tara screamed. Brye cried out. They joined a roar of voices that crescendoed until, like a wave, it crashed in horror.

With one last attempt, Lenna clapped her inflamed hands together, submitting the animal for good. It disappeared in a wave of heat, ash, and smoke. The ground trembled, forcing the crowd to take a step back.

Then silence.

The only sound was the crackling of the wheat and trees. The villagers stood unmoving, too frightened to do anything but stare at the aftermath.

Lenna wobbled on her feet, her head lolling to the side. Aiden burst out of the crowd in her direction, screaming her name, but she hit the ground before he arrived.

The whispers grew in volume. The king and queen immediately took charge, ordering villagers to bring buckets of water to extinguish fires. The crowd froze as a crack rang. A burning tree fell over, crashing away from the forest.

Brye ran toward her sister, her hand still in Gareth's. She let go when she stood over Lenna's unconscious body.

"Her hands!" cried Tara, reaching her second later. "Brye, her hands."

Aiden crouched beside Lenna, moving the hair from her forehead with trembling fingers.

"Brye? What do we do?" he pleaded. Both he and Tara waited for commands.

The smell was horrid, pungent and sweet, yet nauseating. Lenna's hands had turned white and leathery, with patches of charred skin and slowly forming blisters. Some had already burst and were oozing liquid all over. The fire had charred her fingertips and palms, and the damage extended to her wrist. Brye had never seen such instant decay.

Oh, Lenna.

Brye softly touched her sister's forearm to gain a sense of the injury. She breathed a sigh of relief, thanking the Founders that her sister was unconscious. The pain would be excruciating. The absence of pain hinted at places where the burns were too severe, the flames having caused damage right to the nerves.

But there was more. Brye bit down on her lip as she passed her fingers over her sister's forehead. Her heart hammered, and a cold tingle ran up her spine.

She is too weak.

"I must—" Brye's voice cracked. All eyes pointed at her. She couldn't lose her focus now. She took a breath, regaining her composure. "We must get her home as fast and carefully as possible."

"You will not take her yet."

The royal advisor appeared behind the small group. Desperation oozed out of the woman, barely concealed by her drawn complexion and untamed hair. Brye almost flinched at the sudden emotions. As quickly as they appeared, they vanished.

"You can examine her later, Roweena," Gareth hissed.

She came to stand next to Brye, who was still kneeling. "I need to see her back," she said.

"Can't this wait?" Tara snapped.

Roweena frowned. "I want to see her for a moment. It won't take long."

"No," Gareth ordered. He searched the crowd and locked eyes with Beltran, who appeared. "Accompany them back to their home."

Beltran blanched when he saw Lenna lying on the ground, but he nodded and reached down.

"I can carry her," Aiden pushed him aside.

Gareth hesitated, then nodded.

"All official warriors must stay to work the field. We need to know what happened," Gareth ordered, nodding at Aiden. "Tara, could you stay a moment?"

Brye sensed her sister's hesitation. "I'll send Aiden back so you can come."

Her younger sister's jaw worked, but she gave a curt nod.

Aiden lifted Lenna, trying not to jostle her. She groaned. Brye placed her head on his shoulder, crossing her arms gently over her middle.

"Thank you," she whispered to Gareth.

He nodded, and the crowd parted as they left.

Charred

Tara

TARA GROUND HER TEETH as she watched Aiden carry Lenna away, Brye rushing to keep pace with them. She was divided between staying and going. But she needed to find out what happened to her sister. She needed answers, and for once she would try to gain them first. She narrowed her eyes at Roweena, who stood tense next to Gareth.

"She is my charge," she said, "under my training."

"Then you can explain what happened here tonight," he growled. "Since she is your charge and under your training."

Roweena pinched her mouth, giving Tara and Beltran a dark look.

"I believe this event merits a private conversation," she whispered in the prince's direction. Gareth crossed his arms, staring down at her.

"I don't believe so. Her sister has been seriously injured, and Beltran knows Knot Magic. Knowledge you are not willing to share."

Roweena crossed her arms over her chest and stayed silent.

"I will talk to Lenna when she awakens," the royal advisor said slowly. "Before I pass judgment on what happened." She gave a short bow and left.

Tara let out a breath and released her clenched fists.

"Do you think she knows anything useful?" Tara asked.

Gareth shrugged, uncrossing his arms. "It's irrelevant at present."

"I guess there will be no mating ceremony today," Tara pointed out.

Gareth exhaled, looking at the sky. His voice was drawn tight when he turned towards Beltran. "Based on your knowledge, what do you think happened? We know the knot magic broke, but the animal?"

Beltran rubbed the back of his neck.

"I arrived late. I only caught a glimpse." He stayed silent for some time before letting go a deep breath. "I believe it was a Wraith. A creature that resembles an animal or insect, with an affinity to an element. They cannot be dominated by normal means."

"Are they common?" Tara asked.

"Not on the Continent. According to records, they disappeared thousands of years ago. They only formed in places with dense, ancient magic."

"What do you mean dense, ancient magic?" Tara asked.

"Places where magic is tied and threaded together. Places dependent on the stability of magic in the land to even exist."

"A place like Avalon," Gareth said.

Beltran nodded. "They take advantage of unstable magic to form, and they can create havoc wherever they go. They can even destroy entire cities. They disappeared around the time the Founders came here," Beltran continued, his gaze scanning over the disaster around them. "The chronicles of the time only registered one event, a mighty Wraith shaped like a dragon that destroyed part of the capital city."

"How did the animal disappear?"

"The chronicles are vague. Too many accounts contradict each other. Some say the Mad Shifter King transformed and fought the beast, winning the battle. Others believe a powerful magic holder stabilized the magic, and the beast disappeared."

"There is no way to know which account is accurate?" Gareth asked.

Beltran shook his head.

"Then Lenna is the only source we have. We will have to wait until she awakens." Gareth rubbed his face and turned to Tara. "I need you to speak to Badar and Aiden. We should consider that the southern-west field will also fall prey to whatever happened to this one. We might need to plant an emergency crop to see if it will grow before winter."

"I don't understand," Tara said, frowning.

"Magic will not help the crops grow. We will not be able to use the field again till spring." Gareth touched her shoulder gently. "We will not be prepared for winter if we don't take action soon."

Tara slowly realized the implications.

This is one horrible mess.

She sighed and looked around her. The fires still burned, and the ash rained toward the village. It was as bright as the sunrise that was still hours away. Warriors and villagers were moving buckets of water to prevent minor fires. Most of the harvested wheat was gone. What was left had been sent to be processed. Farmers who had worked the entire year on the crops walked around aimlessly, their faces filled with dread and trepidation about the future.

Tara's stomach turned.

"That's not the only issue," Gareth gazed around. "We have more to worry about than the crops, Tara."

"By the Founders, now what?" Tara groaned.

"The mists have been inconsistent. If this continues, the island might be visible from the Continent," Beltran answered.

Visible from the Continent?

Tara rubbed her face. They had been isolated for... what? Way too long for her to even remember. Little was known about Avalon prior to the mists and the Founders. What would happen if they were found out? Would they be invaded? Would they be able to survive? What did Avalon even have to offer the Continent to merit war? Or did people over there not care? The constant training and insistence on having so many roles now made sense. Gareth wanted them to be prepared, but for what? Beltran gave them very little information about the Continent. Was it indeed a place of nightmares?

"Tara?" Gareth called her back to the present.

"I'll go speak to Bader and Aiden so he can supervise. We must start at once to plant the southwest field."

"Training will be suspended until then," Gareth stated.

"Can we afford to?"

"No, but we can only tackle one problem at a time."

Tara nodded.

"After you speak to him, go home and help your sister. Tell Aiden to report back to me," Gareth ordered. "Share what you've learned with Brye. I'll come to see you all later."

He dismissed her and walked toward the king, who was in an audience with the royal advisor and the queen.

Tara gave one final look at the burnt field. With a heavy heart, she then headed out to do her duty.

Brye

The walk back to the cottage was slow and tense. Once they were close to the house, Aiden broke the silence.

"Is she in pain?" Aiden gave Brye a side look as he huffed from carrying Lenna.

"Not at present, but I would prefer to get her home to have a closer look."

"She should…" his voice cracked. "She should have come home! Had I known what she would do, I would have dragged her back."

"It's not your fault." Brye opened the door and motioned inside.

Aiden entered and settled Lenna tenderly on the bed. The room was dark, and without a word, he reached for the fire's dying embers and started to bring them to life. Meanwhile, Brye took out her kit and placed it beside the bed. She lit a candle and observed her sister. The light was too soft, and the room too cold. It seemed like an eternity until the hearth was lit, and the room warmed and lightened.

Aiden stood, lost, with his face smudged with ash and water.

"Aiden, you didn't know what she was going to do," Brye whispered, preparing her tools.

"I should have known she was going to do something stupid. With all her ridiculous training," he whispered, running his hands over his face.

"I'm sure Lenna would take offense to that comment."

Aiden cursed and turned away. Brye winced at the sight of his back. The tunic was scorched, and there were holes where the fabric had burned out. Underneath, his hair was singed, and his skin was full of small blisters.

"Aiden, your back is a mess. If you are going to stay, I need you to wash your face and hands. This whole place needs to be as clean as possible."

While he cleaned up, Brye focused on what needed to be done. She carefully passed her hands over Lenna's body, examining the extent of her external and internal injuries. Brye's shoulders relaxed. Only Lenna's hands had received the worst of the damages.

She was preparing the mixture for the burns when Aiden returned. He had removed his dirty tunic and wore only his sweaty but mostly clean undershirt.

"Help me keep the candle close enough for me to see," Brye said.

Aiden relit the candles and placed them near her head. A jolt of fear passed through Brye's fingertips, and Lenna whimpered. He pressed his lips together and moved the candle farther away.

"Sit on the stool." She motioned to the one next to the cot. "Keep the candle close but not enough to startle her. She doesn't like the fire."

"How do you know?"

"Wouldn't you if it attacked you?"

Aiden sat down carefully and attempted to smile. "Stupid question."

"Only a bit." Brye gave him a worried look. He then sat with his elbows on his knees, staring into the distance.

"Brye?" Aiden asked, his head in his hands. "Will she be all right?"

"I don't know," Brye whispered.

Aiden took a deep, choppy breath and nodded.

Brye got to work. She focused on the skin, attempting to restore health to the damaged areas. Using her abilities, Brye enhanced the healing properties of the herbs in the mixture and slowly dipped strips of cloth into it, and set out to clean the burns.

She kept her mind clear as she worked, but flashes of what happened in the field filtered into her vision.

Aiden found Lenna.

Both their tones were off. His irritated and hers defensive.

Lenna's discomfort at his touch.

Then she was in the field and was working with threads? Colored threads that she had tied around her hands? Was she pulling the threads or working against them?

Was she weaving something? What was she doing?

Lenna's thoughts and ideas were garbled together and came in spurts. A wolf in a cave, talking to her.

Moving water.

Standing barefoot and cold on a misty beach.

The thoughts were disconnected from one another.

None of this makes sense.

Once Lenna's hands were cleaned satisfactorily, she lifted them and tried to map the scarring.

They sat in silence. Aiden's concern filled the room to suffocating levels until Tara walked in. Then the concern mixed with a familiar consistent sense of annoyance.

"The prince summons you," Tara said, reaching for Aiden's hand. Tara held it as she recounted the conversation with Gareth and Beltran. Brye only half-paid attention.

"I'll go then." Aiden gave Tara a crooked smile and patted her shoulder. "I'll have Enid tend me so you can focus on Lenna."

Tara gave him a worried look.

"His back is a mess," Brye mentioned. Aiden rolled his eyes.

"It hurts, but there are more pressing matters right now." He gave Tara a quick kiss. "I'll head straight to Enid's and then to the field."

Tara nodded, then raised an eyebrow as Aiden shut the door behind him. "He couldn't get out of here fast enough."

Brye shrugged as she finished wrapping Lenna's wounds.

"Help me, Tara." Brye pushed Lenna into a sitting position, and Tara shifted to help. They bathed Lenna with a wet cloth, changed her shift, and unpinned her hair. She made no sound except for a short whimper when the cold, humid air hit her skin.

As they made Lenna comfortable, Brye explained the extent of her injuries and concerns to Tara. "The burns are not what have me worried. She hasn't woken up yet."

Tara cleaned her sister's face with a cloth, carefully removing the soot. She was motionless, her freckles contrasting with her pale skin. The dark smudges under her eyes spoke of exhaustion deeper than what had occurred tonight.

"She feels drained. Her magic must have been depleted to a dangerous level." Brye gripped Lenna's upper arm softly. "The only evidence I have she is alive is her breathing and heartbeat. But, as I touch her, I don't know how this will turn out." Brye's voice became quiet. "Oh Tara, if the last words I said to her—"

"Don't think about that." Tara took her hand.

"I can't stop thinking about it," Brye whispered, voice quaking. "I can't heal her, Tara. I can't bring a person back from death."

Tara pinched her lips and took a deep, shaky breath, her voice cracking when next she spoke. "We have to believe in Lenna."

"Tara, she has always been so sickly, I fear—"

"Don't say it, and don't believe it!"

"You don't understand." Brye stood and paced. "I have been able to heal almost all injuries or ailments. I know her body is alive. I can't feel the life force." She fisted her hands and stared Tara down. "It's as if she is not here."

Tara looked away, her mouth opening and closing like a fish. Finally, she sat, her hands fisted on the table.

"Brye, she will wake up. She will recover. We need her to recover," Tara's voice cracked, before tears ran down her cheeks. She hugged Brye close, pressing her head into her stomach. Brye bit her lip and inhaled a stuttered breath as Tara's sense of loss filtered into her system.

"Let's tend to her. Let's help her," Brye whispered. Tara sniffled and nodded. Once again, their thoughts were on the small figure in the room. Whatever unanswered questions they had would have to wait.

"We will take turns watching her. Let's hope she wakes soon," Brye said.

"I'll take the first watch." Tara sat down next to Lenna, smearing her tears with the sleeve of her tunic.

Unfinished Conversations

Brye

CONCERN BECAME FEAR WHEN the sun rose over the horizon, and Lenna had not awakened. Her breath was shallow, and her complexion translucent. Her body temperature grew low until she was ice-cold to the touch. They slept beside her to warm her body and it was Tara's turn to wrap her arms around their sister's shivering body.

Brye sat on the table rubbing her face, trying to stay awake, when a figure passed by the open window. She quietly wrapped a shawl around her shoulders and gave a single glance to ensure Tara was still asleep before she stepped outside.

The mists had not returned during the night, and the dim, early morning light made its way over the horizon. Gareth stood with his back to the house.

Brye hugged the shawl tighter around her shoulders, attempting to ignore the ache in her chest. Gareth's clothes were covered with soot and ash. His face was grimmer than usual, worsened by the streaks of dirt and sweat.

"How is she?" the prince asked.

Brye's lips trembled. "I don't know yet. She hasn't awoken."

Gareth nodded, rubbing his face and hair with his dirty hands.

"You look terrible," Brye pointed out.

"I feel like shit." He winced.

She bit back a smile.

"Your sister contained the wraith but the fields were a mess. We spent the rest of the night putting out fires."

He pressed the palm of his hands to his eyes before letting out a long breath. "We will wait until your sister is well to set a new day for the mating ceremony."

"If she gets well," Brye whispered.

He did not answer, only stared in the direction of the Royal Tower.

Brye followed his gaze. "It seems like a lifetime ago we got into this mess," she said, breaking the silence between them. "Was it just yesterday we spoke? I'm starting to wonder what the whole point of this is?" she asked in a low voice. The mating felt like a sham, a bandage to soothe the people while larger problems flirted on the horizon. What was the point, when it seemed like Avalon was literally coming apart at the seams.

Gareth's jaw tensed, and he turned away, grumbling under his breath.

"I beg your pardon?" Brye cocked her head to the side.

"This would be so much easier if..." his voice trailed off.

"If what?"

He fisted his hands while his answer came through clenched teeth. "Forget it."

"No, you started it. If what?" She closed the distance between them to avoid being overheard by the neighbors.

"Nothing, Brye."

"It isn't nothing. Tell me. What would make it so much easier for *you*? If I was obedient and agreed with you all the time? Content to play the happy woman who's just *so blessed* to be chosen by the prince?" Her voice grew tense with each word, and her body trembled with tired irritation. Part of her recognized that she was at capacity—so stressed out about Lenna, about the strangeness of Avalon, worried about her sisters, worried about the dreams they were all having, worried about the implications of it all. She was tired of carrying the weight of everyone's emotions. It was time for someone to carry hers.

And Gareth was an available target to channel all that angst straight into.

Unfair? Certainly.

But she didn't care at the moment.

"That's... that's not at all what I meant," he continued to speak through a tight jaw. "You have a shallow perception of me." By now, they were so close Brye could see the ash stains connected to the tattoo that peeked from the loose collar of his tunic.

"You have no idea what I truly think of you, Gareth," she argued. "Because you didn't try to get to know me before you barreled forward with this mating. What is it that you want? I still don't even know. Do you want a partner or a pretty object for your arm? Because I'll have you know right now that I will not be the latter."

Gareth's demeanor grew tenser as they spoke. His arms trembled at his side, and his shoulders remained stiff.

"So tell me, *Prince Gareth*, enlighten me on how to make this—" she pointed her finger between them, "—*so much easier*."

"Do you even know your own mind, Brye?" Gareth finally broke his stoic silence. "One moment, you are agreeable, and then the next you want to call off everything. This would be *easier* if you could make a decision and hold firm to it. This would be *easier* if I knew what you truly wanted out of this."

She stared at him, jaw agape. "Do you even *hear* yourself? What part of 'I would like to get to know you before we mate' did you not understand? If you want to know what I truly think, *get to know me*, for Founder's sake."

"I do know you!" The words burst out of him in a flustered rush.

Brye frowned. "What?"

He growled, the rumble nearly subvocal and deep in his chest, almost animalistic. "Nothing, never mind." He rubbed his face until his skin became streaked with black and red. He then flicked his arms in her direction. "You want out, say so, Brye."

A hollowness settled in the pit of her stomach. "Is that what you want? What are you saying?"

Or, rather, what wasn't he saying? She hated the stone that settled in her stomach as insecurity wormed its way through her. Did he just want a pretty woman for his arm? Someone beautiful to warm his bed? Brye had always hoped that she would be so much more than that. She wanted a mate who treated her with compassion and respect, someone to share a life with rather than simply exist in his.

And she realized now, with a sickening sense of hurt, that she had begun to hope that she could find that with Gareth.

Perhaps she'd been wrong.

"Your constant contradictions are impossible." He placed his hands on his hips and stared her down.

"What I find contradicting is your manner toward me. One moment you are as cold as ice, formal and indifferent. Another moment you are warm, empathetic, and..." her voice trailed off.

Oh dear, I was going to say attractive.

"Brye," he sighed, his tone filled with longing and frustration.

She swallowed, her ire petering out at his tone. Founders help her, this man was confusing. "What do you *want*, Gareth? Avalon is falling apart and your mother—" She paused. Was he rushing because of the queen and her health? Could it be that she grew sicker? No, if she had Enid would have told Brye.

Tentatively, his hand went to her face. His touch trailed goose-bumps on her skin. "It's not that..."

"What, then?" she asked, her voice barely a whisper. His hand toyed with a lock of hair by her neck. His eyes never left her lips. Brye found herself staring, her mouth parted. "Why are you rushing this?"

"I want..." he whispered against her mouth, silencing himself. The kiss started sweet but mutated quickly, becoming a crash of lips and heat. With a moan, Brye let herself be swept away. His arms wrapped around her waist and dragged her against his chest. In return, she ran her hands up his torso to his neck, pulling him closer. When he deepened the kiss, she met his need with her own, nipping his lower lip.

The growl that emanated from his throat erased the longing, replacing it with a need to consume. To be consumed.

She could taste it on his lips and tongue. It drove her mad. Her hands fisted in his hair. He gripped the back of her dress, and the fabric ripped.

More. I want more.

Desperate to feel him, her mind opened without her volition. Unblocked emotions and images filtered into her, filling her mind and body. A faint voice echoed inside her head.

Oh, Brye, please remember.

The voice was too distant to recognize or attach meaning.

Time stood still. Brye did not know how long they were locked in the embrace until he let go of her with a groan, removing the grip of her hands. He pushed her gently away, his breath haggard. For a moment, he looked dazed, and she certainly felt that way.

"I no longer know why we are even fighting," Gareth admitted, a smile playing on his lips. His knuckles played with her jaw. "I think we are only exhausted. Let me know when Lenna awakens." He took another step back and walked away.

Brye stood at the door, touching her swollen lips, confused.

Remember? Remember who?

In Between

Lenna

WHERE AM I?

Lenna found herself barefoot on a beach. The mists gave the air a chilly but thick, humid taste, with the sun attempting to breach the haze. The waves crashed over the sand, roaring and rolling in and out. The mists thinned enough that she could see over the water and the entire perimeter of the wall.

Or so it seemed.

She was not dressed for the cold, misty morning. Her gray cloak was gone, and she wore an old thin dress that did not keep her body warm. She flexed her hands, the fingers stiff and odd and needing continuous stretching.

She tried to make fire but failed. No matter how much she attempted to draw her magic, it was weak and distant, as if she were removing it from a deep, dark pool. Voices occasionally came from far off. She called back, but they never answered. How much time had she been on this beach? If the sun never sets, do the days even pass? Was she dead?

Lenna didn't feel dead. Her heart continued to beat and the rise and fall of her breathing were evidence enough of life. Wasn't it?

Tired, she sat on the beach, watching the waves, her legs tucked under her dress and curled into her chest for warmth. Lenna wrapped her arms around herself and shivered.

The mists thinned out, and a landmass came into view. Large towers made of smooth stone sat on opposite cliffs. The smell of spices and sand hit her nostrils, and her breath caught in her throat.

Is this the Continent? Has it always been so close? It didn't seem like it. Then again, how was she to know? This was all so confusing.

Lenna stood up and turned full circle. The cave still sat encrusted on the tall cliff side of the wall. The wall in this place was made of black stones covered with thick vines and branches. The vines penetrated the wall in different places, exposing cracks in the rock. What she had mistaken for grass on the dried river was, in fact, roots from a tree that grew on the other side of the wall.

"You promised me."

Lenna's mouth dried. Her heart beat rapidly in her chest, and her hands became clammy. Slowly, she searched for the voice and a figure appeared a few feet away.

No.

Elsywth was as vibrant as Lenna remembered. But still different. She was dressed strangely in long pants and a tunic with slit sides. On closer inspection, her clothes were made of a crackling fabric that resembled leaves woven together.

Her mother should appear to be Enid's age, with silver in her hair and wrinkles decorating her skin. But this version of her mother was younger. Her hair was still a bright crimson, with curls escaping her braid. It was oddly decorated with dried, auburn leaves, and her skin was a touch lighter, like fresh blossoms.

Something is not right.

The woman stood with her face crumpled and blotchy from tears.

"*Maither?*" Lenna whispered in disbelief.

"Oh, Lenna, you promised to hide your magic."

Lenna huffed out a breath. "I don't understand."

This couldn't be her mother. She died almost fifteen years ago. Or so they thought. Her body was never found.

But there was something too familiar.

"The more magic you use, the more the island will bind you. You should have never been trained."

"How can you say that?" Lenna cautiously walked toward the woman, her eyes darting in all directions. "Did you not see what I did? I tamed the fire."

"Yes, I did. But it is only the beginning of what you can do. And you will pay the price for it."

"What price?" Lenna's voice grew.

"You are here," she said. The woman wiped away her tears with a sleeve. The tunic shed small leaves onto the ground.

Thunder rumbled, and lightning shot in the sky as a storm formed over the ocean. The clear day was erased almost instantly by ominous dark rain clouds. The woman jumped back.

"You are in the In-Between, not there and not here," she continued, ignoring the darkening clouds.

"Am I dead?"

"No, not yet." The woman ran a hand over her face. More leaves fell to the ground, this time with small cream-colored petals. "Those trapped in the In-Between do not belong in the land of the Above or the Unknown, my sweetling. They are cursed, trapped to live in a loop forever. You cannot stay here."

Lightning struck the sand around them. The smell of sulfur and burnt metal invaded her senses. In the distance, a warning bell went off, as well as screaming voices carried by the wind. An imposing storm was approaching fast. The woman's eyes flicked from the mainland to her.

"You need to go back," she sputtered.

The dark clouds burst as they reached them. Heavy drops of cold, icy rain fell. In moments Lenna's skin turned to gooseflesh, and her teeth chattered. Her thin dress was little protection from the elements. She kept her arms rigid at her side to hide the trembling.

The woman's clothes shriveled and more leaves crumpled to the ground.

Lenna, exhausted from the physical and emotional ordeal, narrowed her eyes. "Who are you?"

"Lenna," the woman groaned.

"Why do I need to hide my magic? Why can I not be trained?"

"It is a dangerous idea," she thundered. "A foolish idea."

"Because I am not strong enough?"

"No." The woman rubbed her forehead. "You need to calm down, Lenna."

The wind picked up debris from the beach. Sand, twigs, branches, and leaves pelted over them. They mixed with the rain and salty air, scratching her skin.

But Lenna felt nothing. The storm could take her for all she cared. "Because I am not good enough?"

"No."

"Because I am not worthy?" Lenna yelled, frustrated with the woman's tone and persistence in not answering her questions.

A cone of water and debris formed over the horizon. A part of the funnel came down from the sky to meet the other rising from the ocean. By now, the sound of the bell going off on the shore was lost in the roar of the tornado.

"You need to stop this, Lenna, right now! You need to go!"

Lenna ignored the woman's insistent warnings, unaware of the increasing danger. The slanted raindrops pelted her face, and she screamed over the sound of the wind. "Then tell me, what have I done? Why must I hide who I am? What am I?"

They stayed in a tense standoff until the woman lost her composure. She ran toward Lenna and held her close.

All doubt left her. The body that held her smelled of dried herbs and a clear sunny day.

Lenna's lips trembled.

Maither.

"Because you will get hurt," Elsywth sobbed. "And I cannot endure it."

Lenna struggled with her emotions. She trembled in her mother's embrace, and ragged sobs escaped her control. Her arms involuntarily wrapped around her mother's waist.

It's her.

Lenna repeated over and over. Even though her mother was covered in leaves and flowers, it did not matter. It was her.

The arms that held her trembled, and her chest heaved with deep, ragged breaths.

"*Maither,* I—"

"Shh..." Elsywth ran a hand down Lenna's hair, pressing her cheek over her head. "It's all right, my sweetling."

The sobs worsened, but Lenna did not have time to say more. She did not have time to react to her touch and warmth or to say she loved and missed her.

The mists returned, quickly engulfing her. Someone called her name from far away. She tried to keep hold of her mother a little longer, but she was gone.

Healing

Lenna

Lenna's eyelids were heavy and sticky. She attempted to raise her hand to clear them, but her arms were stiff at her sides, and her head ached. Through the discomfort, she could sense the light and warm room, with the usual smell of dried herbs and burning peat. The scent of burning grass brought back a series of vague memories.

A fire? There was a fire. No, a giant fire beast that burned down grass. Was it grass?

Her mind was unfocused, trying to connect thoughts and ideas. Why was she in bed? Where was she supposed to be? Nothing made sense. Something unpleasant happened to her. The exhaustion and a dry, acidic taste in her mouth were evidence enough.

All these ideas passed her mind, but a movement by her side drew her attention. Tara's drawn face came into view.

"Brye!" Tara croaked. "She's awake!"

Brye appeared beside Tara, whose shoulders trembled as her hands covered her face. Brye was wane, with smudges under her eyes. Both her sisters seemed fragile, on the verge of breaking.

What happened?

"Water?" Lenna's voice cracked from lack of use. She licked her chapped lips and grimaced at the aftertaste. Brye's features relaxed, and she let out a long sigh.

Brye gave her water from a cup. Lenna sipped, wetting her tongue. The water went down with difficulty. Her mouth and throat were raw, almost like dry wood. She laid back down, spent.

"What happened to me?" she finally asked.

"Oh, Lenna," Brye choked back a sob. "You've been asleep for almost five days."

"It was the longest five days of our lives!" Tara cleaned her blotchy face with her sleeve.

"I had to trick your body into taking nourishment. You'd choke and almost drown. But we lost hope yesterday. You were wasting away."

For her part, Lenna could not believe it had been that long. It felt like she was in the field only a few hours ago, but her body's decrepit state and weakness only confirmed her sisters' story.

Once they recovered from their shock, her sisters took turns narrating what had happened since the night of the fire. Brye sat with a bowl of thick broth and fortifying herbs. The smell made Lenna's mouth water, even if only a bit.

Tara propped Lenna up, and Brye began, "We had visitors daily asking for you." She brought the bowl close to Lenna's cracked lips. The warm spoon made her lips itch. Lenna winced when she raised her hand to scratch them. She cringed at the sight of her hands. The bandages were thick and awkward; the pain and numbness were disarming. Due to the lack of nutrition, her hands were healing slowly.

"Enid came once to help feed you," Brye said. "We both took turns tending your hands, but one became inflamed, and we feared it would putrefy. It is so good you woke up. Once we get you hydrated and nourished, you will heal faster."

"Anyone else came to see me?" Lenna asked. She placed a bandaged hand over her growling and twisting stomach. Some liquid dripped down her lips, and Tara picked up a cloth and cleaned it away. Lenna leaned into Tara, too tired to stay upright.

"The most interesting visitors were Gareth and Beltran," Brye answered.

"Aiden came once, but since then, he has been detained in the fields," Tara's voice trailed off. "We spend most of our time there, getting the land ready for planting," Tara rubbed her arm, and Brye lifted another spoon of broth.

"Planting?" Lenna searched Tara's face. "Are the fields that bad?"

"The fields are taking shape, and an inventory of our winter supplies has been done. We will survive the winter if we get the extra grain from the southwest field. If we are careful, no one will grow hungry."

They shared Gareth and Beltran's worries about the waning knot magic and their theory of how it might be connected to the wall.

Lenna nodded, her head on Tara's shoulder. "You've been busy."

"Yes." Tara gave her a tight-lipped smile. "We also believe Roweena must know something."

"Well, there are many questions." Brye helped Lenna finish the bowl of soup.

"And little answers," Lenna said as she pushed the bowl away. A debilitating sense of exhaustion settled over her. Her sister helped clean her up and change her clothes and bandages. Lenna was asleep moments later.

Lenna's schedule centered on regaining her strength and accepting her current condition.

Initially, she spent all her time sleeping and only awoke to eat broth and drink liquids. Sometimes it would be early morning before Tara went to the fields or mid-afternoon when Enid would arrive to help Brye. Lenna slept during the first few days and took small steps around their room to regain strength.

Lenna's frustration with her body grew. The tiredness she was experiencing was significantly more acute than ever before. Even after two weeks, she still grew lightheaded by walking around the room.

The more magic you use, the more tightly you will be bound.

Was this what it felt like? To have your magic so tied up, you could hardly move or breathe without losing consciousness?

To make matters worse, her hands were healing too slowly. Lenna was afraid to look at them. Brye or Enid would change the bandages, but she kept her gaze away from their work.

Until one night, Lenna sat with her back against the wall. Her sisters were asleep, exhausted from the day.

With a heavy sensation deep in her chest, she slowly removed the bandage on her right hand and grimaced at the sight. The skin was raised and pocked from where the blisters had been. Her left hand was the worst, a large piece of skin had been scorched, and now the new piece looked crusty and dark. Her palm prints were gone, and so were the fingerprints. The new skin was stiff and itchy in places. Brye had covered her hands in a salve to keep her from scratching.

They were a complete mess.

Lenna mustered a deep breath through her tight lungs. She didn't care what her hands looked like, really, but the lack of functionality alarmed her to her core. Her strength was in her embroideries and tapestries that were sought out and cherished. Her patience in sitting for long hours with her sketches and needles was a skill she excelled at.

How am I going to accomplish that?

She wasn't showing her usual patience. Lenna wanted to return to doing what she loved, but it would have to wait. Other things took precedence.

Lenna closed her eyes and summoned her magic, weak as it was. It took effort to bring it to the surface. The magic grew inside her belly, and tingles ran up her chest and settled around her heart.

When she opened her eyes, the bindings were around her hands. The tiny, thin threads of magic made of many colors had changed shape and design since the night in the field. As if of their own volition, the bindings connected with the burn scars over her hands and fingertips.

They were exquisite. Lenna raised her hand closer and rubbed the skin with her tender fingers. The threads of magic vibrated with her touch, alive and beating.

One detail had her biting back a moan. The gaps from where her elemental magic seeped through had narrowed. The bindings had tightened over her. It made sense why she was so tired and taking so long to heal. Her body was bound tighter than before.

Lenna rewrapped her bandages and let out a shaky breath. Her mother had been right. Her magic was hurting her.

But then, how could she use magic to see the bindings? Was this type of magic different from the elemental? Was the source the same?

She couldn't stop now because there was so much left to answer. Going back to repressing her magic was equally painful. She debated telling her sisters what truly happened in the field and her dream about her mother.

If it was a dream.

What Lenna experienced seemed too real for it to be a dream. Perhaps it was best to keep this all to herself until she had more information. The embers dimly lit the dark room, and Lenna made out the back of Brye's form on the opposite cot. Tara mumbled in her sleep and turned away as she hogged all the covers. Only a bit of her head was visible.

Lenna laid back down with a long sigh. She scuttled closer to Tara for warmth. She needed answers, and soon.

Mending

Lenna

GARETH AND BELTRAN VISITED at the end of Lenna's second week of recovery.

Lenna raised a brow as Brye stood at the door, wiping her hands on her apron and then fidgeting with her hair.

But the door remained closed.

"Is the door going to open itself?" Lenna bit back a smile.

"Of course not!" Brye pulled herself up straight and reached for the handle. Her face stayed with a pinched smile when both men entered.

Gareth was just as tall and imposing as ever, with a dark green tunic and black pants, all pressed and clean. His hair was brushed back, and his beard trimmed to perfection. But something about his demeanor was different. She couldn't place what it was.

He cleared his throat twice while his hands stayed stiff at his sides. His gaze remained on Brye longer than necessary. Her sister raised an eyebrow, and only then did he turn to Lenna.

Uhm... What do we have here?

"How are you faring?" asked Beltran, who appeared worn and thin. His clothes were wrinkled, but his beard and hair were trimmed.

He looks worse for wear. I wonder if it's the weight of all the secrets.

Lenna gave him a warm smile. "Better, thank you." She then turned to Brye, motioning to the chairs in the room.

Brye blinked, then her eyes widened. "Oh, yes! Please be seated."

"Thank you." Beltran chose a space near Lenna, leaving Gareth to sit next to Brye, who placed her hands nervously in her lap. The tension and discomfort in the room grew as the couple gave each other edgy looks.

Lenna turned toward the Beltran. "Tara mentioned you had some information about the fields. The knots? I would love to discuss this with you. Is that all right?"

Beltran's face and ears quickly pinked, and he focused on her bandaged hands. A confused expression passed over his face, and he quickly hid it with a smile. "Of course. Your perspective as a Mist Maiden is most valuable."

The answer seemed like a strained lie. Was he hiding something? Lenna narrowed her eyes.

Gareth cleared his throat again. "We are pleased you are better. We would like to ask you some questions from that night?"

Brye leaned closer and spoke in a low stern voice. "I thought you said you would wait until she was fully recovered."

"That is why I am asking her," he snapped, gritting his teeth.

"More like interrogating her," Brye hissed.

Lenna chuckled while Beltran cleared his throat awkwardly. The arguing pair stopped mid-sentence and turned away from each other. Brye crossed her arms over her chest. Gareth looked at the ceiling letting out a deep breath.

"Will you?" Beltran repeated the question. "Answer some questions, that is."

Lenna sighed and nodded, nerves tingling through her heart.

"Why don't you start by telling us why you were out so late?" Beltran asked encouragingly.

Really? Are we going to pretend you don't know about my training?

Brye tilted her body in her direction.

"I train near that field," Lenna began.

"Alone?" Gareth interrupted.

She avoided Beltran's inquisitive gaze. "Yes."

"Don't you train with Roweena?" he asked. Brye scowled at him. He gave her a pointed look. Sensing another disagreement, Lenna rushed to answer.

"She has assigned me to self-train at present. Once I complete certain tasks, she will continue training me."

Her stomach knotted at the thought of that painful reality. "I was finished and was heading home. I met Aiden along the way, and we came upon the fire. He went to get help. I stayed behind."

"How did you contain it?" Brye asked.

"I don't know." Lenna shrugged. It wasn't a lie. She honestly did not know how to explain how she did it. It all seemed part of some strange story adults use to scare children: Bindings, magic knots, fire beasts.

"I attempted to reduce it, but my magic tends to be sluggish at the best of times. It was a slow and uneasy task."

"How have you been training with fire?" Beltran asked. Lenna ground her teeth and chose her words carefully.

"I light small fires and test my abilities in reducing them," she said, choosing her words carefully. They were all silent for a few moments. Gareth was about to ask a question when Lenna interrupted him. "I am sorry, your highness, I seem to be a bit more tired than I expected. Perhaps we could continue this conversation tomorrow?"

"That's all right, is it not, *your highness*?" Brye gave Gareth a forced smile.

"Yes." He stood, and Beltran did so as well. "We will leave you."

He motioned for Brye to follow. She stood stiffly from her seat and met him outside. Lenna walked near the window, hiding behind the half-open shutter. Beltran patted Gareth on the back and walked away. Alone, Gareth and Brye spoke in hushed tones.

"Roweena wants to see her. I have kept her away for as long as I can. Unfortunately, word has gotten out that she has mostly recovered. It won't be long before she is summoned."

"She is not ready," Brye said.

"I know." He leaned in and lowered his voice even more. "But, she belongs to the royal advisor and is under her training. If she is summoned, she must go."

"Lenna is not a tool," Brye hissed. "She doesn't belong to anyone."

"I agree." Gareth went to reach for her arm but stopped. "But the one who needs to prove that is Lenna."

Gareth gave her a waned smile. Her sister nodded.

A heaviness settled in the pit of Lenna's stomach.

Roweena.

Lenna heard the fading footsteps of the prince, and she hurried back to her seat before Brye entered their house. "Everything alright?" she asked her sister.

Brye nodded, but Lenna didn't miss the flush across her sister's face. "Yes, of course."

She watched as Brye returned to her herbs, a different heaviness settling in her. Brye and Gareth... Tara and Aiden... where did that leave her?

Tara

Tara thought Beltran and Gareth's visits were unusual. They came almost every day while Lenna was asleep and asked for her daily. But Lenna did not comment on their visits. It was Aiden's absence that drew her attention.

"I find it odd he hasn't come to visit."

"We've been so busy, Lenna." Tara grabbed some breakfast before heading out the door. "With training and the fields, there hasn't been any time." Lenna gave Tara a pained expression but nodded.

Tara left for the training field with a nauseated feeling in the pit of her stomach. She grumbled and kicked the small pebbles she found along the way. Her emotions chaffed her raw.

She did not have the heart to tell her sister that she was the one who had kept him away. Aiden had wanted to see Lenna from the moment she woke up, but Tara had convinced him to wait until she was better. It was getting harder to keep them apart. And why should she? They were friends! If they want to see each other, they should.

But it wasn't okay.

Tara never gave Aiden and Lenna's friendship a second thought. Aiden spent most of his time with Tara. But his relationship with Lenna was different. Thinking about it gave her a sour taste in her mouth.

It was how he spoke to Lenna, touched and held her when she was injured or didn't leave her side.

Why can't they stay away from each other? Why can't he leave her alone?

Tara froze in the middle of the path, near the village exit.

Jealous. She was jealous of her sister. Aiden and Lenna had done nothing to merit her feelings.

Or had they? Aiden treated Lenna differently than Brye. Even different than how he treated her. Almost protective. Perhaps?

No. He is in love with me. He wants to be with me!

Aiden stood with his sword as she arrived at the training field. His gaze warmed and unsettled her.

"Good morning to the fiercest warrior in all of Avalon." He gave her a wink. That was the limit of their display of affection. If the others found out, they would use it as leverage in training.

"Har, har." She rolled her eyes but still gave him a half smile.

"I was thinking that today after we visit Lenna, we can spend some time together in the northern woods." He ran a finger down her arm. Tara's body warmed from her scalp to the tip of her toes.

"Sounds like a plan." She bit her lip. "Lenna would like to see you."

His smile only grew.

Yeah, I'm a fool—a complete idiot.

Tara was dying to spend time with him. They had been finding moments the last few days, but except for some hot kisses and intense but frustrated touching, they had not been entirely alone. There was no time between the fieldwork, training, and Lenna's recovery. No privacy.

As she trained that morning, Tara tried to keep her mind on her skill, but it returned to her feelings of jealousy. It was not the only point on her mind. She still hadn't told Lenna about her relationship with Aiden. She had ample opportunity but avoided it by working in the field or training later.

Not only a fool but a coward.

When she was set on her ass again in sparring, Duncan yelled, "Tara, your head is not on your shoulders today."

She ground her teeth and held her tongue because he was right. She couldn't concentrate.

Why don't I tell her?

Training proved a failure. She was too distracted to do her best. Even though she still bested everyone in archery, she was off in the rest of the skills.

"What's up with you?" Aiden asked as they headed directly to her home.

"I'm fine," she snapped.

Aiden didn't push her. He ran his fingers down her arm and took her hand. She sighed, content. What was the point of denying herself the pleasure? The caress did not help her state of mind, but she enjoyed it nonetheless.

Maybe I do deserve this happiness. He chose me over all the other women on the island.

Her thoughts were cut short by Aiden's sudden stop. She followed his gaze down the path and sucked in a sharp breath.

Lenna and Brye stood outside, with Brye holding Lenna's weight. Her sister's appearance was a shock in the afternoon sun. Her skin was translucent, and her undereye bags were pronounced, giving her green eyes a glassy look.

Like a walking corpse.

"Lenna!" Aiden called, sprinting the rest of the distance.

Lenna's face brightened as soon as she saw Aiden running toward her.

Tara's stomach sank, and the pressure in her chest suffocated her. She bit the inside of her mouth. For the first time, she was grateful to be covered in dirt to hide how the blood drained from her face.

The real problem wasn't Aiden's relationship with Lenna.

It was her sister.

Lenna had feelings for him.

But why is that a problem? I shouldn't be jealous of my own sister.

Tara's eyes met Brye's briefly, and her sister cocked her head to the side, examining her.

She knows.

"Aiden, we were coming to find you," Lenna said warmly. "You have been avoiding me." She pointed one bandaged finger in his direction and raised an eyebrow.

He narrowed his eyes at her before glancing at Tara as she finally caught up to them. "Well, you found me. I am so relieved you are well." Aiden picked Lenna up in a tight hug before setting her down gently. His eyes twinkled as his arms settled on his hips.

"Me too. It seemed I've missed quite a bit, being so cooped up." Lenna's gaze pinged between Aiden and Tara before settling on

Aiden. "I believe you finally had the gumption to confess to my stubborn sister."

Tara stepped back as if slapped.

How did she know?

"Yes, well…" Aiden reached for her and pulled her forward. "She finally realized what was good for her."

"My words exactly," Lenna said, laughing. She stepped in their direction, and Tara immediately reached out to steady her, the action as unconscious as breathing. Lenna hooked her thin arms around her neck and hugged her tightly. "Don't be afraid to be happy, Tara," she whispered. "I am happy for you both. I love you."

Tara engulfed Lenna's fragile body with her long arms. Tears clogged up her throat. "I'm sorry," Tara whispered. A powerful sense of relief washed through her, but the horrible dread and guilt remained as the tears overflowed her eyes and ran down her cheeks. Deep down, she knew she needed to hear those words. She let go of Lenna, turned, and dashed away.

As if she could run fast enough and far enough from all the painful emotions.

Wants

Lenna

LENNA WATCHED AS AIDEN sprinted after Tara, calling her name. He turned back once to give Lenna and Brye a quick wave before rushing out of sight. Lenna let out a tired breath.

"Are you happy for them, Lenna?" Brye asked.

The hairs on the back of Lenna's neck rose, and she sensed a tingling sensation where Brye's hand made contact with her skin. She quickly removed it. "Of course. They were always meant to be together. Aiden complements Tara well."

What a liar I am. I couldn't compete with Tara's vibrancy and energy.

"Do you envy them?" Brye interrupted her thoughts.

"I know I shouldn't, but I do. I envy what they have and what you will have," Lenna explained, her tone matter-a-fact. "Both of you will be mated."

The afternoon sky was cloudy, but it did not feel like rain. The paths filled with people finishing their afternoon tasks and heading home or to the village proper near the Royal Tower to drink with friends and family. Their laughter and voices echoed around them. Even though everyone seemed to enjoy themselves, the energy was subdued. There was too much uncertainty for anyone to relax completely.

"Do you want a mate?" Brye asked, rubbing her sister's arm and leading her home.

Lenna looked down at the ground as she walked. Did she? Was it something she truly wanted? Or, perhaps, she only was feeling left behind?

"It must be nice to have someone look at you the way Aiden looks at Tara," Lenna said. Her heart ached, and her feet grew heavy as she walked. "But I am a Mist *Maiden. I'm not supposed to have a mate.*"

"You can still want one."

"It is silliness to want things I know I can't possibly have. I know what I am, Brye. Please don't pretend I will have what I want. You, however, are another matter." She observed her sister. "When did your feelings for the prince change?" Lenna held back a smile.

Brye rubbed her forehead and sighed. "It's complicated."

"If you say so," Lenna punctuated each word.

"Now, you are being as insufferable as Tara."

Lenna chuckled. "I will try to take it as a compliment."

She gave Brye a side glance, and they both laughed. The sensation in her stomach was still there, but it was the first time she had sincerely laughed since waking up even if it was her sister's discomfort.

"The tension is palpable," Lenna said casually, as if she were merely discussing the weather. "One can't help wonder when all the *sexual drama* will explode."

Brye stopped in her tracks and gaped. "Lenna!"

"I was referring to Aiden and Tara, of course." Her eyes twinkled, and she shoved Brye with the side of her hip. The disparity in their height only made Lenna wobble. Brye smirked.

"Now, that is an image I do not want to think about." Brye let go of her arm. "Are you coming inside?"

Lenna shook her head. "I'd like a few more minutes of sunshine."

Brye nodded and went inside the house. Lenna leaned against the door, watching people pass by and give her a hello. She closed her eyes, and let the sunshine hit her face.

She enjoyed bothering her sister. They were getting closer to being back to normal. As normal as they could under the circumstances.

Lenna was happy that Aiden had finally spoken to Tara. They both seemed to be a great fit, and it was only a matter of time before they were mated. She had not lied to Brye about her feelings.

But it was so bittersweet. An ache grew in her chest at the thought of loving someone, of being loved.

Why couldn't she have it as well? Why did she have to smile, even when she felt like breaking? Lenna had made it all into art, hiding and playing a part.

But oh, how nice it would be to relax. To break without fear of never being put back together. To prove her mother wrong, that she was not weak. That her magic was part of her, and it made her stronger. She did not want to be afraid of who she could be.

"Lenna," Brye called from the window. "Come back inside. You need to get some rest."

"Of course." Lenna pushed away from the door as Brye opened it.

One day she would let go, and it would be glorious freedom. *But not today.*

Interweaving

Tara

Tara ran, unthinking about where she was headed but unsurprised to find herself at the north field. The tall, thin trees provided little protection compared to those denser near the wall and village. The lone White Thorn Tree stood sentry by the river, its heavy, fragrant branches swaying in the evening breeze.

Her lungs ached, and her chest burned, and still, the emotions blazed through her, hotter than any physical pain. She ran to escape the feelings, to tire them out of herself, but they were still there.

Jealous. Jealous of her own sister.

Lenna was beautiful and smart and powerful and resilient and she was everything Tara wasn't—

Tara reached the tree and sat with her back to the trunk. Sweat dripped down her back and hairline. She pulled her knees to her chest and dropped her forehead down.

But even as she thought it, it wasn't *Lenna* that was the problem.

It was that Tara had staked her claim. Aiden was *hers*. Aiden belonged to Tara.

And perhaps... perhaps Aiden deserved someone better than Tara. Tara, who ran head first into everything, who wanted everything everyone else had, who wasn't content to sit at home as a dutiful partner. She wasn't soft and sweet and kind and content like Lenna.

Lenna fancied Aiden. Tara could've let him go, could've nurtured that relationship.

And then Lenna had to go on and say those things to Tara.

Don't be afraid to be happy. I love you.

All the while Tara had been seething with jealousy.

Footsteps crunched through the undergrowth coupled with heavy breathing. Tara didn't lift her head, but she knew it was Aiden by how he huffed out a breath as he plunked down beside her. They sat silently under the late afternoon sun, with skies slowly changing color. Pinks and oranges reflected over the water, and shadows framed the clouds.

"Do you want to talk about it?" he asked into the stilted silence. He slithered his hand into hers, taking it and threading their fingers together.

"I don't deserve you, Aiden," Tara whispered finally, the words leaching out of her like poison. She wiped her face with her sleeve. "I know there must be a worthier woman out there for you. I keep thinking about how another would appreciate you better, but a huge part of me doesn't want that. That selfish part of me wants to keep you forever." She peeked her eyes out from her knees.

Aiden sighed and turned toward her. He watched her with his intense blue eyes, gently rubbing the palm of her hand with his thumbs. "Do I get a say in this?"

"I just think you might not be considering all your options," she reasoned, voice thick. "You could have someone nice and gentle—"

"Where is all this coming from?" Aiden interrupted.

Tara propped her chin on her knees, staring out over the river. She could feel Aiden watching her still. "I just... I thought maybe Lenna—"

"Lenna?" Aiden chuckled.

"It's not funny, Aiden!" she shouted, the tears spilling over her eyes again, her voice cracking. "I think... I think about all the time you held onto your feelings for me, not acting on them... I would explode, if that were me. My sister was on her deathbed and I didn't want you to see her because I was *jealous*. It consumes me, fills me up until I'm sick with it. How *selfish* I am, to be jealous of the idea of you spending some time at my sister's bedside than with me. I don't deserve you."

By the Founders, it sounded worse out in the open than it did in her head.

"That's why you didn't want me to go see Lenna? Because you were jealous?"

Tara burst to her feet, suddenly too restless to stay still. Her skin felt too tight over her bones, her blood a thrum in her veins. "You deserve someone better, someone calmer and sweeter and softer—"

Aiden pushed himself to his feet and blocked her path, grabbing her by the arms. "Listen to me. No, listen, Tara," he added as she tried to twist away. "I have spent *years* trying to ignore my feelings for you. Years! In the beginning, you were like an annoying little sister. But those feelings changed. Before I realized it, I had fallen for your stubbornness and your fire." He let go of her and framed her face. She could feel the calluses on his palms against her cheeks. "Every woman I have flirted with, kissed, and fucked, has been to try and erase you. Don't tell me to consider my options. Don't tell me that because, the way I see it, you are the only option, Tara."

Tara shook her head. Founders help her, she wanted him with every fiber of her being. She was a selfish ass and she didn't deserve him, but she could not let him go.

"I don't want you to want anyone else," she whispered, wrapping her hands around his wrists.

"Good thing I don't want anyone else then," he said. "I want you and your jealousy and your impulsivity and your stupid stubbornness—"

She finally cracked a smile.

" —and your selfishness and your pride and your strange desire to fight everything bigger than you—"

She laughed out loud, wet and crackling.

"—and your fire. That's what I love the most. The fire in you." He touched his nose to hers. "I want to chase after your chaos for the rest of my damned life."

She tipped her face forward, kissing him gently. "I want that too," she said against his lips.

He let out a suppressed groan and wrapped his arms around her waist, pulling her flush against his body. Heat spiked through her, warming the space between her blood and bones. She shifted her hands until she could grab a fistful of his tunic. He broke their kiss and looked at her, bouncing his gaze back and forth between hers. A question. An uncertainty.

"Make love to me," she demanded.

He closed his eyes, a breath escaping him. "Are you sure? We can wait."

Tara bit his lower lip, a sudden wave of nerves flooding through the heat. Should they wait? Find somewhere else—a loft in a barn, the back of a wagon, somewhere not in the middle of woods where anyone could stumble along...

"Yes, I'm sure," she whispered, pulling his sweaty shirt over his head. She chucked the garment away and grabbed his face to kiss him again, devouring him, tasting him. He was hers, and she wanted to own him. Every part of him. All hers.

A chuckle rumbled through his chest. "So impulsive," he said, trailing his mouth down her jaw and along her neck. Tara melted, gripping his shoulders hard as his hands looped behind her waist, reaching for clothes fastening.

Slowly, between kisses and caresses, they undressed. Aiden set the pace. Where Tara was ready to rip off all his clothes, caught somewhere between driving arousal and sheer nerves, he was steady. He scooped her up and laid her down in the grass, their clothing a makeshift blanket, and Tara thought she might just implode as he ran his hands over every inch of her.

"You're shaking a little," he said against her mouth. "Do you want to stop?"

"No," she said, running her palms over his spine and shoulders.

"Do you want to slow down?"

"No, I said." She could not have loved him more than for those words alone, for giving her all the power. But the words still came out a little clipped and a little heated. She needed him desperately and wanted to be consumed by the fire he wrought through her.

He notched himself at her entrance, and a small string of curses left him. She squirmed against him, but he shifted his hand to her hip, stilling her underneath him.

"Tara."

She opened her eyes, locking her gaze on his.

"Still alright?" he asked.

"Don't stop," she assured him, digging her fingernails into his shoulders. "Never stop."

He cupped her cheek with his free hand as he filled her body, and the fire inside her burned and burned until all that remained was a deep pleasure. She could drown in those ocean eyes of his, watching as his pupils dilated, hearing him groan her name as he rocked into her, slow at first, then building up to a steady, deep pace.

This, this, this. This was all she wanted. Him. All of him.

No one else could have him.

He slowed his rhythm and gently flipped them over until she straddled his hips. Once more, he guided himself inside her, and he moaned as she rocked into him, settling into position. Taking his pleasure, making it her own.

"By the Founders, look at you," he groaned, skating his hand up her ribcage, over her breast, and along her collarbone. "So beautiful." He looped his hand around the back of her neck and tugged her down to kiss her. She let him, tangling her tongue with his until they both were gasping for air.

Aiden gripped her hip with one hand, but the other grabbed hers, threading their fingers together. He let her set the pace until words were forgotten and the world around them slowed. It was a race to feed her need for pleasure.

It was selfish, but she didn't care.

She wanted him.

She wanted to keep him.

As she climbed the peak of her pleasure, Tara arched her back, tossing her head back with a cry. She gripped his hand hard, squeezing his fingers. Aiden's climax followed hers until they both tipped over the edge, her name spilling from his lips over and over like a prayer. It became a chant that ricocheted through her chest.

He tugged their joined hand down until she was sprawled across his chest and kissed her. Kissed her so thoroughly, she felt every emotion swirling through her—love, contentment, arousal, all blended together with a fierce, near-crippling possession.

Hers. He was hers.

She broke their kiss, resting her forehead against his, their rapid breaths mingling.

"I love you, Tara," he whispered.

Her heart constricted, something unnamed closing around her throat, trapping the sentiment inside her. She couldn't say the words. Founders help her; she felt them right there but couldn't say them. Not yet.

"It's alright. You don't have to say it," Aiden assured her. "Only when you are ready."

Tara sighed, nuzzling herself against his naked chest.

"Thank you." She spoke against his skin. "Thank you for being what I needed."

"Always." He kissed her forehead and hugged her tighter against him.

Perfect.

It was all so perfect. Nothing could take this moment away from her.

Cracked

Tara

Tara didn't know what woke her. She was cold but a general sense of urgency invaded her, snapping her eyes open.

It was dark, and she could hear the running river close by. Insects called in the night, but it was quieter than usual. As her eyes adjusted, she realized it was not the absence of light that made her heart race.

It was the absence of the mists.

She sat on high alert, her body still naked and sticky. She picked up the sound of falling rocks and an animal groan. A crash came moments before tremors shook the ground under their feet. Aiden jostled awake.

"Get dressed." Tara stood quickly, finding their clothes. She searched, using the light of the half-moon for guidance.

"What was that?" Aiden pulled on his pants as the sound of stone hitting stone echoed, mixed with an unknown crackling.

"Nothing good."

They ran in the direction of the noise. Their footsteps on the grass and heavy breathing filled the air, only interrupted by the growing sound of crashing and breaking.

They approached the stretch of meadow just before the north-west side of the wall. Aiden pulled Tara to a hard stop at the edges of the trees, and the sight before them had Tara gasping. "Another one?"

A wraith shaped like a stag formed by compressed earth and stones stood at the opposite edge of the field from them. Its antlers were made of thick branches and eyes of blazing blue fire. The earth stag kicked the ground moments before it lowered its head and rammed the wall. The ground trembled, and the wall slowly cracked on impact.

"It's breaking it," Aiden said, eyes wide. "Why?"

The wall was not the only piece the wraith wanted to destroy. It rammed its enormous antlers at the nearby trees before bashing against the stones.

Slowly, the trees around them began to fill with people. Men held torches and lanterns, carefully angling them to avoid catching the trees on fire. Tara dared to drag her eyes off the majestic yet horrifying sight of the stag to glance around them. It seemed the entire village came running, likely drawn to the crashing. Tara immediately spotted Brye, half-dragging a very tired-looking Lenna. She slapped Aiden's shoulder and gestured toward her sisters. Aiden quickly jogged over to them and picked up her recovering sister, guiding Brye and Lenna back to Tara.

The prince arrived with the royal family and Roweena. Beltran was curiously absent. Around them, people stood murmuring and crying as the beast, ignoring the growing audience, continued its quest to smash the stone structure.

"If it continues, the wall will fall," Brye said.

"I think that's the goal," Tara said. Lenna's eyes darted in different directions.

"What is it, Lenna?" Brye asked.

"I don't know," she whispered. "I think it wants to break the bindings."

Tara's skin crawled at her words.

The wraith rammed itself against the wall, pieces of it falling. It became clear that, like the fire lizard, the main objective of the beast was not to attack the villagers but to destroy the wall and surrounding woods. The villagers were an afterthought. It did not stop the increasing sensation of panic or dread that tainted the meadow.

Lenna

Lenna couldn't believe what she was seeing. The wraith continued, and with each strike, the wall weakened. Stones fell in every direction, and debris followed.

Roweena stood close by and gave Lenna a curious look. It was the first time the woman had set eyes on her since her confrontation with the fire lizard. During that time, Roweena had aged. She had lost her composed appearance, with hair streaked with gray and patchy, dry skin.

"Well," she snapped at Lenna. "What are you going to do now?"

Brye pulled her back, and Aiden inserted himself between Lenna and Roweena.

"What do you mean, what am I going to do?" Lenna replied evenly, brow furrowed.

Roweena snapped her fingers without saying a word, and a small flame appeared.

Lenna's stomach twisted, and she ground her teeth as the flame grew in size and strength.

The earth stag sensed the danger and expanded its body, bellowing in rage.

Lenna doubled over, crashing into Aiden, standing in front of her. Her body crumbled in on itself, and her energy leaked out of her like an open wound. She panted as she kept her eyes on Roweena's form. The woman appeared pleased with her discomfort, and Lenna forced her mind to work. To understand why this was happening to her.

"Lenna," Brye made her sit down. Tara stood by her side, rubbing her back as Lenna gripped her stomach.

"Let me help." Brye reached for her hand, but Lenna pushed her away.

"Don't touch me," she hissed. "Please don't. Not now."

Roweena was in total control of the situation. She strode confidently out of the crops of trees and into the meadow proper, molding the flame in her hands. It grew and grew, becoming a giant bow and arrow. She drew the bow back, aimed for the stag, and shot.

A perfect shot, right between the eyes.

But she was not quick enough. With its dying strength, wraith rammed against the wall, succeeding in bringing it down in a cascade of stones.

A groan echoed over the field as the wall collapsed from its weakest. Mixed within the fallen stones were strange vines, thick, torn ragged, and black as ash, as though they'd been burned and charred. The wraith disappeared in a ball of flame.

Roweena returned to them, pale and shaken, and she stared Lenna down with her cold, gray-streaked eyes.

Lenna lifted her chin. No matter how weak or sick to the gut she might be, she refused to show weakness in front of this horrid woman.

She stayed on the grass, with Brye beside her. Gareth arrived and stood beside Aiden, blocking Roweena's line of sight. He crossed his arms over his chest and returned the woman's deathly stare.

Roweena hissed and left with her head high.

"She doesn't seem happy," Tara observed. Lenna shrugged in response.

"She never is," Gareth said. He reached and helped Brye to her feet. "She's under a lot of stress."

Lenna refused his help. She didn't want anyone to touch her. Why couldn't they leave her alone? Didn't they see how much their touch affected her?

Tara mumbled something about a stubborn woman from behind her. She lifted Lenna with a jolt offsetting her balance.

"You should go rest," Aiden said, giving Tara a pleading look.

"I'm fine," Lenna hissed.

She needed to think. They didn't help by coddling her.

Lenna wanted to wobble home, but before she got a few steps away, Tara and Brye grabbed an arm and led her back home.

Her sisters began to speak, but she ignored them and tried to think.

The earth stag appeared a month after the fire lizard. In that time, Lenna convalesced and regained her strength, while avoiding the royal advisor and her training with the wolf.

But the wall started to fall. The knots were breaking, and if this continued, it was only a matter of time before the bindings completely broke. The mists were dwindling, and the island was losing its protection.

And then what? What did they mean, and how were they connected?

Lenna had so many questions, but one fact was unavoidable.

The respite was over.

Backstitch

Lenna

WHEN LENNA AWOKE BEFORE dawn, she discovered herself cold and alone. Tara snuck herself under the covers with Aiden, who came back that night. From where she huddled in a fetal position, Lenna could see how he held her close, with Tara's head resting on his shoulder and her arms wrapped around his middle.

A familiar heaviness settled over her stomach. Her eyes stung, and she rubbed them with her numb hands. She went over the events of the previous evening, trying to organize her thoughts and feelings.

The appearance of the wraith was a bad omen. As Lenna walked home with her sisters, she became aware of how melancholy the air had become. Each of them was lost in their thoughts, and spoke very little as they got ready for bed. Aiden went to check on his parents and returned during the night.

Equally subdued were the villagers who spoke in hushed tones or remained silent. The only sound was the closing of doors and the shuffling of feet over the path. The good cheer that had slowly been recovered was now nonexistent. The mists stubbornly remained absent, and only a cloud of apprehension and dread remained. It settled over Avalon like a weighted blanket.

Not wanting to dwell in her dark thoughts, Lenna pushed the blankets off her body, and the cold, humid morning air hit her clammy skin. Biting back a shiver, she quietly snuck out of bed and dressed. She tightened a sash around her thin waist. She still had not recovered her weight from before the fire lizard.

Then again, I wasn't very healthy to begin with.

Once dressed, she slipped on her sturdy boots and unwound the bandages from finger to forearm. She moved her fingers, stretching the new, tight skin. The scars were healing nicely, but her hands looked terrible. They used to be small, with thin fingers and attractive freckles. Now they were a crisscross of lines and overlapping scar tissue. It would take time to get used to, but she had little choice in the matter.

Once her hands were covered in a thick white poultice, she rewrapped them.

Dawn was fast approaching, streaking the sky in blues and pinks. She needed to leave now. Biting hard on her lip, she reached for her satchel by the door. It stayed there since that fateful night with the fire lizard.

"Where are you going?" Brye whispered groggily from her cot. Lenna bit back a squeak. Her hand flew to her mouth. Thankfully, Tara and Aiden did not stir.

"I need to go train," she said quietly.

Brye immediately stood up, stumbling toward her sister, eyes wide. "No! I forbid it!"

"Shh! Keep your voice down," Lenna hissed. She shot a glance back at the couple on the floor. Aiden shifted slightly, but he went back to sleep. "I'm too old for you to forbid anything."

"You recently recovered from a serious injury. Last night you were depleted for no reason. Training is out of the question," Brye whispered agitatedly.

"Is this your professional or personal opinion?" Lenna flicked her hair to the side. She returned to the cooking area, filled a water sack, and placed it inside her satchel. An apple from the basket on the table followed.

Brye gripped her upper arm. "We just got you back."

Lenna sighed. "Brye, neither you nor Tara can protect me from everything. Like you, I am old enough to make my own decisions. What happened to me is connected to Knot Magic, and I need to know how it works."

"Lenna, please."

Lenna removed Brye's hand from her upper arm. "You need to trust me."

Brye cursed under her breath and exhaled. "Alright, but let me at least braid your hair. You always leave it a mess."

Lenna left Brye wrapped in a blanket and closed the door quietly behind her. She headed north to the hole in the wall. Around her, nature awakened with the call of birds, and small animals searched for their morning breakfast. She trudged along until she came upon the aftermath of the fire lizard.

It was the first time she had ventured to see the destruction. The farmers and warriors had done an excellent job cleaning it up. The only evidence of the fire was the scorched trees, black and ashy in the distance, and the patchy ground where the wheat had burned.

Lenna closed her eyes and took a deep breath, willing her magic through her core. She opened her eyes and saw tiny threads cut and hovering over the earth. They were colorless and ethereal, like spider webs floating through the sky. Lenna released a tired breath, and the threads vanished.

Whatever this new magic was, it came from a different source than my elemental magic.

More questions to find answers to. Clutching her bag closer, she continued her path north. She passed through the woods with their tall trees and underbrush. Mossy stones followed the well-worn path to the northern field. The crush of fallen leaves and twigs accompanied the awakening woods. She took a deep breath, and the scent of earth and herbs invaded her senses. Lenna forgot how much she needed this.

Her sisters were both outgoing. They needed to be surrounded by people to talk to and interact with. Tara more so than Brye. Tara flourished in the spotlight, and Brye warmed when helping others.

Lenna needed to be alone. She enjoyed the company but felt best when she had time to herself. To breathe and regain the energy she lost from the social interaction. It was something her sisters had difficulty understanding but accepted. Even Aiden, whom she cared for deeply, searched for human interaction. He thrived in it, but Lenna wilted.

She reached the northern field by the river and stopped in her tracks. The White Thorn Tree stood before her in the distance. She had seen it countless times, but today it stood out more acutely against the early morning light. It was not like other trees of the same species. This one had grown to an extent as if it wanted to occupy space, and its branches spread out in different directions, engulfing everything. The thick roots also spread around the area, almost reaching the river bank.

Lenna stood under the tree and closed her eyes. The smell of the white five-petal flowers tickled her nose as the rustle of the leaves soothed her.

Where had she smelled this before?

Deciding to come back later, Lenna left the tree and quickened her pace to the break in the wall. Her heart pounded the closer she got. She knew she was moments away from the freedom of the bonds that held her magic.

As she passed the break, her lungs expanded, and the world's weight was lifted off her shoulders. Even her hands were less numb. Emboldened by the sudden spike in energy, Lenna set out in a sprint to the cave. A laugh broke from her lips, a sound foreign to her. She smiled against her bandaged hands and slowed to a walk.

Lenna reached the cave only to find it cold and empty. It seemed no one had been there in weeks. Her good cheer left, and her heart plummeted.

The wolf was gone.

Was he even on the island? Where could he be?

With no answers in sight, Lenna stood back up and ran her hands over her skirt. She took a deep breath, releasing it slowly and carefully. She came back here wanting answers. Finding none, there was only one thing left to do.

Train.

With or without help.

Hidden Nature

Tara

"Look at all these vines..."

Tara threw another stone onto the growing pile. She, Aiden, and a few dozen warriors had spent the morning shifting through the rubble that was once the southern wall. The collapsed wall had left piles of rocks and debris that needed to be sorted and removed. Some would be reused in the building of houses, others on a new containment for what was left of the wall. Warriors and farmers worked side by side, supervised by Badar, Gareth, and the king, though Tara hadn't failed to notice that the prince was quick to get his hands as dirty as the rest of them.

Thick vined branches were hacked and pulled down. It would be reused for wood during winter. Nothing would be wasted. Gareth sent a group of warriors along the perimeter to identify the origin of the vines. They came back shaking their heads.

"The vines are rooted deep into the wall," one warrior reported to the prince. Tara kicked Aiden lightly with her foot, and at his questioning look, she tipped her head behind her. They both slowed down, pretending to work while they listened.

"How much of the wall is covered?" Badar asked.

"We only walked around the southern perimeter, but what we saw was covered in vines."

"They were not there before Beltane," Badar commented.

Gareth nodded and let out a long breath. "Did you find an origin point?"

"No," the warrior answered. "There is a group checking the northern section."

The rest of the reports did not bring better news. By the end of the morning, it became clear that the vines were slowly infesting the entire wall.

Tara and Aiden exchanged looks but continued to work.

"What do you think it means?" Tara whispered as she lifted another stone and placed it in a pile.

"It means we are in deeper trouble than we thought," Aiden answered.

"What do we do?"

Aiden shook his head. "I don't know. Wait for answers."

By mid-afternoon, ladders and clay were brought to re-enforce cracks in the stone structure. The temperature rose, and men removed their upper tunics. Sweaty, bare-chested workers decorated the field. Tara wiped her wet forehead with her sleeve. Aiden appeared, drenched in sweat, squinting against the sun as he hauled some stones. He too, was bare-chested and the sight of him was quickly becoming an unproductive distraction.

Tara followed him with her eyes. She couldn't get enough of him. The sensations were so new to her but, at the same time, familiar. The warm flutter in her chest traveled down to her stomach and lower.

How can one person become so important in such a short time?

No, that wasn't the right question.

How can he, my best friend, become the most important person in my life?

Because, whether irritated or playful, Aiden was the most important person in her life. Just as important as her sisters. Or perhaps more.

Tara hadn't noticed she had stopped working and was staring at Aiden as he moved about.

"See something you like?" he whispered as he crossed her path carrying some stones.

"Maybe." Tara smiled warmly. "I think—"

"Tara!" Gareth's voice echoed across the field. Tara jumped back, and her face turned as red as her hair. She ignored him, returning to work. He only called again and motioned her forward.

Now, what does he want?

Unlike the rest of the men, Gareth remained clothed, covered in grime and sweat. The heat and humidity plastered his shirt to his chest. Beltran, who had been absent the last few days, looked even more uncomfortable. Dressed entirely in black, his tunic stuck to his skin, and sweat kept dripping into his eyes.

Why do they torture themselves?

Tara stood before them, arms crossed. "What—"

"Come with me. We have some extra training for you." Gareth signaled Duncan and set out to the training field. Beltran followed behind. Tara glanced back at Aiden. He just shrugged at her and went back to his work.

"What's this about?" she asked as she followed the men. "I thought morning training had been suspended for today."

"It has, except for you," Gareth replied cryptically. Tara raised her eyebrows and walked unhurriedly, but her hands started to sweat. She placed them in her pockets to hide the trembling and made sure to walk a step behind them.

Something doesn't feel right.

Lately, training had been different. Each session was easier than the last, which sounded exactly like how training was supposed to go, but it felt almost too easy. Her body adapted quickly to variations in style and weapon. She outpaced the men by leaps and bounds. She was faster and stronger and smarter. Duncan tried to keep her on her toes by making her spar with every warrior, including himself.

Everything felt effortless. Boring, she dared to think.

She studied the backs of the men in front of her. Tara smirked. She hadn't sparred with Gareth or Beltran.

Maybe we are on the same level.

They reached the deserted training field. Tara strode to the center.

"So, how will this go?" she asked, gesturing around her. The hairs on the back of her neck stood to attention as Gareth circled her, as though he were sizing her up. She couldn't shake the feeling that something was wrong.

Out of the corner of her eye, she spotted Beltran over by the wooden weapons rack. The man opened the chest at the bottom and rifled through it. He procured two weapons—a small single-hand ax and a dagger.

"We're going to fight," Gareth said, still circling around her.

Tara stiffened as Gareth disappeared out of her line of sight. An instinctual part of her didn't dare turn around, didn't dare move, as though her body were locked, waiting for permission. "That's fine," she replied. "But why don't we fight when all the men are also here? I'd like an audience when I kick your ass, prince."

"You think you can best me." It wasn't a question.

"I've bested every other man. You might be a prince, but at the end of the day, you are still just a man."

She anticipated the blow, but she didn't hear it coming until there was a foot against her spine and she stumbled forward. She caught herself and whirled around, bringing her hand up in a guard.

Gareth launched himself at her again, and Tara realized with a shot of panic that he was fast. Faster than any of the other men. He peppered her with blows, and it was everything she could do to guard, block, and evade.

"Do you feel different, Tara? Strong? Fast?"

He swept her legs out from underneath her and she hit the ground hard, the shock vibrating up her spine. She rolled out of the way just in time to avoid his boot smashing into her face.

She scrambled to her feet, resuming her position as her ass and back screamed at her. "I am different."

Gareth beckoned her forward. "Prove it. Fight me."

She growled and charged forward, a fury of fists and feet. Gareth was effortless, blocking her and redirecting her, shoving her back on her ass again and again.

And again.

And again.

And every time she hit the ground, the prince would say, "More. Fight me, girl."

Until Tara was dragging herself back up, chest heaving, covered in dirt. She spit blood onto the field and watched as Gareth shook his head. He gestured for Beltran. Tara flipped her gaze to the sage. She'd completely forgotten he was here with them.

Beltran tossed the ax and the dagger to Gareth, who caught them easily, before helping himself to a short sword.

"Not enough," Gareth said, making eye contact with Beltran. The sage nodded, and Tara gasped as both men came at her.

This time with steel.

She sidestepped Gareth, dodging a backswing with the dagger, only to be tripped by Beltran. She rolled, and felt the tip of his sword graze her shoulder, catching and ripping the material of her shirt.

"Fight us, Tara. Let's see what you're made of," Gareth egged her on once more.

"Both of you?" Tara stuttered in disbelief.

She rose, keeping them both in her line of sight, breath sawing in and out of her lungs. Gareth attacked again with the ax. Tara evaded, only to be punched in the stomach by Beltran. She fell forward, trying to draw breath.

They're too fast.

They worked in sync and used their advantage in experience, speed, and strength to corner or throw her down. The other would take the opportunity for a hit if she evaded one attack. She was outnumbered and weaponless.

I should have kept my mouth shut! I'm not ready for this.

The chest. If she could make it to the chest.

Because she would never disarm either of them. She couldn't even get close. But with a weapon, with something with a longer reach...

Tara evaded the attacks, attempting to get closer to the weapon's chest. As Gareth lunged with his ax, Tara rolled near the open trunk and took out the first weapon she could—a dagger. She barely retrieved it before Beltran flung his sword at the lid. It buried itself into the old wood a mere hairsbreadth from her head.

"Are you trying to kill me?" she screamed. With a yell, she wrenched the short sword out of the wood and launched to her feet, twirling the dagger and the sword in her hands.

Good. Having weapons felt good.

Something stirred to life inside her, like a single eye of a sleeping monster opening. Watching. Observing. It growled softly.

Tara felt that same growl crawl up her throat as the men circled her, closing in.

"Let's go, boys."

And she launched herself at them.

Having weapons helped, but the seamless routine of the men was still overwhelming at best. They had the advantage, bullying her, pushing her. They shoved her to the ground over and over again. Blood ran down her nose and arms. She might have twisted her ankle on one of the falls. She hissed through her teeth in pain, but what made her blood boil was that neither of the two warriors were tired. They seemed barely winded while she fought for every breath.

"Is this some sort of lesson on humility?" Tara spat out, trembling, her hands white-knuckling her sword. She'd lost the dagger moments before and didn't dare try to retrieve it.

Gareth charged. Tara parried with her sword. Clash, clash, crack. The sword spun through the air in a deadly projectile, landing point-down in the field some dozen feet away. Gareth shoved her, swinging for her with the ax. It missed her neck but clipped her cheek as she stumbled backward. The twisted ankle unbalanced her, and she fell back against one of the tall stones that delineated the perimeter of the training field.

Gareth was on top of her in a second, pressing his forearm into her throat. The impact of her head against the stone made her teeth chatter and her eyes swim.

"No," he growled, putting pressure on her throat. Tara gasped for air. "You have to fight as if you mean it. I want to see what you're truly made of." She banged her hands over his ears, but he kneed her between the legs. The pain brought tears to her eyes.

I can't breathe!

"This is not enough, brat." He banged her head against the stone. Stars swam before her eyes, her vision tunneling. "You are not enough as you are."

"Shut... shut up," she gasped, rage pouring into her stomach.

"Fight me to the death."

Tara gripped his forearm, clawing at the skin. Her fingertips burned, seeking to dig deeper into his flesh.

"Or else I will kill you right now."

"Asshole..."

He pressed against her harder and she gagged. Her feet barely touched the earth anymore, and she pumped her legs in an attempt to get leverage.

"More, Tara. Fight me harder."

A scream twisted through the air at the edge of the field. The rustling of running feet, pounding the ground. A desperate cry across the field, "Gareth! Let her go!"

Brye! It's Brye! Brye was coming. She'll make him stop.

"Mercy will be in the killing, Tara," Gareth growled low in her face.

His eyes became two dark pinpoints that she couldn't escape. They crawled under her skin, awakening that sleeping creature buried inside. Another part of her, dormant but deadly, wanted to bring him to his knees. To make him know who was in charge.

Another bang of her head against the stone and Tara's eyes rolled back. She collapsed like a puppet whose threads had been cut.

Loose Loops

Brye

BRYE REACHED THE FIELD as her sister fell unconscious.

"Stand back," ordered Gareth. Brye ignored him. Beltran grabbed her around the waist.

"Let me go!" She pushed against Beltran's body.

"You can't touch her, Brye." Gareth blocked her view of Tara.

"What did you do? What were you doing?" She wrenched herself free of Beltran's grip, launching herself toward Gareth. Was this what he called training? This couldn't be—this was so much more violent than she ever imagined.

Gareth stepped in her path, blocking her from approaching Tara. "Brye, no—"

Snarling. Something was snarling, and cold shivers ran up Brye's arms. They all turned toward Tara, watching as she slowly, smoothly, pulled herself to her feet.

Gareth pushed Brye behind him toward Beltran.

"Stand back." Gareth's face paled even under his stony appearance.

Brye gasped, her hand on her mouth.

Tara's eyes were completely black, and her face, which had been turning blue, regained its color. She let out an aggressive howl like a wild animal. Her canines extended, cutting into her already bloody lips.

"Get Brye out of here!" Gareth's voice edged with panic. Brye took only a step back when Tara lunged at the prince with lightning speed. She picked him up by the neck, his legs suspended, and tossed him fifty paces back.

Beltran pushed Brye behind him, picking up a sword. Tara stopped the blade with both her hands. The young woman took advantage, side-kicking him in the face. He fell to the side with force.

"The body follows the head," Tara hissed out, her voice hoarse. She picked Beltran up by the hair and tossed him face-first against the stones. His body collided with a brutal crack.

A scream burst out of Brye, her hands flying to her mouth once more as Beltran collapsed, dazed.

Hearing her own breathing in her ears, Brye turned her attention back to Tara as her sister shifted her gaze from Beltran to Brye.

"Tara?" Brye croaked out.

Tara turned and cocked her head to the side, studying Brye with black, empty eyes. She tugged Brye forward by the strap of her crossed satchel. Brye stumbled, and her heart hammered.

Who is this?

This wasn't Tara. Whoever or whatever was here was not her sister. Her face had no emotion, only a sneer of anger and hatred.

Tara was pulling back her fist when Gareth tackled her to the ground.

"Move back, Brye," he yelled.

She didn't think. She simply did, her feet pushing underneath her and she bolted back. She reached the stones at the edge of the training field and whirled around, finally daring to look behind her.

The battle was not over. With swift movements, Tara straddled Gareth with her knees. With his arms pinned down, she took no time in inflicting a succession of punches to his face. Bones cracked with each smack of her fists. Blood gushed from Gareth's broken nose.

Brye screamed Tara's name until her voice was hoarse, but whatever creature now inhabited Tara's form didn't listen.

She was going to kill Gareth. Her sister was going to kill him.

Beltran appeared and pulled Tara back by the hair. She went limp, only to use the momentum of her falling body to bring the sage down with her. He made the mistake of letting go.

Tara jumped up with eerie speed and grace. Brye watched, horrified, as her sister grabbed a dagger from the ground and used it to cut Beltran across the chest. He yelled out. She kicked him with the heel of her boot. Beltran crashed against the stones once more. This time, he didn't get up.

"Gareth... Gareth!" Brye screamed, a piece of her primed to launch herself across the field once more, but an instinctual fear and self-preservation locked her knees.

Tara turned and returned to the prince, who pulled himself to a stand, his arms in a defensive position. Both his eyes were swollen, his face unrecognizable, with his lips cut and bleeding. They circled each other for long, tense moments. Brye shrieked when Tara launched herself at him, and they went down to the ground together in a twist of furious limbs and growling. Tara flipped him, gaining the advantage. She grabbed a fistful of his hair and slammed his head back into the ground. Once. Twice.

"Fight to the death?" she snarled close to his face, raising her dagger. "Would you like to be the first, then?"

Brye screamed, "Tara, no!"

With a yell of rage, Tara slammed the dagger down, aimed perfectly at Gareth's chest.

But she missed her mark.

A gust of wind howled through the training field, whipping Brye's skirts. Tara was lifted off Gareth in a surge and thrown across the training field, landing in a twisted heap.

She did not rise.

Lenna

Lenna panted, arms outstretched, face pale. Across the training field, Tara lay immobile, sprawled out on the grass.

She dropped her arms heavily, vision spotting. She studied her hands, gently flexing her fingers.

Growling, shouting, the sound of Brye screaming—

She'd slipped through the gap in the wall, back into Avalon proper, without being noticed by the men tending to the depleted structure. She'd spotted Aiden, but something inside her had hollowed out when she hadn't seen Tara. Call it sisterly intuition, call it magic, but when she'd asked Aiden where Tara was, and he'd responded that Gareth and Beltran had taken her to the training field, a deep sense of wrongness settled into her heart. She'd hurried that direction, and perhaps her expression had alarmed Aiden, because the man had been on her heels.

She'd arrived as Tara raised the dagger over Gareth's chest. Fear choked through her, and she'd thrown out her hands, summoning enough wind to lift Tara and send her across the field. She didn't know how she accomplished it, but now that the adrenaline was fading, her vision flexed and tunneled. She took deep breaths to regain some of her composure.

Crashing in the undergrowth. Aiden appeared at Lenna's side, and he inhaled sharply.

"By the Founders..." he let out a string of foul curses. "What happened... shit. Tara."

Lenna managed to grab his wrist before he bolted around her. "Wait for me," she said.

Aiden glanced at her hand, then at Tara's prone form. He swallowed visibly and nodded.

Lenna led the way across the field, her legs jelly beneath her. She touched Brye's shoulder. Her oldest sister sat like a statue in the grass, pale as marble, staring at Tara. Lenna wasn't certain Brye was breathing.

"Tend to the prince, Brye," Lenna ordered.

"Lenna, Tara, she—" Brye stuttered. Her freckles stood out against her pale face like blood on snow.

"Not now." Lenna placed her hand on Brye's head and pivoted her face toward Gareth. "Go help the prince. Now." Once Brye was propelled into motion, Lenna strode toward Tara, who laid face up on the ground. Aiden was already behind her, crouched in the grass by her head.

"Don't touch her," Lenna said.

Aiden sat back on his haunches. He flicked his gaze from Lenna to Tara but did as she ordered.

Lenna crouched down behind her sister. She gently touched her arm. Just as she'd suspected, Tara too, had bindings wrapped around her, though at the moment, they were loose.

"You don't see those, right?" Lenna asked Aiden.

He frowned. "See what?"

"Nothing…" Lenna murmured, tracing a finger over the bindings. Tara's appeared more like thorned vines, wrapping around her, spiraling up her skin. Claw marks also appeared on her arms and neck, shifting like living threads. Lenna bit her lip. Whatever had been contained was now momentarily free.

"See what, Lenna?"

However, as Tara regained consciousness, the bindings slid back in place. They stretched taut and then disappeared under her skin.

Tara's eyes snapped open and for a moment were jet black. The ground around them hissed with power. Aiden froze in place, and Lenna touched her sister's arm.

Tara released a painful moan, and her eyes melted back to their usual nutmeg brown. "What happened? Am I done training?" she groaned.

"Take her home, Aiden. Don't let anyone see her," Lenna said. Aiden nodded slowly, helping Tara to her feet.

"Ugh, everything hurts," Tara complained, leaning into Aiden, but as her eyes tracked over their surroundings, her face pinched. Lenna twisted around to follow Tara's gaze. Beltran leaned heavily against a rock, and Gareth was sitting up, his face a patchwork of blood and bruises.

"What happened to them?" Tara gasped.

"Aiden," Lenna repeated. "Take her home."

Tara twisted out of Aiden's hold, limping a few steps away from him. "Who did that?"

Lenna pushed herself to her feet and stopped Tara with a firm hand on her arm. "Go home, Tara. Now. Please." She glanced over Tara's shoulder at Aiden and nodded.

"Lenna—" Tara's eyes tracked back to her. "Lenna, what—"

But Aiden scooped Tara up without warning. Tara squeaked, but she looped her arms around Aiden's neck. She gave Lenna a long, haunted look before she rested her head against Aiden's shoulder.

Lenna sucked in a deep breath and whirled, feet moving toward Beltran. She paused mid-stride. He had disappeared. The bloody rock was the only evidence he had been there.

How did he—?

"Lenna! I need you," Brye choked out.

Brye knelt next to Gareth. One of his eyes was swollen shut, and his nose was visibly broken.

"I need help getting him to the Royal Tower," Brye said.

"No," he mumbled. "No tower."

Brye spoke in whispered tones to her sister. "He might have some broken ribs, and I must take him somewhere to examine him."

Lenna took deep breaths. "We can't take him home. He'd have to walk through the village. It would raise more questions. The old fielder's cottage at the edge of the northeast wall? The woods grow thicker there. No one will disturb you."

"It's a long way there," Brye said, hesitating.

"We can take him between us."

"You're sure?" Brye gave her an assessing look.

"Yes, Brye. Come, let's go."

Brye groaned, helping the prince get his feet under him. "Gareth, you have to walk. Lenna, hold him up from the other side."

It was a slow, struggling pace to the abandoned cottage. Brye supported most of the prince's weight while Lenna kept him upright around the waist. He ground his teeth and put one foot in front of the other.

They followed what was left of the wall as it pitched north, skirting all the workers and passing by unnoticed. On their right was the tall, stone structure covered in thick vines; to their left, the woods. The afternoon sun was hot on their skin.

During the trek, the only noise was the crush of their feet over the path, the whoosh of the trees, and Gareth's haggard breathing as he stubbornly moved along. It was quickly joined by Lenna's, but she did not falter.

They stopped a couple of times to catch their breath, but kept moving. Lenna ignored her discomfort, only focusing on helping Brye and the prince as she thought about what she had seen.

It was clear that only she could see the bindings. The others had not noticed Tara was different once the bindings loosened. Was Tara the only one bound besides Lenna herself?

She sighed in relief as the small cottage appeared, just as the sun sank lower in the sky. It was built using the wall as part of the structure. No one had lived in it for a while, leaving the cabin to the elements. The roof had caved in, and the entire house was covered in thick branches and thorny vines similar to those that now covered the wall. Even the door had been closed over.

After ensuring Brye could support the prince, Lenna went to the covered doorway.

"The vines are not as thick here. I think I can cut a small path."

"Let me, your hands are still recovering," Brye said.

"No, let me try something." Lenna closed her eyes, taking a deep breath. Upon opening them, she discovered the bindings over her hands were not as tight as before. The closer they were to the wall, the looser the bindings became.

The breaking of the bindings on the island has affected my own.

More questions and no time to answer them. Gareth wobbled on his feet, and his eyes glazed over.

Letting out an exhale, Lenna passed her right hand over the vines. She pulled the moisture from the small branches, and the vines instantly became brittle. She broke them off once they were dried out, creating a small entrance.

Inside was dark, with the furniture and floor covered in dead leaves and earth. They gently placed Gareth near the door while they made the cottage presentable. Brye found some candles and flint stones the previous owner had left. She lit them and put them on an old ceramic plate. Lenna located a wooden bucket in relatively sound condition and went to the nearest stream to bring back fresh water.

"I will go get your kit and check on Tara." Lenna placed the bucket of water near the door and cleaned her hands on her skirt. "If she is unwell, I will return and stay with the prince. You can go check on her."

"Enid can tend to Tara. Bring me supplies for the night." Brye crouched down by Gareth, who was breathing haggardly, eyes closed.

Lenna nodded. With one final look at her sister, she headed home.

What we are capable of

Brye

Finally alone, Brye took a long breath and cleaned Gareth's face. He sat against the wall, holding his side and fighting for every breath. There was no clean place. The cot was covered in dirt and dust. Animals must have used it for warmth. She would have to tend him right here, leaning against the wall near the door.

Standing, she wiped her hands against her skirt and went for the stool on the other side of the room. Making sure it was sturdy enough, she brought it closer to Gareth. She placed the candles on the chair and inspected the damage Tara had inflicted.

His right eye was completely swollen shut, but his left was slightly less. He probably favored his left side and turned his face away while Tara pummeled him. Brye cleaned her fingers in the water and rubbed them together. Once they tingled, she carefully touched and probed his face and skull. She took care to be gentle, but he still let out a painful moan.

"Shh... I know, it hurts. Let me help you."

Brye continued speaking to him in quiet, soothing tones. With her heart and mind open, she let his pain filter into her through her fingertips.

There was a lot of it focused on his face. Underneath the swollen cheeks, his jaw and cheekbones were cracked and broken. His nose needed to be reset. The break only increased the swelling around the eyes. If not tended well, he could have vision loss in his right eye.

Her hands went to his skull, feeling for any cracks or swelling along the brain. She found none. Brye exhaled slowly, relieved by that score.

It could have been worse.

"Your head is as thick as Tara's," she whispered, her knuckle running along the bottom of his jaw. The beard tickled her finger.

"One can only hope," he ground out.

Brye bit down a smile and sat back on her haunches. She tried to find the anger or resentment she felt in the field, but it was absent. In its place were worry and distress for him and her sister.

Was she even certain what she saw? What had even happened? She felt she was missing pieces, because the version of Gareth in her head didn't match the version she saw on the field today.

The same could be said for Tara, she supposed.

It was all too strange.

"I need to check your chest and ribs."

Getting on her knees, Brye gently removed his tunic and undershirt sticking to his skin from sweat. She bit back a gasp. He was well-muscled, with thick arms and marked abs, but that did not draw her attention. His chest, waist, and upper were decorated with intrinsic designs of tattoos with knots and lines. An open-jaw wolf design was open around his heart. It formed from the knots from his left shoulder.

"Let me." She lifted his left arm away, extending it over her head. He immediately winced at the effort. She bit down inside her mouth when she noticed considerable bruising over his ribs.

Brye probed the area gently but firmly. There was pooling blood under the skin, forming a monstrous bruise and hiding two cracked ribs.

This explains a lot.

She sighed in relief.

At least they are not broken.

A broken rib would mean a risk of a punctured lung. Cracked would be bruising and tenderness. She gently placed his hand down.

"Your face is the worst part." She leaned back on her knees. "I can heal it, but you will need some days to recover."

"We shall see," he replied hoarsely, closing his eyes and leaning back.

Brye sat opposite, watching him. What happened today terrified and confused her. None of it made any sense.

Both she and Gareth had started to get to know each other, just like she'd wanted them to from the start. She'd come to find that while he was stoic and mysterious, underneath, he had a wealth of goodness, even if he was hiding something... maybe somethings. Then why did he do it? What was the objective? She rubbed her face.

Everything changed. In one breath, her sister transformed, and whatever she became was deadly.

Gareth and Beltran reacted to Tara's transformation. Almost as if...

As if they'd expected it.

"You provoked her," Brye whispered, bringing her knees to her chest. "You knew she would react the way she did. That was why you told me to get away. But I think you did not anticipate how much she would change." Gareth opened his one good eye. He turned his head toward her voice but said nothing.

He drew a slow deep raspy breath. "It shows what we are capable of," he muttered, turning away.

We?

Brye grew silent. He was in pain, and she had other ways to get answers. She sat beside him, her back against the wall and her long legs stretched out. She rubbed her face again and closed her eyes. The only sound was his ragged, short breathing.

There are more ways to get answers than asking questions.

She only needed Lenna to get back with her kit.

Soothing Wounds

Lenna

LENNA STOPPED AT THE training field before heading home. She searched for Beltran. He, too, had been injured and needed tending. When she found no trail near the rock where he had fallen, she looked around the woods nearby. There was no trace of him or anyone else. Exhausted, frustrated and a touch concerned, she turned toward home.

By now, the sun had almost set, and villagers were crowding the streets, going on with their business.

Lenna waved to some people on the path and smiled at others. Appearing as if all was well when deep inside, she was in turmoil. Every face around her was taut with worry. The air was filled with heavy dread, even with all the bustling. The previous happiness was gone, replaced with apprehension. People spoke in whispers and hushed tones, a certain chaotic hustle to them, as if they all desired to finish their business and be home quickly.

The mists still did not descend.

She arrived at the house and opened the door carefully. From the door, she could hear soft voices coming from the bathing room. Inside, Tara sat in the tub, hugging her knees with her face buried in them. Her shoulders trembled as she hid her sobs. Aiden rubbed her back, murmuring to her.

Lenna's eyes prickled and she pinched the bridge of her nose. Her sister's sadness weighed heavily in the room. She didn't want to intrude on the intimate moment but had to. Letting out a long sigh, she coughed into her hand. Aiden lifted his head, and a nervous smile spread across his face. Tara did not raise hers.

Lenna kneeled next to the tub, and Aiden stepped back, giving her some space.

"How do you feel?" she whispered to Tara.

"Everything hurts." Tara's voice came out muffled. She sniffed against her knees, and a broken sob came escaping her. Lenna rubbed her hand softly on her sister's bruised back.

"Brye said to call Enid." She motioned to Aiden, who nodded.

"No! I don't want to call Enid." Tara raised her head. Her eyes were swollen and puffy, full of agony. "What did I do, Lenna?"

"Defended yourself," Lenna whispered, rubbing her bruised back.

"Then why don't I remember anything?"

"I don't know, but we will find out." Lenna kissed the top of Tara's head. "I need to take Brye her kit and some supplies. She won't be home tonight. I'll be back late."

"Is she afraid of me?" Tara asked, her voice quaked.

"Brye loves you." Lenna wrapped her arms around her sister's naked body. "So do I."

"That is not an answer."

"We don't know what happened, but we are not afraid of you, Tara."

"I am afraid," Tara whispered.

Lenna did not know what to say and chose to say nothing. Tara took a quaking breath.

"I'm staying tonight. She won't be alone," Aiden assured.

"Has she ever?" Lenna smiled, and Tara let out a soft chuckle. "If you feel poorly, call Enid. Promise me."

"She won't have a choice," he answered.

Aiden went to Tara and helped her out of the bath. He dried her bruised body which, Lenna noticed, was healing faster than expected. He wrapped her in a towel, carried her to the cot, and helped her into a clean shift. Tara let herself be dressed and tended to before lying down and falling asleep almost instantly.

Lenna watched from the cooking area, where she got Brye's healing kit and a basket to fill with provisions.

"Let me help," Aiden whispered. She gave him a wane smile, and they quickly prepared food and drink for Brye and the prince.

"I'll be back as soon as I get this to Brye," she said in low tones. Aiden made to bump her nose with his knuckle, but seemed to hesitate. His hand went directly to his pocket. "You better."

She took the satchel and Brye's kit and turned to the door.

"Lenna,"

"Yes?"

"Be safe," Aiden called out.

Lenna cocked her head to the side and smiled. "I will endeavor to do so, my dear friend."

Brye

Brye took a nap as she waited for Lenna to arrive. Once she did, both girls cleaned and aired out the cot using an old broom, a cloth, and a bucket. It was dark, and the moon was out when they finally placed Gareth on the low bed.

Brye was relieved as Lenna left, and she watched her sister walk away, guided by the moon's light. She did not want anyone to be around as she worked on Gareth. It would cause more questions. She suspected Lenna already had a fair few, based on the number of glances she gave them. But Lenna had stayed quiet, biting down on her lip.

Behind her, Gareth slept on. Brye kept her hands steady as she measured amounts, mixed, and poured. She enhanced the herbs and the tonics a bit more than usual. With everything ready, she kneeled next to the prince.

"Drink this." She lifted his head and gave him a green tonic mixture.

"What is it?" he asked doubtfully.

"It will reduce the pain and help healing."

He kept his eye open on her the entire time as he sipped. She sensed his reluctance and did not blame him. If it were reversed, she would feel the same.

"You will feel less pain. Still, it would help if you were careful. Just because you feel less of it only means you can cause more damage," she warned. "Now, let me get to work."

Before dipping her fingers in the ointment, she rubbed her hands until they were warm. Then she reached for the green lotion and, as before, probed his face.

This time, instead of inspecting, she focused on healing. Her hands moved over the cracks and bruises. When she reached a break in the bone, her fingers would warm even more, and she would put them back in place. With each small snap and crack, his face mended.

His nose was one of the worst injuries. She dipped her hands in the ointment again and snapped it back into place with an audible crack with her index and middle finger.

He hissed out a breath but kept his eyes closed. She left the bruising for now.

After ensuring the bones were set, she cleaned her hands and put some ointment on a pair of leaves. These she placed over the swelling in his eyes.

"Keep them closed. I am going to work on your ribs."

Taking up the ointment, she rubbed her hands over the cracked ribs on his right side. He inhaled and winced.

It's time.

His pain was dull enough for her to use her abilities for something more invasive. She knew she could do it. However, she rarely, if ever, intruded on others' thoughts and feelings. If she did, it was unintentional.

Except for today. She needed information.

And she would steal it.

Lulling him into sleep, she opened her mind and saw flashes of unfamiliar thoughts and ideas. New voices entered through the connection. One memory rose from the backdrop. She grabbed onto it, focusing until her mind cleared, and dove deep into the memory.

The light blinded her eyes. The sun was high in the sky, and the air was hot and humid.

I hate summer.

It made her sticky and sweaty. Worse, she had been waiting for the woman to arrive in the sun.

I can't wait to play in the snow this winter. Maybe my mother will let me come with my friends.

A vision of a tall, blond woman came into her mind. She had a warm smile and a twinkle in her eyes.

Brye struggled with the memory. It took hold of her, swallowing her up until her body shrunk, but her limbs were long. She was stronger and faster for only being eleven years old. Her father was proud of how much she had grown up.

She couldn't wait to continue training. To be a strong warrior.

No. I don't want that. Tara does. Who am I?

A tall woman with a mass of red hair that ran down her back was walking down the field. Brye looked over the rock she was hiding behind, her heart hammering in her chest.

But it wasn't her heart. This body wasn't hers. It belonged to someone else.

He. I'm a boy.

A wild young boy stood hiding as the red-headed woman headed north.

The boy lost sight of her. For a moment, he cursed and rubbed his face. He turned to head back home and pulled up short. He was face to face with the person he had been waiting for. A person Brye never thought to see again.

Her mother.

Reading Memories

Gareth

GARETH COULDN'T HELP HIMSELF. He liked the way she walked, boasting confidence and security. It drew him like a moth to a flame. He was not the only one. Men and women from the village would stare as she passed by. They would never engage her in conversation, but their jaws would twitch with unsaid words.

The wild one, they would call her. Gareth always wondered why they said those mean words. He asked his mother; she said it was because she was wild and had three little girls with no secure mate.

But he knew the truth.

They were envious because she was more vibrant than them.

Today, he followed her out to the northern field. He thought he was being quiet and stealthy, but the path was empty.

"What are you doing, little man?" A deep throaty voice appeared behind him.

Gareth jumped out of his skin, his ears turning red as the woman appeared behind him. Her face was round, covered in freckles, with deep, forest-green eyes framed with thick blond eyelashes. Her sparkling eyes and easy smile made the boy's mouth go dry.

"I'm only walking!" he stuttered.

The woman raised a light eyebrow and pinched her plump lips. "I see."

She ignored him and continued on her way. Gareth hesitated a moment before following her long strides.

"Are you walking in the same direction I am, little man?" She glanced down at him without missing a step.

"I always walk this way. I am surprised we have not met," he continued.

"Really?" She suppressed a laugh.

Gareth tried to seem uninterested, but it lasted as long as his hesitation had.

"Why are you walking alone?" he asked.

"I am now walking with you. I am not alone."

"You left your little girls behind. Why don't you bring them?"

"When I train, I don't bring them. They stay at home with their lessons."

"I am training as well!" he exclaimed, puffing his chest. "I am training to be a warrior because, as you know, my father is the king!"

"Is he now?" she asked. "So, you are the little prince?"

"Yes! And I have a name. It is not a *little man* or *little prince*." He snorted.

The woman stopped and turned to him. Her gaze narrowed. "What is your name then?"

"I am Gareth!" he exclaimed, giving her a confident grin.

She laughed and extended her hand. "Well, little prince Gareth, I am Elsywth.

Gareth looked at her hand. The skin there was fairer than on her face. When he placed his smaller hand in hers, it tingled.

Her hands are so strange.

But he liked the strangeness in her. The oddness made him curious and warm.

"I think we will be very good friends, little prince."

Days later, Gareth was waiting again in the northern field. He was dirty and grimy from training. Duncan had been tough on him because he had been too distracted, thinking about Elsywth and her little girls.

He saw them that morning. Elsywth held a small one's hand while the other two ran around. It seemed like fun. Gareth wanted to talk to her and play, but he was not free to do so when his mother and father were with him. The king and queen invited formality and expected him to behave. He sighed heavily when he lost sight of them as they reached the training field.

Duncan, noticing his distraction, demanded more from him. The expectations were high. He fell so often that he could not sit down, and his ankle ached.

He was reluctant to go to his mother, who would coddle him and keep him home. And Gareth did not want to be home. He left training and headed north. He wobbled, head low and brow furrowed.

As Gareth sat by the river, he knew he had made a mistake. He should have gone to his mother and rested.

But what kind of warrior would he be if he showed weakness? *And why is it wrong anyway?*

Why do men always have to be strong and control their emotions? He had seen his father sometimes cry, hidden away from his mother. Why did he have to hide?

Gareth almost did not notice Elsywth's approach. He hid his excitement under a bored face.

"I was expecting you," he said, avoiding her gaze.

Elsywth stopped, placing her hands on her hips. "Is that so, little prince?"

"It is so. You are late." He narrowed his eyes at her.

"I make my own time, little prince," she said and resumed her walk to the wall. Gareth stumbled along behind her.

She stopped and turned. "You're not as sprightly as usual."

"I'm fine," he replied, biting his lip.

Taking his arm, she gently examined his features.

He pulled his arm away. "I said I was fine. I am a warrior. Warriors don't feel pain."

She placed her face at the same level as his. Her eyes blazed, becoming dark, jagged stones on her flushed face. "Everyone bleeds, Gareth. Everyone feels pain, even warriors. Denying it will only cause you more harm than good."

Elsywth placed her hand on his face. Her tingling fingers burned his skin. Her eyes turned darker still, and he couldn't stop staring.

"It is all right to feel pain and joy. They make us stronger when we acknowledge them, not weaker."

When she stood, he blinked, rubbing his eyes.

Did she read my thoughts?

"Tomorrow, I will bring my daughters to the river to play. We will expect you."

She ruffled his messy blond hair, then left.

He stared, too surprised to move.

The pain was gone.

Gareth returned the next day, excitedly carrying his new sword and dagger to show Elsywth. He slowed his pace when he saw them at the river bend. She stood in the river, her dress tied around her waist, the water reaching her calves. A little girl with a mop of curly red hair was playing in the water, squealing and yelling.

"*Maither,* look what I can do! Look, look!"

Another stood at the bank's edge. Gareth stopped short, his breath caught in his chest, his heart pounding. She was tall for her age, with russet-colored eyes and freckles like her mother. He couldn't breathe. Her playful and intense eyes focused on him.

Time stopped.

"Brye, bring Gareth over!" Elsywth called.

On closer inspection, the girl called Brye was peachy-skinned, with a round face like her mother's and old eyes that read into him. Her voice was strange for her age, too thick for a child.

"Hello," Brye said. He rubbed his clammy hands on his pants. Brye took his hand in her tingling fingers and gave him a confused look.

"You are strange," she stated in a matter-a-fact voice.

"So are you," he replied hoarsely.

"Are you afraid of me?"

"No!" Gareth snapped. "I am not afraid of girls."

"Brye, no reading without permission," Elsywth reprimanded from the water. Gareth stood by the river, still holding hands with the strange girl. He pulled it back. Brye cocked her head to one side, regarding him closely.

"It's not polite to invade other people, Brye," the third little girl said, coming out from the shallow end of the river. She had a small, thin body, held down by the weight of her wet dress and long brown locks. Her deep forest green eyes were round and her plump lips pinched in concentration. She looked younger than her years, her eyes older than time settled on him.

"I didn't do it on purpose." Brye shrugged.

"I find that hard to believe," Elsywth replied, raising an eyebrow at Brye.

The small wet girl extended her tiny hand. "Hello, prince, I am Lenna."

"His name is Gareth, Lenna. He does not like to be called prince," Brye replied. "I think he doesn't really like being the prince."

"That is not true!" Gareth called out.

Elsywth gave a knowing smile. She let the wet little redhead go. Like an arrow being shot, she plowed into Gareth. She wrapped her little arms around his middle, crushing him with unnatural strength. He groaned.

"I am Tara the Terrible! Are you a warrior?" She looked up at him, blinking from the water on her face and the sun. Her eyes were deep brown like Brye's, but her lashes were light and fair.

"I am," Gareth replied.

"You seem small for one," she said. "No matter, I will beat any warrior!" She let go and gave Gareth a toothy smile.

"You are pretty small for that," he smiled. He couldn't help himself.

Elsywth stood with her hands on her hips. He looked around, realizing they were all waiting for him. His chest buoyed up, and he couldn't erase the smile on his lips.

It was Brye who took his hand gently in hers. Her tingling fingers reached into his thoughts. He was so thrilled. He had waited so long to be here.

"You want to play with us, don't you, Gareth?" Brye asked. Someone let out a laugh.

Yes! Forever.

❦

"Do you think we will always be friends?" Brye asked as they sat by the river.

He had been teaching her to swim, and she had mastered it. Gareth sighed and sat back, watching Tara run from side to side. Elsywth was with Lenna by the shore, both in deep conversation. Tara could not keep still. She ran from one side to another, jumping and splashing. Gareth had already taught her to swim and Tara proved to be a natural, like with everything she did. Lenna refused to learn.

"Of course! Why wouldn't we be?" He cocked his head to the side regarding her.

"Because you are the prince, and you are bigger."

"That is true. I am bigger." He laughed. "And stronger than you."

"Gareth," Brye whined.

He didn't understand his feelings at the moment. They seemed too hard for a boy of eleven to grasp, but he knew this girl was important. She was the most important friend he ever had or will have.

"Of course, we will be friends. Forever," he pointed out.

"Do you promise?"

"More than that." He looked out at the water. "When we get older, you and I will be mated."

"Mated?" She made a face. "Isn't it when people get together to have babies?"

"No!" Gareth responded, equally disgusted.

Have babies with Brye? Gross!

"Mating is when two people who are best friends decide to spend the rest of their lives being best friends."

"Oh!" Brye bit her lip.

He played with the grass at his feet, pulling it with his hands. "Do you think that's a good idea?"

Brye smiled up at him, her face bright. "Yes! It's the best! Let's get mated!"

Longing for
the Past

Gareth

PAIN! OH, SO MUCH pain.

Everything hurts.

It was late and Gareth was in a field surrounded by dense mists. He sobbed uncontrollably. His body shook from the burning sensation around his chest, waist, and shoulder as if his skin had been flayed. He couldn't control the emotions that consumed him. They came like wave after wave. He staggered under the weight.

Pain, rage, loss.

Why am I in the field? How did I get here?

The only thought in his mind repeatedly was that someone was gone. Someone important was gone, or had gone missing. But who? From where he sat against a tree in the north field, he heard the voice of a small child.

Brye? Whispered a voice near his head. He turned to see who spoke but found no one there.

His vision ebbed and flowed. The pain consumed him, fogging over his mind. Thoughts became harder and harder to grasp and string together.

Wait. *Whose voice is that?*

The girl called again. She was calling her mother.

His mouth filled with bile, and his stomach cramped. He tasted the blood on his lip and moaned.

The girl was alone. She was crying, and it wasn't safe. Wait, didn't he know her? He couldn't remember. By the Founders, everything hurt. His body, his mind...

How did he get here? The last thing he remembered was...

Was what? Where had he been before this? He remembered... he remembered... did he train this morning? Or did he play at the river? Did he play with people? Who was he with? Thoughts slipped through his mind like a sieve. Like dreams whisked away at dawn's light, never to be recalled again.

His head hurt.

The girl's voice called out again.

Why did her voice sound so familiar? Do I know her? Why is she here alone?

He tried to stand and reach her but stumbled over and over again, finally collapsing face down on the ground. Tears ran down his face as he heard the girl's desperate cries, looking for her mother in the middle of a misty field. He closed his eyes hopelessly.

Why am I here? Why can't I help?
Why?

"Her Majesty wants the maypoles out in the field by the lake," Roweena said to Badar, her voice clipped and commanding.

Gareth walked alongside them, only half listening. Roweena's voice was a bit shrill on celebration days. She would talk an octave higher, especially when his parents were absent. And this morning was such a day. His father stayed behind with his mother and Beltran, the mysterious young mage.

He knew about Avalon, arriving like a ghost from the Unknown.

If he knew about the island, how long before others came? How long would their isolation last? All the questions they asked this morning were answered with half-truths. Gareth would need to talk to him again without his parents.

The positive point to Beltran's arrival was that another young man would be in the mix for Beltane. The poor bastard had no idea what he was getting into.

Maybe Gareth's mother wouldn't be as adamant that he chose a mate this year. It was getting worse and worse each year.

"Do we have enough wood for the fire? Last year it almost did not last the entire night." Roweena continued her questions with Badar. Perfection. That was what the woman prided herself on. Perfection on every celebration, especially Beltane.

Gareth never really understood her obsession with it.

He rubbed his face, pretending to pay attention to the people passing as his mind played over the strange dreams he'd awakened from that morning. He couldn't get past them. They chewed him up with every passing hour. Dreams that had left him aching and hollow and nostalgic for things that hadn't been. Dreams of playing with children by the river toward the north.

Dreams of... Brye the Healer, as a child. But Gareth had no memories of playing with Brye or any other children, for that matter. He'd been devoted to his books and training with Duncan.

He knew Brye, of course. Who didn't? She was easily the most beautiful young woman in Avalon, and a budding healer apprentice. His mother would go on long yarns about her mother, Elsywth, but Gareth had no idea who the woman was. She supposedly disappeared from the village some fifteen years ago.

"Prince Gareth."

He checked back into the present. "Yes. Those large logs on the edge of the wheat fields... Can we use those?"

"Of course," Badar agreed. "I believe my son is just running out with Tara to grab more flowers for my wife and Lenna to continue the flower crowns, but once he returns, I'll have him rally some young men together."

"Lenna and Tara?" Gareth said. "They are Brye, the Healer's younger sisters, right?" Something inside him pulled and pulled, nagging at him like a sense of already lived. What was it? Two little girls squealed past him, and the sound vibrated in his skull.

What was it he was supposed to remember?

"Yes." Badar nodded. "Lovely girls, though Tara is a spitfire. In fact," Badar pointed down the path, "there's Brye now. She must've walked Enid to my home to make crowns with the ladies."

There she was indeed.

She had a satchel over one shoulder and waved back toward the window of Badar's house with a small smile. Her hair had darkened to deep chestnut and she wove dried flowers in her braid. An odd fashion that he hadn't noticed before.

She glanced up the path, and when she spotted Badar, she also gave him a small wave.

"She's certainly beautiful," Roweena commented. "Now, about the table placement. I have made some changes to last year's layout..."

Gareth stopped listening, rooted to the spot. This version of Brye was much older than the one from his dreams, but somehow still the same—old eyes and many secrets. Freckles and knowing smiles. Harsh words and soft pranks. It mired together until Gareth's ears rang, and a strong snap, like the plucking of a well-tuned instrument vibrated inside his chest. He quickly pressed a hand over his heart as a burning sensation raced through him.

And quite suddenly, he knew her.

He knew Brye.

When we get older, you and I will be mated.

He'd played with her on the river bank. Taught her how to swim. She... she could always see into him, reading his thoughts and feelings and anticipating his every need. He knew her. She stood out in vast contrast to every other memory from his childhood, until he was left aching for every moment he was without.

But why now? What was happening? Why were these memories coming to him now? Did Brye remember these things?

"Prince Gareth? Gareth? Are you quite alright?" Roweena asked.

"Yes..." he managed. "Yes... I am."

The royal advisor gave him a calculating look, but nodded. "Well, in that case—"

Smoke billowed out from Badar's house, followed by feminine shrieks.

Brye

It was foggy coming back from the memories. A persistent sense of dread and emptiness for what was invaded her. She felt deprived and yet hopeful. The emotions settled temporarily and she became aware of the dullness around her face and a gritty, herby taste that coated her tongue. She tried to open her eyes, or one eye, but discovered two smelly objects weighing them down. Using hands that seemed bigger than she expected, she removed leaves with ointment. Her face was wet from tears that had fallen as she'd slept. Her body was in persistent, underlying pain.

Licking her broken lips, she sensed a warmth that radiated from her stomach. It was unexpected but welcome.

A long thin hand was settled over her stomach. A familiar crop of dark hair and a freckled face came to her line of vision.

That's me!

As if by realizing it, feelings collided with unimaginable strength inside her. There was an ache that spread all over her body. A desire for more, that drove her breath to hitch. What she wanted the most in the world was right beside her, and she couldn't have it.

Then she blinked, tears coating her swollen eyes and her view changed.

Gareth's features appeared before her and he narrowed his eyes, wary. His eyes were prickled with unshed tears.

He feels embarrassed and betrayed.

If only those were the only emotions.

"What did you do, Brye?" he whispered, trying to rise, but Brye pressed down softly on his chest. She didn't want him to go. There was so much left unsaid, and so much to say.

"Don't." Her voice was quiet, the words struggling to come out of her mouth. "Please, stay. I should apologize, but I won't."

He averted his eyes.

"I wanted to know why you provoked Tara. I wanted to know your intentions."

"Did you discover them?" he groaned.

"No. I couldn't control what your mind was doing." She swallowed hard, fighting the messy emotions lingering around her heart. "I didn't know that you knew my mother."

"You lost her very young, Brye," he responded. "It makes sense that you don't remember everything."

"That really isn't an excuse, is it?" Brye wiped a tear that fell from her eyes. "I was eight years old. I should remember more. I was not as young as Tara or Lenna, but..."

Brye turned his face in her direction, only to discover the swelling diminished and his bones fully healed. Gareth's gaze was intense, cold, and demanding from his good eye. But underneath, he was as moved and unnerved as she was.

A careful mask for others to see and no one to recognize.

Oh, Gareth.

"I think I was not the only one that lost something when she disappeared."

His breath wobbled, but he nodded softly in her hand.

"I think," her voice was a whisper close to his face. The scent of the ointments tickled her nose, but the strange earthy scent was underneath. One that only belonged to him. She fought the desire to move closer, to wrap her arms around him. "You lost something as well."

"Yes," his voice wobbled slightly, but he whispered, "I lost you."

Brye let go of him, examining her own emotions. She wanted to cry, the sense of loss suffocating her. Loss of her mother, of the memories that were vivid and pure in his mind. The possibilities and wonder of having a childhood full of hope and happiness.

It was all gone for no real reason.

And she couldn't escape the sense that there was more. So much more she did not know. Exhaling, she leaned back and stared at the ceiling.

After some time, Gareth relaxed, and he drifted back to sleep. She listened to his soft snores and smiled.

Something changed tonight. It was as if the mists around her mind dwindled. She had a whole past with Gareth erased from her memory, and she wanted to know it all. She wanted to learn more about him, and she couldn't continue to ignore that her dislike was slowly changing into something more.

Something she was not ready to admit to herself yet.

Rubbing her face, Brye closed her eyes, fighting the temptation to look at him. Shortly after, she joined him in sleep, dreaming of her mother's face.

Childhood Affections

Lenna

"I'm glad we finally managed to get her to sleep," Lenna whispered as she sat beside the small mattress by the fire. Aiden sat with Tara's head in his lap. He played with Tara's curls, and slowly massaged her back. They spoke in soft tones not to wake her. "Aiden, don't you think it is a good time for a mating ceremony?"

"That would depend on Brye and Gareth. If I recall correctly, they were waiting for you to get better to set a date."

"I wasn't talking about them." She rolled her eyes.

"I know."

They were silent for a few moments before she spoke. "With all that has happened, do you have second thoughts about Tara?"

He did not respond immediately. "Should I?"

"No, you shouldn't."

It was his turn to blink in surprise. "I think Tara is rubbing off on you."

"It is always beneficial to learn from the best traits of others." She pinched him. "Don't change the subject."

He winced. "Right... What was your point?"

Lenna played with the fabric of her dress. She needed to word this carefully. Aiden knew Tara the most, but love could blind you. Lenna needed Aiden to be sure that he loved Tara and would never abandon her. She wanted to take care of her little sister. "I think Tara feels insecure and out of place in Avalon, wanting to be a warrior in a society trapped in time. With what happened, she will be plagued with doubts. Perhaps even begin to be afraid of herself."

"I am aware Tara is not as strong as she appears."

Lenna nodded, biting her bottom lip and wrapping her arms around herself. "I ask you again, do you have second thoughts about your feelings? After seeing what Tara can do."

He did not answer, only regarded her. He extended his hands in her direction, but she ignored it. It stayed that way, palm open.

It was what he always did. Search her out. Make a connection to see if she was alright.

But it had to stop.

Lenna couldn't keep doing this to herself. She kept wanting someone that she couldn't have. All this time, he was oblivious to her feelings. She was well aware of that.

It was time to let Aiden go.

After a moment, he dropped his hand and exhaled. "I have no doubts. Tara is still Tara. There are no other choices."

The finality of the statement was brutal for Lenna to hear, but she accepted it. It hardened her resolve.

"Then set a date, preferably before Brye sets hers." She stood and walked to get her blanket and cot.

"If she'll have me."

"You might have to do some heavy convincing."

Aiden chuckled. "What about you, Lenna?"

What about her? With Brye moving to the tower with Gareth; Aiden and Tara would need privacy; where was she destined to be?

"I will find my way, Aiden," she said after a while. "I will always find my place."

Sometime later, Lenna lay beside the fire on her blanket, tired and empty.

Where did she truly belong? Did she even belong to herself? Would she ever find someone who wanted her?

It was only a matter of time before the royal advisor called her back. Heaviness filled her stomach, but how could she avoid it? Was she prepared for a life of service to the island and its people? Did she genuinely want to spend the rest of her days alone?

Restless, she decided to go for a walk. She dressed, leaving her gray cloak behind and taking up her old green one. With one last look at Aiden and Tara wrapped together underneath the blankets, she closed the door.

The village was clear and silent—the calm before the storm. No hushed whispers or villagers were drinking in the square. Everyone had gone to bed earlier than expected.

A tiny waning moon accompanied her as she reached the gap in the wall. She crossed, exhaling as the weight lifted off her body.

With each step, the sea air filled her with peace, and the breeze moved her messy locks around her face. Her hopes plummeted when a cold empty cave received her. It was the second time she came and found herself alone. The wolf had promised to train her.

Now we know what his promises are worth.

Lenna wanted to pinch the bridge of her nose to stop the tears but decided against it. She was alone. Why not cry to her heart's content? Why not feel sorry for herself, like she was supposed to?

I can't stand all these feelings. Of being overwhelmed, annoyed, and jealous.

She fell on her knees at the first intake of breath. She hugged her arms close to her stomach. The second exploded with a cry, and she let the messy tears fall down her cheeks.

Lenna buried her head in her knees and let everything go.

Proposals

Tara

TARA SCREAMED, CAUGHT IN an endless nightmare. Each moment was worse than the last. In the haze of her dream, she stood over the crumpled bodies of Gareth and Brye. Her hand still held the bloody dagger. They were dead.

She killed them.

Her eyes flew open, and she found herself in Aiden's arms, safe and warm. Outside, the sky was slowly turning blue.

"Nightmare?" he asked in a groggy voice.

Tara nodded. "I can't escape what I could have done." She hid her face against his neck.

"Talk to me, Tara," Aiden pleaded softly.

If she spoke it out loud, would it make it real? Gareth's voice echoed in her head. *"Fight, Tara. Fight to the death"*.

Whatever happened yesterday, she fought without reason or compassion. She remembered nothing, only the moments before her head snapped against the stones and after Lenna appeared in her line of sight.

Terror gripped her lungs.

The damage I could have done.

"I want to help Tara, but you need to talk to me," Aiden whispered against her hair.

"I am afraid," she whimpered, but she told him about the nightmare.

Aiden listened, holding her close and rubbing her waist with his traveling fingers. When she was done, his chest was covered in her tears.

"Tara, with all that is happening, I am not surprised you have nightmares," he whispered. He removed a curl from her forehead, running a finger down her face. "But holding them to yourself and putting everything on your shoulders shows a lack of respect and faith in your family and me."

"It was never—" She was cut short by his fingers on her lips.

"Let me finish, please. We both know you can be stubborn." She smiled hesitantly. He responded in kind.

"If you truly want to protect those you love, talk to them. Don't make the mistake of keeping it all to yourself."

Tara let out an unsteady breath. "I know. I'm sorry. I just can't right now, because I don't even understand what I am feeling."

"I forgive you. I think..." He gave her a coy smile.

Tara snorted and rolled her eyes.

"Now, I have been thinking about something for a while," he began kissing her softly. He slowly rubbed her cheek with his fingers, cleaning the remains of her tears away.

"Oh? This sounds serious." She bit back a smile.

"Very, and it involves you," he whispered against the hollow of her neck before nipping a sensitive point with his teeth, "and me."

Shivers spread along her body, and a familiar ache pulsed between her legs.

"Does this involve clothes?"

"Yes, in the beginning, at least."

"Sounds uncomfortable. You just said, "I enjoy you without clothes."

"Tara." Aiden took a deep breath. "Would you be my mate?" Tara blinked, and the warmth immediately left her body. She sat up abruptly. "Did you see what I did? I almost killed the prince and my sister, and you are proposing to me?"

"As usual, you look at one side of the information." He sighed, sitting up.

"Are you aware of what you're asking?"

"Very," he continued, speaking in a matter-of-a-fact tone. "I want to spend the rest of my life with the woman I love. The question remains. Is it what you want, Tara?"

Tara looked at him as if he had grown another head. "This conversation sounds familiar."

"And it will continue on a similar loop for the rest of our lives because it is how you and I are, Tara." He placed his arm over his raised knee. His smile was back. "Let me know when it sinks in."

Tara crossed her arms over her chest, wincing at the still-tender muscles.

Oh, it hurts when he is right.

It came down to her being a ninny. She tried to imagine a life without him, not only as her friend but as sharing every experience with him.

She couldn't.

Looking past him, she asked, "When do you propose this ceremony take place?"

"I was thinking, as soon as we talk to your sisters and my family. We only need witnesses and the bonding ceremony." His voice was as casual as her own.

Tara bit back her smile, then licked her lips.

"I agree with your proposal." She sighed in feigned resignation.

"I'm glad it pleases you." He held back a grin.

They broke out laughing. Tara wiped her tears. Aiden leaned in and grasped her face gently. "I love you, Tara."

"I know you do. Let's take advantage of the moment to show me how much."

"That is an order I will gladly obey," Aiden responded as he bit her lip and gently worshiped her.

Brye

Brye awoke with the rising sun. The cot next to her was empty and cold. She quickly rubbed her eyes and stood.

"If he hurts himself more because of foolishness, I'll kill him," she mumbled, going outside only to find Gareth walking toward her from the stream. He carried the bucket, but the look on his face was what disarmed her. He was relaxed.

She had never seen him that way.

Her heart grew in her chest, and she pinched her lips not to smile.

"I thought you would like some water to wash before heading home," he said.

"You should have awoken me." Brye rubbed her hands together. "You must rest. If you strain your injuries, they won't heal properly."

He raised an eyebrow, and Brye examined his face more closely. His eyes were open, and the swelling was now a pale yellow. She blinked.

"Let me see your ribs," she ordered, placing both hands on her hips. Gareth sighed, putting the bucket on the ground and lifting his dirty shirt.

Brye found the tattoos and symbols more intriguing in the soft morning light. They were too intrinsic for someone in Avalon to be able to produce, and the wolf was magnificent. Detailed to perfection. It almost jumped out of his skin.

Clearing her throat and wetting her lips, she placed her hands on his ribs, where the bruising was now a greenish-yellow. His heart rate increased as she probed, and his body tensed at her touch. She forced herself to concentrate on the task at hand. The ribs were mended entirely, and the pain was minimal. They seemed more like old wounds.

"How is it possible?" she asked, baffled. "My abilities are not this advanced for healing to happen so quickly."

Gareth took a step back and pulled his tunic over his torso. "You are an exceptional healer."

"There is more to that." She waved a finger at his face. "I have many questions you could not answer yesterday. Clearly, you have no excuse today."

"Is that so?" His lips twitched slightly. "Did you not get enough information last night?"

"Oh, definitely not! If anything, I have even more questions."

He scoffed. "Sounds daunting. Give me your hand."

"Why?"

He reached for it, placing it on his stubbled cheek.

"My hands tingle," she mumbled nervously.

"I know," he replied, his lips twitching again. Her thumb was close to his mouth. She could rub the pad of her thumb across his lips if she wanted. "Read me, Brye."

Brye blinked, her brow furrowed, but she reached into Gareth's mind.

Be careful what you say. The woods have ears.

Her eyes opened wide and she bit hard on the inside of her mouth. Curiosity won, and she pushed her thoughts toward him.

Where can we speak?

Only two places are safe in Avalon—your home and my room.

She inhaled and exhaled slowly. Gareth removed her hand from his face. Brye's heart fluttered in her chest as he lifted it to his lips and kissed her knuckles. He rubbed them before letting go.

I can't breathe.

"Time to head back," he said gravely.

"Four days," Brye said, grabbing his hand again.

It was his turn to look confused.

"The mating ceremony," she continued. "I think we waited long enough, don't you? I mean, we already spoke about this. A long time ago." Her voice sounded strained. She pushed her thoughts to him through their hands.

If the woods have ears, it's best to keep appearances.

His gaze turned suddenly cold. His control over his emotions was extraordinary. But he couldn't hide from her. She could sense every feeling behind that cold mask. And he was relieved, and... hopeful. A hope that filled every space around her heart.

Brye let go of his hand and wrapped her arms over her chest.

"I am glad you finally made a decision," he said.

"Yes. My mind is set. Go," she ordered. "I can find my way just fine."

Gareth hesitated but stiffly nodded and left, not looking back.

Brye let out a breath and went to fetch her kit. Her hands trembled as she put all the pots and bottles back inside the basket. She marched home, her mind running through the previous day's events.

There was so much to process. The memories she had experienced showed a history where Gareth was part of her family.

A past that included her mother.

Where they had been friends.

He taught her to swim.

He played with Tara.

Soothed Lenna.

Smiled and cared for them, especially her.

One day when we get older, you and I will be mated.

She blushed even though she was alone. That particular vision certainly explained quite a bit. With each of his memories, more and more questions arose. There was one fact that remained at the forefront of her thoughts. Gareth had known her mother. His memories of her were so clear.

Why can't I remember?

Oh, how unfair that he could see her so clearly, but Elsywth's own daughter struggled to remember her hair color. Was it always so vibrant? Was she always so fair and covered in freckles? Were her eyebrows and eyelashes so light that they got lost in her face? Brye had forgotten how much they resembled her. Each had an aspect of their mother's appearance or temperament.

Tara was so similar in color to her mother.

Lenna had her deep green eyes.

They had so much of their mother, and neither of them knew.

Brye stopped in her tracks. If Gareth had been so close to her mother, he perhaps knew what had happened to her. But his memories were tinted with grief. During those last moments, his heart had beaten erratically. Gareth had been so distraught that he could not process what was happening.

But he knows more. Not only about maither *but of who we were before.*

Brye had been able to read people's thoughts and emotions from a very young age. Tara showed unnatural strength and speed. Yet, none of them demonstrated their abilities till now. Even Lenna's gifts were sporadic until recently. What changed?

We are all connected, Tara, Lenna, Gareth, and I.

Bindings.

Lenna mentioned something about bindings the night of the earth stag. The royal advisor grew tense and violent when her sister said it.

Frustrated, Brye picked up her pace. She needed to get home and prepare for the four-day mating ceremony.

This time they couldn't afford to distance themselves. They needed to accept what was to come.

She was to be Gareth's mate, and his future queen.

Tingles ran down her body at the image. They became more acute when she remembered a twitching smile and a gentle kiss.

Sisterly Bonds

Lenna

LENNA AWOKE WITH A start about mid-morning. The fire that kept her warm extinguished to almost embers.

"Damn," she hissed, rubbing the grit and dried tears from her swollen eyes. "Damn, damn, damn!"

Lenna extinguished the fire without a second thought and headed home as fast as possible. She tripped and stumbled after passing the break in the wall. She avoided the group of villagers that were still working on organizing the debris. Her body attempted to recover its rhythm as she marched south.

Damn the bindings, and damn this wall. And damn all of it.

After a night of crying and self-pity, the long walk allowed her to face reality. Wishing things were different was unhelpful. She needed to accept the painful truth that her sisters were going on with their lives. And she was stuck.

Lenna had made few connections with men her age. She was awkward and shy around strangers, preferring to observe than participate in events. She enjoyed watching her sisters move around with their energetic strides, social graces, and strengths. It came naturally to her to stand by as others shined.

Now, her role as Mist Maiden required her to develop skills unnatural to her. One she did not fully understand.

Perhaps it's time she took her role seriously. It would mean controlling the mist and understanding how the island's binding works. She did not trust Roweena to train her fairly. However, if she wanted to gain knowledge, she had to return. Lenna's stomach cramped at the thought.

I will have to use her more than she uses me.

With a long sigh, Lenna picked up her pace.

Easier said than done.

Lenna ignored the villagers as she got closer home, but the atmosphere was oddly bright and filled with expectations. She opened the door quickly and jumped back as Tara, Aiden, and Brye stood simultaneously from the table.

"You had us worried." Brye took her cloak and Tara her satchel. Lenna smiled at Aiden, who had rolled his eyes.

"I said I was going to be late," she said, drying her bandaged hands on her skirt.

"Of course, but late and the next day are two very different things," Tara said.

"I expect a bit of trust in this family." Lenna unwound the dirty bandages. Brye extended her hands and helped.

"We do." Brye raised Lenna's hands to check. She nodded and let her sister clean them gently with soap. "You still need to put the ointment on it."

All three still stood around her, expectantly. With her back to them, she asked, "So when is the ceremony?"

"Which one?" Tara answered, smirking knowingly.

Lenna dropped the ointment on the table. She blinked at Brye, who gave her a cautious smile.

"Both of you?"

Her sister nodded.

Lenna pinched her lips and massaged her forehead, smearing the smelly cream on her face.

I knew that it was going to happen, but...

"This is quite unexpected," she stated.

"Well, a date had to be set," Brye reasoned.

"No, of course! It's just two dates. So quickly..." She sat down on the chair Aiden had vacated. He was standing close to Tara with an arm around her waist. Brye wrung her hands.

"Why are both of you so nervous?" Lenna raised an eyebrow.

"We wanted to know how you felt about everything," Brye continued.

"Me? I think you all have memory problems." Lenna pointed to herself. "I'm very happy for both of you! If I am not mistaken, I spoke to Aiden last night about asking Tara."

"She did." Aiden quirked a smile.

"And I told you," Lenna pointed at Brye, "Gareth seems like a sensible match. I think you two suit each other very well."

"Then why do you look so shocked?" Brye asked.

Lenna ignored the question. "When are the ceremonies?"

"Ours tomorrow. Brye's in four days," Tara replied.

Lenna's jaw dropped. "Then what are we waiting for? We have a ceremony to plan for!"

Brye let out a sigh.

"Really." Lenna waved a hand. "You think I was going to make a scene? Me? When I have the both of you to make one?"

Aiden and Tara laughed as Brye smiled.

"Wiser words were never spoken," Aiden said, giving Tara a smacking kiss on her forehead.

"No, never," Tara answered back.

❧

The following day, at breakfast, Lenna made an announcement. "I will inform you, dearest sister, that I know exactly where I want your ceremony to take place." Lenna beamed, clapping her hands, wincing when the tender skin hit. "Ouch... It will be perfect! Just leave it to me."

And that is what Lenna wanted most of all. For her impulsive sister and her best friend to have the perfect day. And it needed to start with getting Tara ready. She stank. Lenna pushed her into the scented bath Brye had prepared.

"I'm going to smell like a field of flowers," Tara sighed in pleasure as she contorted her body into the tub.

Lenna laughed, leaning against the door frame. Tara's tall, lean body barely fit in the tub. And with Brye and her together in the small bathing room, it was a tight fit. "I am sure Aiden will appreciate the change in odor."

"Especially since lately, you smelled like the dung heap," Brye muttered as she crouched beside the tub. She touched each part of Tara's body; as if checking her injuries.

Oh, her polite sister. A bit too polite.

"Shit," Lenna said. Her sisters turned in her direction, wide-eyed. "You can say shit, Brye. The word is a bit more accurate than a dung heap."

Brye and Tara burst out laughing. Lenna chuckled to herself.

"You have healed surprisingly well," Brye remarked. "I am a bit surprised at how rapidly you have healed, Tara. Your face is no longer puffy, and your ankle is only tender. You should not have healed so quickly."

Tara turned, forcing water to slosh over the rim. Brye shrieked as her skirts were sprayed.

"I feel very little pain. You're right, it is odd, though."

Brye continued to rub. "Gareth also healed quite rapidly for the extent of the injuries he sustained."

Tara slipped into silence, and her body tensed. "I still don't remember."

"I don't think you're supposed to," Brye whispered, "but—"

"What, Brye?"

"Maybe I can help you." She rubbed her hands together.

"How?" Lenna asked.

"I know you both believe I am only a healer," Brye hedged nervously, she exited the room and Lenna entered.

"You are more than any healer, and you know it," Tara stated, dropping the sponge into the scented water. "Time to get out. I am all shriveled."

She stood, her long, toned body dripping over the tub. Lenna wrapped her in a towel.

"More is an understatement," Brye continued.

Tara sat by the fire while Lenna dried her sister's hair with the towel. Brye's tense stance gave her pause.

Brye sat on the chair and said, "I can read with my hands."

"Read?" Lenna's eyebrows squished together. What did that mean?

"I can detect injuries, heal them, and read people's thoughts, feelings, and emotions."

Tara's jaw dropped. Lenna repeatedly blinked, her plump mouth forming an O.

That explains the tingling, and how the bindings were limited to Brye's arms. Lenna concentrated on Tara's hair, but something nagged her about what Brye confessed.

"Remember when I told you that neither of you could sleep in my cot anymore?"

"My ribs still hurt from Tara's kicks," Lenna mumbled. "I will not miss that."

"Hey!" Tara snapped.

"I feel so sorry for Aiden," Lenna teased, tugging at her sister's wet hair. Brye rolled her eyes slowly, and Lenna bit her lower lip in contrition. "I'm sorry, Brye, continue."

"A conversation in this house is such a challenge." Brye let out a long sigh. "Like I was saying. I decided it would be best not to sleep together because I would go into your dreams. If my hands touched your skin at night, I would dream about whatever you did. Feel what you feel." Brye massaged her temples.

"Since when?" Lenna asked, but she had a feeling she knew when it all started.

"It happened randomly. I couldn't predict with whom or when it would occur. But my abilities have gained strength since... Since Beltane."

When Lenna's magic was discovered. Beltane had significance in all this. She knew it. By the Founders, she just didn't know how they all connected. Lenna concentrated on Brye once again.

"I am confident that I can help you reach the memories of the other day."

Tara stared at the fire for a moment. "I don't know if I want to remember."

"Then you don't have to." Lenna left the towel and brought a comb to run through her sister's fiery locks.

"But," Tara continued, "I want to know why I did what I did."

Lenna combed a bit more forcefully, her eyes focused and narrowed. Tara winced.

"Sorry," Lenna rubbed her sister's shoulder, continuing carefully. Should she tell them? Would she be able to explain something she didn't understand yet? All this was so confusing.

Brye tapped her sister's arm with her finger. "Lenna, is something on your mind?"

Lenna brushed Tara's hair and then placed the comb on the table.

It's now or never.

"I have some ideas, but I don't have any way to prove them or know if they are truly connected."

"Any ideas are better than none." Tara sat with her back to the hearth as the fire dried her hair.

Lenna stood and paced. "I believe there is a connection between the island and the bindings, but I am unclear what it might be. Avalon's wall is akin to thick roped threads that bind the magic to the island and inside of it." Lenna disappeared into the bedroom briefly and grabbed a cloth she had been working on. She came back into the room holding it out.

"Like my tapestry work, only much more detailed and complex." She ran her hands over the small decorations. "Once the tapestry work is done, it would take enormous time and effort to break it apart and leave the cloth beneath."

"Is that why we have been protected for so long? The mists, the magic fields, is it all knotted magic?" Tara asked.

"Yes, but that magic is breaking. Somehow, the wraiths are breaking the bindings. Or perhaps because the bindings are breaking, the wraiths appear? Whatever comes first, the magic is seeping out," Lenna continued.

"How is this connected to us?" Brye inquired.

"I don't know. Each of our abilities are bound differently."

Tara scoffed. "I have no magic."

"Yes, you do," Lenna remarked. "You are unnaturally strong, Tara. You are agile and heal far too quickly compared to the rest. And you, Brye, can heal and use herbs with precision. Not only that, but you can read into others. An empath, I think it is called. Your abilities will develop more with time."

"If so," Tara countered. "Why haven't we developed them sooner? Even your magic, Lenna, has been off most of our life. What has changed?"

"We did have them earlier. When we were younger. From what I know, both Tara and I openly displayed our abilities," Brye said. "We just don't remember."

"How do you know about this?" Lenna raised an eyebrow. Was she the only one that had secrets?

Brye rubbed her hands together and then clasped them in her lap.

"I..." She hesitated, looking up, and then let out a long breath. "When I spent the night taking care of Gareth. I took advantage of my growing abilities."

"And?" Tara leaned in.

"I drugged him and read his memories," Brye said in a rush.

"No!" Tara exhaled. "He must have been furious."

"No... strangely, he was more relieved," Brye mumbled.

"Wait a moment." Tara tapped Brye with her finger. "How much does he know?"

"Enough for me to tell you that we were not always as bound as we were." Brye flicked Tara's finger away. "I can't tell you more."

"So, he gets to remember, but we don't? That seems extremely unfair."

Lenna placed her hands on the table. Tara was right. It was unfair that Gareth could remember his past, and they couldn't. She rubbed her face. Did the bindings affect their memory? If so, then no one in the village should be able to remember their mother, but they did. Lenna had not taken the time to check each villager's bindings or even if Gareth had any. The magic was still new to her. And it was all so terribly confusing. Each piece of information was tangled together like a ball of yarn.

"Whether we had abilities before or not right now is unclear. And we will go over the topic again at a later date," Brye interrupted Lenna's thoughts with a squeeze of her hand. "However, the biggest question remains, what do our bound abilities have to do with the breaking knot magic?"

"Well," Lenna bit her lower lip. "I might have an idea about that." Her sisters looked at her expectantly. "Dear me, I never thought we would have so much difficulty having a conversation."

"Out with it, Lenna," Tara stabbed her with her finger. Lenna flicked her sister's fingers away. She hated when Tara did that.

"All right. It might be because the three of us are also covered in these threads."

Tara scoffed again, but Lenna reached for her hands. "You can't see them, but they are there. They are like long invisible tattoos that run almost around your body."

Brye's head snapped up, and her eyes narrowed. "They look like tattoos?"

Lenna nodded. "Yes. Tara, your bindings are like long thorny branches, and, for some reason, claw marks run down your heart." She ran her finger over her younger sister's arms. "And Brye, yours are thorny branches as well, but with small unopened flower buds. They cover your hands and run up to your chest." Lenna demonstrated with her own hands.

"And what about yours, Lenna?" Tara asked.

"Mine? They cover my entire body and are a mix of thorny vines and many intrinsic knots. Like the bracelet the queen gave Brye, but even more, knotted together."

"How do you know about all this, Lenna?" Brye asked.

Lenna took a deep breath and reluctantly told her sisters about her training. She commented on how the binding became restrictive coming back into the wall. She also confessed to using her magic to tame the fire lizard, pushing the magic through the bindings. She omitted the wolf and his participation. They didn't need to know that. Her sisters were smart and would immediately know it was Beltran. And Lenna wanted to confront him herself first.

If he showed his face again. He was technically avoiding her.

"You have been hiding all this for this entire time?" Tara asked, her voice full of disbelief.

Lenna nodded. "I think our magic will be less constrained as the bindings break. That is why you transformed, Tara. Whatever your true abilities are, they are bound and knotted in you, and Gareth knows how to release them. He is hiding the why."

"I think he hides a great many things," Brye acknowledged.

They fell into silence, and Tara was the first to break it. "Well, we now have an insider who will discover what the prince is up to."

Lenna laughed while Brye scowled.

"So unbecoming of a future princess, Brye," Tara chuckled.

"That will be the day after tomorrow and not today." Brye stood, wiping her hands on her apron. She went to the trunk and pulled out the blue dresses. "We must continue this discussion later, for we have a ceremony to prepare!"

"Don't think about the reasons for now. Whatever happens, we will solve it together. As we always do. As we are meant to," Lenna said, as she squeezed Tara's shoulder.

"Yes, together," Tara answered. "Now, do you think I smell better?"

"You smell edible, dearest sister," Lenna smirked. "A delectable, flowery feast."

"Lenna!" Brye's indigent voice vibrated through the house while Tara sat dumbstruck.

And Lenna enjoyed every moment of it.

Binding
Ceremonies

Brye

BRYE AND HER SISTERS set out to the location a few hours before sunset. Tara was dressed in the same emerald-colored dress sent by the queen for Brye's proposal ceremony, with the addition of a metal belt decorated with knots and symbols. Lenna embroidered a few quick decorations around the sleeves and neckline.

Tara's long red hair was halfway down, with a coronet of braids discreetly twined with wildflowers. Brye walked close just in case Tara needed help, but she didn't. Aiden seemed to have everything under control. Tara's ankle was better, but she still leaned on Aiden as they walked. He whispered something that made Tara laugh and Brye smiled.

The bridal party was small and intimate, with only the sisters, Enid, her husband, and Aiden's parents in attendance. They left in small groups so as not to draw attention to themselves. Once they passed the village, Lenna led them north until they arrived at the river and the White Thorn Tree.

Aiden and Tara froze before reaching the tree.

"Is something wrong?" Lenna asked.

Tara's face flushed while Aiden pulled the collar of his dress tunic.

"No." Tara chuckled. "No, this is beautiful, Lenna."

Lenna raised an eyebrow but nothing more.

The tree served as a backdrop for the event, and the gushing river as music. The White Thorn Tree was in full bloom. It seemed more magnificent in the late afternoon light as if it grew with the attention and visitors. Its fragrance was intense, and the soft rustle of its branches seemed to convey excitement.

Lenna and Brye dressed down in simple blue tunics and a few flowers in their hair. Lenna was adamant that Tara needed to be the center of attention. "No matter how beautiful you may be, older sister, today you must be an ornament."

"Stop saying it like that," Brye groaned. "You are not a scare-crow."

Lenna patted her hand, and a dull sense of happiness entered Brye's system. "Relax, I was just teasing. You are a beauty with brains. I am very proud of you."

Brye was about to remark when a figure came jogging towards them. Her breath caught. Lenna raised her hand over her eyes to hide the sun's glare and smiled.

Gareth came.

He dressed simply in a green tunic with black pants. His beard was untrimmed, his hair windswept, and his brow dotted with a fine sheen of sweat. He recovered his breath after the sprint, giving a forced smile and nod to everyone present.

"We did not expect you," Brye said, breathlessly, her hands clasped tightly in front of her. Her heart unexpectedly hammered in her chest.

"The queen found out when she sent some more gifts to your home," he said, but then he leaned down and whispered for her only, "One of your neighbors mentioned that you were on your way here. My mother insisted I needed to be present."

Brye smiled kindly and gazed at Tara and Aiden under the tree. Gareth crossed his arms over his chest. Brye took a handkerchief from her inside pocket and extended it in his direction.

"For your brow." She motioned to his forehead, her face flushed.

"Oh." Gareth stared at the fabric. "I'll dirty it."

"That's what it's for." Brye took it upon herself and wiped his face. Gareth tried not to move while a visible flush crept up his neck. He grasped Brye's hand, and his intense emotions wrapped around her heart and tied themselves there. The longing had grown stronger, and with it was one that weakened her knees. She pulled her gaze away, gripping the handkerchief tighter in her grip.

It wasn't the time to examine these feelings. They were too intense, and she needed to focus. If only he would stop looking at her that way. As if the universe was in her eyes.

"Where is Beltran? Lately, it seems you are tied together. We can't find one without the other," Brye asked, placing the handkerchief back in her pocket and looking ahead. Aiden and Tara spoke in low tones with Caitlin.

"He had to go back," he answered grimly. "There seems to be some unrest with the present Shifter King."

"What kind of unrest?" Brye asked.

"The Shifter King is new to the throne, and the transition is not going as smoothly as they thought. We expect him to return to Avalon soon, though."

"Should he not stay?" Lenna asked, flushing to the tips of her ears as Gareth gave her his full attention for the first time. "If he is so important at this particular time on the Continent, shouldn't he stay?"

"He still has to come back." Gareth lowered his voice. "The occurrences in Avalon are rare. He might be of use."

He turned to Brye and exchanged a knowing look. One that portrayed that they couldn't continue the conversation. Out in the open. Where some mysterious force or person could hear them. Brye still had questions about that, but she trusted Gareth enough to know he wouldn't lie.

"I would think—"

Brye cut Lenna off by motioning to Aiden's parents. "Time to get this ceremony started."

Lenna's brow furrowed, but she didn't continue the conversation. Caitlin and Badar stood next to Aiden and Tara under the tree.

"Today, we celebrate a binding that brings us great joy," Caitlin began, her soft voice rising above the rustle of the leaves. "A love tended, persisted, and warmed through the years has finally blossomed. As their friends and family, we are here to witness this moment in their young lives and to bind them together. Who will knot the thread?"

Lenna and Brye raised their hands. Aiden's mother motioned them forward. Lenna pulled a long string from her inner tunic pocket. Between Brye and Lenna, they slowly tied Tara's left hand to Aiden's right with the thread. The joy was like a drug to Brye's body as they passed thread and recited, "We bind the love you share."

"We bind the time that will come," Lenna followed.

Together, they continued to recite the ceremonial rites.

"The laughter and joy
The sorrows and rile
We bind the flesh and the bone
The soul and the mind
For now, you are one
One until eternity,
We bind you together
One, over two, over three."

Once tied, Lenna and Brye stepped back, hands clasped together. Brye's hands touched Lenna, and glimpses flooded her mind. The smell of brine and wet fur mixed with loneliness and disappointment. Lenna raised an eyebrow and removed her hand. The sensations stopped, and Brye was left hollow.

What was that?

"Brye." Lenna pulled at her sleeve and motioned with her head. Aiden stood tall, looking at Tara with his whimsical blue eyes.

"Tara, I'd say you are the light of my life, but we both know you are more than that," his voice broke. He coughed to clear it and continued, "I bind you, the blood of my blood, and bone of my bone. I bind my body, my spirit, till our lives are done. And even then, I wish to be reunited, for I walk beside thee in this life and the next."

Tara's face lit up when it was her turn to speak, and her deep eyes bored into Aiden's.

"Aiden, I bind you, the blood of my blood, bone of my bone. I bind my body to yours, and our spirits entwined, till our lives are done. For all we have been together and all that will come, I ask, please, don't walk in front of me. I may not follow. Don't walk behind me. I may not lead. Walk beside me, be my friend, lover, and equal."

Aiden pulled Tara closer and kissed her smiling mouth. Then, the White Thorn Tree gifted the newly bonded couple with a shower of fragrant flowers and the music of its moving branches. In response, the audience applauded. The smiling couple laughed and beamed as petals fell over like water.

Brye smiled and raised her hands to catch them. As she touched the petals, her mind filled with happy moments and sensations, as if the tree was gifting them to her.

She could see little girls playing at a river, supervised by a tall, burly boy with serious eyes. A long-haired girl carried flowers and gave them to the tall boy. It was her and Gareth together. Always together as young children.

Why couldn't she remember? The memories grew in strength with each petal she touched until happy tears pricked her eyes and she smiled.

She opened her eyes and found Gareth's gaze. He watched her so intensely, and his mouth twitched. It was as if he knew. He could see in her eyes that she was slowly remembering who he was.

Who they were.

The almost smile warmed her to the core, tugging at the edges of her memory, to those feelings still locked away and waiting to be accepted.

To take root and grow.

Twisting

Lenna

A TIGHTNESS SETTLED IN Lenna's chest as she stood, hands clasped. Beside her, Brye and Gareth exchanged glances. If Brye had not fallen in love yet with Gareth, it was only a matter of time. It left Lenna feeling something she did not want to at one of the happiest moments of her younger sister's life: envy.

The newly mated couple needed to stay tied until it was time for bed. Brye came up with the idea of the old cottage. "It is hidden and private. You will not be disturbed."

"What about tomorrow and the day after? We need to prepare for your ceremony. I wanted to spend time with you," Tara insisted.

"And we have and will, but tonight is for you," Brye ended the argument.

The walk to the village was lively, with Tara and Aiden leading the celebration group. The mists had not yet fallen, and the sun was finally setting over the horizon. Brye walked beside Gareth, deep in conversation.

Lenna walked behind them, listless. Her hands clasped together.

Once they reached the village, people were out on the paths. They clapped and congratulated the couple. Whistles and calls came soon after, with hugs from neighbors. With the happy couple's news, the dread that weighed over the village lifted momentarily. Gareth took Brye's arm and placed it in the crook of his. Lenna sighed at the sight.

To be in love.

"Miss Lenna."

She turned at the sound of her name. Edgar—the attendant from the Royal Tower—edged through the passersby until he reached her side.

"Edgar." She nodded to him in greeting, even as her stomach hollowed out at the sight of him.

"The royal advisor requests your presence." Edgar gave her a slight bow.

"I am sure she can reconsider," Gareth replied sternly. "It is her sister's bonding ceremony."

"The royal advisor sent her congratulations. She also said the meeting would not take long." The older man motioned for Lenna to follow. Gareth, Brye, Aiden, and Tara stopped outside the house, waiting for her. She didn't want to go, but she knew it was inevitable.

"It's better to get it over with." She patted Brye's arm. "I will be back soon."

Lenna followed Edgar into the crowded streets and did not look back.

Inside the Royal Tower was quiet and dark, with only a few candles lighting up the path up the spiral staircase. Lenna rubbed her arms and bit her lower lip at the sudden drop in temperature.

"She is waiting in her room." Edgar motioned to the stairs.

"Thank you." She nodded and went up.

She found a door on the short landing on the fourth floor. It was the one leading to Roweena's private rooms. Her training had always been on the landing on the top of the tower. She had passed this door many times but was never invited in.

Until today.

Lenna took a deep breath and raised her hand to knock. It creaked open before her knuckles hit the wood.

"Enter." Roweena's commanding voice came from inside.

Lenna gripped her skirt to keep her hands from shaking and walked in.

The small apartment was made up of two rooms connected by an archway. The first was a small living area with tables and chairs next to the windows. There were fabrics against the walls to keep the warmth inside during the winter. The materials were simple, not like the tapestries in the royal chambers.

The floor was adorned with well-worn, colored rugs. Whatever was in the bubbling cauldron over the fireplace made the room smell of herbs and something spicy.

One side of the room contained a shelf of mostly empty bottles. Lenna carefully walked over to the table. On it was a large dark book open with detailed pages and illustrations. Small scribbles and notes were all over the paper. Beside it was a glass dagger decorated with silver symbols.

There were very few personal effects in the room. Everything was clean, organized, and coordinated except for the large book. As if it could belong to anyone.

Roweena appeared from the sleeping chamber. She wore a black robe tied at the waist. Her long, curled dark hair fell down her back, untamed by any style.

Lenna's skin crawled like tiny ants. It took a great deal of self-control to keep her features neutral.

"Finally," Roweena stated, bored. "Strip."

"I beg your pardon." Lenna gripped her skirt until her knuckles cracked.

"You heard me. Remove your clothing." Roweena looked down at her with dark coal eyes, the strips of gray intensifying her gaze.

"I need to see if the marks on your back appeared. I don't trust you to tell me." Roweena pointed to the carpet.

Lenna removed her dress, and all the flowers in her hair fell to the floor. In her underclothes, she shivered with hands stiff at her sides.

Did it suddenly become colder?

"How was the ceremony?" Roweena walked around her as she spoke.

"It was beautiful, as can be expected when two people love each other."

Roweena scoffed. "Love? An emotion that is highly desired but goes sour very easily. Like bad milk."

"Do you speak from experience?" Lenna's voice cracked.

Roweena stopped and raised an eyebrow. She reached for the strap of Lenna's stays and tugged. "Everything, Lenna."

The tone left no room for opposition.

Lenna's fingers fumbled with the front lacings of her clothes. She wasn't prudish, but she had never undressed in front of anyone but her family. As each layer of her underclothes fell to the floor, Lenna's stomach became even more knotted. She trembled with humiliation as she noticed her protruding ribs, and jutting hips. She had regained some weight after recovering from her burns, but keeping it on was harder than expected.

Why was Rowenna doing this to her? She had done everything the woman wanted. She had gone to train by herself. Her magic was improving, at least, outside the island's wall.

What did Roweena want?

Power. The idea came to her as she removed the last of her underclothes. Completely naked, she bit hard on her lip and fought the urge to cover her breasts. The older woman wanted power over her. But it made little sense. The only reason that she would go to the extent of humiliating Lenna for power, was if she was powerless in comparison.

But how could Roweena, a woman who was clearly an Elemental, be powerless?

"Now, I can look at you properly."

Roweena observed her with intensity. Gooseflesh appeared all over her pale body, and even the tiny hairs on her temple stood out.

Roweena ran her hands down Lenna's arms, picking up her hands and examining them.

"They have healed very well. Your sister is very accomplished." Roweena ran a finger along Lenna's arm and shoulders down the other arm. She retraced the path to reach the marks on the spine. The finger stayed, circling. The intimate touch only increased Lenna's sense of discomfort.

"Tell me about the first wraith, the fire lizard." Roweena let go and sat in a chair, crossing her legs and arms.

"I was practicing with fire, as you instructed—"

"I instructed you to tame the mists, not fire," Roweena interrupted.

"I was not having any success, so I thought if I could concentrate on the basics, it might be easier to build up to it," Lenna replied, keeping her gaze averted. She attempted to relax by breathing carefully.

"The night of the fire lizard, I was coming home from training. I saw it destroying the field. I had practiced increasing and decreasing small flames, extinguishing them by removing the air that feeds them. I don't know if I succeeded in taming the beast or if it was luck. The last thing I remember, my hands were on fire."

Lenna looked down at her feet. Her pink toes were pale against the dark carpet.

"Elemental magic is more complex than the simple dominion over the four elements," Rowenna explained. "The interaction between these elements and the forces around us make elemental magic. What are their opposing forces? What feeds the flame but reduces the amount of air? What can cause a tremor in the earth but keep structures standing? Elemental Magic is not a toy to be played with or guessed about. It requires knowledge."

"Yes," Lenna whispered. "I agree. There is much I do not know yet."

But how was she supposed to know this? How was she expected to learn anything if no one took the time to teach her? Roweena only tortured her. The wolf disappeared after the fire lizard, probably licking his wounds.

A strange sort of anger settled in the pit of Lenna's stomach. Anger was good. It was much better than fear.

"Well, it was quite a spectacle." Roweena stood and narrowed her eyes as she approached again. "It seems you are full of surprises."

A sudden tightening sensation increased around Lenna's body. No matter how much air she tried to breathe, she couldn't catch her breath. Her hands flew to her throat.

What is happening to me?

Lenna fought the desire to double over by gritting her teeth and focusing ahead of her. The dagger on the table, its silver symbols, blurred together. A faint glow.

"But I know you are lying, Lenna. You lie through your teeth. You know more about magic than you are telling me," Roweena hissed in her ear.

Lenna doubled over on all fours on the cold floor from the pain. The carpet burned into her knees and hands. Breathing hard through clenched teeth, she kept her gaze locked on the cracks in the fabric in front of her. Focus. If only she could focus, maybe it would stop.

But it grew worse.

"Please," she begged.

"Please?" The voice sounded distorted, as if coming from inside her head. Lenna shook it.

The cracks on the carpet before her became a twisted, spiral knot. She followed the knot as it spread all over the floor, like the tentacles of a spineless animal. Lenna raised her head and discovered they were coming from Roweena's legs.

She repeatedly blinked, trying to erase the image but could not.

What? What?

A hand grabbed Lenna by the hair, making her stand on wobbly legs. She bit back a scream.

A face covered by threads and knots that stretched and raised the skin, marking it with a dingy color appeared before her. The eyes of the creature were deep gray, and unnaturally colored lips sneered in her direction.

A monster.

"You are not the only one full of surprises," the voice growled low.

Lenna trembled violently. She was pushed back down onto the floor. Her knees hit the hard stone, and her hands reached for support.

"Get dressed," Roweena ordered. "We will resume training after your sister's ceremony. Be prepared."

It took Lenna two attempts to put on her underclothes. She kept her back to the woman but felt her gaze crawl up her spine. With her heart in her chest, Lenna grabbed what was left of her clothes and walked stiffly to the door. She did not turn back to see if the royal advisor had returned to her former self.

She did not want to see the creature again.

Outside the door, Lenna paused. The tightening around her and the sensation in her stomach slowly receded. Profound exhaustion and a persistent need to vomit were left in its wake.

On bare feet, she made her way down one level to the royal living area and was surprised to find Gareth standing at the bottom of the stairs. His raised eyebrow was the only change in his impassive face. He motioned her to follow to what appeared to be a bedroom. She did not have the energy to question.

He pushed her gently inside and closed the door.

Lenna gurgled compulsively. "I'm going to be sick," she groaned and was pushed into the bathing room. She managed to get on her knees and she vomited. She retched until only water was expelled, but the tremors and gooseflesh did not dissipate.

She flushed and stood up, finding Gareth leaning on the room's door frame. His eyebrows drew together, and he came closer. The warmth of his body reminded her that she wasn't alone.

"Lenna—"

"I'll be fine in a minute," she croaked. She pushed past him and exited the bathing room. Her throat throbbed from the vomiting.

"I'll leave you to finish getting dressed. You can clean up and I'll accompany you back," he said softly.

"Thank you." Before he pulled away, she grabbed his arm. He stiffened under her touch.

"Please, don't mention anything to Brye. She will tell Tara, and they will both worry. Today was such a nice day. The next two days are important, especially for you and Brye. So, let's focus on the good things to come."

"Are there no good things to come for you, Lenna?"

"Of course! My sisters will both be happy, and I am training. Many good things," she replied.

Gareth removed her hand from his arm and gently held it. "That is not what I meant. Lenna, there is more to life than the happiness of others."

Lenna looked down at their clasped hands. He let go, and the lack of warmth instantly brought back the shivers. She crossed her arms over her chest and examined the small room. It was cozy but bare as the one above.

"This room seems to have no identity."

"I don't like clutter."

"My sister is all about clutter. She will give this room many identities," Lenna sighed. He did not answer immediately.

"I hope she does." He gave her a long look.

"You really do care about my sister. Don't you?"

Gareth crossed his arms. "I'll wait outside to escort you home."

"I'll take that as a yes." He was about to open the door when she stopped him.

"You are right," she admitted, her shoulders slumping. "There is more to life than my sisters' happiness. If I focus on that, I might find some of my own." Her chin quivered, and she pinched the bridge of her nose. "I need time."

Why does it feel like I'm running out?

There was so much she wanted to say and couldn't. The words stayed trapped in her scorched throat.

Once dressed, she found Gareth standing in the hall with his back against the wall, arms crossed. He placed a finger on his lips and accompanied her home. There was a moment when he took her arm and put it in the crook of his.

The strange sensation of kinship returned. One that Lenna now understood was connected to their long, bound past. She wondered what it was like to be his friend.

He leaned in when they were outside her door and whispered, "See you tomorrow."

Lenna took a deep breath and decided to do what she always did, what she needed to do to protect those she loved.

She needed to lie.

Lie to her sisters and to everyone else.

Roweena did not suspect that her sisters had any sort of magical ability. Even if the older woman knew, her attention was clearly on Lenna. She needed to keep it that way. Tara just mated her best friend, and Brye will have the prince at her side.

She couldn't hide the truth from them forever, but maybe until after Brye's mating ceremony.

Yes, Lenna would tell them after. And maybe together they could find a way to protect themselves from Roweena.

Lenna gripped the door handle and stepped inside. Her stomach was a mass of knots. She pushed the fear down, and pretended for one moment that she had everything under control.

Yes, it was necessary to lie.
Especially to herself.

Part III

Marked

Brye

IT WAS EARLY MORNING on the day of her mating ceremony, and light made its way through the windows. Brye laid in bed, drumming her fingers over her stomach. Her eyes darted to Lenna, whose mousy brown hair came out from under the blankets. A hollowness settled in her stomach when she remembered Lenna's face the night of Tara's celebration. She'd come home from the Royal Tower, escorted by Gareth, looking strained and pale.

"Stop fussing! It is Tara's day! Let's not make it about me." Lenna went inside ignoring Brye's questions.

That only left one option, being nosey in the traditional way. Brye grabbed Gareth's hand.

"I would suggest talking to her directly." He removed her hand from his before she could read him. "And no reading to find out what you want. I don't know what she talked about with the royal advisor, but she was unwell and I brought her home."

He hesitated a moment, putting his hands in his pockets, With a curt nod farewell, he left. Brye watched him go, drumming her fingers over her mouth.

"It's not polite to read people without their consent," he called back as he disappeared into the empty paths. There was a short chuckle that drifted away.

Gareth didn't understand. He was an only child. The three of them grew up very close, yet still so different. Tara was impulsive and brave, willing to fight for what she wanted and believed. She was independent and now mated to a good man who could manage her strong will.

Lenna used humor to deflect attention from herself. Over time she had become more reserved and closed off. Her sister was hiding something. It was dangerous and raw.

"You're awake?" said a groggy voice. Lenna sat up, rubbing her eyes. "What time is it?"

"Very early," Brye replied as she prepared a simple breakfast.

"It will be a long day. It would be best if you got more sleep." Lenna stood, stretched, then grabbed her stomach.

"Are you still unwell?"

"A bit of your herbal tea will solve that, and then we shall make you irresistible." Lenna hugged her sister from behind. The top of her head reached Brye's neck.

"Repeating what we did for Tara?" Brye laid her hands on her sister's arms around her waist. Through the touch, Brye sensed a weak emotion that caressed her heart.

Longing.

It disappeared as quickly as it came.

"Well, I'd say even better. But we must wait and see if Tara will be helpful." Lenna mumbled into her back, "Or if she can walk straight."

"Lenna!" Brye gave her arms a swat.

"What? I am not naive, and you shouldn't be either. I am quite curious," Lenna let go and sat at the table.

"Well, I'm not!"

Lenna gave her a knowing look. "Liar! I intend to quiz Tara about the mechanics, if not the details. She has been at it for at least two days!"

Brye rolled her eyes. "Since when have you been so crude?"

"Always," Lenna rubbed her stomach. "You just haven't asked me."

Brye placed the herbs for the tea. "Well, I am still not curious."

"I am sure you are trying hard to believe that."

Brye chuckled as Tara arrived a few hours later. She floated into the house, arms spread out as if to embrace the world. Her eyes, smudged with dark circles, seemed to brighten as she smiled. "I am here! Let's begin."

"Where's Aiden?" Lenna asked, handing Brye the oils.

"At his mother's. It is only us girls, as it should be." Tara picked up some cider that was on the table. Brye looked at her left hand and gasped, dropping the herbs.

"What happened?"

"I thought you could tell me."

Tara put down the empty cup and lifted her sleeve. Her hand was covered in faint marks of raised skin. "The night of the ceremony, we cut the rope you used to bind us. That's when we noticed the marks."

"Both of you?" Brye reached for the hand and traced the lines, checking for injuries.

"Yes," Tara replied. "It doesn't hurt. We thought it might be because both of you have abilities." Tara gave a sheepish shrug. "I am sorry, but I did tell him about what we discussed. I kind of had to, given... well. This." She gestured with her left hand.

"That's all right," Lenna said, but she still bit her lip.

"You are correct. These are not injuries. They feel like part of your skin. Lenna, why don't you take a look?"

Lenna scrunched her forehead as she examined Tara's wrist. "It does feel different, like a magical imprint of some sort? I don't know."

Lenna let go of Tara's hand.

"Well, since it isn't painful, we should focus on other matters." Tara reached for Brye and tugged on her clothes.

"Hey!" Brye pulled her dress down.

"Brye, be helpful. We need to make you into a sensual feast." Tara continued to undress her.

Brye groaned as both her sisters stripped her naked. A hollowness settled over her at the thought of Gareth and her... naked and... If the kisses were any indication of what was to happen, she was too nervous. Or excited, or both?

Her face flushed and she shook her head. "I don't see the point. It's not that type of ceremony. The royal advisor will be the one to bind us," Brye muttered as Lenna helped her into the tub in the bathing room. Tara stood at the door while Lenna poured the scented water over Brye's loose hair.

"What kind of ceremony should it be?" Lenna raised an eyebrow.

"Like yours, Tara. A ceremony for two people in love announcing to the world their commitment to one another." Brye avoided their gazes and focused on one of the herbs that floated in the water. She played with the leaf, twirling it between her fingers.

"How long will you continue to lie to yourself and everyone else?" Lenna said, handing Tara the oil to rub over her sister's skin.

"I'm not—"

"Yes, you are," Lenna interrupted. "I see those looks you give each other. If you had no feelings for him, you would have done everything possible to ensure this did not happen."

Tara placed her hands on Brye's shoulders. "I will reluctantly add that Gareth tried to protect you from me. He values you."

Brye shrugged. Should she tell her sister what she knew? No. They were Gareth's memories. He hadn't openly shared them.

She stole them.

Strangely, she didn't feel guilty about it.

"I think we have had too many sober conversations lately." Tara removed a bottle of ale from the cupboard, and poured it into three small cups. "Today, we should celebrate! No matter how it started or how we feel about this ceremony. It was your choice, Brye. I will attempt to respect it," Tara continued, holding her cup. "Please note the emphasis on the word *attempt*. I can make no promises if he hurts you."

"Your faith in me is astonishing, little sister." Brye narrowed her eyes and tapped Tara with her finger.

"Whatever is to come, we will solve it together." Lenna raised her glass and smiled warmly.

"For Founders' sake! I am the eldest. Am I not supposed to be the wise one?" Brye grumbled, sipping the ale as the oils and lotions took effect.

"It would depend on what you think is being wise," Tara set the empty glass on the table. "Can we start now? You are as juiced as a pig on the spit."

"Tara!" Brye covered her face with her hands.

"Well, she is supposed to be edible. Is she not?" Lenna pretended to whisper to Tara.

Brye threw a wet sponge at her sisters before breaking out in a heartfelt laugh.

Mating Ceremony

Brye

A FEW HOURS LATER, there was a knock at the door. Brye jumped.

Lenna peeked outside the window. "Edgar is dressed impeccably! I have never seen him in that dark tunic. He has even combed his balding hair to the side with what I think might be wax."

"Great," Tara mumbled. "What we all need. Even more formality."

The knock came again with more strength. Lenna came away from the window. "Aiden's here."

Lenna opened the door, and Aiden pushed past Edgar, patting the more petite man on the back. His gaze went directly to Tara, who wore a green tunic and tiny beads in her hair. The heat between them became tangible.

"Should we leave and give you the room?" Lenna chuckled, crossing her arms over her chest.

"Lenna!" Brye bit back a reluctant smile.

"It seems twenty-four hours was not enough," Lenna continued. Aiden fidgeted with the collar of his tunic while Tara gave her sister a small smack against the shoulders. Lenna laughed.

"Well?" Brye sat as regally as a queen in a deep green tunic and plaid. Her hair was braided on her head and decorated with a crown. Her eyes were smudged with some oiled charcoal, and her lips were tinted with berry juice.

"Your highness." Aiden held out a hand for her to stand.

Brye scowled and refrained from swatting him. "That will take some getting used to."

"If anyone looked more the part, it would be you." Aiden let go of her hand and stood back. "If the prince does not break out a smile, then he must be blind."

"Or stupid," Tara pointed out, her eyes humorous.

"Or both," Aiden continued.

"That's enough, you two," Lenna interrupted.

"Spoilsport," Aiden mumbled. Lenna rolled her eyes.

Brye's nerves were at the edge, and the lovebirds were not helping. Their familiarity with each other and the sexual chemistry was nauseating.

What have I gotten myself into?

Brye gave them a wane smile and rubbed her hands. Lenna reached for her arm and squeezed.

Aiden said, "As I did before, I shall escort the most beautiful women in Avalon to the ceremony."

He took Brye's hand and placed it in the crook of his arm. Tara automatically reached for his other side. Lenna held her head high and led the way, following the royal retainer.

Outside, the sky was slightly overcast, but it did not smell like rain as Brye made her way to the lake. Villagers congratulated Brye and wished her well. But there was a tension and strain in their tones. Brye gripped Aiden tighter. "Something doesn't feel right," she remarked in a low voice.

"Yes," he answered back softly. Tara leaned in as he spoke. "This morning, the farmers noticed that what was left of the northwest wall was covered in thorny vines. They are thicker than before, and no one can identify the source. Some farmers have pulled a sample to see if there was a way of destroying them without taking down the wall."

"And?" Brye asked through a clenched smile as she waved to one of her former patients.

"The vine crumbled the wall." Aiden's eyes darted in different directions, making sure not to be overheard. "I was in the field this morning with my father. The king and Gareth were there too. Someone suggested bringing the royal advisor, but she was indisposed, supposedly. The king insisted on leaving her be. The prince was not happy about it. He wanted her to be more involved in what was happening."

"How do you even know all this?" Tara asked.

"I am an excellent listener."

"Or were you at the right place and time." Tara narrowed her eyes.

"Of course," he smiled. "How can you doubt me?"

"But the vines were there the other evening. Is there something else?" Brye asked, keeping her eye on Lenna ahead.

They reached the end of the path. The lake was in sight, sparkling and glittering in the distance. Brye's nerves jacked into her throat. Soft music drifted in their direction along with the hushed tones of conversations.

"If you get close, you can hear the vines creak as if they are still growing."

"Why not cut them down?" Brye whispered urgently.

"Some tried, but they are too thick, and the thorns are sharper than a blade." Aiden stopped and released Brye at the edge of the lake. "Don't concern yourself with this now. You have other important things to think about."

"But—"

"Like the man over there," Tara motioned with her head.

Gareth was standing near the altar dressed in dark pants, a light dress shirt, and a tunic with a thick metal belt. His hair was pulled back with wax, and his beard trimmed to soften his stony features. He stood, arms crossed, while he listened to his father, his eyes occasionally searching the crowd.

Until his gaze landed on Brye.

Everything faded away slowly, like a blurry image in the water. Her heart hammered in her chest. She forgot to breathe. Around her, voices dimmed, and she could hear the soft wind in the trees and the sound of steps on the rocky gravel shore.

What is this?

Brye placed a hand over the pressure on her chest, and her lips slowly parted. The sensation grew as Gareth pushed people aside to get to her, ignoring their good wishes.

Without a word, he extended his hand in her direction. His face was serious for only a moment. Then there was the twitch of his lips—the threat of a smile.

Brye was unable to control her erratic heartbeat. What did the tightness in her chest, the sudden warmth, mean? An echo of a memory resonated in her brain.

One day when we get older, you and I will be mated.

Brye reached for his hand. The fog of memories around her mind dissipated as his thoughts drifted through her fingers, loud and clear.

It will be alright, Brye.

His face was impassive, but his eyes scorched hers. Brye gripped his hand tighter and leaned into him. He seemed to hesitate a moment before relaxing.

Brye's nerves slowly drifted away as his body warmth seeped in. She wished her memory was as clear as his, but it wasn't. All these experiences were new and familiar at the same time.

The altar was a large square stone near the lake's edge, covered in moss and lichen. The green, moist plant life only partially hid the decorated knots and loops chiseled long ago into the stone. No one knows when the stone was placed or who worked on it, only that it had been there since the Founders.

Over the altar was a long cord made of different colored threads. Brye and Gareth stood hand in hand. The king and queen were on either side of them, while Roweena and Lenna were behind the altar. Everyone waited for King Manus to commence the ceremony.

Lenna's nerves reached Brye in short, tense waves. Her sister's eyes kept darting toward Roweena. It was enough to churn her stomach. Lenna's eyes shifted to Brye. Within a heartbeat or two, all of Lenna's emotions leached away from Brye like the ebbing of a tide.

Standing tall in a matching tunic, the king clapped his hands together. His eyes crinkled, giving the queen a wink before turning toward the villagers. He lifted his voice to be heard far and wide.

"Today, we are united, as one people, to witness the binding ceremony between Prince Gareth and Brye, daughter of Elsywth. I know these have been times of uncertainty, but we must embrace moments of joy whenever they appear. This is one of them. Whatever will be, we will face it together. Avalon is our place of safety, and we will rejoice in the present and the future. Together!"

The villagers clapped, some whistled, and the tension over the people lifted momentarily. The king clapped Gareth on the back and motioned the royal advisor forward.

The woman looked increasingly more strained since Brye had seen her last. Her dark locks were pinned up, but strands of gray peppered her temples. Her eyes, deep and streaked, were now marked with wrinkles that were absent months prior.

Roweena carried the long-colored cord and bound Gareth's left hand to Brye's right with Lenna's assistance. Her voice rang out in a loud, clear voice. "We bind you, the flesh, body, and bone: the soul and the mind. For now, you are one, and one until eternity. We bind you together. One, over two, over three."

Brye's heart dropped. Even though Roweena spoke strongly and with enough authority to give the ceremony the solemnity it deserved, the words rang hollow.

This woman! Can't she bring some presence or warmth to the ceremony? Should it at least not have some words to hope for?

You think very loudly.

Brye, who had been focusing over Gareth's shoulder, snapped her attention. His gaze was on her face with one eyebrow slightly raised.

Was she that transparent?

Not usually, Gareth's voice was as deep in her head as it was to her ears, but you are today.

Do you have some thoughts of your own? Or are mine more interesting?

A soft, internal chuckle that turned her organs into temporary mush. But his face did not change one iota. *I have plenty of thoughts. I just don't let them show. You look like you want to throttle me.*

"Brye, are you alright?" Lenna hissed between gritted teeth.

She gave a slight nod.

"Now, it is time for each to pledge with your binding vows." The royal advisor stepped back and waved Lenna to her side.

Nerves crept back in, slowly, like crawling spiders over her skin. Brye's mind went blank.

Gareth squeezed her hands. He spoke every word loud and clear, with reverence and warmth. His face lost its coldness with a bright and wholesome smile. He leaned in and whispered, "And even then, I wish to be reunited, for I walk beside thee in this life and the next. You are, and will be, the only partner for me."

Brye's mouth dropped. *He wants to be my mate. He wants me.*

Of course, I do. Haven't you realized it yet? I always have. I always saw you, Brye.

The sensation spread around her heart, and her voice cracked when it was time to repeat her binding vows. Gareth massaged her bound hand in his, and an unexpected giddiness invaded her senses. She wanted her happy ending.

The ending will be what we make of it, Brye. This will be what we decide it to be.

Her eyes filled with tears, and she smiled. Hope filled her heart. His eyes betrayed the same emotion, even if his face did not.

"You are now bound and mated," Roweena announced. "May this union provide Avalon with security and prosperity."

The king clapped Gareth's back again, and the queen grinned. Brye searched for Tara and Aiden. They were at the crowd's edge, holding on to each other. Lenna jumped up and down with a sincere smile and a twinkle in her eyes.

Before the well-wishers approached them, Gareth turned Brye by their clasped hands. He took her face gently with his free hand, rubbing her cheek with his thumb. Her lips parted.

The overwhelming longing from Gareth's dreams filtered into her body, and her heart contracted in response. He did not make her wait. The kiss was delicate, a temptation. So soft it made Brye's knees weak. She pulled at his tunic, wanting him to deepen the kiss, but he pulled away. The sensations grew stronger, and she discovered the feelings were not Gareth's. They were hers.

I want him.

With a roar in her ears, reality set in. Gareth looked unperturbed by the kiss but cleared his throat and looked away.

"Let us feast!" boomed the king.

Queen Celine's smile illuminated her face with a healthy glow. The woman wrapped her arms around Brye. When she let go, her eyes were wet with tears.

"I hoped this day would come, and now I am overwhelmed. Welcome to the family, dearest."

The queen's emotions spilled into Brye. Immense happiness and joy mixed with unwanted sorrow gripped her heart and made her eyes tear up.

Too many emotions and feelings entered her from different directions. It was like being an open wound. Dread invaded her. The line of well-wishers was growing. How would she manage a whole afternoon of people hugging, touching, and suffocating her with emotions? Her abilities were getting stronger and she still hadn't developed a way to tune them out.

Some of her apprehension must have read on her face, because Gareth pulled Brye closer. "Mother, I am sure you will have ample time to coddle Brye after today." Their bound hands forced them to stand side by side, separating her from the group. His calm protectiveness covered her like a blanket, soothing her nerves.

"You are right, my son." The queen let Brye go, wiping her eyes.

The king leaned forward. "Thank you for joining our family."

After that, Gareth intercepted each party member, keeping Brye from interacting physically with some.

Enid came through the line with both hands extended. "It was about time! Your mother would not be surprised at this turn of events. She would have been the happiest!"

A soft tingle ran over Brye's bound hand as if someone were rubbing her palm. She ignored it and concentrated on Enid.

"*Maither*?"

"Yes! Every mother wants their children to find happiness. I told you how important it was to be mated, and here you found one of the best catches in Avalon."

Brye hid her disappointment with a pinched smile. The tingle ceased. She hoped Enid's reference would trigger some memory of her mother. But it did not.

The last to come was Aiden and Tara, who waited back on purpose to avoid the crowds. Tara gave the prince a nod and only reached for her sister. Gratefully, Tara's emotions were not invasive. They didn't need to. They were written all over her face.

She was weary.

"I won't call you princess," Tara scowled.

"I would be insulted if you did," Brye replied quickly.

While Aiden hugged Brye, Tara whispered something in Gareth's ear. The prince tensed slightly.

"Where's Lenna?" Brye asked, searching through the crowd.

"We haven't seen her since the binding ceremony ended," Tara said.

Unease once again tickled along Brye's spine.

"Could you look for her?" Gareth asked, tugging at Brye's hand. "My mate might feel better knowing she is alright."

"Oh?" Tara cocked her head to the side and raised an eyebrow. Aiden wrapped an arm around her waist before she could voice another opinion.

"We will do that. See you soon." He maneuvered Tara away, heading toward the festivities.

Brye exhaled. "Thank you."

"We survived." Gareth pulled her to the side to look at the field of people.

"Yes, so far," Brye examined his face. "What now?"

"We celebrate."

"Oh, that sounds nice," Brye replied dryly.

His mouth twitched at the side in response. "Very." He guided her into the celebration. "Let's get it over with."

Vines and
Stones

Lenna

LENNA COULDN'T CONTROL HER pleasure in seeing Brye mated. Her hands trembled as she held the long ribbons. She repeated Roweena's words under her breath, hoping deep in her heart that they would forge a genuine connection.

Once finished, Lenna stood back and kept her hands clasped as they both faced each other and said their vows. Gareth's voice was firm, each word set in stone. It seemed Brye would falter for a moment, but then she smiled with tears in her eyes.

It was all the evidence Lenna needed.

My sister is falling in love.

Lenna searched the crowd and found Aiden and Tara holding hands. There was a moment when Aiden leaned into Tara and whispered something in her ear. She smiled and elbowed him. He chuckled under his breath.

It was beautiful to see her sisters happy. Lenna's feelings were overpowered by the one that laid beneath it all. Deep in her core, it slithered down her veins and wrapped itself around her heart, crushing it under the weight of its power.

Envy.

Lenna's face burned, and she gripped her hands tighter.

Was it a betrayal to be honest with her feelings? To say and mean what was deep in her heart? She wished she could erase the dangerous feeling taking root in her heart. But she couldn't.

Lenna wanted that type of happiness for herself.

Gareth's words came to her mind, *"Are there no good things to come for you, Lenna?"*

The ceremony ended, and Brye and Gareth were pronounced bound and mated. The crowd erupted in a frenzy of applause. Lenna joined, wincing when she clapped too ecstatically.

"Time to go," Roweena said, pinching Lenna's arm.

"But, there's a celebration—" Lenna replied, confused.

"It can go on without us," Roweena said as she walked away. "We have more pressing matters. Come..."

The music started with the king's enthusiasm. Aiden and Tara stood back, conversing, while Gareth and Brye waited by the altar for well-wishers.

Lenna debated rebelling, standing her ground, and staying with her sisters. It was an important day, and leaving was not her choice. An unexpected tug pulled her in Roweena's direction. She placed a hand over her chest, confused by the sensation.

"Well?" Roweena waved a hand in the direction of the village.

Lenna crossed her arms over her chest underneath her cloak and followed. A heaviness filled her stomach, and she bit down hard on her lower lip. She kept glancing back, watching as the crowd got smaller and smaller. With each step, her trepidation grew.

One thing was sure, whatever her training would be, it would be unpleasant.

Brye

The afternoon celebrations dragged on, and Brye was exhausted from the small talk. The rope pinched her bound hand, and sweat prickled the back of her neck uncomfortably. Gareth also lagged. He shuffled from one foot to another while keeping Brye from physical contact with others.

By the time the sixth barrel of ale was cracked open for villagers, Brye had enough. Her feet ached, her head slightly throbbed, and all she could think about was lying down to rest.

But there was more.

A tension built in the pit of her stomach that did not leave her all afternoon, no matter how much ale she drank.

"I don't know why I feel so uneasy," she finally admitted.

"You are tired. It has been a long day," Gareth whispered in her ear. His breath played with the curls that fell from her braided hair. Tiny shivers ran down her neck.

"Perhaps," she croaked, sipping the ale to clear her parched mouth.

What is the matter with me?

"I might have some ideas." He chuckled, drinking and giving her a side smile.

"You are getting too comfortable with that."

"With what?"

"Reading my mind."

Gareth examined his glass with a furrowed brow. He took some time to answer. "I can't read your mind, you know."

"It doesn't feel that way," she answered, turning in his direction. "The whole day, you seem to anticipate me. It's unnerving."

"I find it refreshing," Gareth said as he studied their bound hands, rubbing hers carefully with his fingers. Small warm currents ran up her arm, making her heart ache. She attempted to push the emotions aside, weary of feeling everything he felt. She paused, her heart skipping a beat.

They were hers.

The depth of the feeling shocked her. She looked away, studying the lake and the villagers mingling, anything to distract her from her own emotions. What business did her feelings have, getting involved in a promise she didn't even remember?

"We will cut the bindings once we return to the tower," he spoke low, still looking down. "I know they are increasing your discomfort."

She glanced at him again. "It's not so bad."

"Really?" He looked into her eyes, and his mask was momentarily gone. Before her was the boy of those borrowed memories, insecure and vulnerable, wanting to have a friend. His free hand went to her face, trailing down her jaw with his fingertips. She leaned into his hand and closed her eyes.

"Am I..." His soft voice caressed her heart, invading her senses.

"Yes?" Brye whispered back and opened her eyes. His hand stayed there for a moment longer.

Then his eyes shifted, becoming wary. He repeatedly blinked, standing back and cocking his head to the side.

"The music stopped."

Like a bucket of cold water, Brye straightened, and her senses returned to the present.

The conversations had dimmed, and people around them searched for the origin of the interruption. Gareth did the same, and his eyes settled behind Brye to a group of men, the king among them.

"What is it?" Brye turned and saw Duncan—the head training instructor—appear in the crowd, making his way to the king and queen. His stony face was grimmer than usual. They spoke in hushed tones. The queen paled, and her hand flew to her mouth.

Gareth tensed by her side. His nervousness and restlessness vibrated into her, increasing her heart rate. She placed a hand on his taunt arm.

"Something's wrong," he said under his breath.

The king dismissed Duncan and spoke rapidly to the people around him. They tensed and reacted in hushed tones to what he was saying, but the energy immediately changed. The whispers grew like a sound wave, and only one word crashed into them.

The wall.

Gareth went through the frozen crowd to Duncan, Brye keeping pace with him. His hand was so tight in hers that her fingers grew numb.

"Gareth—" *You're hurting me.*

His grip instantly readjusted, letting blood flow back to her fingertips.

They found Duncan giving orders to the contingent of warriors and farmers drinking by the table. They all quickly finished their drinks and made their way out.

Brye couldn't breathe. It only worsened when Gareth grabbed the older man by the arm.

"Tell me," he ordered.

"Your highness." His tone was low and urgent. "The wall--"

Brye felt it first in her chest, a rumbling so low, she didn't hear it with her ears. Slowly, it grew in tenor, filtering through the ground and filling the air. Surprise turned to terror as the noise grew in intensity.

The king yelled an order, but it was lost in the rising commotion. Women and men picked up small children. People began to scream—first a young woman, then a few older people. The vibrations intensified until the ground underneath them flipped over tables and barrels of ale.

Drinks and food fell to the ground. Wide-eyed and terrified, people ran in every direction, trying to find the source of the noise, while others headed back toward the village.

"Take them to safety," the king ordered the warriors as he exchanged a look with Gareth. "Get the children out of here!"

Those braver than most decided to head toward the quaking and thunderous groans. Brye was not particularly brave but still picked up her skirts as Gareth bolted toward the west field.

They did not speak, Brye stumbling along as the tremors continued. She gritted her teeth in an attempt to regain control over her body. After another stumble, Gareth half-dragged her to keep her upright.

Once they passed the woods and the wall came into view, Brye bit down on her free hand to prevent the gasp from escaping her lips.

"What the..." Gareth gaped.

The thorny vines and branches that had grown into the wall were now breaking and pulling it down. A screeching came from the small group of yew trees that stood parallel to the wall.

This can't be happening again.

A crack echoed, and one of the yews uprooted itself, transforming before their eyes. Another wraith shaped as a bird towered over the gawking mass of people, with eyes of blue flames and a beak-shaped by sharp thorny branches. Its large and dangerous wings spread and stretched, preparing to take flight.

At the first flap, it lifted debris and dirt from the fallen wall. Gareth dragged Brye against his chest, shielding her as pellets of small rocks flew, hitting bystanders.

Groans and cries of pain rang around them. Gareth flinched. Brye winced as his pain filtered into her body through their bound hands.

The wraith took flight and made its way along the wall to the west fields, raining branches and leaves.

"Are you alright?" Gareth ground out, checking her for injuries.

Brye did the same, running her unbound hand down his arms. "Yes, I'm fine, but you—"

"I'll heal quickly. It's nothing." He pulled back. Brye's hand went to her forehead as she examined her surroundings. The onlookers who came were now splayed all around in different places. Cries of children and the wounded echoed around them.

Gareth winced, rubbing the back of his head.

"Let me," Brye said, but he waved her away. He then looked down at their bound hands.

"I'm sorry." He retrieved a small knife from his boot and cut the bindings. Brye flexed her fingers, massaging them to regain some feeling. Frustration and disappointment were brief companions in her chest—the untying of the bindings was supposed to be sacred, a special moment between newly mated people.

A moment now robbed from her.

The heaviness in the pit of her stomach did not go away. So many unsaid words were on her lips, but none came out.

Aiden and Tara appeared, eyes wide and pale.

"Aiden, get the rest of the warriors. We need to find the creature and get it down," Gareth ordered, rubbing his free hand. "Tara, stay here. Keep an eye on the king and queen. They insist on staying. You are in charge."

"Got it," Tara responded.

"I'll tend to the injured with Enid," Brye said.

Gareth's mouth worked as if he had words to be said. But he only nodded and set out to follow the tree bird.

Tara dragged Aiden toward her and planted a desperate kiss on his lips. His arm went around her waist to deepen it.

"Aiden!" Gareth bellowed. "Leave the girl, damnit!"

Aiden whispered to Tara, making her laugh before letting go. He ran behind Gareth and the other warriors.

"What did he say to you?" Brye asked.

"That Gareth's jealous."

Brye blushed but remembered something. "What did you say to him before? When you and Aiden came to greet us?"

Tara sighed, but her tone and voice grew serious. "That if he hurts you, I'd kill him."

"I can handle myself, little sister."

"Just because you can doesn't mean you have to."

Brye huffed out a breath and motioned to the crowd with her head. "Come on. We have to get to work."

Know your
place

Lenna

LENNA SAT WITH HER back against the battlements of the Royal Tower. Her head pounded and her ears rang. She had been right about the training.

She hated it.

Lenna placed a cold hand over her forehead. She would trade training with Roweena for the dullest of celebrations. For Founders' sake, she'd even take making flower crowns at Beltane again. Even being stuck in the In-Between was better than the torture of having her magic pushed beyond its limits.

"Again," Roweena ordered. "You have rested long enough."

Lenna rubbed her face and stood up carefully, keeping her eyes on the royal advisor. She had been ordered to create the mist, and that was hours ago. Lenna knew creating the mists to shield the island from the outside was imperative. The mists had been absent for days, and with it, the island's protection.

Was there a connection between the bindings and the mists?

Could the magical bindings around the island draw them in naturally? But as the bonds broke, the mists would not form. Roweena couldn't create them and was now focused on Lenna's magic. Could it be that the older woman was being pressured for answers about the magical animals and the lack of mists?

She probably doesn't have them.

"What are you waiting for?" Roweena hissed. "Do as I say."

Lenna released a long breath and rubbed her face again before extending her hands. She closed her eyes, concentrating on the moisture in the air. She imagined it expanding into tiny floating droplets. She visualized each drop merging and being shifted by the wind.

As the moisture took form, the tightening and pressure around Lenna increased exponentially. She struggled, biting hard on her lip. The strain was too much, like having her entire body in a vice.

Lenna grabbed her stomach. She licked her broken lips and winced. Opening her eyes, she discovered a small cloud of mist overhead. It was consistent and covered most of the top of the tower.

But not enough.

Roweena stared at her with clenched teeth before starting to pace.

Never enough.

"Better than when we started after Beltane, but still pathetic."

"I can gain more experience if I train on my own," Lenna suggested.

"We can't waste any more time. We need you to do this."

"Why?" Lenna wiped the sweat from her brow.

"Don't ask questions."

"I think I am entitled to them. Why do I need to do this? Why can't you?"

Roweena's nostrils flared, and her jaw tensed.

Lenna wobbled over to Roweena. "What is going on, Roweena?"

The royal advisor took a step closer, her eyes dark. "How dare you question me?"

Lenna's head snapped back, hitting the wall behind her with a crack. A sharp pain radiated from her head and her cheek. She touched her face and felt warm liquid and a jagged cut along her face.

Roweena had backhanded her with her ring.

"Why—"

An angry screech exploded, followed by a prolonged squawk. An empty feeling filled her stomach as Lenna walked on trembling legs to the edge of the battlement. She squinted as the setting sun was in her eyes, but a dark form appeared on the horizon even at this distance. A growing body with wings, ready to take flight.

Roweena stood behind her, wide-eyed and full of fear. Her hand hovered over her open mouth. "No, not another one."

"What do we do?" Lenna asked.

The woman stood frozen with her face drained of color. Lenna placed a hand on her sleeve and repeated the question. Roweena jumped at the contact and grabbed Lenna's arm. "We have to go."

The sun had almost set once they reached the west fields. Lenna and Roweena were equally dazed at the sight before them.

A giant tree-like bird came into view, shadowed by the waning light. Its nails were long and destructive, while its wings threw pellets of twigs and rocks in every direction. It took flight and landed on top of the further south, right on the wall. The pressure of its toes and claws crumbled the stones. It studied them with small eyes made up of blue blazes.

Roweena pushed Lenna toward the winged creature. "Tame it!"

"What?" Lenna backed up in shock, but Roweena shoved her again. She lost her footing and fell with her hands hitting the stony grass.

"A little incentive will be beneficial. Tame it!"

Lenna trembled, holding herself tightly together. The tree bird screeched loudly, projecting branches and leaves from its beak. Lenna covered her face while Roweena moved away.

Lenna gripped her fists and bit hard on her bloody lower lip, tasting blood.

What am I to do?

Unlike the fire lizard, taming this bird seemed impossible. What element would counteract the magic? Would water, fire, or earth debilitate it? How was she supposed to know?

The tree bird used its claws to crush the remaining parts of the wall. The structure fell into a heap of rubble and ripped vines. Once it had a small amount of discarded stones, it hopped slightly and flapped its wings, launching more debris in Lenna's direction.

Lenna ducked and moved back, protecting her face from the projectiles. She could not save her body as small stones collided with the back of her cloak.

Element. I need an element... But which one?

Fire echoed an unfamiliar male voice inside Lenna's head.

Who was that?

She searched, trying to find the source of the voice. It had no accent. It wasn't the wolf.

A group of warriors entered the field, carrying bows and arrows, Gareth and Aiden among them. Lenna ran in their direction, Roweena following behind her. She ignored Roweena's piercing gaze. She ignored the bile in the back of her throat. Gareth's eyes widened, and Aiden grabbed her arm.

"What happened to you?" He reached for the cut on her face, holding her chin to look closer.

Lenna flicked his hand away. He frowned down at her.

"Fire. We need fire," she spoke directly to Gareth, who scowled.

"Explain."

"We need to burn it with fire. It's made of wood. Launch fire-covered arrows at it."

"We can't risk missing the bird and burning the fields or the trees," Aiden said.

"Not if you are good with arrows," Lenna pointed out.

"It's a risk we must take," Gareth exhaled. "Unless the royal advisor can come up with a better idea." He spoke directly to Roweena.

She paled, her arms crossed over her chest. "I will remind you, I have had this role since before you were born."

"Prove it." Gareth waved a hand towards the tree bird. It continued to hop and destroy what was left of the wall. "Do your job!"

Gareth's hostility toward the woman only increased Lenna's discomfort. Roweena was dangerous at the best of times. Something about the woman smelled of desperation, and Lenna knew it would be directed at her.

The bird flapped its wings repeatedly, launching even more debris in their direction.

Gareth reached out for her, but Aiden shielded her from the brunt of the flying debris. He pulled her against him, covering her head with his arms. She could feel the erratic beating of his heart against her cheek, and warmth flooded her body, pushing away the terror. She gripped his tunic and held him close, smelling him.

"Are you alright?" he released her and ran his hands down her arms. She pulled away as quickly as she could.

"Yes, are you?"

"Nothing I can't endure."

Roweena pushed him aside. "Move!"

She grabbed Lenna's arm and dragged her toward the bird. Lenna winced as Roweena's nails dug into the flesh.

Gareth called out, but Rowenna ignored him. By now, they were close enough to the creature for it to look down and squawk madly. Lenna flinched, but Roweena made her stay firm. The tree bird flapped its wings twice and took flight.

"It's getting away," Lenna exclaimed.

"He won't get far," Roweena said. She held her palm up in front of her and widened her stance.

It was like being hit by lightning. No matter how much she fought for breath, Lenna couldn't get enough air in her lungs. She recognized the symptoms as her knees gave out. She softened her fall with her hands. Her eyes searched for Roweena only to discover the monster in her place.

She stood tall, imposing, with thick, black tattoo-type knots around her body. The knots pulsed and tentacles reached along the ground in Lenna's direction. They attached themselves to her hands and ankles, burning into her skin. Like leeches, they drained the magic out of her.

A scream crawled up her throat, but she bit hard over her broken and bloodied lower lip. The copper taste filled her mouth.

Aiden and Gareth tried to reach her, but more and more debris flew into the air, preventing them from doing so.

Roweena raised her hand and drew the wind to her. As she did, her eyes grew intense, and she regained color to her waned cheeks. She placed her palms together and then pulled them away from each other. A bow and arrow made of fire appeared from the space between her hands.

But the fire's intensity was too dim to cause any real damage. The tree bird settled itself further down the wall.

Lenna was lying on her back, losing strength as another tentacle grabbed her leg. Black patches formed in her vision. She was so tired and cold. All she wanted to do was sleep.

Stay awake, Lenna. See the threads for what they are.

The same male voice as before called to her. She attempted to answer, but no words came out. Exhaustion made its way through her body, but Lenna's heart fought to keep her alive. It beat erratically in her chest, pumping blood to her cold limbs.

Is this what it is like to die?

The voice dissipated from her mind, echoing once again for her to stay awake. She obeyed and refocused her attention on Roweena.

Like a parasite, Roweena drank up her magic to fuel her own. The more she drained, the bigger the bow and arrow became until it was half the size of the bird. Before the bird made one final attempt to fly away, Roweena launched the arrow and, this time, hit her target. The bird erupted into flames.

The dying animal did not go quietly. With its last breath, the bird flew into the newly planted fields, and the wheat seedlings took to the fire like water.

The world erupted into flames once more.

A snap of tension released inside Lenna. She closed her eyes, taking ragged breaths. Her hand went to her face, and she knew. It was a knowing that was becoming overly familiar.

Another island knot broke.

She kept breathing slowly, one breath after another, until she could force herself to sit up. Her eyes scanned the field. The corpse of the mythical animal only served as a wick for the fire.

Roweena was drained, with overly bright eyes and a clenched jaw. The knots and bindings around her body receded, as well as the tentacles attached to Lenna's ankles and hands. She glared down at her, making her clammy skin crawl.

"Know your place," Roweena hissed. She picked up her skirts and left Lenna facing the inferno in front of her.

Gareth finally reached her, Aiden on his heels. He leaned down to help her stand. His mouth was moving, but she couldn't make out the words with the roar still in her ears. Aiden's hands were on her shoulders, keeping her straight, and his eyes, intensely blue, focusing on her.

The roar receded, and his voice penetrated with too much clarity.

"Lenna? Lenna, talk to me!"

No.

She didn't want to talk to him or anyone. She let out a frustrated moan and took a step back. His hand fell away from her.

She shook her head and bit down hard on her wounded lower lip.

"Lenna, you need help."

Lenna wrapped her arms over her stomach, turned, and walked away. She ignored Aiden's cursed calls and Gareth's orders to come back.

She had nothing to say to them. How could they possibly understand what she had experienced and seen?

The field was filled with warriors calling for help and water to turn down the fire. Gareth bellowed orders, and there was a sense of organized chaos. A snap and a hiss of the growing fire behind her only reminded her of the inevitable.

There was nothing she could do as everything went up in flames.

Brye

Brye and Tara were the last to reach the fields. They stayed behind, tending to the wounded while all the healthy were called to the wheat fields. Gareth was further away, speaking to the king and a group of men. He gave Brye a pained, tired look. Her heart ached for him.

Tara hauled her in Aiden's direction, where he was collecting charred wheat with a pitchfork. His body was covered in soot and sweat from work.

"Where's Lenna?" Tara asked.

Aiden pointed with the pitchfork to the woods at the edge of the field, farther away.

"Are you well?" Tara gripped his arm.

He nodded. "Go see your sister. Something odd happened to her."

Lenna was sitting with her back against the tree, facing away from the field. Her body curved in on itself as she hugged her knees to her chest. Brye knelt and took her hands. Instantly the sense of cold and exhaustion invaded her senses, almost unsettling her. Tara placed a warm hand on Lenna's forehead.

Lenna shook them off. "Leave me alone. No reading."

"Lenna, you are not well," Tara pointed out.

"Stop it, both of you." She stood up with support from the tree. "Stop treating me like a child." Her voice cracked.

"We will when you stop acting like one!" Tara snapped back.

Lenna looked away, her cheeks burning.

"Lenna?" Brye took her hand firmly.

"Tara, why don't you go help Aiden? The warriors are in over their heads, and you are stronger than most." Lenna ordered. "Brye, you are a princess now. It would be best if you tended the wounded. Some of the warriors have gotten too close to the fire. "

"What about you?" Brye asked, pulling away. Lenna didn't meet her gaze, only looked north, her posture stiff.

"I am of no use right now. I have done my part. It's time you both do yours." She walked away. "Don't wait up for me."

"Lenna." Brye went to grab her, but Tara held her back.

"Leave her."

Brye watched as Lenna's form grew smaller and smaller until she lost sight of her through the thicket of trees. "You saw her. She is as pale as a ghost."

"She doesn't want to be coddled right now. Whatever happened with Roweena has left her empty. She wants to be alone."

"What she wants and needs are two different things."

"I know, Brye!" Tara snapped. "She won't get far. Let's give her some time, and then we can look for her. We both know where she is going."

Brye exhaled and glanced around, orienting herself. "The White Thorn Tree."

"Yes." Tara patted her sister's back. "The White Thorn Tree."

Behind them, more wheat popped, hissed, and exploded as it rose in flames.

Unraveling

Brye

BRYE'S BODY WAS EXHAUSTED when the moon cleared the sky, and the fire died out. They managed to save the field, but with the magic gone, it was useless until the following season.

Gareth and the king were covered in soot, speaking in low tones. His eyes settled a moment on her, and her chest ached. Brye gave him a pained smile, and his lips twitched before he returned to his conversation.

It was an endless, horrible night. Brye wiped her sweaty brow and took notes of those injured by the tree bird. The queen and Enid stayed with the wounded from the ceremony, ensuring they had what they needed.

Aiden and Tara supervised the cleaning up. They worked with pitchforks, carts, and water barrels to ensure all fires were out. By the time they were done, both looked like shadows of their former selves. Every time Tara wiped her brow with a cloth, her face became a dark mask, with tiny tendrils of red peeking through. Her good dress was stained and torn on the sides to make it easier for her to move.

Everyone was taken care of, and the mood was sober and sad. All the celebratory feelings had burned with the fire. The crowd returned to the village, dragging their feet and holding their heads down.

Gareth finished his conversation with the king and walked toward Brye. She stood, equally covered in soot and grime, against the tree Lenna had vacated some time before. She held her kit close to her body. Gareth released a long breath and took the kit. She reluctantly gave it to him, too tired to care. Aiden and Tara joined them by the tree.

"I think you can all head home," Gareth said. "We will report early to assess the damages and retake inventory tomorrow. Aiden, let your father know we will need him here too."

"I will do so, your highness." He took Tara's hand to leave, but Brye spoke, stopping them.

"Lenna has gone out by herself." She looked at Tara. "I think we gave her enough time to think."

Tara nodded and released Aiden's hand.

"I think you should leave her be. If she wants to be alone, it would be best to respect her wishes," Gareth insisted.

"You don't know her enough to make that statement," Brye said.

"No," Gareth regarded her. "I don't. But I would want my word taken seriously if it were me."

Tara let out a sigh. "He is right, Brye."

"So, neither of you is going to look for her?" Aiden asked. Tara squeezed his arm, and he exhaled a long breath.

Gareth rubbed the back of his neck. "I will send someone to fetch her and take her home."

Tara ground her teeth and gave a curt nod. Both left, hand in hand, at a quick pace.

"She hates agreeing with you," Brye said as she watched them leave. Tara was arguing with Aiden.

"Tara hates easily. It's Aiden's insistence that surprises me." Gareth rubbed his face and the back of his neck again, spreading soot over his features.

"Why?"

"I... I can't explain it very well."

"Try," Brye insisted.

Gareth hummed under his breath, gaze bouncing around the trees. "There was a short time I thought there was something between Aiden and Lenna."

Brye chuckled wryly. "You're not wrong. Though, I think it is more on Lenna's side. Aiden's love for Tara is too deep to look at anyone else."

"Which makes one wonder if the whole concept of mating is what we think it is," he spoke slowly, looking down at her kit.

"What do you mean?"

"Avalon is so isolated. I am wondering, if choosing a mate is destiny, or is it a choice?"

"Can't it be both?"

Gareth shrugged.

"Having second thoughts?" Brye asked.

"No, you?"

Brye crossed her arms and gave Gareth an assessing look. His tunic was torn, stained, and unsalvageable. His well-trimmed beard had degraded to a dark black, and his eyes crinkled. Compared to Dagonet's symmetrical features or even Aiden's quick wit and smile, Gareth rang short.

But there was something about Gareth that drew her. His steadiness centered her, rooting her in a place of comfort.

"Not anymore," she smiled. "Then again, ask me tomorrow."

Gareth's chuckle sounded off and almost as if he rarely used it. "We should head to the Royal Tower. Tomorrow promises to be a long day." He motioned for her to walk ahead. Brye tentatively placed her hand in the crook of his arm. He stiffened, then relaxed at her touch.

"I'll attempt not to read you. I promise," she whispered. They walked side by side. The only sounds were the hushed conversations of villagers and their steps along the paths.

Gareth broke the silence. "I am sorry that the ceremony was not up to your expectations."

"That's all right. I don't believe the tree bird helped." His features tightened. "But, none of it was your fault, you know?"

He sighed and nodded.

Edgar received them once they arrived at the Tower.

"Your highness, the king and queen have retired and asked for their meals to be sent to their rooms. Would you and the princess like some food as well?"

"Yes, Edgar, that would be appreciated. Thank you," Gareth instructed. Brye's mouth dried as realization slowly came back. She was going to share a room with Gareth and all it entailed. She cleaned her clammy hands over her already dirty skirt.

Once they were in his bedroom, Gareth closed the door and leaned his head back against the wood.

"Finally," he whispered.

"Is it true what you said? That everything we say can be overheard?

"Unless it is in your head, yes." He sat on the chair, extending his long legs in front of him. His shoulders and face relaxed.

"How do you know?"

"Beltran pointed it out," he said with a shrug. "He sensed there was no real privacy inside the walls of Avalon. But there was no way to confirm it. As a precaution, I prefer to keep things to myself."

Brye nodded, her gaze wandering around the room. The fireplace was lit, and the windows were open to let in the cool night air. The result was a warm and cozy atmosphere. On the far side, there was a privacy screen made of cloth. The fresh flowers on the table filled the room with the familiar scent of home.

The bed was made up of deep, burgundy blankets with embroidery that she recognized instantly. Lenna's delicate hand decorated the cloth with vines and flowers all over the hem of the fabric. It was not the only recognizable thing. At the edge of the room sat the trunk she had made up that morning with her sisters.

"What are you thinking?" Gareth asked.

"The room. It's different," she said, opening her trunk and pulling out a small square of soap and a jar of scented oil.

"I would expect it to be. I am going to be sharing it."

She looked at him over her shoulder as she set her things on the closed trunk.

He was filthy, and his blonde hair was standing on end, but his dark eyes, lost in thought, drew her attention.

"And what are *you* thinking?" she asked.

There was a knock on the door.

"Enter," Gareth called.

Edgar entered carrying a tray with a bowl of fruits, bread, cheese, and some cold meats that he placed on the table with a pitcher of ale.

"Thank you," Brye smiled.

"You're welcome, your highness," responded the retainer before leaving. Brye's cheeks burned.

"That will take some getting used to."

"It does, but you will still be Brye to those that matter." Gareth stood and stretched. "The bathing room is through that door. I'll give you some privacy."

"Where are you going?"

"I need to speak to someone. I will be back later. You get some rest." He reached for the door.

"I thought..." her voice trailed off.

He turned, one hand on the door handle. "Yes?"

Brye blushed and realized she did not have anything to say. She did not want to be alone. She had slept in the same room with her sisters for most of her life. The thought of spending her time alone tonight tied her stomach in knots.

"If you wait, you can take a bath after me." She gave one look at her mucky complexion and winced. "I have some oils to help you relax."

"That's all right. I'll bathe in the stream."

"Will you be long?" she asked, striving for nonchalance, her hands stiffly pressed together.

His mouth twitched. "Not very long."

"Would you like me to wait for you?" Brye reran her hands over her skirt.

Gareth leaned back against the door and crossed his arms.

"Brye, is something the matter?"

"No." Brye placed her hands on her hips. "We were mated today. I think I am supposed to ask these questions?"

He gave her an assessing look. "Really?"

"Yes! Really."

"And here I thought you simply wanted my company," he remarked. "Now I have discovered it's just you fulfilling your role as the dutiful mate."

"Only part of it," she mumbled, looking away.

Half a chuckle escaped Gareth's lips. Then he sighed, rubbing his face with both hands. It only made him grease the soot in new directions.

She was tempted to clean it for him.

Especially the stubborn lock that stands on end.

"It's been a long day. I wanted to give you some time to yourself and leave you to rest. I want you to feel comfortable."

"So... you will not be sleeping here?" she asked slowly.

"Would you like me to?" His voice was cautious.

"If I said no, where would you sleep?"

"I usually spend nights sleeping under a tree in the woods. I rarely sleep here."

"Why?"

"I like sleeping out in the open. It soothes me."

"If I said you could stay, would it continue? I mean, the sleeping outdoors."

"Brye." Gareth rubbed the back of his neck harder and groaned. "I can't read you. You need to be clear with me, like you have always been. What do you want?"

Brye cocked her head to the side. He was weary and tense, waiting for her to decide. It was a critical moment for both of them. He was letting her set the tone for their relationship—all that power at her fingertips.

But she already knew what she wanted. She knew it when she said her vows. She confirmed it every time she searched for him, and her chest ached. It was a path she started walking a long time ago. Of course, she lost her way, but now, as she looked into the dark eyes of her newly mated companion, Brye knew this was where she wanted to be.

She wanted to be with him.

Gareth reached for the door.

"I'm not a light sleeper," she blurted out. She inhaled swiftly, gathering herself. "Sometimes it takes a good shake to wake me up, but…"

He stopped, his gaze leery and confused.

She continued hesitantly, "But I think you should know. I tend to share dreams. I can't wake myself to sever the connection, and I have no control over it. How do you feel about that?"

"I don't mind," he replied thickly, looking down at her face.

"You don't care if I dip into your dreams? See your secrets? Know what you might be hiding? A person's mind is not their own when they dream. We both know you have many secrets."

"No," he replied coolly. "Once I remembered who you are, I knew it was a possibility."

"And you still pursued me?"

"I did and would do it again. Maybe I am tired of secrets."

"Then." Brye stood taller and looked at him squarely. "I would like you to."

"You would like me to, what?" He looked expectantly.

"Sleep here with me." She flushed. "Preferably starting tonight."

Gareth inhaled, frozen for a few heartbeats as if trying to process her words. He then took Brye's face softly in his hands. It was what always confused her, his gentleness. He was so large and grim, yet his soft touch was disarming. He leaned his forehead against hers. She shivered.

"I'm all dirty," he whispered.

"You worry about that too much," she replied.

He rubbed his mouth tentatively against hers as if asking for permission. She gripped his wrists close to her face. His mouth pressed harder, and she let him in. The kiss changed to an exploration of taste and sensation.

And she wanted it all. Not his feelings, hers.

Her hands wrapped around his neck, and he gripped her waist. Her body fit along with his, warm and hard. It ignited the spark kindling inside her. His tongue explored her mouth until she forgot how to breathe. He was the first to regain some composure, untangling her hands.

"I will be back soon."

She nodded, not trusting herself to speak.

He let go of her, and his absence left her unstable. He shook his head as if to clear it and gave her a scorching gaze before leaving the room.

Brye sat on the bed and took deep breaths. She placed a trembling hand over her chest and was not surprised to feel her heart racing.

Destiny or choice? Which one was it?

"Both," she whispered to herself. "It's both."

❦

Lenna

Propelled by anger and resentment, Lenna marched up the north field. In her condition, she wasn't going to get far, but she needed to get away, to think.

Her mind raced to process what she knew.

One, the island was bound by magic.

Two, the bindings are like the threads of tapestries.

Three, Roweena's magic seems to be unstable. Or is it diminishing?

Four, Roweena's drains my magic to use for herself. This was by far the worst part.

The tentacles wrapped around her ankles and wrists had left red, painful welts on her skin and had drained her entirely of magic. It explained why she had been constantly tired after training or the mark on her wrist during the first couple of sessions. Roweena had been draining her magic all along.

But then why did she let me train by myself? What could have been her goal?

She wrapped the cloak tightly around her, cold to the bone. But it was not caused by the temperature outside. Thanks to the absent mists, the night was warmer than usual. She was trembling from the inside. Her teeth chattered, and her hands clammed up. She rubbed them together under her cloak.

The bindings around the island, her, and Roweena were similar. They appeared like threaded tattoos. Both she and Roweena were bound in some way to the island. The woman had found a way to use the bindings to her benefit.

Did the same person make the bindings? Was she then a Bondmaker?

No, all evidence pointed out that she was an Elemental. If she were a Bondmaker, then she would have been able to restore the knots in the field. Everything pointed to Roweena being powerless to stop the breaking of knots and bonds.

Then how can she suck the magic out of me?

There was no evidence that an Elemental could accomplish such a task unless she were a Bondmaker.

But what do I know about Elementals and Bondmakers?

Lenna stopped stiffly when she reached the White Thorn Tree.

Maither.

Had Roweena done something to her? What would happen to her sisters if the woman learned about their abilities? Lenna massaged her temples and took deep breaths. Anxiety pitted her stomach.

She'd use them. Drain them, just like she was doing with me.

No. She couldn't let that happen. She would not let her sisters fall prey to the vicious woman and her needs. Lenna would protect them. More now than ever.

She paced. The White Thorn Tree loomed over her, its branches swayed lightly, and the fragrance of the flowers filled the air.

Lenna rubbed her achy eyes and head. She needed to rest. She pulled the cloak around her tightly for warmth and laid down under the tree. Fallen flowers and leaves softened the ground. The fragrance was intoxicating, wrapping her up like a blanket. She curled into a fetal position and immediately fell into a deep sleep.

Making
Connections

Brye

BRYE LOOKED UP AT the dark ceiling. It was too late to ask herself if she was prepared. She had followed her instinct, and it led her to Gareth. None of the men she encountered made her feel anything except a passing fancy. Perhaps a few ignited a small flame, but it dwindled quickly. Even Dagonet, her longest flirtation, did not move her.

He did not make me burn.

Wasn't that what Tara had said when Lenna asked her?

"If you could describe it, Tara..." Lenna had picked up the embroidery on the table, playing with the small designs, "in like, a phrase or word...."

Tara had stood, stretching her hands to the ceiling, her joints popping. "Oh, that's easy. It is like being on fire."

The room had grown silent, swelling with tension, and Tara paled. "Oh... Oh Lenna, I'm sorry. I didn't think..."

"It's all right." Lenna stood up, setting her work on the table. She smiled at her sisters. "I understood your meaning."

Brye was so confused. Her body was tight as a string, stretched to the limit, ready to snap. Being on fire? Is that what it was like? How would she know if Gareth did not come back?

Brye looked out of the window again. "Back soon... Soon needs to be redefined...."

Deciding she had waited long enough, Brye got up from the blanket and prepared for bed. She ran her hand over the new sleeping dress the queen had given her. It was short, with no sleeves and a plunging neckline. It barely reached mid-thigh. It was one of the most revealing garments she had ever worn.

She braided her hair to keep it out of the way and went to bed. Unlike the ones in her own home, this one was raised on what seemed like rows of rope that ran diagonally and across a frame. The mattress was filled with soft material covered in blankets. She laid under the covers with her hands over her stomach.

The blankets were cool but not itchy. The pillows were plump and soft. She closed her eyes and focused on her breathing. She forced her body to relax, first her achy toes and feet, then her tight calves, thighs, and hips. She breathed in slowly and exhaled. The room grew warm, and her lids heavy. The blankets smelled musky, with an earthy scent that played with her senses. It invaded her dreams only to drift away.

Sandalwood.

A creak woke her up with a snap. Her head was heavy with sleep, and her eyes were sticky. Embers played with active flames in the fireplace. She had fallen asleep, but not very long ago.

The creak came again, and the door handle moved. It opened quietly, and Gareth crept in. He stopped in his tracks when he saw Brye sitting in bed.

His dirty blond hair was still dripping water and curled around his head. His clothes were moist from putting them back on before he had finished drying. Gareth kept playing with a dirty shirt, gripping it from one hand to the next.

Brye flushed as an unexpected warmth ran through her system.

"You're awake," he whispered.

"Just now," she groggily replied, rubbing her face.

Nodding, he cleared his throat. "I need to change for bed,"

"Of course." Brye laid back down and turned away. "Is there a side you wish to sleep on?"

"Not really."

She closed her eyes as he shuffled and moved around the room. A few moments later, the bed dipped, and her body tensed.

"Good night," he mumbled.

Brye jerked up. "Good night?"

"All right, good morning? It seems appropriate, I guess. It's only a couple of hours till sunrise," Gareth muttered, keeping his eyes closed.

Brye groaned and laid back down.

"I will remind you, I can't read minds," he pointed out. "You hold the advantage there."

She turned on her side, focusing on his profile in the fire's dim light. His face appeared relaxed, but his chiseled chest drew her attention. The tattooed wolf was a dark mark around his heart. The long claw marks and scars on his torso created shadows over his skin.

"Who made your tattoos?"

"I don't know. They appeared on that terrible night."

The way his voice dipped at the end was enough to know what night he was referring to. The night her mother disappeared. But Brye didn't want to remember the pain.

"Who makes your soap?"

"Is it unpleasant?" He quirked a smile.

"No," she spoke softly, her hands playing with the blanket's edge, close to his bare arm. If she extended one finger, she could touch him. His body heat came out in waves in her direction. She was too aware of him in the bed.

"Is there something on your mind, Brye?" His voice was barely above a whisper.

"I don't know how to ask," she admitted. He turned his body on his side, facing her. "But maybe I can show you."

She took his hand and closed her eyes. She sent her feelings and emotions toward him through her fingertips as if they were words caressing his skin.

Brye shared the erratic beat of her heart, the heat that grew in her chest and traveled down her body, centering itself between her legs. As she opened up to him, he tugged at her thoughts and emotions, reading into them.

Gareth exhaled slowly, his breath tickling her face. She opened her eyes, and he moved closer. She shivered, biting down on her lip.

"Brye, can I touch you?" His mouth whispered close to hers.

"Yes," she pleaded. "Yes, please."

He pulled her flush against him. His hand rested on her waist as he dipped his mouth to hers. Her free hand settled on his face. The kiss was different yet the same as all those that came before. His tongue explored, tasted, and teased.

It wasn't enough for Brye. She needed him closer. Laying back, she pulled him half on top of her.

Gareth groaned as her hands explored his naked chest. Her tingling fingers tapped into his emotions. His need was explosive. A build-up held back by sheer control.

She wanted to break it free.

His mouth found a sensitive place on her neck. She almost came out of her skin. His hands roamed her waist to cup her breast over the sleep dress. He was taunting her, sending shocks down her body.

There was too much fabric between them. She shifted, dragging the sleep dress up until it gathered at her hips.

"In a hurry?" He chuckled breathlessly.

"A bit." She nipped his lip as her fingers fumbled with his pants. More skin, more... she needed every inch of him against every inch of her. "You?"

"No." He pulled the dress up and over her head and tossed it aside. Gareth's eyes roamed her naked body with reverence. "I've waited too long to rush."

He sat back, working the laces of his pants. Her breathing escalated, mouth dry, as she watched his fingers. She reached forward to help, but he swatted her hands away gently.

"Patience," he said, shimmying out of the pants and kicking them to the end of the bed.

Everything south of her brain went molten, even as nerves tangled through her throat. Not that she had anything to compare it to, but he was impressive. This was really happening.

It's like being on fire.

She was certainly burning for more. Patience was not her virtue tonight.

Brye pushed a hand underneath her to lean forward, her other hand reaching for him once more, but he was swift. He captured her wrist, his large hand dwarfing hers, and pressed a kiss into the center of her palm. Warmth pulsed through her, seeping through her blood and settling in her core.

"More," she demanded as he settled her hand on his shoulder and crawled back over her. He kissed her at the same time as he pressed his entire body into her from chest to knees. Brye moaned into his mouth, her hands tracing the line of his shoulders.

He savored every part of her, taking his time. When he kissed and played with her breasts, she nearly came undone, arching her back and strangling the life out of his hair. It only intensified when one of his hands made its way between her legs. He paused, running circles on her inner thigh with his fingers. Brye squirmed, but he did not yield her to demands.

"Gareth, please..."

"Please what?"

"Anything," she nearly sobbed.

He had the audacity to chuckle at her, the infuriating man that he was. But he finally placed his fingers between her legs, and Brye cried out, the pleasure nearly unbearable in its intensity. He slipped a single finger inside her... then another, and Founders' help her, it was so tight, and still it wasn't enough.

She wanted more.

She wanted it now.

Brye's hands gripped his shoulders, and without control she pushed her need into him. Gareth groaned, and his fingers continued to work her closer to the edge, the rhythm faster and deeper, and it was still not enough.

Brye arched back and muffled a scream, her entire body tensing as ripples of pleasure raced over her.

"You're magnificent," he whispered against her mouth, kissing her flushed lips. "A goddess."

It was an effort to string words together. "And you talk too much." Brye ran her hands through his hair. "I need you inside me."

He settled his weight in the cradle of her hips. She gasped as he entered her, stretching her body, filling her past capacity—

"Breathe deep, Brye," he said against her mouth.

She did, inhaling until it hurt, and with a final thrust, he seated himself inside her to the hilt. Her breath rushed out of her in a half-moan, half cry. Each part of skin that made contact brought new, heightened sensations. They were tangled together, as close as two people could be. It was confusing, terrifying, and mind-blowing. It was too much, yet not enough.

Gareth groaned. "Brye, I need..." He moved inside her. Brye adjusted her hips.

"I know," she said against his lips. "I know what you need."

He still held back. The animal inside him wanted to break free and claim her. To bite, and command her body into submission. With every contact of skin, her body knew. She nipped his shoulder, sharing her need once more, wanting to overpowering him.

She wanted him to break too, to snap that tether of control.

She fed his need over and over with her own, taunting him and pushing, pushing, pushing—

A tortured growl escaped his lips.

"More, Gareth, please."

"Brye."

He broke.

Finally.

The wick exploded, and they were on fire. Gareth leaned back and popped her knees up until they nearly kissed her shoulders, his large hands bracing on her shins as he claimed her savagely. Every emotion burned inside her, vibrantly alive. Their bodies begged for more. More pleasure, more pain, more connection. There was no tenderness, only mindless need.

Brye couldn't tell if it was her desire or his. He groaned her name and released her legs. She immediately locked them around his waist, trapping him to her. His mouth came to her neck, biting her, his tongue caressing the sting left behind. The force of Gareth's release echoed into her body, slamming her with waves of pleasure. She arched her back and gripped his hips as they crashed down together. She muffled her scream with his shoulder, wrapping her arms around him, so close that every angle was imprinted in her curves.

Gareth collapsed like a fallen log, nearly his entire weight pressed into her deliciously. Brye was equally spent, processing as best she could the whole experience. Her body was relaxed and achy in new places.

There was no distinction between their emotions and selves. It was too much for Brye, but still not enough. It would never be enough.

"I'm sorry."

"What for?" She sighed, still dazed in pleasure. She traced her fingertips over his spine. "You have exceeded expectations."

He chuckled, his face pressed into her shoulder. "For not taking precautions. To avoid any...." His voice trailed off. "I should have asked."

"Oh... oh that?" She patted his shoulder. When he peeled his face out to look at her, she smiled at him. "I have a special contraception tonic. I made some for Tara and kept some for myself. Just... just in case."

At the time, she'd considered it awfully presumptuous of her, to keep some of the tonic for herself. But her practicality won out and she had squirreled some away in her trunk. Better to be cautious now than sorry later.

He chuckled. "I am sure Tara needs a great deal. The way they keep at it, I'm surprised they can walk." He eased off her and flopped his large frame onto the bed beside her, propped on his side, facing her.

"Is that so?" Brye turned on her side and narrowed her eyes.

"It is so," he replied humorously.

"Maybe we might need as much... or more." She winked, pinching his shoulder.

"I did not imagine you being such a tease." Gareth attempted to hold back a laugh as he got out of bed. He almost succeeded, but his mouth twitched too much. He handed Brye a wet cloth.

Suddenly self-conscious, she quickly went into the bathing room to clean herself. She came out and raised an eyebrow. Gareth sat naked on the edge of the bed with his elbows on his knees.

Her heart gave a small jump.

"It was your first time," he said, concerned. It wasn't a question.

Brye reached for the sleeping shirt on the floor and put it on before answering. "How did you know?"

"You tensed up for a moment there..." He shrugged. "Call it instinct."

"Does it surprise you?" she asked.

"A bit. I just didn't expect it." He rubbed his face. "You are very popular. I was sure you had many... admirers."

Brye wanted to run her hands over his untamed hair and scruffy beard. The need to continue to touch him overwhelmed her. "You mean lovers?"

"Yes."

"I've had some proposals, but none have been appealing. Is that a problem for you?" She asked, taking out the vial of tonic from her kit. She took a sip of the herbal liquid and grimaced. The acid aftertaste burned her tongue.

"No. I am not one to judge your past." He examined the floor. "You just keep surprising me."

Brye walked up to him and stood between his knees. He was forced to look up, and she ran her fingers through his hair, giving a small tug. Gareth settled his hands on her hips, a slow grin decorating his stony features.

It felt natural and right to be here with him. There were no lingering feelings of doubt or regret. She could not deny it any longer. Her heart was whole.

"That's good. I'm tired of being predictable."

His eyes twinkled. "Are you ready for some sleep?"

She stopped playing with his hair. Her fingers sensed emotions underneath the surface: doubt and uncertainty.

"Gareth." She paused, trying to find the right words. There was no right way to ask. "Is there something else? Something you are not telling me that I should know?"

He sighed, his shoulders hunching over. He placed his forehead against her stomach.

"I sense serious thoughts are turning around in there," she continued. "I am trying not to read you, but it is not easy when your feelings around those thoughts are so loud."

"How loud?"

"Very."

His attempt at a chuckle fell flat. His arms went around her waist, tightening the embrace as if he needed her support. The pain and worry sat in the pit of her stomach. She was tempted to take a peek—a small one to settle the nerves.

But she suppressed the desire. She wanted to give him as much privacy as her gift could provide.

Brye kept her hands steady on his head until he let out a long breath, releasing her.

"I can't tell you, yet." A new level of uncertainty wrapped around her heart, settling a weight inside her chest. "I will tell you everything, Brye. I promise. I need to concentrate on this crisis. The knots are almost broken. We have no protection and might not have enough wheat and food for the winter. We became too dependent on the knot magic. My father and Aiden's are trying to find solutions."

Brye kept her hands on his shoulders. "What are they proposing?"

"Nothing that can solve the issue right now. I am waiting for morning to speak to Beltran and see if he can give us any useful advice. The Continent does not rely on magic as we do. They might have better agricultural systems."

Gareth stood and reached for the pants he had thrown on the floor. He put them on and got under the covers. He patted the place next to him. He seemed relaxed, except for the worry line on his forehead.

Brye followed, covering her legs and sitting back against the headboard.

"That is not what is bothering you," Brye said.

"It is one of the many things on my mind." He exhaled. "The other is entirely different, but I promise if anyone should know and will know, it is you."

He reached for her hand, taking it gently in his. He raised it to his lips and kissed the knuckles softly.

"You do so much with these hands," he said.

Brye's heart thumped wildly, and another wave of warmth spread through her limbs. He rubbed her knuckles and then turned her hand over, exposing her wrist. He ran his thumb over the delicate skin before bringing it to his lips. He left his mouth there for a moment, closing his eyes.

It was an intimate act, even more than they had shared. Gareth kissed his way up her forearm. Brye's mouth parted.

"We are not going to sleep yet, are we?" she asked, as her limbs turned to liquid and her skin burned under his touch.

"No." Gareth closed the distance between them. "No, we are not."

Promises

Lenna

"Lenna, do you see them?"

"See what, Maither?"

It was twilight, and they sat together under the White Thorn Tree. The crisp air around them filled her senses with the smell of dry leaves. The tree was full of magnificent colors, reds, yellows, oranges, and browns. It was Lenna's favorite season, and she loved exploring with her mother and sisters.

However, lately, Maither was reluctant to take them out. Since Beltane, she hid them at home. It had been months of playing close to the village and no long walks. Lenna would not have minded it if only her mother were home, but she would leave at night and return with the rising sun.

Brye could not sleep with them, claiming her dreams had become nightmares every night. Tara would whimper, waking up screaming and then crying herself back to sleep. It was up to Lenna to soothe her baby sister, hug her close, and calm her until morning. Lenna had nightmares that she couldn't share. She needed to be strong for her sisters.

"The bindings around your hands. Do you see them, sweetling?"

Lenna sat on her mother's lap. She came close to her shoulder, her breath tickling her. She took Lenna's small delicate hands in hers.

Lenna's hands were long and thin for a child, with soft freckles on the outer part of her skin, like her mother.

But that was all she saw.

"I don't see anything, Maither," she whispered nervously.

Elsywth sighed and kissed her on the cheek. "Look over there to your sisters and Gareth at the river."

Gareth had his hands on his hips and sternly talked to Tara, who seemed indignant. Brye walked around them. She took Tara's small shoulders, whispering something in her ear that made the little girl scream. Gareth appeared to have lost patience and was saying something to Brye. Her older sister ignored him and shrugged. Gareth, older and wiser, retreated to sit by the river. Tara stopped wailing and pushed the boy into the cold water.

They seemed far away in their little world. A world made for strong children. Lenna's heart went heavy in her chest. She placed a hand over it, trying to make the sensation disappear. It did not. It settled there with all her dark secrets.

"I see them."

"I need your help, my sweetling." Maither rubbed Lenna's arms, pushing warmth into her cool body. "I need you to bind them with your magic."

"Bind them?" Lenna repeated, her brow furrowed.

"Yes," Elsywth continued. "You need to tie their magic up so they can be safe."

"But you made me promise not to do any magic." Lenna pinched her lips.

Her mother rubbed her fingers. "Yes, I made you promise, and you must continue to do so. But this magic is different. It does not make it rain, cast mists, or fire. I promise, once you do what I say, you will never have to do it again. You won't even remember it."

Lenna bit her lip. "Will I forget all my magic?"

"No, your magic will be here." Elsywth pointed a finger at Lenna's chest. "Tucked away so it won't harm anyone, especially you."

"Is someone trying to hurt them?" Lenna bit her lip.

"Not yet, but someone will soon. That is why I need your help."

"And Aiden? Does he need me to bind his magic?"

Elsywth laughed, hugging Lenna close to her and kissing her cheeks.

"No, my sweetling, no. He is very clever and smart, but he has no magic."

"Will he have magic one day? Like me?"

"No one will have magic like you, my sweetling. No one. You are the most gifted of us all."

She placed Lenna in front of her. A pair of forest green eyes mirrored her own. Lenna's mouth dried, and her stomach ached.

I have to be strong. Strong like my sisters.

"Alright, Maither. I will help you," Lenna replied as her siblings and the prince ran and played around the field.

"Thank you." Her mother wiped away tears from her cheeks. She gave Lenna a deep smile. "Thank you, my sweetling."

***

That night, while the fire was lit, her mother put Tara, Brye, and Gareth to sleep. He had come, invited by Elsywth to dinner. She made everyone's favorite food and told them the stories of the once powerful dragon shifters who lived on the Continent. They asked for their favorite story about the Three Founders of Avalon, but Elsywth was reluctant to tell it.

Lenna listened with her tiny knees against her chest, upset that Aiden had not been invited. Tara had repeatedly asked for him. She threw a tantrum and begged her mother to fetch him. But Maither did not relent, insisting he would be invited tomorrow for a picnic.

Lenna's stomach turned to lead, and a familiar sensation fell over her. It made her wonder if she was helping her mother do something good or bad.

Or something terrible.

"Come, Lenna." She made her stand in front of Tara, who slept curled around a pillow. "Place your hand over your sister. I want you to imagine she is wrapped in soft threads."

Elsywth took a thread and slowly curled it around her finger. She looked at Lenna to make sure she understood. Lenna nodded, and her mother continued. "As you imagine it, you will repeat the words I say with all your might."

Lenna extended her hand.

"I bind you, Tara of Avalon. I bind your true form. I bind you until the knots of Avalon break. I bind you, one knot, over two, and over three."

As she spoke her mother's words, small, dark vines with sharp thorns wrapped themselves over Tara's legs and arms. The vines gripped the little girl's skin and glowed dull yellow. Tara whimpered louder, growling and foaming at the mouth. She clawed the air around her, trying to free herself from an invisible threat.

Claw marks, raw and painful, appeared on Tara's chest. The marks slowly healed and then disappeared under her skin. Elsywth touched Tara gently, running her hands down her hair. Her sister went back to sleep. It lasted less than a minute.

"Did I hurt her?" Lenna cried softly.

"No," Elsywth responded quickly, but Lenna doubted her mother's sincerity. Whatever she was doing was not good. She could tell her sister was shivering and in pain.

Why doesn't *maither* heal her?

Brye slept next to Gareth, her hand reached out toward him. Lenna had noticed how for the past months, Brye would find ways to touch Gareth and make his serious face smile. They would always find moments to speak and talk before playtime.

A dark sense of foreboding filled Lenna's tiny body.

"I don't think I should do this, maither," she whimpered, holding her hand away. Elsywth took Lenna's hands and rubbed them.

"It will be alright."

Lenna repeated the words slowly. As before, long, thin, thorny vines wrapped around Brye's hands, arms, and chest. The thorns dug into her skin, and prinks of blood appeared.

Brye thrashed out, crying in her sleep before the vines bloomed and disappeared. Brye shook and turned away from Gareth. Seeing her sister turn away from a friend was the worst part of all.

Elsywth ran a hand over Brye's head and spoke in low tones. Brye relaxed somewhat under her touch and went into a deeper sleep.

Lenna's body trembled and was weighed down by a tight sensation. Her mouth tasted of blood, and her head throbbed. She recognized the signs. Her magic was making her sick.

"Only one left," Elsywth whispered.

"Maither, I don't feel well," she cried. "Can we stop?"

"We will, after Gareth." Elsywth placed her hand on Gareth's chest. Underneath her fingers, she sensed the pounding of his heart and the evenness of his breath.

"Can't we let him sleep," Lenna begged, but Elsywth covered her hand. Her mother's hand tingled, then grew warm.

The warmth brought no comfort.

Her mother's power moved along the connection, and Gareth began to squirm, a moan trapped in his half-open lips.

"Lenna, say the words."

"I bind your true form, I bind—"

Lenna jumped at the knock on the door. She tried to pull away, but her mother kept firm and barked, "One moment!"

"Finish it!" she hissed in Lenna's ear.

"I bind your..." she was so tired, and her stomach hurt, "... your true form until the knot breaks. I bind you..." she swallowed hard. "Maither..."

"Just a little more, sweetling..."

"One knot, over... over two and over three," Lenna quickly said, the magic moving sluggishly through her, a trickle compared to the wave she'd used on her sisters.

Gareth bucked under her tiny hands, growling and yapping like a dog. The thorny vines ran up his legs and arms, cutting his skin. He struggled against the magic, but it was impossible. When they reached his torso, long claw marks slashed his chest, and he whimpered.

"Maither..." Lenna trembled so hard that she could barely catch her breath.

Finally, the vines merged into the shape of an open jawed wolf. Its teeth settled around the hand Lenna had over his heart.

Gareth stopped struggling and curled around himself. Lenna sat back, her breath coming in short gasps, her hands clammy. Cold wrapped itself around her body as tears ran down her cheeks.

"What did I do, Maither?" she whispered, biting her lip.

Elsywth breathed a sigh of relief before the knock on the door came back, insistent.

"I'm coming." She stood and left Lenna sitting on the floor.

Gareth started to wake. "What? What am I doing here?"

"Gareth..." Lenna whimpers, taking his hand. His dark eyes were groggy and full of pain.

Elsywth finished speaking to who was at the door and returned to kneel next to Lenna and the boy.

"I must go," she whispered urgently. "Gareth, go home. Lenna, get in bed," she ordered.

Lenna nodded wearily, too confused and scared to speak. Gareth stood on wobbly legs and left the house.

"Maither, I don't think he is well," Lenna cried, wiping her nose with the sleeve of her dress.

"He will be. He needs to adjust. Now, close your eyes. No more crying. It's all over. You did well." She placed her hand over Lenna's eyes. "Remember, tell no one. I love you, Lenna."

Lenna's last memory was the warmth of her mother's hand over her eyes.

A few hours later, she was woken up by Brye, crying over her. Tara whimpered by her side. Brye's voice barely made sense between her broken sobs.

"Maither's gone. She is never coming back."

⁂

Lenna couldn't open her eyes. They were sticky and leaden by the dried tears. She placed two cool hands over them, willing them to open.

What was that terrible dream?

It seemed too real to be her imagination. No. It was a memory of a long time ago. One that made more sense than she expected.

Rubbing her eyes, she focused on her surroundings. It was darker than when she fell asleep. The air was clear and crisp, and a light came from a fire nearby. She could smell the burning wood, and her stomach clenched.

"Finally. You're awake.'

Fraying

Lenna

The accent gave him away.

Lenna rubbed her frozen hand over her limbs, attempting to regain warmth. Her hair and clothes were covered in rich sweet petals. She untangled them with numb fingers.

"I was worried you might not wake up. You looked unhappy."

Beltran sat hunched over by the fire, tending it with a stick. The shadows and his uneven beard darkened his face. His eyes, usually bright and alert, were surrounded by dark circles. She recognized that face. She saw it every morning in the mirror.

He was exhausted from living.

Lenna plopped down next to him, close enough to see the detail of the crinkles around his eyes and the plumpness of his bottom lip. It was odd. She hadn't noticed it before. Blushing to the tip of her ears, she asked, "What are you doing here?"

"Gareth sent me to find you and make sure you got home safely," he replied, his eyes examining her face.

Gareth had unfortunately seen her in some of her worst moments. Lenna wrapped her arms around knees and closed her eyes. She massaged her temples in circles to numb the slight ache.

"Are you alright?" Beltran asked.

"Not presently," she sighed.

Beltran leaned toward her and lowered his voice. "Is there something I can do?" Lenna considered him.

"More than you have already done?"

"I have done very little," he responded wearily.

"We can both agree that is... bullshit."

"Lenna," Beltran muttered under his breath.

"You are my..." she stopped herself before she said more. "The Wolf Shifter. Admit it."

Beltran rubbed the back of his neck, tapping the stick on the ground. "Is this even important? You are not training with the wolf any longer."

"Only the wolf would know that."

"When did you realize? There are no unbound wolf shifters here."

"Since the beginning. I'm not that stupid. I can make connections." Lenna kept her gaze on his face. "And you can't hide an accent."

Beltran grimaced and swallowed. "I am sorry. I shouldn't have gotten so close to you or anyone. After the fire wraith, I thought it was best for you to focus on other things."

"Why?" Lenna demanded.

Sparks jumped from the fire, falling on Beltran's exposed flesh. He winced. "I think you have answered your question."

Lenna dipped her chin. She was terrible at confrontations or handling anger effectively. Her face heated up to her ears. "I apologize. You must have your reasons. I wish I knew them. You can't get my hopes up and expect me to do nothing."

"I never expected any less of you." He threw the stick into the fire. "And my reasons for stopping are not what you think."

"You do not know what I think."

"Yes," he growled. "I do."

He moved his hands as he spoke. "You think I stopped training you because you are weak."

Lenna ground her teeth as he barreled through the rest of it, his tongue stumbling over some of the words. "But you are wrong. Initially, I thought you were only a Fire Elemental, but Lenna, you were so much more. You are one of the most powerful Elementals I have ever encountered. I read about people with your abilities in ancient scrolls and books. The only other registered in the Utreqira is the Avalon Founder, and before her, only the one of the Forgotten Gods. That makes two powerful Elementals in history, with you three."

Lenna blinked, her mind grasping the last few words he said. "The *udrukira*?"

"It's pronounced *oot-dray-kee-rah*. It is the government building and the home to the Grand Register, the Book of All Names. It has every person born on the Continent. No matter what side you are on, the...." he paused, trying to find the words, "the Shifter or Yuansu side, as you call it. When you are born, your name and abilities will be automatically registered in the book."

"Is my name there?"

"No," he exhaled. "Avalon is protected. The island does not appear on any maps. The knot magic prevents those born here from being cataloged and registered."

Lenna brought her cloak closer around her. Her mind tried to grasp the magnitud of the information. There was so much she did not know about the Continent or even her island.

One thing at a time.

Lenna ran her tongue over the scar on her lower lip. "What do you know about the Knot Magic on the island?"

After a long moment, Beltran spoke, in starts and stops, as if trying to decide what to say. "I learned about the binding magic through a specific book from the Vallerium, the Great Library. According to the book, the only way an island can protect itself is if it bound to limit its magic. That is to say, someone or some people must have put a binding spell on the island's perimeter for it to keep magic. The knots in the fields are extensions of these spells."

"The Bondmaker Founder."

"Yes."

"Are they permanent?"

Beltran shook his head. "They are unique to the Bondmaker and what is being bound. The Bondmaker can limit or extend the bindings. All this has been theoretical at best because there have been no other Bondmakers since Clothos. This is the first time I have had first-hand experience with it."

What was the last thing Beltran said? *The knot magic protects…* Lenna's clammy hand flew to her mouth.

There are barely any knots left. The magic that kept the island safe dissipated with each fallen stone.

When the knots of Avalon Break.

No. This was no coincidence. This was happening because someone had made sure it did.

"If the knots break, will the Avaloneans also appear in the Book of All Names?"

"It would depend if Avalon falls within the Grand Register's limits." There was a hitch in his voice when he spoke.

"But?"

"But it is likely that they will. Even those who have passed will appear and their abilities."

"What would be the consequences?" A deep, dark weight settled in her stomach.

Beltran looked back at the fire, his jaw working. His hand bunched into fists on his upturned knees.

"The villagers without magical abilities would be reassigned to a new home to make a place for themselves. The royal family would lose their titles. There are no other monarchs except the Shifter King and the Zuanshi Empress. If they are lucky, they might be given honorary titles and lands. I think it is unlikely."

"And those with magical abilities," she spoke tentatively. Images of Gareth and Tara's shifting and Brye's healing hands came into her mind.

"Depending on the magic of the others, they would be sought out." He responded slowly. "However, you and Roweena would be in a delicate position. It would depend a great deal on politics and laws."

Lenna paled. "Speak frankly."

"Lenna, there has been no one else like you in almost a millennium. The Shifter King and Zuanshi Empress would want you to take their side. The peace they have is new. They would want to guarantee you as an ally."

"And if I do not want to be involved in political games?" She was already tired of the one she was playing now, and her kingdom was small. The scale of what he was presenting grew in her mind.

No, that was not a reality she wanted to navigate.

Beltran physically aged, his body curling in on himself. He stared at the fire with sad eyes. "Then you would be a threat."

"How does the Book of All Names know what to include?"

"I don't know. Only Clothos knew the extension of his magic."

"Of course."

Around them, the White Thorn Tree moved with the soft, calm wind as if listening, waiting for the information to unravel.

Beltran hinted that her Elemental Magic was rare. How much more dangerous would it be if he knew the extent of her magic? If she told him about the binding spell her mother forced her to do.

"You mention bonding, binding magic, and such. Based on what you know, theoretically...." Lenna measured her words, her mind trying to grasp the details of the conversation. "Is it possible to bind someone's magic?"

His features changed, darkened. "What do you know of Bond Magic, Lenna?"

"Nothing," she reassured, her hands extended. "That is why I asked. You said the Knot Magic protects Avalon. It is only fair to assume that magic is bound inside of it. Nothing comes in, and nothing leaves. Based on that assumption, I wondered if it could bind a person's magic inside them."

Beltran ran his hand over the fire, making it grow and diminish. "A Bondmaker is a rare individual. Binding a being's form and abilities is forbidden. They become a shell of what they could be. It was considered a punishment saved for only the worst transgressors."

Lenna wrung her hands, hidden underneath the cloak.

"What kind of transgress?"

"That varies from each point of view. For some, it can be using magic to murder the innocent; for others, using magic at all. It is more common to be born Shifter and Yuansu, with little or limited magical abilities, than to be a pure Shifter, Elemental, or Bondmakers. Those abilities have been extinct for centuries. Until now." He gave Lenna a pointed look.

"I don't understand."

"Let me be plain," Beltran explained. "I, for example, can manipulate fire and some elemental magic. But to an extent, my magical source is limited. To be a Pure One is to know nearly limitless magic akin to the Forgotten Gods. To compel other shifters, manipulate all the elements or reality with complicated spells. That has been extinct since the Founders."

"Nearly limitless?"

"No source of power is eternal. When they have used up all their magical supply, they need to take them from others. If they do not have access to magic, they can leech the life out of an individual. It extends their life cycles, but they carry the essence of those they take. It can play on the mind."

A deadly chill fell over Lenna. The image of the royal advisor and the tentacles grabbing her arms and legs flashed in her mind, tormenting and torturing her.

"Is there a way to undo it? The bindings," she whispered, licking the blood that seeped from her lip. She pressed down on it with her fingers.

"Usually, the Bondmaker will set a condition for the binding to break. But it takes a skilled and powerful individual to create one, equally to break them."

"What would happen if the person was unskilled?" Lenna's voice cracked.

"It would be so much worse. If an inexperienced Bondmaker created the bindings, the bond conditions would not be complete. For example, if this person were to bind someone's memories about an event, they will still remember some of it, if only distorted."

Lenna nodded and considered. It made sense that Brye could still heal and read people with her hands, but her memory of her mother was incomplete. Tara would still be strong but could not shift. It would leave Gareth? Why would her mother bind him?

Beltran gave her a great deal of information and more questions, but time was catching up. An urgency grew in Lenna's chest. Whatever began that night in her home long ago with her mother was coming to an end. The knots were almost broken. There were no mists to protect the island. If her mother had her reasons, she died with them.

Lenna stood up, shook out her dress and cloak, and wiped her clammy hands.

"Thank you for the enlightening conversation."

"Where are you going?" Beltran stood, wary.

"Home." She picked up her skirts and headed to the village. "I need to speak to my sisters."

Beltran cursed, extinguishing the fire with a sweep of his hand, and went after her. Fueled more by the increasing sensation of danger, Lenna moved as quickly as she could.

It wasn't fast enough. Beltran caught up with her. The sudden grip of his hand tripped her, and she fell on her face. Lenna winced as her body, already bruised from the previous evening, rebelled. Beltran extended a hand. She flicked it away.

"Why does everyone insist on helping me?"

"Lenna, you fell. I helped you stand. It is not such a big offense," he snapped back.

"You say I am supposed to be powerful, but you do not treat me as such." She pulled away, her hands fisted at her side.

"Of course, I do."

"Why are you here, Beltran?" she demanded.

"As I mentioned before, Gareth wanted me to make sure you got home safely," he restated, exasperated.

"Exactly," she pointed out. "I have lived here longer than you. I know my way home. I do not need an escort."

She resumed walking.

"You can honestly say that?" He cut her path. She narrowed her eyes, fighting the urge to stomp her foot. "Being gallant and a decent person does not make the other weak. It makes a person foolish not to accept help."

"Noted." Lenna continued past him towards the village. Beltran muttered under his breath and followed. She didn't invite conversation, and he didn't pursue it. They walked in mutual tense silence in the dark.

Beltran stopped. "Do you hear that?"

Lenna strained her ears. They reached the forest that connected the northern field and the southern part of the island.

"I don't hear anything—" she cut herself off. She didn't hear anything. The forest, usually filled with the song of crickets and hoot of owls, was quiet. Even the trees, slowly moved by the wind, barely made a sound. The absence of sound sent goosebumps running down her spine.

A sense of urgency exploded in her chest. It forced her to turn and see what was left of the wall to the west. In terror, she gripped Beltran's hand. The wall was too far to distinguish, but, in her mind, she could see.

Thorny, thick branches slithered into the small gaps in the stone. The invading roots vibrated, pushing against the rock until a long, resounding snap echoed over the field.

"The wall," she whispered, her mouth agape.

Beltran's large hand gripped hers tightly, and it took a moment for Lenna to sense the warmth of his touch and the vibration of his worry.

What was left of the wall crumbled under strain. A cloud of dust and debris floated around the stones. The wind took it farther into the field.

The snap that resonated inside Lenna's chest took the breath right out of her.

"Lenna?" Beltran rubbed her back. She took ragged breaths to regain some air. Her pounding heart did not soothe her. She paled as a realization washed over her like cold water.

The heaviness and tightness she perpetually felt were absent. Only the tiredness and dull pain of the last hectic couple of days was in its place. The bindings were still present. They were still wrapped around her like an old blanket. But something was different.

"They're gone." Lenna let out a shaky breath, and her eyes searched Beltran's face.

"What is?"

"The island's knots." Her voice trembled. His eyes grew wide as he, too, heard the weight in her words. She gripped his hand.

"Do you realize what happened?" Her voice grew. "The magic knots are gone!"

Thread Tension

Tara

Tara and Aiden were awoken by the house coming apart. Tremors shook the foundations as glasses and ceramics cascaded onto the ground in a field of shards. One of the tables moved to the side of the room, and chairs toppled over. The slow-pitched rumble rattled every object, even Tara's teeth. Once it ceased, they bolted off the bed.

"What was that?" Tara quickly grabbed her clothes. She tossed her dress to one side, picking out a pair of work clothes. Her fingers shook, and she dropped her belt twice. Aiden picked it up the second time and wrapped it around her waist.

"Nothing good," Aiden said, kicking her boots in her direction before reaching for his over-tunic and belt.

As they scrambled to dress, voices came from outside the door. Whispered conversations grew, and people stood outside in the paths. The crack that came a few moments later was so loud it silenced the village. Tara's face paled, and the voices raised into nervous chatter.

"The northwest field!" someone yelled. "The wall has fallen!"

"Aiden..." Tara's mouth went dry.

Aiden nodded and went for their weapons placed next to the door. As they stepped outside, another low rumble slowly approached the village. The vibrations pushed them back into the house. They gripped the door frame until the waves passed.

The nervousness from the villagers around them turned to terror. Screams of disbelief, confusion, and desperation rang out. People were running in the direction of the northwest field. Every able-bodied person made their way there, searching for the origin of the tremors. Only some stayed behind, especially those with younger children, who were too small to help.

"We better get Brye and Gareth," Aiden said.

Tara nodded as he led her into the moving sea of people. It took only a few moments for the villagers to become a mob, making their way in the opposite direction of the tower. Aiden lost his grip on her arm. She could see his dirty blond hair above the crowd a few feet before her.

"Let me pass!" Tara yelled, trying to find a path through.

A long beastly howl rang through the chaos.

A cold and definite chill ran up her spine, freezing her in place. The cry demanded her to obey. Wide-eyed, Tara stood, unable to move in any direction or feel the press of bodies pushed past her. She tried to breathe, to regain control over her arms and legs, but the call forced her to listen.

Aiden appeared in the sea of terrified voices. He gripped her face with both hands. She concentrated on his sky-blue eyes, then his moving lips. He was calling her and repeating her name over and over. In one quick, sharp moment, his voice invaded her senses loud and clear.

"Tara, sweetheart! Focus on my voice, please!"

She nodded, grabbing his hands that cradled her face. His warmth centered her. She regained focus.

"Brye and Gareth." Her voice was muffled against his hands.

"Yes." Aiden put his forehead against hers. Even in the growing confusion, he slowly breathed in and out.

It became clear why Tara needed him so much. He centered her when everything seemed to be falling apart. She breathed along with him until her heart came back into her chest.

"We need to go to the tower," she said slowly.

"Yes, we do." Aiden exhaled. He grabbed her and pressed his lips to hers, using his touch to bring her back to the present. Everything around them disappeared for one moment. The communication wasn't gentle. It was a need for her to be there, with him. To imprint herself in him.

The kiss ended as abruptly as it started, and Tara took a haggard breath. Aiden gave her one final searching look before leading her in the direction of the Royal Tower.

As they neared their destination, the crowds dimmed. The door opened, and the royal family walked out into the paths.

The king and queen were dressed in mismatched clothes. Their hair was in disarray, like they had been pulled out of bed. The king had his sword inside his belt, and the queen clung nervously to his arm.

Brye was beside the queen, placing a hand on her shoulder. Tara had never seen the king and queen so lost, so aged.

Brye and Gareth were better dressed, both alert and ready. Brye carried a bag with her kit, and Gareth had his sword in place. He was adjusting knives into his boots when Tara crashed into her sister. Aiden by her side.

"What is happening, Aiden?" the king asked.

"We don't know yet. People are running toward the northwest field," Aiden informed.

"That is where the commotion is coming from," Tara continued.

"We better go then," the king commanded. "My love, you stay in the village with the older woman and children, ensuring they are calm. Son, you will—"

Another long howl exploded around them. It echoed into the valley, too far and too close simultaneously. It seemed to be coming from everywhere.

Tara sensed Aiden's firm grip, but it wasn't enough. Whoever was making that call was screaming the same message over and over. The sound awoke a deep part inside her. A part that understood the message loud and clear.

Invasion.

Gareth took a step back and tensed. His whole body became rigid, and a long, low growl came from the back of his throat.

The long howl ended. Gareth, stony-faced once more, took Brye by the hand. She blinked up at him, her face pale and concerned.

"Aiden, get the warriors and go to the White Thorn Tree. I will go south," Gareth said. Aiden nodded, and Garth turned to Brye. "I think we might need your kit."

Brye looked down at his hand and squeezed. "Leave it to me."

Aiden had to leave, but Tara did not let go of his hand. She couldn't.

"I'll go with you," she said.

"Tara, you have to stay here," Aiden said. "You need to stick with your sisters."

Tara shook her head without letting go. Behind them, the king and queen went off to do their duty. Brye and Gareth waited, speaking in low tones. But Tara did not care about them. She only cared about Aiden, her mate.

"Tara." He took her hand and raised it to his lips. "I will be fine."

"I..." she hesitated.

"I know, sweetheart." He ran his thumb over her lips. She hated when he did that. She brushed his hand away, and he chuckled.

"I love you," he said. "Everything will be fine." He let go of her hand before disappearing into the crowd to sound the alarm.

A sense of warning grew in her chest. She kept her eyes on Aiden's retreating figure on the paths until he turned north and made for the woods. There she lost sight of him, and the panic only grew worse.

Without peeling her eyes away from the spot where Aiden disappeared from her sight, she addressed Gareth. "You act like you're expecting a battle." Finally, she swung her attention around and focused on the prince.

"We must be prepared for everything." Gareth's nostrils flared, and his eyes darkened into two small dark pools. His tone did not change, but it felt like a scream. "Are you ready, Tara?"

Tara's mouth filled with a sour taste. She looked around her for a moment. Beyond them, there were cries and screams. The square was almost abandoned, and time was slipping away.

But Tara wasn't ready. Deep down, she knew she had been playing to be a warrior. She did not know if she could do the right thing. Her mind went back to Aiden. If she was unprepared, then how prepared was he? He never wanted to be a warrior, yet he set out to do what was right.

"Yes," she responded with apprehension. "I am ready for battle."

Distant terrified screams rose in the distance. It was only a matter of time before the threat came to the village.

Tara jerked as Gareth gripped her by the collar of her shirt with his free hand. He stared down, eyes ablaze. She couldn't look away, no matter how much she tried.

"No matter what, Tara." His voice vibrated in her head, echoing until it merged with the pounding in her ears. "No matter the cost, you protect your sister. Your priority will only be your sister's safety."

"I..." Tara's mouth opened, but no other word came out. Gareth's face changed. His eyes became dark deep pools, and two sharp canines descended; one nicked his lower lip.

Tara clawed with her hands, but it was no use. He was stronger and more commanding than her. The strange yet familiar creature inside her moaned and whimpered. It crawled under her skin, attempting to flee.

Her vision blurred, and memories of Gareth invaded her mind. They flashed quickly, jumbled with little sense.

She knew him. By the Founders, she *knew* him. Far longer than after her mother disappeared. His spirit, his essence, his presence. He was an essential aspect of her life. An older brother, a trainer, a leader, but most importantly, someone who had to be obeyed by authority.

His word was law.

She could not rebel.

"Gareth, please…" Brye placed a hand on his arm. He ignored her.

"Do you understand?" Gareth insisted, shaking Tara like a rag. Her teeth chattered.

"Yes." Tara nodded repeatedly. "I understand."

He let go, and she stepped back, shaken to the core. She wrapped her arms against her stomach, attempting to regain some of her dignity.

"Stay with Brye. Keep her safe," his voice was gruffer. Tara nodded, then turned away.

"What about Lenna?" Brye held Gareth back a moment.

"Beltran should be with her," he replied. Brye pulled his mouth to hers, kissing him for dear life.

Tara flushed, and a chilling anger filled her limbs at their embrace. Her eyes strained with tears.

"I will be fine. You come back," Brye said as if they had an internal conversation.

"Yes, princess."

"I will remind you how I detest being called princess." She bit his lip, then let go. Gareth suppressed a laugh.

The screaming and sound of battle brought them back to the urgency of the present. Tara grabbed Brye's hand, holding her in place as Gareth ran toward the training fields.

Shadows

Lenna

Lenna stood, horrified, as the wall broke piece by piece by the long thorny vines covered in white flowers. Their scent alerted her to the true origin of the vines.

"The White Thorn Tree," she stammered, her scarred hand coming to her chest.

"What?" Beltran turned her to face him. "Lenna, make sense!"

"The branches! They belong to the White Thorn Tree," she pointed.

The tremor underneath their feet overshadowed the rumble of the wall. They grasped each other, trying to stay upright as an earthquake shattered what was left of the island's boundaries. Terrified birds took flight. Sleeping animals searched for shelter.

Beltran held Lenna firmly against his chest as the ground vibrated. She gripped him while his erratic heartbeat pounded in her ears.

Once the movement ceased, they ran toward the White Thorn Tree. They did not get far when another crack reverberated. Lenna's ears rang and her eyes widened at the painful view before her.

The White Thorn Tree split in two, and smoke rose from the torn trunk. The tree decayed in less than a few heartbeats, turning black and charred before their very eyes.

Figures emerged from the middle of the tree. They were dark and made of shadows. In the dim moonlight, you could confuse them with the shade of the fallen tree. They moved in jerked motions and spoke in garbled noises. The largest one came last. He hushed the growing group of shadows by waving a large object. One of the decayed branches fell to the ground with one smooth swing.

"What are they?" Lenna whispered, her skin crawling.

"I don't know, but we must return to the village." Beltran dragged her toward the woods. They made it some distance when villagers came from the south, speaking in hushed tones. None of them were warriors.

"Get back—" Lenna attempted to cry out, but Beltran covered her mouth with his hand.

"You'll betray their position," he hissed in her ear.

Badar and Caitlin were among the group, carrying tools with other farmers. They stood in a circle speaking in low tones, observing the wall.

Lenna bit hard into Beltran's hand. He cursed, releasing her. She wasted no time heading in Badar's direction. She had to warn them. She had to warn them about the shadow monsters...

Heart pounding, Lenna crashed into the older man. "Go back." She clawed at his tunic. "It's not safe—"

"Lenna, breathe." He took her by the shoulders. Lenna attempted to take a full breath. Caitlin rubbed her back.

"What is it, Lenna?"

"The wall has fallen. The White—"

A piercing howl of a wolf came out, vibrating around the field. Lenna covered her ringing ears. Beltran growled under his breath, and his hand paled over his weapon.

The call disappeared.

"I have to take you to the tower." Beltran tried to get her to move. She tugged her arm away.

"Wait," she pleaded.

"Yes, take her to the tower." Badar let go of her and gave her a push. "We will see what is happening and see you later."

"No," she cried out. "You don't understand."

Beltran half-carried Lenna into the woods. Behind them, the villagers stood in the same position, some even walking closer to the fallen wall.

Can't they see the danger?

The shadow creatures were gone, hiding—except one that made its way south.

"What is wrong with you? We have to warn them!" she spat out, trying to free herself, pummeling his chest and arms.

"No, we need to get you to your sisters." He winced.

The wolf howled again, and behind them, the crowd became restless.

A scream woke them up from their confusion. A flash of a shadow creature came full speed into the unexpected group. Lenna's blood drained from her face. Beltran didn't wait. He hoisted her on his shoulder and ran.

No! No!

Terror and screams were heard in the distance, mixed with growling and screeching. It was too dark and the trees were too thick for Lenna to make out what was happening with her eyes.

Her ears had no such issues.

And she heard—violently, horribly, vividly—as the monsters descended upon the villagers whose only crime was to be in the field. She heard the shouting, the shrieking of agony, the clash of metal pitchforks, the thumping of clubs, and the cut-off screams as crazed victims begged for mercy from monsters they could not see.

"No!" Lenna screamed, bile rising, panic tightening the skin over her scalp. Badar... Caitlin...

Around them, the woods were silent of animal life as if they were hiding in fear.

And slowly... agonizingly slowly, the screaming of the villagers near the wall faded.

Lenna kicked Beltran, screaming, crying, and squirming until he let her down near the path at the edge of the woods and the village perimeter.

"Lenna, you have to think," he begged. She pounded against his chest, trying to free her magic, but it was useless. "You need to survive this. We have to get you off the island."

"Survive?"

There was no way she would survive this. There was no escaping the hell that erupted around her.

What good is having magic if I can't use it?

The sky rumbled above them, but he held on to her. She scratched his face with her nails.

The village lights were ahead of them. A large group of men stood at the path, waiting. They were so far away that she could still make out their features, but the surrounding trees hid her. Some broke off and headed north. Lenna's mouth dried out. North... north toward the White Thorn Tree... toward where those shadow creatures were...

Aiden appeared along the trail and spoke to one of the villagers.

Her stomach sank.

"No," she mouthed. "No! Aiden, *no*! Don't go!"

Lenna fought even harder, but Beltran held fast. In one move, he turned her back against him and choked her. Why was he holding her back? She could save him!

She had to save him!

She struggled with her gasping screams as they turned to sobs. Aiden disappeared from view into the dark woods.

When she bit down again on his arm, he loosened his grip.

He's heading toward his death.

"Let me go!" Lenna's throat burned. "Aiden, come back! Please."

"I can't." Beltran dragged her back, his face a mask of regret.

Another howl echoed in warning, this one long and desperate.

Beltran cursed. He turned Lenna and carried her over his shoulder. He gripped her thighs tightly against his chest. Lenna twisted in his arms, but his superior strength kept her firmly in place. She wiped the tears that ran up her forehead.

The sky was still dark in the early hours, but rain clouds formed, and lightning fell in the distance. Thunder echoed over the valley. The waning moon was obscured, and the valley's only light was the lightning cascading from one cloud to another.

She was causing it. She could bring a storm but couldn't free her magic long enough to help the man...

The man her sister loved.

Selfish Acts

Lenna

THE VILLAGE WAS MOSTLY empty, except for the queen and some women with children. They stared as Beltran carried Lenna up the path. Once they reached the Royal Tower, he dropped her in front of her sisters.

The sky thundered. "You had no right!" Lenna's hand collided with his face and the sky erupted in flashes of light. He covered his marked face and took a step back, avoiding her gaze.

Lenna grabbed Tara, shaking her frantically. "Tara! You have to get him."

"Lenna, calm down," Brye said, her healing hands running down her arms. The tingling sensation attempted to calm her.

"You're not making any sense," Tara said as she examined her from her tear-stained face to her dirty hem.

"Aiden!" she stuttered hysterically. "He is heading for the northwest field, and the shadow monsters are there. He's in danger."

"Shadow monsters?" Tara repeated.

Lenna shook her again, fear eclipsing every other emotion inside her, drowning her. "Shadow monsters! They came out of the tree!" Why was Tara not listening? "They killed everyone—" Lenna's voice cracked, her throat thick and closing tight around each word. "Aiden's headed right for them."

Tara paled, and her eyes widened.

Brye gasped. "Oh no!"

"You have to go to him, Tara," Lenna pleaded. Above them, a storm circled the island, a testament to her lack of control. Lightning lit up the sky, followed by a roll of thunder that shocked the earth. "You need to bring him back."

"Didn't you try to stop him, Lenna?" Tara cried out.

"I did!" Lenna quaked. Tara's anger made hers fizzle out. "But I couldn't."

"I had to bring her back," Beltran interrupted, placing himself between the dazed Tara and Lenna. "We need to get the three of you off this island. It isn't safe for you here anymore."

Tara punched Beltran on his already bruised face. The crack was enough to make Lenna wince.

"You should have gone back for him!" Tara roared as she stormed down the path. With each step she took, her body wobbled. Lenna gaped as Tara fumbled and stumbled, until her sister screamed in frustration and came storming back.

"You are coming with me." She dug her nails into Brye's arm.

"Why?" Brye grimaced, freeing herself from Tara's grasp.

"Because Gareth compelled me to protect you. I can't leave you behind," Tara persisted, snatching Brye again. She grabbed Lenna with her other hand. "You too."

Lenna let herself be dragged by her reluctant younger sister, her eyes darting back to the tower. The tension in her stomach grew.

We won't get far without protection. We need the mists.

And only one person could accomplish that.

"Wait," Lenna planted her feet. "Stop!"

"Walk, Lenna!" Tara ordered, gripping Lenna's wrist in a bruising hold.

Brye was physically affected by Tara's rage, trembling and growing pale. Beltran followed close behind, but even he was wary of Tara's reaction. Lenna stood her ground, planting her feet. Tara tugged, growling, and Lenna bit hard into her sister's hand.

Tara hissed and grabbed her hand. "What is wrong with you? I'm already wasting time. If anything happens to Aiden, I will never forgive you."

"Please, Tara, let me make it right."

"Make it right?" Tara bellowed, her eyes darkening to almost midnight. "You can set fire and move things with your anger and create fucking storms with your temper, but when you are truly needed, you are worthless!"

The screams became louder. The sense of urgency intensified, and time sped up. Tara paced like a caged animal, growling and muttering under her breath.

"Lenna, you can't stay here," Brye begged.

"I have to, Brye." Lenna looked back at the Royal Tower. "I'm the only one who can do it."

Brye grasped Lenna's hand, and the tingling sensation alerted her.

"No reading."

"Lenna."

"We have to go." Tara took Brye's arm once more.

"Go, Tara," Lenna said. "I'll see you soon."

Tara nodded once before she turned and strode purposefully down the path, dragging Brye behind her by sheer will.

Lenna swayed slightly as her sisters headed northwest. Panic rode her hard. They would be alright. They had each other.

"What are you up to, Lenna?"

That stupid accent.

"Haven't you done enough?" Lenna walked to the tower and stood before the doors, Beltran at her heels.

"The island is dying, Lenna. You can't stay behind."

"I can't leave either. You said so. I won't be part of some ridiculous political games."

"It might not be like that."

"You don't—"

"I can't leave you to die!" he roared, pinning her to the wall. Lenna's eyes widened. Beltran heaved ragged breaths above her. His face was a mess of bruised skin and darkened patches of exhaustion. He carried the world's weight on his shoulders, and Lenna softened at the sight.

"Beltran," she whispered. "You know I need to do this."

His jaw tensed, and he shook his head while tears fell down his cheeks. Lenna reached for his face, cleaning the tears with her thumbs.

"Lenna," he pleaded, leaning into her hand. Her heart ached painfully. "Please, come with us."

The sense of danger was suffocating. Time slipped through her fingers, but she wanted one thing.

One selfish thing.

It might mean nothing, but it meant so much to her.

Lenna raised on her toes, wrapped her arms around his neck and gently pulled his lips to hers. He tensed. All she needed was one moment. One moment of being wanted and not used.

Please don't push me away. Give me this.

Beltran's arms circled her waist, plastering her against his muscled body. He smelled of fur and brine, and her mind danced with memories of playing with water and learning about magic.

Of being free.

He moaned and changed the kiss, exploring her mouth until Lenna's knees gave way. She gripped his short hair and sensed the burn of his beard along her face. She tasted the blood of her torn lip, and the salt of his tears. She bit his lower lip, forcing a growl from deep in his throat. Her heart pounded, and an incredible warmth spread all through her limbs. A fire that did not terrify nor harm.

It was bliss—one pure moment of joy.

A terrifying scream in the distance brought reality cruelly to the forefront. "Thank you," she whispered against his lips.

"What?" he asked, his breath ragged.

"For this." Lenna pushed against his chest. Beltran blinked down at her, still holding her tight.

"Lenna—"

"Do something for me, Beltran." She unhooked his hands as the screams grew closer.

"Anything, but come with me," he pleaded, looking north. Lenna took advantage of his distraction and pushed him aside.

"Take care of my sisters," she called out, reaching for the large wooden doors.

His face grew slack before he made a grab for her. She banged the door closed, the wooden bar locking her inside. It was the last memory she would have. Beltran's tired, surprised look right after she kissed him.

The wood vibrated as Beltran pounded on the door and screamed her name. She was tempted to go with him. To flee this horrible place.

Finally, there was a dull silence, and Lenna leaned her forehead against the wood. She placed a hand on her swollen, broken lips. They still tingled at the memory. Outside, the sky threatened rain, but not one drop fell. Inside the tower, the noise from the chaos was muffled, almost as if it were happening someplace else.

To someone else.

Letting out a deep, long breath, Lenna took stock of her appearance on a mirror by the edge of the wall.

Her face was flushed, and her hair had fallen out of its braid. She removed the cord and brushed it with her nervous fingers. She could do nothing about the open cut on her lower lip or the bags under her eyes. It did not matter. What she needed to do had nothing to do with her appearance and everything to do with her ability to appear unmoved.

She locked away the kiss, along with her wishes and failed dreams. She had enough accumulated for a lifetime. Her short lifetime. Lenna tried to erase the worry for her sisters and Aiden.

Beltran and Gareth would help them get off the island. They had to.

Now, I need to do my part.

With one final shaky breath, she headed down the corridor.

It was time to face Roweena.

Raw Edge

Tara

Tara guided a reluctant Brye south first, following the fallen wall. A heaviness settled permanently in the pit of Tara's stomach, and her eyes burned with every torturous step. The mountains of crumbled stones gave enough cover as they made their way north, but Tara's apprehension. Any moment the shadow creatures could discover them, and then where would they be?

Fucked, that's what.

Brye followed her silently, apparently lost in her thoughts. Their steps were the only sound as they trudged along the uneven path. It was slow, and Brye forced Tara to stop every so often to the sounds of death that echoed over the valley. "I don't like this," Brye whispered, wrapping her arms around herself. "I don't like that we left Lenna behind."

Chills ran down Tara's spine at the thought of Lenna. The determination in her eyes, and the flash of hurt as Tara wounded her with words. But she stayed behind. "I don't either, but we need to keep moving."

Finally, they found their way to the edge of the western crop fields where the first wraith appeared. There, Tara forced them to crouch and hide behind the piles of fallen stones and twisted vines.

It was still early dawn. There was still at least a couple of hours of coverage.

Tara gave Brye a signal and approached the edge of the pile of stones. Keeping her body low, she gave her eyes time to adjust to the contrast between the lit torches and the shadows. The field never fully recovered after being set on fire. The ground was scorched through, and debris was settled in small piles here and there.

A new pile in the center was more significant than any other. The shadow creatures kept carrying large pieces from one side to the pile. They talked, poking what appeared to be large logs with their lower extremities. She waited until they brought a log closer.

Tara's stomach dropped, and bile rose to her throat. She bit down on her knuckles to keep from screaming as the face of a villager came into view. She recognized him as a man who worked the fields with Badar. His eyes were wide open, unseeing, and his mouth was set in a silent scream. His body was slashed to the bone, torn and covered in blood.

Tara tasted metal from her cut knuckle as her gaze darted in every direction. It was not a mountain of rubble and debris.

It was a mountain of bodies.

Bodies slain and covered in blood.

Bodies that still moaned out in pain, pleading for help.

How had they killed so many and so quickly? It made no sense. It took them less than thirty minutes to get to the field. In such a short time, they killed more than a dozen. Why didn't the villagers run and take cover?

A hand came over Tara's shoulder, and she flinched away. Brye appeared close, and Tara tried to protect her sensitive sister from the carnage. But she insisted. Brye stiffened, and a choked noise came from her throat. She covered her mouth and face, taking heaving breaths to recover.

There was no way to do so.

With a nod from Brye, they both returned to the tree line, hiding behind rubble. It was impossible to escape the coppery smell of blood and the sweet scent of the vines' white flowers.

Tara rubbed her face as dread and terror collided, increasing the stretching sensation inside her skin.

"I need to see if he is there," Tara whispered in her sister's ear.

"We need to be careful," Brye hissed.

Tara growled low, and the force inside her extended her canines, nicking her bottom lip. She struggled to regain control while the black shadows finished making the pile of corpses. They spoke in their gurgled whispers for a moment, pausing occasionally. Half of the group headed south toward the village a few moments later.

The others stayed behind, huddled together farther down a field. They appeared in deep conversation. Tara let out a long breath, slowly so as not to be heard. They were too close. A tall wall of stony debris was the only thing separating them from danger.

Soft tears fell down Brye's cheeks, and Tara, now calmer, wiped her face with her sleeve.

Tara breathed deeply and tried to distinguish between the scent of brimstone and acid from a new one brought by the breeze. The bushes rustled ever so slightly, and Tara, still crouching, positioned herself in front of Brye.

A second later, the scent crashed with full force.

Wet dog smell.

Tara relaxed as Beltran's bulky figure appeared before them.

It was new. To have her senses heightened was terrifying and distracting, even more so than the strong smells. She raised her arm and gave herself a sniff.

She didn't smell any better.

Beltran crouched next to them, a grim frown on his colored features. He was covered in dirt and grime from his walk through the woods. His right cheek was sore, and he started to sport a black eye.

After leaning over the pile of rubble, he sat back in silence, his gaze lost. Brye motioned with her head in his direction, and Tara shrugged.

"Lenna?" Brye asked in a low whisper.

"She stayed in the tower to talk to the royal advisor," Beltran explained.

Tara cursed.

"We should have forced her to come." Brye sniffed.

"She made a choice, painful as it may be." Tara ran a sleeve over her runny nose.

"Tara." Brye placed a hand on her wrist. "One day, we will reflect on this moment and regret it."

"I know, but not today." Tara removed her sister's hand. She didn't need Brye to read too much into her emotions. She barely could understand them herself. "And not right now."

"We need to get you off the island," Beltran said. He ran a hand through his dark hair, then over his face.

"Not without Aiden," Tara stated.

"Or Gareth and Lenna," Brye insisted.

Beltran glanced around uneasily. "Lenna wants you off the island."

"No!" Brye hissed. Tara shushed her. "We all go, or none at all."

"So, you expect us to wait and die here?" Tara snapped back. "Lenna said she would meet us."

"I don't see you proposing to leave Gareth and Aiden behind."

"Gareth won't be left behind," Tara sighed.

"What makes you say that?"

"If he's alive, he will find you," Beltran said.

"How?"

"He will track your scent," Beltran explained. "He will find us. All Pure male Shifters can do so."

Brye blinked repeatedly, and Tara's mouth fell open.

"Pure what?"

"Can you repeat that?"

They mumbled over each other. Beltran rubbed his face harshly before releasing a long breath. "It is a long, complicated story, and this is not—" He froze, his eyes darting in the direction of the field.

It was too quiet. They were so engrossed in the conversation that they failed to notice the lack of garbled noise. Too terrified to move, the three stayed in their places, ears strained. Beltran motioned with his hand around the pile. Tara shook her head.

He then took crab-like steps over the soft grass mixed with the gravel. Once he reached the edge, he knelt and leaned his body carefully around the pile. Brye and Tara waited with bated breath. Brye reached for Tara's hand. They stood motionless until Beltran returned.

"They are starting a fire," he whispered. His face became pale.

"With what?" Tara asked. There was a slight whoosh and then a soft crackling noise.

Tara went for a better look.

And regretted instantly.

Her eyes widened at the sight of the pile of bodies, some still alive, slowly going up in flames. Terrified screams rose in the air. Cries for mercy and help rang out until they needed to cover their ears.

The shadow creatures struck those still convulsing and in pain before the fire got them in what appeared to be genuine sympathy. Little by little, the cries died, and only the nauseating smell of charred flesh remained. The smell was so suffocating they could almost taste it.

Sweet, putrid, and steaky.

More shadow creatures made their way toward the village. A few remained talking among themselves around the bodies. They passed the torches over the mountain of corpses. Tara moaned as the figures of their friends and loved ones went up in flames.

Between Needles

Brye

"THIS DOESN'T MAKE ANY sense," Brye shook her head, rubbing her face with her sleeve, cleaning the tears away. "Why would they slaughter innocent people?"

"How will I find him?" Tara buried her head, her body softly shaking.

Beltran leaned over once again to the side. "Four stayed behind."

"Probably to make sure the fire doesn't die out." Brye's voice cracked.

Beltran nodded. "We should head north to the break in the wall."

"Tara?" Brye whispered, pushing the locks of her sister's hair away from her hidden face. A snap of tension and grief ran through her fingers; she rubbed the sensation away. Tara's grief was too much to handle at the moment.

Tara took a long, shaky breath and wiped her eyes. "I'm ready."

"A distraction would be nice." Brye pointed in the direction of the shadow creatures.

The fire had grown and consumed more crumpled bodies—the smell of burnt fatty flesh mixed with tiny ashes of charred skin floated in the air.

Brye could not wait to escape the torture, her eyes burning. Tara kept wiping her face, trying to clean away the tears.

Beltran extended his hand in the direction of the fire. His eyes deepened as the smoke from the fire rose and changed direction. He then flicked his wrist, and an active flame jumped onto one of the shadow creatures. It squealed like a pig, throwing itself on the ground. The other watched, too surprised to move. Infuriated at its companions, it grunted and punched one of them.

They fought and wrestled on the ground until a tall black figure grabbed both creatures and bashed their heads together. They collapsed, and the more towering figure garbled. In response, they moved further downwind of the fire.

Beltran nodded at Brye and Tara. They followed the collapsed wall north, away from the improvised funeral pyre.

The stench was insufferable. Their clothes and skin were covered in sooty grease. Brye continuously wiped her nose with her sleeve. She noticed Tara doing the same.

Once they cleared the fields, Brye turned to Beltran.

"That was helpful." She rubbed her hands together. "It's the first time we've seen you do magic."

Beltran opened his mouth to speak, but Tara cut him off. "It was about time you did something useful, but we still need to find Gareth and Aiden. Time is running out." Tara motioned to the faint light over the horizon.

Locating Aiden in the semi-darkness, with shadow creatures walking about, killing off villagers, was a risk. Even if they found Aiden and Gareth, there was no guarantee that they could get off the island.

Brye bit the inside of her mouth to keep her teeth from chattering. She hoped Gareth would find them soon. Maybe he would bring Lenna?

Tara rubbed her face again, the tears making another appearance. Brye took her sister's hand.

"I..." Tara whispered thickly. "I wonder about Caitlin and Badar. They would have gone north."

"I couldn't make them out in the pile." Brye swallowed an uncomfortable knot in her throat.

"I couldn't either." Tara sniffled.

A snap ran up Brye's arm, cutting her concentration. She examined the grooves over Tara's skin.

"Tara, is this your marked hand?"

"Yes."

Brye ran her fingers down the thin, scar-like marks on her sister's wrist. The marks moved under her touch. Another jolt ran up her arm. Brye calmed her agitated mind, and narrowed her gaze until the emotions cleared and images appeared.

She was in a humid, shadowy field. The metallic smell of pooled blood filled her senses. The haggard, shallow breathing of someone in pain echoed in her ears. The coolness of the stone behind her back helped her focus. Her eyes blinked, and she saw piles of bodies around her. Some she recognized, and others were new to her. They were scattered around her in clumps. She held a sword covered in thick crimson liquid in her hand, and her other was pressed against her side. Each breath was more painful than the last.

I should have stayed behind.

Aiden's voice rang clear in Brye's mind. His regret filled every part of her, emptying the air from her lungs and tearing her heart apart.

Brye ignored Aiden's invading emotions and focused her attention on his surroundings.

She could hear the rustling of the water over the uneven breathing. The cracked and blackened White Thorn Tree in the distance came into view. The smell of its sweet flowers became an intense perfume that mixed with the metallic scent of blood. Brye's stomach knotted over the disgusting smell, and her mouth filled with bile. They were close.

But were they close enough?

Brye pulled back, stunned. Her eyes cleared, and she released Tara's hand.

"What was that?" Tara rubbed her wrist. "You grew still and cold."

Beltran removed his coat and placed it over her shoulders. She rubbed her arms. "I read the bond like I read people."

"And?" Beltran asked, his voice low.

"He's farther north. I don't know how he got there so fast."

"Is he alright?" Tara asked.

Brye gripped the strap of her kit harder than before. Her knuckles went white, and Tara's face crumbled.

"How long?"

"I don't know," Brye replied. "He is near what is left of the White Thorn Tree but further west by the wall. I could see the river and tree nearby."

"Then we go," Tara ordered.

Brye held back. "What about Gareth?"

A howl echoed along the valley. It is faint but still strong enough to distinguish its message. It was deeper, sinister, and angry.

Beltran and Tara stiffened at the sound. Tara yapped, and her hand gripped her sword. Brye searched around them for a threat but saw nothing except the glowing blue light of the sky.

A moment later, the howl stopped, and Tara and Beltran regained some of their composure. Tara groaned and rubbed her face forcefully.

"Gareth is looking for you," Beltran said.

"That's good news, right?" Brye asked wearily.

"Not for me," Tara muttered. "He's epically pissed at me."

"Why?" Brye asked. "No, wait, how do you know all this?"

"He was the one who howled," Beltran responded tentatively.

"If he is a Wolf Sh–"

"Pure." Tara interrupted. Brye rolled her eyes and gripped her satchel tighter. Really, it was just a word.

"*Pure* Wolf shifter, why are you reacting to it?"

"Because, so am I," Tara responded, shaking her head. "I think?"

Beltran nodded. "Both of your true forms were freed when the bond holding the magic to the island broke."

"Island bindings? True forms? I am missing information." Brye's voice became edged.

"Only you?" Tara snapped. "You are not the one ordered around, unable to free herself from his command."

Brye waved her hands in the air.

"A Pure Shifter's order is the law to subordinates," Beltran explained. "It's called compelling. It is rare."

"Not rare enough if Gareth managed it." Tara sighed.

"You seem especially forthcoming now," Brye pointed out.

Beltran raised his hand, silencing them. He waved in the direction of the rubble.

A small group of about ten shadow creatures headed their way. They stopped close, whispering among themselves.

Tara crouched along the rubble, pulling Brye and Beltran down with her. The monsters sat, speaking in low tones too occupied with themselves to notice.

But time was ticking away. With each moment that passed, Aiden was growing weaker. Brye could sense Tara's increasing agitation. It came to her in waves, forcing her to fidget where she sat.

What they needed was another distraction.

Beltran and Brye sat with their backs against the rubble, and Tara plunked herself carefully beside them.

"I'll wait until the shadow of this mound of rubble moves from here..." she marked two lines with her dagger in the sand, "to here. Those monsters are dead if Gareth has not arrived or Lenna does not create the mists. And then I will go find Aiden."

Brye pinched her lips but nodded.

Tara kept rubbing the marks on her hand. "Lenna, please. I hope you know what you are doing."

Brye wrung her hands and painfully counted the seconds left until sunrise.

Lenna

The tower was abandoned entirely. After securing the front and back doors, Lenna made her way up the stairs to Roweena's chamber. She found the woman sitting on one of the massive chairs by the hearth, looking into the fire.

An empty cauldron hung over the flames. The smell of herbs, burning wood, and incense tickled her nose. The fire was the only light and sound in the room. The shutters and windows were shut, giving the space a cave-like quality. It was too quiet for the amount of chaos and destruction that was happening outside.

"I was wondering if you would appear," Roweena commented without turning, her voice a long sigh. "I thought the wolf would help you and your sisters escape."

"The island has been invaded."

"Yes. That seems unfortunate." Roweena waved Lenna closer.

"It is our responsibility as protectors of this island to aid them in their escape."

Roweena scoffed. "What makes you believe I can accomplish that?"

"I don't think you can, at least not by yourself." Lenna wrung her clammy hands but kept a straight face. "We both know what needs to be done."

"Ah." Roweena turned, raising an eyebrow. "You have discovered my secret."

"Just the one?"

"Now, this is interesting."

"One of them is written all over your face," Lenna said.

"Oh!" The older woman rubbed her cheek, pulling her saggy skin. "Magic, or the lack of it, takes a toll. It isn't something I can control, just like this lamentable invasion."

"What do you know about it?"

"Nothing happens on this island that I am unaware of, at least in most places. For example, what was it like to kiss the mongrel? I at least hoped that you'd have better taste."

"As kisses go, it was what I expected."

"Then you have not been properly kissed."

Lenna stole the kiss, wanting to feel one before the end. And she cared for Beltran. He was the wolf, her friend. She did not love him even if she was disappointed in how everything ended. If she had, it would have made her want to escape.

"See? Unexceptional."

"What else do you know?"

"I know your sisters and the unbearably Beltran are heading for the northwest field as we speak. Gareth is fighting with his regained wolf shifter ability and strength in the training fields east of the tower. Some warriors are with him." Her gaze went to the hearth as if seeing what unfolded in the flames.

"Caitlin's son, Aiden, I believe? He fought bravely but was cut down and is now bleeding to death near the White Thorn Tree. He is desperate to say goodbye to those he loves. Well, too late, I suppose."

Roweena tilted her head, regarding Lenna curiously.

Lenna bit down hard on her lower lip, the blood pooling into her mouth. She had been desperate to know about her sisters, Gareth and Aiden. The news was distracting her from her original goal.

"These bindings you mentioned. I think my mother knew of them. But she could not see or make them," Lenna continued, matter-of-fact.

"You are correct." Roweena sighed, waving her hand in dismissal. "I doubt Elsywth was a Bondmaker. It is an ability that can be easily hidden, but your mother was not one for discretion, at least not regarding her powers."

"Can you make bonds?"

"Me? By the gods, no! That was never my magical ability. I can neither see nor make magical bonds." Roweena tapped her finger over her bottom lip. "But, your curiosity over bondmaking magic makes me wonder. Even more so than your mediocre elemental magic."

Lenna tentatively sat in the chair opposite Roweena. It was comfortable and warm from the fire. The room was cozy, even if the sense of safety was superficial. Lenna sighed and leaned back on the chair.

"Did you know that once the door of this room closes, time can flow differently?" Roweena said. "It can move faster or slower depending on the desires of the occupants. It is binding magic at its best. Clothos loved to experiment with time."

"Bending or binding time?"

"Both." The royal advisor regarded her as a specimen to analyze or collect. "How much time do you want?"

Lenna cocked her head to the side, observing the woman. Roweena had aged since the morning. Her skin was wrinkled and sagged, and her hair was almost entirely gray.

"You are the Elemental Founder."

"Lenna, you are becoming more interesting by the second."

"I will say the same about you."

They reached the end, and a sense of finality settled in the room. The faint screams of the dying seemed miles away, but it was only the prelude to one last evening.

One last battle of wills.

One last night for answered questions.

"Well, have you decided?"

Yes, she had.

"I would like to buy time until you tell me everything I wish to know," Lenna stated carefully, one of her fingers playing with the fabric over the armrest.

"And then?" Roweena's eyes darkened.

"I will fulfill my role as a true Mist Maiden."

"You will die," Roweena coldly remarked, snapping her fingers. The wooden door locked, and a hush filled the room. The only sound was the crackling of the fire and their breathing.

"Yes, Roweena. I will die... as my mother did," Lenna replied coolly. "Now, start at the beginning, and don't leave anything out."

History
Lesson

Lenna

"You guessed right, Lenna. I am the Elemental Founder. The Shifter was my sister, Helene, and the Bondmaker was my brother, Clothos." Roweena sat back; her arms relaxed on the armrests. Her eyes grew intense, darker, and more profound. Her voice was rusty with the lack of use. "I will attempt to enlighten your education further.

"The island was not always bound as it is now. After its foundation, Helene became the ruler, aiding those who came and teaching them our ways. She was a natural at it and respected by all. Clothos became a teacher, and I would advise on the fields and the weather. We lived in relative harmony."

"But then the Dragon Shifters came," Lenna interrupted softly.

"Yes." Roweena's features turned downcast. "Initially, they seemed genuine in their need for refuge, but time showed their true intentions. They wanted power and to gain Avalon as a breeding ground for other Shifters and Yuansu to regain control of the Continent. They killed Helene with the Leviathan Dagger." Roweena motioned to the table with the large book. There it was, the dagger that seemed to be a mix of metal and glass. Lenna had seen it before, and had thought it ordinary.

Why would she keep it?

Roweena seemed to have read her mind. "You would think we would abandon keeping an island full of powerful beings. At least, one would hope. But that did not happen. On her dying breath, Helene made us promise to continue protecting the island's magic. My sister was too soft.

"Clothos was the one that came up with the solution. He decided those seeking refuge must sacrifice their greatest strength—their magic. If you were willing to be bound, you were given entrance.

"I don't think he knew the extent of such a spell. By doing so, he would tie generations of magic inside their holders. With time, the memory of what they were would be erased from existence. Shifter's animals would lay dormant. Yuansu would be unable to channel their gifts, losing their ability to heal themselves and others. The price of peace was to become magicless."

"But that is not the only price." Lenna cocked her head to the side.

"Regrettably, no. A binding that strong takes its toll. He gave up his life essence to bind the island and disappeared.

"Generations passed, and fewer and fewer magic holders were born. Mist Maidens—those who showed visible magic and seemed to defy the laws of the bindings—were unusual. I assigned a royal family as leaders, while I became an advisor, a role I assumed without thought."

"And no one questioned your age? No one knew who you were?"

"Bindings take a toll on collective memory. The older you get, the less you can remember." Roweena waved her hand. "And time trudged along. Decade after decade until almost five hundred, if not more, years passed. Trapped by my brother in tribute to my murdered sister. I watched generation after generation of Avaloneans born magically castrated."

"Until my mother," Lenna pointed out.

"Your mother was born during one sweltering summer, along with a plague. Before we could find a remedy, your grandparents died."

"Did you know them?"

"Not particularly. They were unexceptional people, like everyone else. Elsywth was left an orphan and raised by different community members. When it became apparent that she was different, she ended up living in the tower with the previous king and the prince."

"The current king?" Lenna asked.

Roweena placed a hand on her forehead. "You are incredibly slow."

"No." Lenna leaned back. "Only incredibly curious."

"He might have been somewhat infatuated with your mother when they were younger. Everyone was. Elsywth was a force of nature. Imagine an empath who possessed superior strength. It was Yuansu magic at its best. I should have suspected it was the beginning of a series of problems.

"Elsywth was stubborn and strong. She had an opinion about everything and everyone. On more than one occasion, she expressed it freely and unfiltered. As soon as she was fifteen, she moved into the home of the previous healing woman to train and spend time with Enid.

"I saw no harm. I took her under my wing and helped her with tools to further her training. She assisted with the births of all the babies on our island, including the queen's pregnancies. The queen trusted her explicitly, to the point of only consulting her about her health.

"Unfortunately, many of the babies were stillborn. Then the prince arrived. I always had my suspicions about that particular birth. All the stillborns were girls up until Gareth. After what appeared to be a dangerous and waning pregnancy, suddenly she had a happy, strong, overly large baby boy."

Roweena shrugged, waving a hand as if dismissing the idea.

"You don't believe Gareth is the queen's son?"

"Of course not. But I have no way to confirm it. What do you think?"

"I think my mother was very good at keeping secrets."

Roweena narrowed her eyes. "More than that, she was remarkable at it. Not only her secrets but of others. She would be the only one who could truly answer if Gareth was a prince of Avalon or a substitute. And even if he was a false prince, would it have mattered at that point? We had an heir to the Avalon royal family! He was strong and everything a prince should be. No, the harm came later when she got pregnant with your sister, Brye.

"Elsywth trained by herself for hours. Or so she said. What could she possibly be training for? She had no mate and spent a great deal of time with women. She hid her condition for months, wearing loose tunics and robes. You can guess what a surprise it was to find out she was pregnant, and to make matters worse, she did not reveal the father. I demanded that she tell me who abused her, but she was adamant that it was consensual. Brye was born, healthy, and by all accounts, magically unremarkable."

"So, our father was not an Avalonean?"

"Your father is a mystery if you all share the same one. No Avalonean man has come forward to claim you. For all purposes, he could be an outsider or a ghost."

"Ghosts don't impregnate women."

"There is so much of our world we have no information about, you naive little girl."

Lenna tapped her lip, controlling the desire to fidget. The woman seemed to enjoy leading on her tale as people were being massacred outside the door, and her sisters were in danger. But she needed to play this out. With a wave of her hand, she asked, "What happened after?"

"She continued her role as a healer with Enid. Both were inseparable. Then once again, almost three years later, she was with child. Her condition was harder to hide this time around. She was continuously sick and lost a dangerous amount of weight."

Roweena rubbed her arms, her voice serious. "You were draining the life out of her."

Lenna looked away a moment and stared at the fire. The sense of pressure in the room became apparent to her, as if the walls were keeping something out.

Time passed, one slow second after another. But whatever was happening outside was on its way. Second by second, it crawled into the present. Lenna gripped the armrests, waiting for Roweena to continue her tale.

"Many of the villagers wanted to shun her. Imagine an unmated young woman with two children and no father."

"I don't remember being shunned."

"You weren't. If they had opinions, they kept them to themselves. They were too scared of losing the queen's regard, my favor, or Elsywth's healing abilities. It took no time for the villagers to warm to Brye and you. Babies, especially the adorable kind, can do that to people. Make them stupid and ignore all the warning signs."

"Why didn't you use your connection to the island to discover our father?"

Roweena tapped her temple. "Blind spots in my vision. I can only focus on some places at a time if I want to. That is when I suspected she was meeting with an outsider. I could confirm nothing. She stayed on the island for two years, and you and Brye thrived."

"Then came Tara," Lenna whispered.

"Yes, her pregnancy with Tara came as an absolute shock. This time, she did not attempt to hide it. It made her glow. She was stronger and more agile than ever before. After Tara was born, she became a mother to three little girls and a surrogate older sister to the prince. The little cub followed her around, getting underfoot.

"But, Elsywth could not keep magic a secret. Not hers and not her daughters. Rumors spread of Tara's unnatural strength and Brye's cunning intuition in the thoughts of others. You showed no magical abilities except for being on the sickly side. But it did not stop her from keeping you safe. She began to take you out to play near the northern field by the White Thorn Tree. She thought of isolating you, but I found out. I always do."

A sad smile played on Roweena's lips, and she leaned back in the chair.

"One afternoon, I came upon all of you at the river. I saw Tara lift Gareth and throw him into the running water. It was the first time I saw her shift. Her true form was revealed: a small rust-colored wolf. Gareth reacted and shifted as well. His white undercoat with rust overcoat coloring resembled Tara's, but his build was larger. Brye was close to the shore, laughing at their antics. Elsywth sat on the bank with you on her lap.

"I remember how my body grew cold. There have been no shifters born on the island for centuries. All were bound before birth. Do you even know what that meant?"

"It meant that the island's bindings were weakening, even then," Lenna said.

Roweena nodded. Her lost gaze was tinted with regret and melancholy.

The room grew colder, and the rush of blood to Lenna's head made her ears pound.

Both Tara and Gareth were shifters. Brye was an empath, like Maither. *And me? What am I?*

Lenna's mouth dried. "What happened next? Tell me."

Roweena's face grew dark and severe. "You were right. I am not a Bondmaker. I am but a Pure Elemental whose magic had waned over the years. Draining the magic of beings has kept me alive for this long. But with generations born with no gifts to drain, my abilities had plateaued. The only magic that came easy was the mists.

"I cared for your mother, but I knew it was only a matter of time before I would need her magical essence to keep myself alive. I could not see, but I felt the cracks in the bindings. The day Elsywth was born, the wall cracked, and by the time Tara was a year old, there was an invisible bridge and an enormous stone gap."

She knows about the gap...

Lenna thought she kept her face neutral, but Roweena raised an eyebrow at her. "Yes, I am aware of the gap, and I know you trained outside the wall. It was the only explanation for how your magic evolved. It is impossible inside the perimeter, but your continuous trips outside helped you gain a reservoir of magic. As you naturally tap into it, you will gain experience and strength. I lied. You are stronger than I gave you credit for."

"Have you considered leaving the island?"

Roweena scoffed. "Have you been listening? I am bound to the island. I can't leave; it was not for lack of trying. If I did manage to leave, I wouldn't make it a few paces before I shrivel up into a mound of dust and old bones. With all the care I take on my appearance, that is a look I could not manage."

There was a sudden snap of breaking wood. The sound went on and on, joined by a vibration beneath their feet.

"The front door has been breached," Roweena pointed out.

Lenna's heart pounded in her chest. Time was catching up. "What did you do about my mother?"

"I decided to speak to her. I had hoped she would see reason if I told her the truth and asked for help. I went to her one night and invited her to take an evening stroll. I took her to the northern field near the White Thorn Tree. I confessed who I was and how the island magic worked. She denied that any of you had magic. If it were so, it would have been bound at birth. She challenged me to go and see for myself. I didn't go.

"She believed the bindings were cursed and had to break. That no magic should last forever."

Roweena's face grew blotchy, and she gripped the armrests with enough force to make her knuckles white. "I was physically ill. She threatened everything my siblings died for, keeping the island safe. Who was she to question me? She was only a child. A spoiled, ungrateful girl." Roweena's voice grew, and her face contorted in a sinister scowl.

"I panicked, but it soon turned to rage. I knew if Elsywth left, I would lose the source of magic that I needed. I didn't want to take a chance. I gripped her with my tentacles. Clothos helped me develop these abilities, changing my essence and strengthening me."

"I drained her. She fought me, using her magic against my own, but it was not enough. What she had in energy, I had in experience. I saw her bright green eyes, the color of the forest dull before me. The light was gone forever."

Lenna paled. Roweena's words opened up the jagged wounds her mother had left. It made sense now who was at the door that night. Elsywth wanted to protect them from Roweena.

"I have cried very few times in my life. When you get as old as I am, you save your tears for only those who deserve your weakness. I cried when Dragon Shifters murdered my sister. I locked myself in my room and caused a storm when my brother disappeared. I broke when I killed Elsywth. I knew we were different, but I cared for her in my way."

"But you cared for the island more." Lenna pinched the bridge of her nose, taking a shuddering breath. A long, echoing sound came from outside the door.

"I cared more for my promise to my brother and sister." Roweena's eyes held unshed tears. Her voice resonated across the room.

"I promised my siblings I would protect Avalon, keep it safe and hidden no matter the cost. It was a mistake to care for Elsywth. I should have drained her at birth, but she was so charismatic—" Roweena wiped her eyes. "I, too, was in awe of her. I always knew if the island's magic broke, the least of the dangers was an external invasion. The worst was an invasion from below."

Lenna's scarred hands turned deathly white. "Below?"

"There are more worlds than Avalon or the Continent, young Lenna. Some you go to find peace in death. Another is a looped prison for the most dangerous beings that have ever existed. I did not know it then, but when Clothos chose the location of Avalon, he did it on the union of threaded bindings. A tapestry, if you could imagine, between worlds.

"Before we created the island, there was a rip in the tapestry. A path for those on the other side to come here. He linked the island to those bindings. The bound island became the locked door that kept the path closed. Once the bindings break, it would open, and those on the other side would rise to regain their lost lives."

"Lives? Are you speaking of the dead?"

"Oh no, the dead do not rise. Only those trapped in the In-Between, the land of the Forgotten Gods, can rise. They are creatures you do not wish to meet, in any lifetime."

"The dark figures are from the In-Between," Lenna realized. The strange empty beach where she spent her time while her body lay dormant. It did not feel dangerous at the time.

Roweena stared at the door confusedly. "Time's almost up."

In the last minutes, the room grew chillier, even with the crackling of the fire. They could hear the distorted screams from those still left outside every so often.

"Where is my mother buried?"

"Under the White Thorn Tree. She loved that place."

"Then don't you find it odd that the White Torn Tree's branches broke the wall? That the tree snapped in two and became a path for those in the In-Between to come up and slaughter everyone?"

Roweena paled, her eyes wide. "Do you think Elsywth was involved in this?"

"At this point, I know very little. This could have been avoided if you had trusted me to be your equal from the start."

Roweena shrugged. "Had I known you were an Elemental from birth, I would have killed you. I only found out after your public display of magic at Beltane."

So, Roweena had suspected her sisters but never of her. She didn't know the true extent of her magical abilities.

Garbled noises alerted them that the world outside the door was creeping in. The fire dimmed, and the shutters slowly creaked.

"Let's not dwell on 'what ifs'; they are a complete waste of time." Lenna waved a hand.

"Oh, do you have ideas now?"

Lenna sat taller. "Some, but that is neither here nor there. I know that if my sisters have any chance of escaping this massacre, you will have to do your job." Lenna leveled her gaze at the royal advisor. "Summon the mists to give the people the cover they need to escape."

"Why would I do that?"

"We each gain what we want. For you, it will be to fulfill your promise to your siblings." Lenna paused, looking directly at Roweena. "As for me, I am going to die for something I care about."

"The Continent is an unknown place for two untried Shifters and an Empath. You might be sending them to a far worser fate than what they face here. In the end, they might even beg for death."

"I can assure you neither of my sisters nor Gareth can beg. If any three could make their place in the world, it's them," Lenna said with conviction.

"That is being a bit too optimistic, even for you."

Lenna shrugged. "Beltran will guide them on the Continent."

"Oh yes." Roweena smiled knowingly. "The forgettable sage. He will prove very helpful."

"Sarcasm." Lenna rolled her eyes. "Like I haven't heard it before."

Roweena raised an eyebrow, tapping her thinning lips, hiding a smile.

"My, my... I would have loved to have gotten to know this Lenna. She at least has a sense of humor."

"A loss I am sure you will survive."

A cackle escaped the older woman before she stood up and ran her hands on the front of her dark dress. "The price you must pay is heavy. Are you ready, Lenna?"

"Of all people, you should not ask me that." Lenna stood as well and crossed her arms over her chest.

She reigned in her emotions with effort until they were tied down inside her stomach. If she was going to face death, it would be with dignity and the knowledge that she did the right thing. She had protected her sisters, her island, and herself. She refused to feel regret.

Roweena's skin darkened with the marks of her bindings, and her eyes deepened. Lenna gripped her crossed arms tighter against her middle until her nails left crescent marks on her skin. Her face blanched, but her features remained impassive.

Thick tentacles removed themselves from Roweena's legs, slithering along the floor.

"I'd love to tell you it doesn't hurt, but I might be wrong," Roweena said. As the tentacles gripped her ankles and forearms, Lenna ground her teeth to keep them from chattering. The tentacles burned along her skin, but she had felt worse.

Far worse.

"Oh, shut up and get it over with."

Collapse

Lenna

STANDING THERE, AS THE tentacles burned her flesh, Lenna's thoughts drifted to her short life.

What was the point of so much control? Always holding everything inside her: ideas, opinions, emotions, and magic. All contained until they exploded. Did she ever truly express herself? Shared herself with those she loved?

The room grew dark, and her thoughts ran fast in her sluggish brain. Had she ever been happy?

Are there no good things to come for you, Lenna?

Yes. She had. She had been happy with every second she had spent with her family and friends. They were her reason for being happy.

Too bad she would never be able to tell them.

Lenna tumbled onto the stone-cold floor. It should have been jarring, but it wasn't.

Why did dying feel so strange?

What a relief it would be to fall asleep.

Above her, Roweena blurred. Her dark figure faded into the background. Lenna let out a long sigh as the cold invaded her body. She relaxed, too tired to move. Roweena extended her arms, closed her eyes, and pulled the moisture from the clouds.

"The mists were never difficult. They take practice," Roweena explained, her voice a fading whisper to Lenna's ears. "You need air and water magic. You move the warm air over water to a cooler surface on land. You change the temperatures and...."

Connected to the advisor, Lenna saw the island—a bird's eye view of what was left.

The sun rose higher in the early morning, bringing light to Avalon's cruel reality. Slaughtered bloody bodies of men, women and children were piled together. Meaningless death decorated the horizon. Tears ran down her face at the loss of so much life.

Gareth fought near the training field with Duncan and other warriors. A few had fallen, among them the king who, for his age, held his own up until the last moment. A shadow creature appeared behind him and cut his throat with one swift motion. He slithered to the ground. Gareth roared and silenced the shadow creature with a wave of his sword.

Duncan collapsed shortly after, a gash opening his chest. Gareth's head fell back, and he howled. The enraged cry echoed along the valley, reaching Lenna through the connection. It vibrated into her chest, constricting her slowly beating heart.

Gareth reluctantly left the fallen and evaded capture. He made his way through the village to the Royal Tower.

In a blink, Lenna could see the field where the darkened carcass of the White Thorn Tree lay split open. Brye, Beltran, and Tara huddled behind the collapsed wall. Tara growled under her breath; her movements agitated even in the dawning light. Brye rubbed her arms, and Beltran sat with his back against the rubble, holding his sword close. A long, deep howl rang through the island. Angry and commanding, decorated with suffocating grief.

Gareth.

Dark rain clouds formed in the distance, quickly covering the light. A light misty drizzle settled over the island like a blanket, obscuring the view and giving cover.

Lenna's magic became a living entity, a pulse under her skin and a tugging at her heart. Like live threads, she focused on Roweena's tentacles, gripping them with all her might.

There was one person left to find.

Roweena groaned at the unexpected invasion, losing her grip on her power. "What are you doing?"

A connection works both ways.

Lenna blinked, and for a moment, she was outside in the misty air. Time suspended around her, humming a tune only she could hear. Birds stayed floating in mid-flight. Their wings sent tiny water droplets around her.

The leaves torn from the trees by the wind hung like decorations. A beautiful and eerie silence made her aware of the strangeness of the moment.

Time suspended its flow. That was what she needed—a bit more time.

With her mind's eye, Lenna explored the island. She moved from one point to another, searching at every fallen body, trying to find the face she needed. Lenna's heart ached when she recognized Caitlin wrapped around Badar near the scorched field. She held on to him even in death.

The ache only worsened when she found Enid. Her body sprawled out in every direction near an active fire. The greasy smell of burning flesh brought flashes of unwanted memories of fire lizards and pain.

It was too much senseless death.

Lenna found him north, by a still-intact part of the wall near the river. He was slumped, holding his side, his breathing haggard.

Aiden.

He managed to find his way there from the fallen bodies. Wounded but still alive.

Time resumed its pace. Rain and drizzle pelted down, and the wind whistled through the swooshing grass.

Aiden was ashen and confused. There was no mischief or hope in his sky-blue eyes, only resignation. Lenna tore against the constraints of Roweena's magic. Desperate to reach, touch, and let him know Tara was on her way. Brye would heal him. Someone would save him.

He wasn't alone.

"Aiden," she whimpered.

His eyes snapped open. They looked straight at her with recognition. She smiled in relief. Distorted voices came from far away. Lenna opened her mouth to scream when Roweena regained control over her magic.

Like a slingshot, Lenna catapulted back into the mists. She came crashing into her cold, motionless body on the floor. Her heart, which had tried to keep her alive, skipped a beat and stopped.

Angry
Momentum

Tara

A GROWING OVERCAST SKY obscured the calm of the dawning light. Dark, heavy clouds dwindled the blue and orange hues, and thunder followed a snap of lightning. With it, the mists slowly descended over the island. The high wind picked up the strands of Tara's sticky, moist curls. Relief settled over her like a blanket.

Lenna did it. She gave them protection.

But at what cost?

"I've waited long enough," she hissed, getting on her haunches. She wiped her wet forehead with the back of her sleeve.

"The sun hasn't even reached the line." Brye grabbed her arm.

"I don't care!" Tara ground out, removing her sister's grasp. "We are wasting time."

Precious time Aiden didn't have.

She crawled further along the rubble until she reached the side facing the field. Taking a quick look, she counted fewer shadow creatures than before. Some must have headed south while they waited.

Beltran was going to be no help. Gareth was still absent, and his howl of anger and resentment did not make her want to greet him.

The sense of desperation did not go away. She traced the lines along the bound hand. She could not feel Aiden there like Brye.

She ran her fingers over and over for the last hour, but there was nothing there. The only evidence of a connection was the increasing cold and numbness along the hand.

That can't be good.

Tara placed the cool hand against her stomach and un-clenched her fists. She closed her eyes, and her nose twitched as she distinguished between the new sensations: the wet grass and the mix of dead and dried flowers. Brimstone with ash coming from the fire, with an underlining fresh scent.

Spices and earth. She ran her hand along her nose as it itched. The shadow creatures were covered in sweet, twangy spices and earthy scents. The new smells were suddenly overpowered by one that made her eyes water, and she bit back a sneeze.

Wet dog smell.

"You're trying too hard." Beltran crouched beside her, rolling his shoulders. "Your senses can be overwhelming in the beginning. You need to learn to distinguish between the assault of information."

"Easy for you to say," she scoffed.

"I'll let you believe that." He gripped his sword tighter. Beltran looked up and closed his eyes, letting the droplets coat his dark, curly hair. For a moment, his eyes crinkled, and unshed tears coated his lashes. Then, he rubbed his nose with his finger.

"Wet, dirty, and bloody dog smell."

"Worse than you?"

He bit back a regretful smile.

The bushes rustled, and Gareth appeared drenched in blood and mud. His face was grim, and his eyes bloodshot, but his features softened when he found Brye. Brye reached out to him, and Gareth released a long, jarred breath.

Tara's chest ached upon seeing the prince's love for her sister. She breathed a shaky sigh before peeking to see if the dark warriors were still in the field. There were muffled conversations and even groans, but visibility was impossible. Unless the invaders possessed superior senses, they would not be able to see them.

Tara went back to rubbing her hand. She jumped when Brye's tingling fingers took hold of it.

"Let me see," Brye whispered into her ear. Tara nodded, and Brye's eyes became two midnight blue points as she sat still. She had never seen her sister like this, consumed by magic. She blinked a few moments later, and Byre's eyes returned to their soft brown.

"We need to make our way further north. He is shy of the White Thorn Tree. We will find him if we stay on this side of the wall."

Tara exhaled. She glanced at Gareth, who gave her a curt nod. In silent agreement, they crept around the rubble pile and darted for the cover of the trees, heading north.

Tara scouted ahead, leaving Gareth, Brye, and Beltran behind. But the trees were dense, and no sound came from the forest. A deathly vibrating calm. She sucked in a deep breath, relieved that the smell of burning bodies was fading.

She glanced over her shoulder. Gareth had a firm grip on Brye's hand, and Beltran brought up the rear of their group. She did her duty and protected Brye. The tension around her caused by the compulsion was gone. All they needed was to find Aiden and leave.

No, that wasn't true. Lenna had stayed behind. Tears prickled her eyes, and she hunched her shoulders as she walked. Lenna was trapped in the tower with a crazed woman trying to be a hero. She bought them time so they could get off the island.

Around them, it seemed more night than day, with storm clouds that at any moment would open up and drown them. The consistent thick drizzle was enough to freeze their bones.

Behind her, Brye struggled with her half-dress and cloak. The fabric stuck to her legs and was held down by the mud. Gareth took her aside and cut the dress with his dagger, leaving only the pants. He did the same with the cloak and picked up her kit. Brye kissed him, and they went back on their way.

Only the sound of their steps accompanied them. Even the woods they crossed seemed empty of life, as if it was all waiting, suspended in time.

Tara was left alone with her thoughts and concerns. A place she hated being. She always tried not to dwell on her feelings and worries. No matter how overwhelming they became. But now, as she made her way north, tracing her fingers over the lines on her hand, nothing could stop her from spiraling.

She wondered what would happen if they managed to escape and what awaited them off the island. All their lives, they were taught to fear the Continent. They were fed stories of persecution and death. It seemed like children's stories about monsters that ate little girls at night.

But the monsters were not on the Continent. They were burning the bodies of her friends and family. Tara sniffed and cleaned the tears away over and over.

Anger was an overwhelming emotion threatening to consume her. It was easier to feel anger than the uncontrollable guilt, terror, and loss that bubbled under the surface.

Tara didn't want to blame Lenna, Brye, or her mother. But someone needed to be blamed. This could all have been avoided if they had been open from the beginning.

Why hadn't her mother trusted them with the truth? Why hadn't Lenna or Beltran? Or even Brye, who would know more than anyone, being able to read into their thoughts and emotions? Why did they all need to keep secrets that would only bring them pain?

Tara sped up, taking longer strides as she made her way up the path. She couldn't dwell on that. She needed to find Aiden and get off this dying island once and for all. That pressed down on her even more than all this uncertainty and questions. She thought about what she had lost and regained only when they were finally safe.

Test your Mettle

Tara

THEY MADE IT NORTH to the river. Tara sniffed the air, and the metallic smell of blood raised the hair on the back of her neck. She wiped the water from her face and stopped short. A short figure in a gray cloak stood perfectly still a few feet away. The image distorted itself the closer she got.

"Lenna?" Tara's jaw went slack, and her eyes grew wide. The figure dissipated in the mist. In its place, slumped against the wall, was Aiden.

Tara fell to the ground in front of him. His eyes were closed, and his hand was against his ribs. The iron smell mixed with another so intense, that Tara needed to shake her head to concentrate. She gripped Aiden's face gently, rubbing his deathly cold cheeks with her thumbs.

"Aiden?"

"Let me examine him." Brye appeared beside her, setting her kit down. Gareth and Beltran guarded nearby.

"Lenna?" Aiden mumbled. Tara tightened her lips but still gripped his hand to get his attention.

Tara shook her head. "She's not here. Look at me, Aiden."

He opened his eyes slowly. Brye gasped, and Tara bit her lip to avoid doing the same. His sky-blue eyes, usually warm and vibrant, were cold as ice. She softly touched his cheek and ran her thumb over the bruises around his face.

"What did they do to him?" Tara croaked, rubbing her hands against her damp pants.

"Give me some space," Brye ordered. She pulled Aiden's torn tunic up. The cloth stuck to the large gash that ran from his ribs to his waist. Once the material stopped pressing down, fresh blood oozed from the wound. Brye quickly replied pressure.

As Brye worked, her eyes became two pools of midnight blue narrowed in concentration. Tara held her breath, running her hands over her thighs to keep them warm and dry.

"He has lost too much blood and has some internal injuries. The wound is too deep for me to tend here. I need more than this kit."

Brye shook her head, and her eyes returned to their dark, russet depths. With her free hand, she clumsily searched in her kit for supplies.

Gareth joined them, dropping to his haunches beside Brye. "Tell me what you need."

She placed another cloth on the wound and pressed down harder than before. Aiden moaned, his face drawn and flushed.

Tara felt an ache in the back of her throat. "Brye..."

"Let me work," Brye snapped. Her movements were purposeful as she cleaned the wound. She whispered to Gareth, and he handed her what she needed. The entire time Tara stood frozen, trying only to warm his hands.

But it wasn't helpful.

Only when Brye poured a dark green liquid over the open wound did Aiden's eyes snap open.

He looked around crazed, his attention unfocused, until his eyes fell on Tara.

"Tara?"

"Yes!" She got in his line of vision. "I'm here."

"Lenna? I saw Lenna." His eyes darted behind her, searching. Tara turned back. Her stomach rolled.

There was no one there.

Gareth asked, "I thought we were going to meet her."

Tara gripped Aiden's hand tighter. His bones strained under her fingers. He groaned, and she loosened her grip. "Didn't Beltran tell you?" she said to Gareth, but her eyes didn't leave Aiden. "She stayed behind in the Royal Tower."

"Why didn't you go back to get her?" Gareth growled at both Beltran and Tara. Beltran moved to answer. The smack of Gareth's fist snapped his head back. Beltran cursed and spat blood on the floor as he glared at Tara.

"She was your responsibility!" Gareth ground out.

"No, she wasn't! No one is." Tara jumped to her feet, trembling as something clawed under her skin. It ran up and down her arms, snapping and biting inside her.

Calm. I need calm.

But she was far from it. "She is an adult! Like us. If she decided to stay, it was her choice. Didn't you say we should trust and respect her choices?"

"This is not one of those moments, Tara." Gareth pointed behind them. "This island is dying. You left your sister back there to die along with it."

"I... we..." Tara's voice deflated, and she turned away to stare at the river.

"She locked herself in the tower with the advisor," Beltran muttered, rubbing his jaw. He kept his gaze averted. "She said she would control the mists to help us escape."

"Did you know about this?" Gareth asked Brye.

Brye nodded. "We tried to convince her to come, Gareth. And she was going to, but then she decided to stay. Beltran stayed behind to convince her to leave with us."

"You should have forced her to come. We—" Gareth turned away.

The uncomfortable silence grew. Each lost in their thoughts for a few moments as Brye continued attempting to heal Aiden. Tara knelt and reached for his hand.

His eyes snapped open, pupils dilating. "You have to go."

"What? No! We are going to heal you, then we will go." Tara held his clammy face. He was burning up.

"Brye, can't you do something about the fever?"

"I'm trying—"

"Now, you have to go!" Aiden pushed Brye's hands away. His eyes were wide, and his nostrils flared. For a moment, there was an odd green flash around his iris that quickly faded. "Can't you smell them?"

The stench of brimstone and ash slowly made its way into the humidity. Beltran and Gareth grabbed their swords.

"Work faster, Brye," Tara hissed desperately, her eyes darting around, trying to identify the threat.

"I can't!" Brye snapped, her hands covered in blood and ointments. Her eyes prickled with unshed tears. "It's not that simple."

The grass crunched a few feet away, and the soft wind brought the smell of ash closer. Gareth and Beltran widened their stance as six shadow creatures appeared.

They stopped abruptly a few feet away. Their uneven forms shifted as they moved. The creatures turned to one another and spoke in their gargled language. One broke out in an uneven sound that appeared to be a chuckle. Soon, the entire group burst out in laughter. Tara squinted against the drizzle. Their bodies seemed to be made of the same consistency as the mist.

Tara rose reluctantly, letting go of Aiden's hand and removing her sword from its sheath. Beltran and Gareth did the same. They formed a semicircle with their back to Brye, Aiden, and what was left of the wall.

It was not a good position. They were cornered and outnumbered. With one injured person and another unarmed, they would waste more energy on their protection than on the offensive.

Gareth planted his feet wider and bared his teeth. Beltran gripped the sword and growled under his breath. Tara stiffened, and her body ran hot. Whatever was inside her prickled at her skin, increasing the awareness of her surroundings. Her senses heightened, especially her scent, which was already a source of confusion.

"They're not what they seem," Tara called out, gripping her sword tighter. Her heart pounded, and a roar filled her ears.

"No," Beltran spat out.

"Time to test your mettle, Tara, the terrible," Gareth muttered in her direction. His face was set in stone, preparing for what was to come. "Let's see what you're made of."

Those words from the training field seemed so long ago.

Another person.

Another life.

Tara released a breath and let go of the control she held together.

Something moved around inside. A wolf too weak to shift but present enough to offer strength. It was like greeting an old friend. Tara's eyes turned a deep onyx, and with it, the shadows cleared. In the rising dawn light, people of various sizes with weapons stood before them. They were only disguised by magic.

Four had swords and daggers, and the other two held double-edged axes. Dressed in dark clothing, cut wider along the legs and the arms. Some had cloths tied around their heads and necks, and when the wind picked up again, Tara could distinguish a new scent underneath the brimstone.

Spices and sand.

Three invaders drew away from the group and lunged. The other two tried to reach Brye and Aiden against the wall. They crashed over the wet grass as a flying body pushed them back. Gareth rolled his shoulders and gripped his sword tighter.

Tara sprung on the warrior ax-wielding warrior nearest to her. He blocked her attacks expertly, the long ax giving him the advantage. Tara stumbled back from the clash of steel. She adjusted her technique and widened her stance to support the impact of the ax.

He barely missed her twice. Debris rose around her as her back hit the wall, moments before an ax descended.

Attempted Farewells

Brye

BRYE'S HEART POUNDED AS she tried to focus on repairing Aiden's wound. But no matter how much she attempted to stitch the tissue and muscle back together, they would not stay in place.

The severity of the injury could not be tended to under the present circumstances. It would take more effort, time, and a clean environment. She had none of that. Aiden continued to lose blood and he was moments away from death. It was a miracle that he survived this long.

The battle was so close that she had to duck a few times from being struck. "Aiden, you have to work with me."

His mouth twitched a response, before his face distorted. A burly man yanked her hair, dragging her into the circle of fighters.

Brye's legs slipped on the muddy ground, and she screamed her throat raw. The man muttered to himself the entire time in an accent too thick to understand. Gareth called her and he maneuvered to reach her, but fell back.

Her hands were slick with sticky blood, but she snagged onto the man's wrists, cutting flesh with her nails. Immediately upon contact, a wave of desperation and regret flooded her system. It was overpowered by despair.

This man didn't want to be here. He did not want to hurt her, but he had to. He was anxious to get rid of her.

Why? Why is he even doing this?

Brye didn't want his regret, the burn inside his stomach, or the bile that made its way up his throat at the thought of the murdered children.

How dare he feel regret and remorse!

Brye's screamed her rage into her hands, and brought forth pain. She reopened every wound, every scar on the man's body.

He froze, gargling, and tried to let go of her hair, but she strengthened her grip. The crescent shape of her nails became infected, gangrenous wounds. The lacerations on his back reopened, showing the indents on his spine. His eye bulged out of his skull. His piercing scream turned frenzied, and he tried to raise his leg to kick Brye away. It snapped in two before her eyes.

It took only a few moments, but it seemed to go on forever until the man crumpled to the ground, foaming at the mouth. His eyes glazed over, then he was gone.

Brye's hand trembled. The nails on her hands were chipped and purpled from being twisted by his flesh. New blood mixed with Aiden's.

Aiden.

Brye pushed her stiff body into action and sprinted back. Aiden sat still as a stone, deathly pale, but his eyes were wide as he watched the scene unravel before him.

Gareth and Beltran each managed to slay an opponent before moving on to the others. There were only two left, and they were not easily swayed. Tara still held her own. Her back to Brye and Aiden, she maneuvered the ax-wielding giant away. In the distance, there was a garbled yell. Reinforcements were on their way.

"You need to go," Aiden ordered, punctuating each word with a painful breath.

"You're bleeding too much. I need to stop it," Brye replied.

"You can't," Aiden whimpered. "We both know you can't."

Brye's face was drenched in tears.

This can't be happening.

The air sizzled and crackled. Static electricity raised the few dry hairs on her head, and small snaps of bluish light floated around them. A long crackle of lightning stretched across the sky. Thunder vibrated the earth beneath their feet.

Brye screamed and protected Aiden with her body as a high-pitched screech erupted and a lightning bolt struck the middle of the field.

A female invader fell to the ground in marked, sizzling flesh.

Tara

With an underhanded swing of her sword, Tara opened the giant's chest and cut his throat. The man fell to the ground. Gareth and Beltran finished each of their opponents. They rid themselves of the invaders, but not for long.

All three were scratched and sore, but none were seriously injured.

Tara sheathed her sword and knelt beside Aiden.

"What was that? Where did it come from?" she asked, searching the sky.

"I don't know," Gareth answered. "But we don't have time."

"You have to go." Aiden struggled to stay awake, his voice slurred.

"We are going together, and that's the last of it." Tara made to carry him.

"Damn it, Tara, for once, listen to me!" he bellowed.

Her eyes filled with tears. She bit her lip hard to keep it from trembling.

"Brye's magic isn't working." He grimaced in obvious pain. Tara turned her pleading eyes to Brye.

Brye nodded, her blotchy face evidence of the reality before them.

"No, no!" Tara ranted desperately, gripping Aiden's face. "She needs to try harder,"

"Sweetheart, it isn't about trying harder. It won't work," Aiden whispered, gripping her hands tightly.

His eyes, the warmth of the summer sky, pleaded. "You need to let go."

"I can't leave you," Tara whispered desperately. She kissed his sweaty forehead, the bruises around his eyes, then his cold lips. "We are mated. We belong together." Her voice cracked. "I love you. I need you, Aiden."

Tara couldn't imagine a life without Aiden. There were a few moments when he wasn't by her side, and now she had to go to an unknown place without him.

She never wanted a mate. To be tied down to a man who would not appreciate her.

But she had been wrong.

Aiden was the only one worthy, and now he was forcing her to let go. Tara held him harder as racking sobs erupted from her until her vision blurred, and she gasped for air.

"Tara." Aiden removed her hands, keeping them in his cold grip. His eyes, still full of pain, searched her face. "You will rebuild a life for yourself. A good, long life with your sisters and two very smelly friends." His voice cracked, but he still attempted to give her a crooked smile.

"That's not funny," Tara whimpered.

The gargling conversation grew closer. Small, thin vines slithered their way along the intact wall slowly in their direction. They reached Aiden and covered him gently.

"No!" Tara pulled the vines apart with her bare hands, but they kept coming. "Leave him alone!"

"It will be alright, Tara," he reassured. "Everything will be alright. I love you."

A pair of arms wrapped around her middle as Gareth half-carried her away. Brye held one of her hands.

Aiden was gently covered in long vines and fragrant flowers. The thorns became sharper and more prominent, but the cocoon seemed like a protective chrysalis around his crumpled body.

A vine grave.

"No!" Tara wailed. She kicked and fought against Gareth and Beltran as they tried to restrain her. Didn't they see? She needed to get him. Aiden was not supposed to stay behind.

"We have to go, Tara," Gareth whispered.

"I'm sorry." Brye took her sister's face. "Forgive me."

The last thing she saw before her vision went black was her sister's dark, pleading eyes and the sweet fragrance of white flowers over a vine grave.

Brye

Brye made her sleep. Gareth lifted Tara over his shoulder. They had a few seconds, but they took it to give one final look at Aiden.

He looked peaceful as if sleeping. His long legs were in front of him, his body leaning on the vines that served as a pillow. Brye reached down and kissed him on his cheek. He was cold to the touch.

She couldn't save him. Her magic hadn't worked, and it was the first time in her life that happened. When she needed her abilities the most, they failed her.

Brye's breath hitched. Gareth took her hand gently, but his urgency was impossible to ignore. The voices grew louder. Time was of the essence if they were to escape.

Gareth had been right. Avalon was becoming more than a dying island.

It was becoming a mass grave.

Bondmaker

Lenna

IN THE BEGINNING, THE pain of having the magic sucked out of her was excruciating. Lenna begged for it to be over. Once she zapped back into her body, she fell into merciful nothingness.

But life was not done with her yet.

Opening her eyes, Lenna found herself standing over her unconscious body. Invisible, like the air in a silent room.

A now crowded room.

Why am I still here?

Once the invaders entered, the shadows disappeared, revealing two women and men. All of them with diverse builds and weaponry. All weary-eyed and challenging.

The most menacing of the group was the scarred giant. He entered with a broad smile as bright as his amber eyes. His skin was tan, and his dark, curly brown hair was wrapped in a bun on the top of his head.

A large scar decorated his features from his ear to the middle of his throat. He laughed boldly, waving the ax from side to side. He seemed to be the apparent pack leader, with his whole body vibrating with authority.

"Well," he said with a thickened accent. "It has been a while, hasn't it? A couple of centuries at least!"

"And still not long enough for my refined tastes." Roweena straightened, wiping her hands.

"No, darling." The man scratched his trimmed beard, smiling with enough mischief to make Roweena weary. "Not nearly enough."

Roweena scowled and sat down, crossing her legs and leaning back with her arms over the armrests. Lenna's connection with the woman was still intact. Underneath the bored and uninterested features hid nerves that crawled along Roweena's skin.

The giant walked comfortably around the room. His shoulders were broad, and his arms muscular, flexing ever so slightly as he played with a glass orb from the table.

He was one of the tallest men Lenna had ever seen. He seemed to be born naturally strong rather than a product of training. He wore dark, fitted pants and calf boots tied below his knees. His shirt was long-sleeved and a dove gray, with beautiful embroidery of vibrant colors—all clean of blood.

Angles marked his young face and a strange softness that turned to stone every time he looked at Roweena.

But it was his eyes that gave her pause.

Amber, like melted hot wax mixed with a hint of mischief, as if he held power and secrets of the world.

He dropped the globe on the table and picked up the dagger. He ran his hands over the blade.

"You kept it?" he asked.

"Hard to get rid of something so powerful."

"I'm sure." He motioned to Lenna's inert body. "Who was she?" He replaced the dagger on the table.

Roweena's shoulders relaxed ever so slightly. "A magic holder of no significance."

"Really? A magic holder born on the island?" He smirked, and the smile lit up his features. Lenna's chest burned at the sight.

"Who says she was born here?" Roweena ran her index finger along the armrest. "I needed a power source, and she was available."

"Because I doubt some idiotic magic holder would come from the Continent and fall into your claws." He leaned against the wall.

Roweena crossed her hands over her stomach. "To what do I owe this displeasure? Am I the last one on the kill list? You seem to have slaughtered everyone else."

"If it were up to me, you would have been dead before you opened your pretty little mouth. But the High Priestess wants you taken back alive."

"I am grateful for the invitation, but I regretfully decline."

The giant straightened and sniffed, scratching the underside of his dark beard. He turned toward the guards at the door. "Leave us. The challenge is almost up."

Two guards left. The other pair stood guard at the half-opened door. He sighed and sat down on the chair Lenna had vacated.

Her body was on her side by his feet. He leaned over, and his calloused fingers moved the hair that had stumbled on her face. He ran a thumb softly over the cut on her lower lip. His touch was strangely gentle and almost exploratory as if he wanted to identify the angles on her face. The intensity of his regard brought shivers along her skin. His hand flinched, then curled into a fist. "She doesn't look like your type."

He placed an ankle on his knee, cocking his head to the side, examining Roweena. "Once they finish checking, we can head back. Of course, you could use your vast abilities to inspect the island. It would be so much easier."

"Make it easier for you? Please. We both know I wish you crossed over and rotted in hell," she replied coldly.

"Thankfully, that did not happen. Why the sour welcome, Roweena? I thought you would be glad to see a familiar face." The chair creaked under his weight, and he chuckled. The sound did odd things to Lenna's chest, like plucking cords along a fine-tuned instrument.

Who is this man? What is he?

"Pray, do tell me, Enver. Why should I be glad you betrayed our secrets to the Dragons so they could murder my sister?" she fumed.

"You and I have different versions of those events. Besides, it happened five hundred years ago. Are you still upset?"

"Are you, *Khuzaymah*?"

Enver's nostrils flared, and his amber eyes flashed. A hot sensation filtered from his body, heating Lenna's cold skin. Roweena tossed her head and tapped her finger over her smiling lips.

"We both know that Clothos, your big brother—"

"Only brother."

"—made sure I could never properly shift again, not in any lifetime. After his convenient disappearance, I was imprisoned and sentenced for treason. The royal family you placed in power fulfilled the sentence," Enver ground out. "Since then, I have been stuck in the In-Between, biding my time and competing in the Challenges. Five hundred years gives you much time to think."

"Oh, I think it's very little," Roweena hissed. She stood and walked around the room, ignoring the sudden stares of the guards. The tentacles slithered in her wake.

"I missed this just as much as having my head cut off," he sneered.

Roweena scoffed, flinging her hands in the air.

Enver grew serious. He placed his elbows on his knees. "Do you even know what happens when you do not want to die, Roweena?"

"You become an entitled bore?" Roweena paced.

"You are stuck between places, in an endless loop with no ending in sight. Except for the challenges when they appear. And when you win—"

"Which, with your temper, you must have won only a few—"

"You are granted a boon." Enver forced out. "But all boons come with a price."

Roweena stood still, her hands stiff at her sides. "What was it?"

"I wanted to come up and kill you," he said coldly.

"But you can't." She resumed pacing.

"No, the High Priestess decided bringing you back with us would be best. The Jester didn't. You know how siblings are. They never agree on anything. She wanted to bring you. He wanted to murder everyone. They compromised."

"Oh? So, kill everyone but me? That was the compromise?"

"In their world, death means nothing, only entertainment." Enver sat back, his teeth set. "We are all entertainment."

It was a game of cat and mouse. Each tried to outmaneuver the other with information or comments. Enver sat relaxed while Roweena paced her nerves away. The tips of his rugged boots were against Lenna's stomach. Unconsciously, he leaned down and pulled a lock of her hair, twirling it with his fingers. He played with the lock momentarily, bringing it to his nose to sniff.

Every time Enver leaned over Lenna, an odd tightness came to her chest. Why couldn't he stop touching her? Stranger still, why did she like it?

He didn't lift his gaze even when Roweena's shrill voice penetrated the room.

"Enver, she is lying to you. I cannot leave Avalon. I cross over, and I will disappear. The High Priestess and the Jester are bored and looking for something to do. They have been locked in the In-Between for too long."

"Irrelevant at present. The High Priestess wishes to see you." Enver released Lenna's hair, cocking his head to the side. His smirk increased Roweena's nervousness.

"What use am I to the High Priestess dead?"

"Oh, we both know that is untrue. Clothos must have trained you to be a Bondmaker. It is the only way you could still be alive today."

"I am not a Bondmaker!" Roweena hissed.

"If anyone can decipher bondmaking magic, it's you. And if anyone can convince you, it will be the High Priestess."

Lenna, do you see them?

A voice echoed, drowning out the conversation between Enver and Roweena.

"See what?"

The bindings around your hands?

Lenna recognized the male voice from the night the tree bird invaded.

She refocused on the conversation between the two other people in the room, but it blurred and slurred. Time slowed to a stop.

Can you see them?

Lenna looked down at her body on the floor. Enver was back to playing with her hair, but her face was turned away to the side.

What is with him and my hair?

Crouching down, she examined her hands and arms but found no evidence of the bindings.

Concentrate.

How did she do it last time?

I felt them before I saw them.

She focused her attention until her brain fuzzed, and all was silent. Behind her eyelids, it grew light until there was an unignorable brightness.

She slowly opened her eyes and squinted. Lenna was alone in an empty room with walls, floors, and ceiling covered in a soothing white. There were no doors or windows. She raised a hand to rub her face and gasped.

Her hands were covered in knotted tattoos intertwined around her fingers and scars. Looped designs with no start or finish went up her arms to her shoulders. She traced the line that started on her right hand up to her wrist. They moved with a burning and tingling sensation.

So, these are what have tied her magic all this time.

Break them.

Lenna flinched. The voice whispered close to her ear, moving the hair near the nape of her neck.

"I don't know how," she answered, tugging her earlobe.

Lenna examined the knots on her hands until her vision blurred and her head ached. There was no change in them. She groaned, rubbing her temples.

"This is ridiculous." Lenna paced the white room.

What did she know about making bonds or breaking them? Her experience was limited to a few life-or-death moments. It was not enough.

Where do I even start?

"You start by seeing the threads and understanding what is being bound." A man of a medium and slim build appeared out of the white mist. He was handsome in a scholarly way, like someone who spent more time hunched over a book than outdoors. He was dressed entirely in black, with pants and an open shirt. His chest was tattooed in thin vines with blooming flowers and small thorns. They were delicate and beautiful.

The man's features were relaxed, with a short and trimmed beard and curly brown hair that fell over his forehead. He had strands of gray hair around his temples and beard, but his face seemed younger.

He extended his hand in greeting, and Lenna hesitantly reached out.

"You must visualize the tapestries that make up our time and place."

"Who are you? You look familiar." He lifted her hand and gave it a soft kiss. His breath was delicate on her skin.

"Do I? I'd hope so." He let go of her hand and stuck both inside his pockets. "I am Clothos."

"You are the Bondmaker. Roweena's brother," Lenna stepped back. "You are supposed to be dead."

"You said it well, supposedly," he responded, waving his hand, and two white chairs formed before them. "But no true Bondmaker is ever dead. We live on in the tapestry of the bonds that we make. Some of us are not destined to fade away completely."

He motioned her to sit.

"Is that why I am not dead either?" Lenna asked, biting down on her lip.

"You are not dead because Roweena can't kill you. You are bound to the island." He motioned the chair again, and she sat. He followed.

"The only way you can free yourself is by freeing the island. I attempted to explain as such to your mother, but she didn't let me. She was too strong-willed. She wanted you to use your powers before you were ready."

"You taught my mother how to use a binding spell?" Lenna rubbed her hands together.

"Unfortunately, yes. But she did not think it through," he explained, crossing his legs and placing a finger under his chin. "She should have waited until you knew about your magic. Your mother was always so stubborn. Brilliant, but stubborn." A soulful smile touched his lips.

"Was there something between you two?"

"At one time," Clothos responded.

Lenna's eyes fell on his relaxed shoulders and easy bearing. For a dead spirit, he was exceedingly calm and collected. "Are you going to elaborate?"

"No." He cocked his head to the side. "I will be honest. You are not what I expected."

"I should say the same."

"What did you expect?" he raised an eyebrow.

"For example, do you age at all? You should be close to being a thousand years old, yet—"

"I look a handsome thirty?" Clothos wiggled his eyebrows.

"A dignified forty." Lenna motioned with her finger.

"Ouch." Clothos sat back, waving his hands. "Yes, well, age is different for me. I keep well."

Beside her, the wall shifted and moved. Stones emerged from the soft whiteness, a gaping hole with wood and a grate, with a fire that sparked to life. The chairs were crimson and plush, with high backs and thick armrests. The rest of the room stayed the same.

"Are you doing this?" Lenna asked.

"Yes."

"How do I know I can trust you? Your sister tried to kill me."

He took a moment to answer, his gaze going to the fire. "When I was younger, my sisters, mother, and father were all I had. Then, all I had were my sisters. Then, I had no one. I could never trust others not to use me or myself not to be used." His posture was relaxed, but his face was not so. He looked tired and melancholy.

"I am sure you know what it feels like to be the only one of your kind. To never be wanted for who you are, but what you are."

She did. To be simultaneously powerful and powerless.

He might be telling me what I want to hear.

She couldn't trust him, but she couldn't afford not to. He was the only one who knew what to do.

"What am I, Clothos?" she whispered, her hands rubbing the armrests carefully.

"You are a unique magic holder. At a young age, you showed elemental magic. Those are the most apparent. It rains when you are sad. Thunders when you are angry. Sunny if you are happy. Bondmaking magic is more subtle. If you are not looking for it, others will not notice. However, the extent of those abilities is still unknown."

"And how will I be able to know?"

"By seeing what you can do." He stood up and extended his hand. Lenna gripped his, surprised at its softness.

"Don't be afraid."

"I have little choice. You are the only one who might give me answers."

"Then I hope to be a good teacher." He leaned in and winked. Lenna held back a smile. It was hard to dislike him. He seemed sure of himself and projected too much of a sense of security.

In a blink, his calm features shifted to a stony expression. His eyes transformed into a deep, dark amber.

"Let's begin."

Tapestry Work

Lenna

Around Lenna, the bright room changed once more, returning back to the advisor's chamber. Enver and Roweena sat in the two chairs, frozen in place. Lenna's body was on the floor, unmoved.

Clothos moved his hand, and the room became vibrant, with braided threads and tapestries along the walls, as if each artifact was made of cloth with threads and knots. Lenna forgot to breathe, captivated and suddenly quite overwhelmed. Clothos rubbed her back, grounding at the moment.

"The first time is the hardest. There is so much to focus on. You could get lost in the details for hours."

Lenna took deep breaths. "What do I do?"

"Focus on what you want to work with, and the rest will fade. It takes practice to see them and unsee them."

Enver sat tense in his chair. One of his ankles was over his other knee, and he still held Lenna's hair in his fingers. Twirling it over and over. The heat in Lenna's stomach curled with each pass of his fingers, tightening and tightening.

Clothos swiped his hand. The rest of the tapestries disappeared before her eyes. Except for one.

"Hello, old friend." Enver's body was made up of colorless and dull braided threads. The only detail was the embroidered dragon that covered his heart. Lenna knelt closer, fascinated by the detail in the threadwork. It was glorious and alive. The dragon was curled around his tail, asleep, breathing ever so slightly.

In contrast to the dullness in Enver's threads, Roweena was iridescent. Her threads were a vibrant crimson, with tones of blue, gray, and greens intertwined to form braids of different thicknesses around her heart. They pulsed with power, rushing the magic around her body like blood.

"These..."

"Those are the threads that make up every living and nonliving thing in our world. They are what we Bondmakers access to create our magic." He walked behind Enver, placing a hand on his shoulder.

The threads lit up like tiny lights. The dragon cooed, shaking its head in sleep, as smoke came out of its nostrils.

Lenna's eyes grew wide, and a small gasp escaped her lips as she touched the creature with her index finger. The small, sleepy dragon rubbed against her finger, licking it with its threaded tongue. After a moment, it hissed and then settled once more. She twirled one of the threads attached to its wings with her fingers. It crackled and snapped, the heat intensifying under her touch.

Like fire.

Lenna hesitated. An unexpected but powerful sensation settled in the pit of her stomach, then wrapped itself around her heart. Unaware, she leaned in the man's direction, breathing in the strangeness of his scent.

Hot nights and spices.

"Interesting." Clothos crossed his arms and cocked his head to the side.

Lenna jumped back. "What is?"

"You."

Lenna's face and body flushed, and she looked away. "Was this you're doing? Binding his dragon form?"

"Yes."

"Why? He seems so..." She rubbed the threads again. The dragon opened its sleepy eyes and continued to lick her finger.

"Irritating?"

Lenna let go of the dragon, and it whined, only to go back to sleep. The threads dulled instantly. "Lonely."

"I wonder what he would say if he heard that." Clothos chuckled. "It was not my best work. Usually, they are more elegant, but this one serves its purpose. Let us examine others and compare, shall we?"

He snapped his fingers.

They were standing in the middle of a battle suspended in time. Water droplets and leaves floated around them, and the air was thick. Tara, Gareth, and Beltran were in the midst of attacking four human invaders. Their faces contorted in concentration and exhaustion.

There, in the middle, stood Tara, her sword mid-swing. Her eyes were as dark as midnight, and her two canines were extended. Her wild hair escaped her braid, and tendrils hovered like flames—the only color in the gray, wet morning.

In one swipe, Lenna's sight burned. "I always suspected she would be a bright red."

Tara's bindings were colored and woven in different directions. Some areas were colorless, and others were as bright and blinding as the sun. In the center of Tara's chest was an immense, open-mouthed wolf, with jaws clasped around her heart.

"Her true form is almost unbound." Clothos stood next to Lenna, marveling at Tara as if she were a sculpture.

A work of art.

And Lenna could not disagree. Tara was a warrior goddess in action. Her threads were beautiful, strong, and vivacious, pulsating with restrained power. Once she was completely free, what havoc would she bring? Who would she become?

"If you concentrate hard enough, you'll notice that the woven designs are not as detailed as one with experience. Here." He pulled one of Tara's threads and placed it in Lenna's hands.

As it made contact with her skin, the weightless thread turned an intense shade of orange, burning the tip of her fingers. She held on and lifted to her ear, listening to the crackling and hiss of fire.

"They're alive."

"Yes." Clothos nodded, leaning in as well. The sweet smell of flowers tickled her nose. "All the threads are alive and give you information about the bearer."

"Am I hurting her?"

"Don't worry. She can't feel a thing. She won't even know we are here."

The thread was not as detailed as Clothos'. It was coming loose at the seams, with missing hoops in the design.

Did I do this?

"The first binding of an inexperienced Bondmaker can look similar to this, or worse. When I was younger, my bindings were far less elegant. For your first binding, you exceeded expectations. As her bonds dissolve, the threads that make up her essence will tighten, and she will be complete."

Clothos removed the thread from Lenna's grasp and placed it back in Tara. Her threads and bindings returned to their original crimson color. He motioned to the other side of the field, where two figures huddled against the unfallen wall. Lenna gripped her hands tighter against her stomach.

No.

Aiden was leaning against the wall for support. Brye strained under the weight as she attempted to hold him up. A dark crimson stain painted his shirt, plastering it to his skin. Brye's hands were covered in blood, with red fingerprints on her face and clothes. It was a gory mess and it was a miracle he still survived with all the blood loss.

Clothos' fingers snapped. Lenna's hand flew to her trembling mouth. The wall behind was covered in vines made of frayed and broken colored threads. They floated like cut spiderwebs, touching everything, but lifeless.

Dying.

Snap, and Brye lit up from within with bright emerald threads wrapped tightly around her entire body. Some areas were uncolored, transparent, and ethereal, pulsating as they stretched and attempted to burn bright.

"Oh," Lenna whispered with reverence. Brye was a soothing green, soft and welcoming. Around her heart, there were tiny flowers, open in bloom and swaying in an imaginary breeze.

Beautiful. Brye was beautiful.

A long, shiny thread floated out of Brye's left hand. It braided with a bronze thread that ran up Gareth's sword arm.

Entranced, Lenna examined Gareth. The mating bond trailed across his arm until it merged with the wolf's coat. The full-faced wolf moved, blinking once and panting. It followed her with its unflinching gaze.

"This mating bond is exquisite," Clothos remarked, playing with the braided threads around his fingers. "You did a marvelous job. Love is one of the most potent ways to create bindings."

"My sister and the prince." Lenna nodded. "They were mated recently, just like Tara and...."

Why? Why did it come to this?

Aiden was dying. His once-bright threads, brilliant blue like his eyes, were fading. The seams loosened around his legs, and the vibrancy around his heart dimmed, fizzling out until there was nothing but the dullness of death.

"Help them," Lenna begged Clothos.

"Help them?"

"Yes!" she screamed, gripping his shirt. "Do something?"

"No, Lenna." He removed one of her hands, taking hold of her wrist. "You do it."

A sharp pain erupted in her chest. Anger fizzled under her skin as time resumed its pace, and the battle continued. Blood, death and destruction. It penetrated the air like toxic fumes, and she couldn't escape it. They were going to lose. Aiden was going to die, and Tara would never forgive her.

I will never forgive myself.

Lenna ground her teeth as she reached for the anger, desolation and emptiness. She gripped the pain and loss tightly until it suffocated her. It was all she had left.

"I am not worthless!" she screamed, and the sky erupted in light. Electricity sizzled and snapped, bursting until it magnified. A bolt shot from the sky, and a figure fell to the ground.

It did nothing.

She was too late. Always too late.

Aiden collapsed in Brye's arms, and Lenna watched in horror the final goodbyes. She failed them.

Why? Why can't I do something right?

A gentle finger swiped a tear from her cheek.

"Was he important to you?" Clothos cocked his head to one side, his eyes full of compassion.

"Tara will be devastated." Lenna wiped her face with her sleeves. "They love each other so much."

"I can see that." But his eyes never left her face.

Lenna didn't particularly like Clothos' intense, probing stare. She couldn't shake the feeling that he was using her. Or the fact that he seemed to be reading into her. She felt naked and vulnerable around him.

Then again, who wouldn't? If the man can read into your very existence?

Wasn't she doing the same thing? Watching private moments?

Taking a deep breath, she waved her hand over the vines. A burning sensation hit the middle of her back, but she continued to spool the vines in his direction. This she could do. She could protect him while he rested so no one would come and hurt him anymore.

She increased the fragrance of the flowers and willed him to sleep. The vines obeyed, almost gleefully, wrapping themselves around Aiden. Holding him tight and lovingly.

Tara's screams penetrated the strange silence of the scene, but she was quickly taken away. Others tried to reach Aiden, but the thorny branches protected him. They left him and went off to catch her family.

Lenna crouched in front of Aiden. A tricky vine wrapped itself around his wound. Lenna blinked and willed it away, but it stubbornly disobeyed her. It stitched the wound and then bandaged itself with more vines.

Odd.

For a moment, she thought his threads snapped and sizzled a strange emerald color. Lenna stretched her hand to touch the vines but they flinched away.

"I promise to save her," Lenna whispered. "I promise she will be alright."

But it wasn't over. "The mists are not enough."

"No," Clothos sighed. "It will not be enough."

"Tell me what to do."

"There will be a price, Lenna." Clothos placed a hand on her shoulder. His face was drawn, and his eyes melancholy.

"There will always be a price. And it will only be higher each time."

Nodding, Clothos swiped his hand, and they were back in the tower.

Lenna chuckled nervously at the scene. Enver had his arms on his hips, staring Rowenna down with a quirky smile playing at his lips. She pointed a finger at him, red-faced with a humorless expression.

"They don't seem to get along."

"They never did. They wanted different things for each other." Clothos responded with a tired sigh.

"Then it was destined to fail."

"Destiny and choice don't always see eye to eye," Clothos responded cryptically. Lenna shrugged. It was past time understanding the man's strange conversation. She examined the knots and bindings still attached to her skin.

In the end, what was the point? Bind the island, unbind the magic. What would be the right decision? There was none. It was taken out of her hands the minute her mother forced her to bind her siblings and Gareth.

"I think it's time to let it all go." She exhaled, and the tension in her shoulders relaxed.

Clothos raised his hand, and removed one of the threads from the stone wall.

"I made these to manipulate time." He ran his fingers over the braided thread. "I always wanted more time. Just a little bit more."

"But we have used it all up."

"Yes, we have."

He tightened his grip and the braided thread pulsated. He twisted one side with his right hand, then his left, ensuring the thread was taut.

"I break the bonds that were made in time and pain. I break the bonds and set us free. I break my bonds, three, over two, over one, and unto me." He pulled the bond tighter with each phrase until it snapped.

The thread stopped glowing. Enver and Roweena unfroze in mid-scream.

"What did you do?" Enver yelled, grasping Roweena's hand.

Glass trinkets cascaded to the floor. The furniture toppled over as it hit the wall. Dust rose from the loosened stones. Enver held Roweena up as the building slowly fell apart.

Unsurprised, Lenna discovered her body forgotten under a chair.

Clothos faded away, although Lenna suspected he was not entirely gone. He would never be gone.

Taking a deep breath, Lenna gripped her bindings. She stiffly stretched the threads between her outstretched hands. She fought the desire to throw them away as they scorched her skin like hot metal.

Slowly, Lenna repeated the spell. "…I break my bonds, three, over two, over one, and unto me."

The thread snapped.

The glow receded.

All hell broke loose.

Escape

Brye

THE MISTS DWINDLED AS Brye and the others approached the mouth of the river. Dawn arrived and went, leaving a weak sun that filtered behind gray clouds, and a never-ending drizzle. With each step north, the woods and fields around them were silent of life except for the rustle of the leaves and branches. Even the occasional bird call would make them jump out of their skin.

They were soaked by the time they reached the mouth of the river. Brye rubbed her arms, hissing under her breath as her teeth chattered. The drop in temperature made little sense considering it was late summer.

The river, with its slow-moving current, lay before them. Large stones from the wall stuck out of the water. The rest lay piled up in small groups of large, uneven rocks with an assortment of dried branches and leaves.

How can one tree do all this?

"Brye."

Brye jumped at the sound of Gareth's voice. He gently settled Tara against the stones while Beltran went farther up the river to check the way out.

Brye rubbed her face with her trembling fingers. Nothing kept her warm. Her lips were numb, and she shivered under her wet cloak. Gareth rubbed her arms and hands to bring warmth back to her body.

"It will be alright," he whispered, gazing into her face. Brye nodded but knew he was saying the words to comfort them both. Nothing was going to be alright.

"Brye." His hands cupped her face. "I need you with me."

"Everything is happening so quickly," her voice trembled. "I'm—"

"We'll get through it," he said softly, kissing her. "I need you with me."

His warmth filtered into her, as well as the pain. The sense of loss was always there, underneath the surface. It threatened to take them over if they stood still long enough. Gareth kissed her forehead before letting go, and Brye was left hugging her hands.

"Let's wake up the hellion."

Brye nodded, crouching beside Tara and touching her sister's temples. "She's going to be fit for murder when she wakes..." Brye warned. "She... she's..." the words stalled in her throat, the hurt too deep to be freed yet.

Aiden.

Snapping her energy, Brye pulled Tara back from her deep sleep. Tara stirred, slowly blinking awake until her eyes focused on Brye.

"What did you do to me?" she groaned, touching her head.

"We needed to get out of there." Gareth stood over Brye's shoulder with his hands on his hips.

"And you were being difficult," Brye muttered.

Gareth gave her a pleading look before turning back to Tara. "But from here on, you're walking."

Tara's gaze bounced back and forth between Brye and Gareth, before flipping around to their surroundings. Her hair was a crazed halo around her set face, barely contained in its braid. Her eyes were swollen orbs on her face.

She pushed herself to her feet, hands clawing for purchase in the wall debris. "We have to go back," she said, each word stronger than the last. "We have to—Aiden. We have to go get Aiden—" Anger floated around her like a perpetual storm cloud, violent but so brittle.

"Tara…" Brye started, reaching for her sister.

"We aren't going back," Gareth said, voice firm and commanding. "We are leaving this island. Right now."

"I don't have to follow you anywhere," Tara spat. She gripped the debris to keep herself standing. She winced as a stone cut into her palm. "I kept Brye safe as you ordered. Now, I will do whatever I want. Don't you dare use your compelling shit on me again."

Gareth clenched his fists and ground his teeth. He took a step toward Tara. "Listen, brat—"

But Brye was faster. Her frustration and exhaustion, and bone-deep ache bubbled forward. And she reacted without thinking.

Tara's head snapped to the side as Brye landed an open-palmed slap across her face. Wide-eyed, Tara raised her cut palm to her cheek. It left a bloody print that only drew attention to the red swelling.

"Lenna and Aiden stayed for us!" Brye's voice trembled. "To *save* us. They sacrificed themselves to buy us time to get off this island, you perpetually spoiled brat!"

Tara got in Brye's face, her voice raising over her sister. "Lenna chose to stay behind! Lenna could've saved Aiden earlier, but she didn't! And if you didn't fight me the entire way, we could have gotten Aiden sooner."

"Did you not see the same monsters I did?" Something inside Brye snapped, all her anger and grief coming forward, aimed directly at her sister. "Did you not see the piles of burning bodies? Our friends and community? Lenna brought the mists down to buy us time!"

"And for what? To leave Aiden behind? I won't do it." Tara grabbed Brye by the lapel of her tunic. "We have to go save him. With your magic—"

"Aiden is gone, Tara!" Brye's voice cracked, breaking around the words. Words she said and knew were true, but still, her heart didn't want to believe. "He told us to go!"

"He is not! We can't leave him!"

"He knew his wounds would not heal. I held his intestines in my hands!" Brye shoved her hands tinted with his dry blood at Tara. It forced her to take a step back. "There was nothing to be done, and he knew it!"

Tara's eyes became deep dark pools. Brye reacted in kind, her eyes midnight blue. The air sizzled with power as both women growled and hissed at each other. Beltran gently tried to pull Tara away. She snarled, shoving him. He stumbled but held firm.

Gareth gripped Brye's wrist. He infused as much calm as he could along the bond. But she pushed against the calm. All her emotions were threatening to topple them over and leave them raw.

Anger, loss, and fear mixed with disappointment.

I understand. But I need you with me.

His voice rang in her head loud and clear. It echoed until she managed some sense of control.

She couldn't leave Tara as well. Too many people had already been left behind. But the one person who could manage Tara's stubborn, selfish, impulsive personality was...

Oh, by the Founders, Aiden is gone. Lenna is gone.

Exhausted, Brye took a step back. Her eyes returned to normal as she slowly shook her head.

"Do whatever you want, Tara." Her voice vibrated around them. "Waste your life. Waste whatever freedoms Aiden and Lenna bought for you. I'm done."

Every word pierced her heart. Every instinct screamed at her to grab her baby sister and haul her with them.

But she was so tired. She couldn't fathom what Tara felt, even with her magic to help her. Was it even worth it to drag Tara along with her? Or kinder to let her join Aiden in the Unknown?

Brye walked toward the fallen stones to the river. Gareth sighed and motioned Beltran to follow him.

"Is it still there?" Gareth asked, his hand stroking the back of Brye's neck. The soothing gesture was not lost on her, and she needed it more than ever. She could feel his protectiveness surging through him, an ache inside him that, like hers, was reluctant to leave Tara behind because he had experienced too much chaotic loss today.

"Yes," Beltran sighed. "I don't know how long it will hold."

"Is what still there?" Brye asked, her eyes falling on Tara, who sat hunched over a large stone a few feet away.

"I have a boat," Beltran supplied. "Small and not fit for so many, but we could use it to get to shore."

"Is the shore far?"

"No, not very. If not for the mists, Avalon could be seen on a very sunny day." Beltran looked back at Tara. "What do we do about her?"

"She speaks so much about choices. Let her choose what to do," Brye responded.

"She'll come," Gareth stated. "If not..." he lowered his voice as he glanced at Tara, then focused on Brye. "I'll make her."

"She will hate you for it," Beltran pointed out.

"Tara hates easily," Brye said, looking at Gareth's face. His lips twitched before nodding.

Daughters of Avalon

Tara

Tara sat on the pieces of stone with her shoulders slumped over. She wrapped her arms over her stomach and rocked as tears washed down her face. She cleaned them with her sleeve, but they kept on coming. The ache in her chest was unbearable, every breath painful, every sob a reckoning.

She couldn't unsee it. Aiden's last moments and the vines coming down on him. He was still alive when they left. She knew it. Tara rubbed the lines on her hand again.

Around them, the mists were gone, and the drizzle continued mixing with the sweat and tears. The gaping wound only grew when she realized the lines along her hand were icy to the touch.

Icy. Like death.

Anger surged through her, empty and hollow but also hot and violent. Every beat of her heart was a reminder that it beat without Aiden. How was she supposed to move through this life without him?

What was even left?

The instinct to go after him was strong—he was hers, he belonged to her, and even death itself could not have him.

Yet... yet...

His last words rang through her, the tenor of his voice fresh and accurate even in memory. *"Everything will be alright. I love you."*

Tara's skin itched with the need to fight and rage. Oh, why couldn't Brye humor her? Or Gareth or even Beltran the lapdog? Why couldn't they scream at her? She wanted Brye to keep fighting her. Tara wanted the whole world to know her anger and the injustice of it.

And for once, fate obliged her.

The other three continued talking a few feet away when a group of people came from the south.

In the morning light, they appeared human. Their drawn faces were streaked with mud and dirt. Their clothes were torn and spattered with water and earth and dried blood. Some even had soot from the fires used to burn the bodies.

They seemed unhurried but surprised to find Avaloneans still alive.

Tara was about to call out when Gareth and Beltran appeared by her side.

Both unsheathed their swords, and each was tense and expectant. The group was slow to react. They moved from side to side and muttered under their breaths. The conversation was strained with urgent undertones.

Tara quickly rubbed her face clean and redrew her sword.

"Hide behind the rubble," Gareth whispered to Brye. "Keep the river to your back."

She instantly obeyed, running behind the large mound of fallen stones by the river.

"Keep her safe," he ordered Beltran.

The former nodded and said, "We are outnumbered."

"Yes," Gareth grunted, a dark expression on his features. "Let's hope Tara is pissed off enough to count as two of us."

"Oh, I am," Tara ground out, her hands firm on her sword.

Fate had given her an opportunity. She would not waste it.

Did they want her rage?

Fine.

She would give them bloodshed.

The wolf inside her agreed, infusing her arms and legs with strength and straightening her spine. It was enough to give her an edge and a new bout of energy.

They both needed this fight.

The rage inside Tara ignited; her nostrils flared, and her muscles tensed as a guttural roar escaped her lips. Her eyes became two dark black pools, and her canines descended, nicking her bottom lip. The ground beneath her feet vibrated with energy, lifting stones and dirt. With a howl that promised violence, she lunged at the group.

Brye

Brye stood back as Gareth, led by a crazed Tara, charged at the invaders.

They were outnumbered, and back-to-back, Gareth and Tara fought savagely, each holding their own. Beltran stayed close to her as she huddled behind the crushed rubble of the wall.

The air was filled with the cacophony of violence. The clash of metal and grunts of pain made Brye's heart pound. Gareth roared, driving and twisting his blade into the stomach of a man who fell to the floor with a grunt, dropping his ax. He quickly picked it up and used it as a complementary weapon.

A woman with short hair and a scarred face appeared from behind. She raised her sword. Tara climbed her back, and slit her throat.

"Move faster," Tara grunted.

Gareth threw one of his knives behind Tara. It landed squarely in a man's chest. His body was dumped on top of the last one.

"Same goes," he said, moving on to the next.

Beltran fought with equal speed and skill. He maneuvered the warriors close by, making them believe they had the upper hand. He then used their confidence to slice into them.

I can't sit here and do nothing.

Searching around for a weapon, Brye found some uneven stones. Without thinking, she threw them in the direction of the invaders. Her aim was off, but she made up for it with persistence.

Until one hit Gareth on the back of his head.

He whirled, a ferocity to him that both alarmed her and warmed her, until his dark eyes landed on her and her handful of stones.

"Your head was in the way!" she yelled, picking up more stones. She bit back a hysterical laugh that contrasted with the dread in the pit of her stomach.

"I'll try to keep that in mind," he answered, driving his dagger into another invader. His grim mouth twitched before he continued. The moment of humor made them remember what they were fighting for.

Their lives.

Each other.

And Brye wanted to live a long life. With Gareth. With Tara. Even though, at present, she was flagging, she did not want to give up.

Tara could continue to rage and be angry with her. She and Gareth still had so much to learn about each other, and Beltran was a mystery all on his own.

But it wasn't only them, as her eyes filled. They needed to live despite what had happened. Avalon could not be forgotten.

We can't die today.

But her stomach sank as more and more invaders appeared, like a colony of ants, swarming into the river bank. They came from the south, screaming at each other in their accented voices. They seemed to be giving out orders, even as some picked up the bodies of the dead and wounded and took them away.

Beltran went down. Without thinking, Brye jumped from the bank, colliding with a tall man. He pivoted and rammed Brye with the blunt of his weapon. She groaned as the air left her lungs in a harsh gasp. She gripped her stomach, trying to get a full breath. The uneven stones cut into her back.

Gareth screamed her name, and Beltran attempted to lunge as the attacker's weapon descended over her. She closed her eyes and covered her face with her hands, knowing it was fruitless.

A howl exploded in her ears before a massive animal descended on the attacker.

A wolf with a white and black undercoat came to her rescue. Its jaws ripped into the taller man's arm, making him swing to the far right, missing Brye. Then, in a swift motion, the animal jumped and shifted in the air, turning into a woman. Using the jump's momentum, she cartwheeled over the man's shoulders and landed behind him. Then, she climbed his back and snapped his neck with equal agility.

Brye gasped and stared. The woman was completely naked except for the long dark braid cascading down her back. Her eyes were mismatched, one blue and another green. Her arms and legs were covered in vine tattoos, and over her left breast was a symbol of a howling wolf and moon.

"You are brave, daughter of Avalon. It will be an honor to defend you," the woman said, then shifted back into the wolf, heading off to include herself in the battle.

"Who was that?" Brye croaked, frozen in her shock. She couldn't even process her own relief yet.

"I don't know, but I think she is on our side." Beltran wobbled as he stood up, then motioned for her to return to the rubble pile. Another invader approached them at high speed. The wolf joined the fight and held her own.

But they were still outnumbered.

Picking up another rock, Brye resumed her assault and prayed under her breath. By the Founders, they needed help. She reached down to pick up another stone, but it fell out of her grasp.

We need a miracle.

Connected Souls

Lenna

LENNA'S BODY ELECTRIFIED WHEN the bindings snapped under her fingers. The power took her breath away, leaving her trembling. She looked down where the multicolored bindings connected to her chest.

A golden thread intersected in tiny knots surrounded her beating heart. The same threading burned down her arms, creating long vine-type tattoos with blooming flowers running from her shoulders to the back of her hands and palms. They glowed and were beautiful, delicate, and alive.

Her body, now free of its bindings, regained its health. Her dull dark brown hair turned a glossy chestnut. Her hollow cheeks filled, as well as her figure. Her pale and clammy skin bloomed to a soft petal pink. She turned to one of the mirrors in the room and gasped. Her right eye had drained of its forest green only to become the color of amber.

The transformation was not only on her spiritual self. Her body was also covered in vine tattoos.

Roweena and Enver were too engrossed in staying upright to notice what was happening.

Until the tremors stopped.

Roweena froze with her eyes wildly searching the room. "This doesn't make sense."

"What just happened?"

"I don't know," Roweena cried.

Enver searched the room. "Everything seems the same."

"It isn't!" Roweena's eyes fell on Lenna's body under the up-turned chair. She tossed the chair to the side and extended her tentacles, tightening her grip on the girl.

"What are you doing?" Enver leaned over Roweena's shoulder.

"Checking."

Before Roweena could drain a drop of her power, Lenna used the connection against her.

With the same force, Lenna slowly sucked the magic out of the older woman. The surge of power was instantaneous. It ran down her body, restarting Lenna's weak heart. Enver froze for a moment, sniffing the air around them.

In contrast, Roweena's hair grew white, and spots appeared on her skin.

"Let go!" Roweena screamed as she attempted to remove the tentacles. They did not budge. Enver raised his hands in the air.

"Gods, woman, I am not even touching you," he yelled. Roweena kept stepping back until she hit the table, falling to the floor.

"Roweena." Enver took her hand to hoist her up, but the bones under his fingers cracked.

"Make her stop!" she screeched in pain, and Enver searched desperately, trying to find the source. Spotting Lenna on the floor, he turned her body over but found her unconscious. Lenna's soul could feel his scorching fingers touch her skin.

"The girl isn't even awake," he yelled back, but he paled at Roweena's transformation. Her face sagged and wrinkled. Her lips thinned, and two teeth fell from her open mouth.

Lenna had seconds before Roweena disappeared into dust. Using the tentacles, she slipped into Roweena's body. The woman convulsed, fighting Lenna's invasive presence. Her lean body curved onto itself, and her screams pierced the room.

Everything went bright once again.

When Lenna opened her eyes, she was in the same white-washed room as before.

And she wasn't alone.

Roweena stood, a woman in her prime. Her hair was back to its dark luster, her eyes almost black with gray streaks, and her face young and plump. She was more regal than ever.

Roweena's eyes, two vast pools in her alabaster face, were the only hint that she was as shocked at Lenna's altered appearance.

"You're supposed to be dead." Roweena finally blurted out.

"I can't seem to die," Lenna responded, clasping her hands behind her back.

"But, but—"

"You can't kill me, Roweena."

"Why?" Roweena blurted out as her eyes flicked in different directions.

"A Bondmaker is never really dead. They continue to live in the bonds they make."

Roweena paled so much that her trembling red lips were the only drop of color. "Clothos." Tears ran down her cheeks. "Where is he?"

"I don't know. He's gone for now," Lenna answered quietly, pressing her lips together.

"So," Roweena spoke. "What is to become of me?"

Lenna rubbed her hands and concentrated on the threads that made up Roweena's power. They were still strong and much more stable than her own. She needed a good source if she was going to do what she had to.

Once the idea took root, she could not escape it. How many deaths can one person have?

"Am I to die like my brother?" Roweena asked, her voice cracking.

Lenna gently placed her hands on the woman's cheeks. Roweena flinched but did not escape her grip.

"Yes, but then again, so am I."

Roweena's hands came to rest over hers for a moment, and Lenna's heart filled with all the failed opportunities.

"We could have been friends," Lenna whispered. "If you trusted me."

Roweena trembled and removed Lenna's hands. "Do what you must do."

There was no going back from this moment. The moment she broke her bindings, Lenna knew she was one step closer to the end of her story. She would finally have an answer to her childhood question.

What would happen when the bindings break?

She took a deep breath and stretched out a piece of the golden threading from her arm. The finger movement alerted Roweena, who swallowed. "I've seen that before."

"It's time for us to end this. Together."

Lenna took a thread that connected Roweena's mind. It glowed silver in her extended hand. She tied the gold thread with the silver, and they braided together. A tingling sensation filled her as the two threads became one, merging and knotting.

Roweena's shoulders relaxed. "It was so lonely," she exhaled as her soul dissolved in the white mist.

Here it was, Roweena's essence. A soft silver thread spooled together that sizzled and snapped. It's hum consistent and vibrant. Even as Roweena's soul slept, an entire story still lived on in the threads of her existence. A long story with moments of happiness and tragedy. But so much loneliness.

"I am not surprised you were lonely," Lenna whispered to the silver threads, tears of regret moistening her cheeks. She sniffed, trying to regain her composure. "I am truly sorry, Roweena. I hope one day we can forgive each other."

There was no sense of triumph, only a terrible ache in the pit of her stomach that would not subside. Would there even be an end after this?

Roweena's soul vanished into the growing mists around Lenna. The sucking sensation increased, and the white room disappeared.

The light blinded her, and a consistent pain radiated from her hand. Lenna stiffened. She was on someone's lap, her head cushioned by broad shoulders. A hand moved a lock of hair from her ear. It was surprisingly gentle, and the touch sent minor burning points along her temple. Even with the uncomfortable pain, she was too content to move. She inhaled the scent of hot night and spices.

The dragon man.

Her heart thundered in her chest, and she sat up abruptly, wincing.

"Are you feeling better?" his voice rumbled close to her face. Lenna blinked. Enver regarded her with what seemed like concern. He twirled her hair with his fingers. Again, the winding sensation in her chest grew. Twist. Twist. Twist.

But it wasn't her hair.

Not mine, Roweena's.

Up close, he was even more intimidating. The scars were jagged and covered most of his neck, and the one across his eye could have left him blind. His eyes drew her in, like a moth to a flame. Liquid amber that warmed the weariness in her soul.

Lenna shook her head, trying to regain focus as the bones in her hand reknit themselves. She flexed her hand as the pain subsided. What was left were intense feelings that distracted her.

I need to get going.

"Wait." Enver gripped her waist. "You collapsed."

"Are these her feelings?" Roweena's smoky voice floated out of her mouth. She wet her chapped, dried lips.

"Who?" Enver asked, his hands going slack. Lenna took advantage and stood up.

"Or mine." She ran her hands down the dark skirt. They were covered in vine tattoos. She pulled at the sleeves of the dress to hide them. Lenna's soul was physically affecting Roweena's body. Every emotion and sensation was more intense than before. Roweena's elemental magic pumped through her system, growing stronger now that it was unbound.

Enver sat with his jaw tense. His eyes examined every point shift of her features. "What are you talking about?"

Roweena's body stopped aging and healed itself. Lenna removed her tentacles from her actual body, still forgotten on the floor.

"Who are you?" Enver whispered.

Lenna bit her lower lip and made her way to the door.

"Where are you going?" His hand barely touched her wrist before his body crashed into the wall. The force cracked the stone, and debris floated around them.

"I don't think Roweena wanted to kill you. She could have. I think deep inside; she wanted you to end it."

Enver's eyes widened, and his jaw dropped.

An unexpected tear ran down her cheek. "I suggest you go back to where you came from."

"I can't go back without you," he ground out. "Whomever you are."

"Then you are in for a show."

Lenna snapped her fingers and the guards collapsed on the stony floor, unconscious. She sprinted up the stairs to the top of the tower.

The drizzle continued. She closed her eyes and focused on the different connecting threads on the island.

There they are.

Her sisters, Gareth and Beltran were surrounded, fighting bravely but outnumbered. Her brow furrowed at the sight of a wolf among them. Someone older and stronger.

Someone who felt familiar.

One particular thread, forest green, thick and alive, slithering and multiplying under the island drew her attention. Reaching her right hand down, she flicked her wrist upward and waited.

Unbound Island

Brye

BRYE'S TREMBLING HANDS FINALLY obeyed when a low-pitched rumble shook the battered stones. The river behind her grew louder as it changed directions. The ground cracked, and vines with massive thorns arose from beneath their feet. In one swipe, the vines impaled invaders toward the White Thorn Tree. Gareth cut into one, but it regrew instantly.

Brye jumped from the stones, tripping and landing on the wet grass. She jerked as a branch came close to her head. It speared a man carrying an ax, tossing him in a bloody mess a few feet away. Gareth dodged branches and bodies, while Tara slashed away, still crazed. The wolf pulled at her clothes, tearing the shirt with her sharp teeth.

"Tara, stop!" Gareth grabbed her arm. She twisted out of his grip, and her fist made contact with his nose. It cracked and his face snapped back. Brye went to reach her, and she quickly slapped her to the side.

"Get a hold of yourself!" Beltran ordered, gripping Tara's wrist. She roundhouse kicked him. His hand loosened while he regained some of his breath.

Enough!

The female wolf shifter growled and snapped. Tara turned, her sword arm raised. Brye lunged, and their bodies crashed into the pile of rubble. The stones jarred Brye, cutting into her already bruised back and arms. Tara quickly straddled her to the ground, landing a punch in her eye. Brye screamed as she saw stars. She grabbed Tara's wrists, digging in her nails and assaulting her senses with pain.

Tara roared as her eye blackened and swelled to double its size. She pulled back her fist when Gareth grabbed her by the waist.

"Obey!" His eyes narrowed as his canines extended.

He bit into Tara's ear; blood oozed from the wound. She whimpered, and her eyes turned back to normal.

"Put her to sleep, Brye," Gareth said through bloody lips. "We don't have time for this shit!"

Brye grabbed Tara's face with her bruised hands and forced her unconscious. Tara's eyes rolled back into her head and she slumped her full weight forward, nearly crushing Brye. Gareth shifted out of the way, and Beltran replaced him, slinging Tara's limp form over his shoulder.

"The branches," Brye pointed. "They aren't attacking us."

Bodies fell, and open wounds splattered blood as the invaders headed back to the fallen tree like a swarm of insects.

But Brye was right. The wild branches avoided them.

"It's now or never," Beltran called out.

There were no more enemies. The wolf led the way, jumping over the invisible bridge. Beltran followed, carrying Tara. Gareth cleaned the blood from his broken nose and took Brye's hand, but she didn't move.

A lone figure in a gray cloak stood in the center of the field, with the White Thorn Tree in the background.

"Lenna," Brye whispered.

Gareth ran in the direction of the figure. Vines shot up from the earth, erecting a sharp wall between them.

The three wraiths reformed out of the churned earth and rubble. The tree bird let out a screech that projected leaves and stones in every direction, scaring off any invaders that stayed behind. The earth stag and fire lizard released havoc in their wake, destroying everything in their paths.

Everything in order to make a path for Brye and Gareth's escape.

Brye nicked and cut her hands, trying to get through the wall of thorny vines. Gareth slashed wildly, but the branches grew thicker and stronger than before.

"Lenna!" Brye screamed.

Tears ran down Brye's cheeks, and she screamed, frustration and agony warring for dominance inside her. Her hand grew slick in her blood as the thorns cut into her sleeves. She didn't care about the pain. Her sister was right there. Right in front of her, she couldn't reach her.

She couldn't leave without her.

"Lenna, please!" she begged. "Come with us!"

The figure extended both arms—covered in vine tattoos—to the sky. The sky opened with the crack of thunder, and lightning snapped around them. The air sizzled, and her hair filled with static electricity.

"We have to go," Gareth said slowly, his eyes darting around. "Brye... Brye, we have to go now."

Whatever was about to occur would be a display of magic of deadly proportions. Brye understood this in her soul, in the same way that she understood how air was vital and love and grief were the same emotion.

Gareth grabbed her wrist. The urgency vibrated through her skin. There was no longer a point in wondering what could have been. Brye wiped her tears, wincing as she made contact with her swollen eye. Gareth gave her a nod, and they ran.

Her heart shattered as she left her whole world behind.

Lenna

Tears ran down Lenna's cheeks at the shock on their faces. Above her, the sky was filled with thousands of floating threads. They made up the ground, trees, water, the grass.

And she needed them all.

Like a spool, she closed her eyes and attracted the many bindings that made up the island and its connection to this world. Her hands sparked as the first thread reached her fingers. The sensation was unbearable, but the weight intensified as the threads braided together and the spool around her hands grew.

Behind her, the massive wraiths wreaked havoc. They distracted the invaders, redirecting them to the chard White Thorn Tree.

All except one.

Hot nights and spices.

Stubborn, stupid Dragon.

Enver's clothes were drenched with sweat as he panted for air. Lenna stood, still cloaked in Roweena's body, while hers was left in the tower.

"Why are you doing this?" Enver demanded against the increasing wind. The island's magic became unstable as each thread attached itself to her.

The fierce wraiths attacked but disintegrated as the wind and rain tore them apart. Enver's face was covered in nicks from the flying stones. He did not waver, only grunted until he gripped the thorning wall separating them. "Answer me!"

Lenna gave a humorless laugh.

He is one to talk.

"Some bonds are destined to fray and break."

A breath later, the sky dimmed, and all that could be seen were the glowing stars. The beauty of the multicolored threads hurt her eyes.

They were exquisite.

She would never be able to see something so vast and impressive again.

Tears of remorse fell down her cheeks. The loss of a future that could have been. The lives that bled for no reason. Lenna wavered under the weight of such emotions.

For a moment, she lost a bit of the power boost, and the threads grew exponentially in weight. Enver's gaze bore into her, demanding answers.

She ignored him.

"Go!" She finally ground out as her knees buckled. She was almost there. The spool of threads between her hands was now complete and growing taut. "Go back to where you came from, or you will be brought down with me!"

Enver stepped back, his jaw worked, but no words came out. His legs slowly obeyed, and he ran toward the White Thorn Tree.

With each step he took, the twisting sensation in her chest stretched until it snapped. With it, Lenna's heart broke into a thousand pieces.

Why? Why am I always so alone?

As the spool grew taut, Lenna's mind flashed with images that merged so quickly that she grew dizzy.

An island came out of the sea.

The earth trembled, and time seemed to stop as mountains and rivers appeared from the depths.

The first arrival of refugees.

Clothos' brown eyes danced as he welcomed them with open arms. Roweena stood relaxed by his side. Behind them was a tall woman with pale skin, dark ebony hair, and mismatched eyes. She bowed her head at the arriving group. "It is an honor to welcome you all."

Dragons flew over the fields, expelling ice, fire, and water. Roweena laughed and danced in the Royal Tower with Enver. The room lit up with candles and music.

Then, time flew forward.

Helene was slain in her sleep by a man with the Leviathan dagger. Her eyes glazed over as the sheets became drenched in blood. The man disappeared into the night, never to be seen again.

A room was full of people, all yelling and screaming as they pointed fingers at Enver.

He maintained his innocence but was found guilty. Roweena, eyes blotched by tears, watched an execution by the White Thorn Tree, still a sapling. Enver's eyes, full of contempt, searched for hers in the crowd.

The ax fell.

More than once.

At the final chop, his body disappeared.

Clothos dissolved in mid-air in the middle of the night.

Time sped up once again.

The island's population grew. There were births and deaths.

Beltane fires ignited one after another.

Her mother's first cries into the world announcing the initial crack in the northern wall.

The queen's stillbirths.

A small, strong boy was brought to the island on a misty beach at night.

A dead baby girl was replaced with a vigorous newborn. Queen Celine was confused, but Elsywth placed her hands over her eyes. Gareth was now the strong shifter prince.

A man with a medium build and dark hair was kissing her mother. His face was clouded and distorted by time and distance.

Elsywth and the man were together in the cave, their bodies entwined in the throes of passion.

Time went by faster and faster. Blur after blur of memories and moments converged until Lenna was too confused to follow.

Brye's first cry into the world triggered another crack in the wall.

Lenna's birth in the middle of Beltane, just as the fire was lit.

The wall cracked once more, and chunks fell into the river.

The man hugged Elsywth close, his arms possessively over her swollen belly.

Tara's noisy birth. Her little body huddled against Elsywth's breast as she suckled milk.

Vines dug their way in between the stones, settling and waiting.

Her mother's sobs when she discovered the man vanishing into thin air.

The first time Lenna moved drops of fallen rain onto Tara's face. The sounds of delight from her sisters. The joy and ache of magic at her fingertips.

The pain of Gareth's first shift. Her mother was there, guiding him with a worried look.

Brye's tingling hands were on Lenna's forehead after she cut her lip. The wound healed instantly.

Tara's tiny war cries as she pushed Gareth into the river. His laughter as he watched her antics.

Aiden's mischievous eyes as snowflakes danced around his head.

The storms appeared when she was angry or sad.

Her mother's promise to hide her magic.

The night Lenna bound her family.

Her mother's death as Roweena drained the life force out of her. Her body was buried under the White Thorn Tree.

Tara cried, and Brye held back her sobs, trying to be strong for her sisters. Lenna's uncomfortable guilt over something she had done wrong but could not remember.

The first time her sisters danced in the fields.

All of Brye's proposals and how she turned them down.

Aiden and Tara always together.

Her twenty-first birthday and the lighting of the last Beltane fire.

Gareth's eyes searched for Brye in the crowd. Byre pretended to ignore him.

Becoming a Mist Maiden.

Beltran changed into a dark-furred wolf to teach her magic.

Magic.

All the memories came down to moments of magic that she would never see again. She wanted to be grateful that she had lived them all, but had she?

Had she truly lived her life, or had she been a spectator?

It all went faster until her eyes burned with unshed tears, and her lip was torn apart from her teeth.

She couldn't close her eyes.

She couldn't look away.

The smell of hot nights and spices.

Deep amber eyes.

Lenna, do you see them?

The threads stretched from all around her, multicolored and magnificent. As they braided between her extended hands, they became the color of liquid gold. They burned and sparked.

Tense and ready.

The bindings around your hands? Can you see them?

"Yes." Her voice cracked under pressure. She bit back a sob. She knew what came next, and her stomach grew tense and heavy. Her head shook slowly.

Break them.

She pulled her hands apart with as much strength as was possible.

"I break the bonds that hold Avalon together."

One by one, the threads snapped apart and sizzled out. As they did, she could hear an island coming out of the sea, and a sky of resewn tapestries.

Enormous tapestries with no beginning or end.

Except for a tear that was stitched in between.

Her chest tightened painfully. She forced herself to breathe as the scent of salty air and wet grass filled her nostrils.

"I break the bonds and free the island from its past, present, and future. I break these bonds with the power that was given to me."

All her existence came down to this moment. She was not born a Bondmaker. She was born to break the bonds, a *Bondbreaker*.

Blood ran down her nose, and the bones in her hands snapped piece by piece, but she persisted. She did not cry out in pain, no matter how much she wanted to.

No matter how much she wanted to be anywhere else at this moment.

"I break these bonds one over two, two over three. Avalon, I set you *free*," she screamed out the last words in a choked-out sob. Her elbows grew weak, and her shoulder popped out of its socket.

The last of the braided knots snapped.

The crack rang like thunder as the bindings disappeared.

Her arms fell to her sides, heavy and numb. Her knees buckled and gave out from under her. Her back hit the ground, and the eternal glowing stars sprinkled the night sky. A moonless night greeted her like a cold, old friend.

All became silent and dark as the starry sky descended like a veil.

Lenna finally closed her eyes, a knowing resonating in her with deep and painful certainty.

Avalon was no more.

Avalon was free.

A place called
the Continent

Brye

THERE WOULD BE NO way to describe what Brye saw that morning. No one would believe her, and no legend or myth would be equal.

The wolf led them past the cave to a cove hidden from view. The salty morning air hit their nostrils as they found a small boat tethered in the shallow part of the cove. It was long and made of carved wood that had seen better days. The sail was tied down with ropes, and two large oars were inside.

Beltran handed Tara to Gareth as he pulled the boat closer to shore.

"It's as close as I can get it without running it aground," he pointed out. "I'll hold it while you climb on."

Gareth nodded and hoisted Tara's body higher. Brye lifted what was left of her skirt and kit and waded into the cold water. She yelped and cursed as they made their way to the boat. Her boots stumbled on the rocky shore and sank as she reached the sandy basin.

On the side of the boat was a short rope ladder. Her wet clothes made it difficult to hoist herself up the first time. Gareth's hand pushed against her bottom, giving her enough boost to get over.

She dragged excess water in her wake before collapsing face-first in the boat.

"Grab her!" Gareth ordered as Tara's head and shoulders came over the side of the boat. Brye immediately stuck her arms underneath Tara's armpits and dragged her back. Gareth followed a moment later, and the boat tilted to one side.

"Careful!" Brye warned as she pulled Tara with all her strength. They both fell onto the deck.

The rocking motion almost made Gareth fall overboard, but he climbed back up. He quickly picked up Tara, settling her on the opposite side of a bench.

"Are you okay?" He rubbed Brye's arms.

"Been better," she answered, her teeth chattering. With Beltran's added weight, the boat tilted and sank some.

"It's not made for so many. We will have to be very careful," he said as he handed Gareth an oar.

"What about the wolf?" Brye asked, looking towards the shore.

"She didn't want to come." Beltran raised the sail. "She growled at me and went away." He rubbed his face, frowning.

Brye squinted in the morning light and saw a naked woman standing tall on the beach. The woman placed a hand on her chest and softly bowed. Brye called out, but the figure faded into the mists.

"She's gone." Brye sat back, blinking.

"Then we should get going," Beltran said as they set out to the mainland in the early morning sun.

Brye reluctantly awoke her sister. Tara's eyes snapped open, and she stood quickly, her hand flying at Brye. The sudden movement rocked the boat.

Gareth managed to get in the way of her slap. His stony face, already bruised and bloody from the fight, turned a ruddy puce. "Enough, Tara!" he ordered, his canines extending. Tara's lips trembled. She reached for the wound on her ear before collapsing on the bench with a huffing whimper.

The clear sky darkened quickly, and thunder rumbled. Gareth and Beltran rowed faster. Tara pushed Beltran aside and assumed his position, freeing him to steer the small vessel. The wind picked up, flapping the sail from side to side.

A snap echoed across the water. The blue sky was torn open, with a gaping hole that showed the stars.

They stopped rowing and gasped. The only noise was the waves lapping against the boat hull.

"What?" Tara gasped.

The water vibrated under them, and a soft rumbling came their way. The sound chilled Brye to the core. Above them, the whole cosmos could be seen. Millions of stars blinded them.

Like the collision of two enormous stones, a second crack echoed over the horizon, and Brye screamed as the sky fell. Gareth shielded her. Tara and Beltran covered their faces with their arms as the stars came down like a blanket. The small boat almost toppled over.

Darkness covered and consumed them, drawing them in and shutting out all sound. The sensation shook Brye and brought her heart to her throat. An eternal emptiness, where no feeling, sensation or warmth swirled around them and in them. Consuming all fire and life.

It lasted a moment that seemed like forever.

The sudden light and heat of the sun startled her, and she could sense Gareth's unease through her fingertips. Brye peeled her face out of Gareth's chest and gasped, mouth falling open.

The ocean was empty.

The island was gone.

With the energy they had left, they reached the opposite shore. The sand under their feet was a welcomed steadiness after the rocking boat. They each collapsed, attempting to regain some breath—some sense of sanity.

The sun was high and warm, and it smelled of brine and salt. Brye had never seen the ocean, and she pushed a crusty lock from her eyes as she took in the sheer vastness of it. It was almost frightening in its colossal emptiness, stretching out farther than she could discern.

Everything was gone. Her home. Her friends. Her family.

Caitlin. Badar. Enid. The king and queen...

Aiden.

Lenna.

Gone. Not even a place for a grave to remember them.

She couldn't move, her body heavy with loss.

Lenna. Sweet Lenna.

Brye had failed her. Failed her as her older sister. Lenna was supposed to come with them. She should be here with them.

Tara sat apart, hugging her knees and sobbing. Gareth and Beltran talked to one side. Their clothes were still humid and splattered with dirt, mud, and blood. Beltran looked haggard, and Gareth was stoic as usual, with dark smudges under his eyes and a pained expression.

Their emotions were catching up to them. Was it only yesterday that she was mated? Why did it feel like years ago?

Sand stuck to her damp clothes as Brye stood slowly and painfully. A long groan escaped her lips as she settled beside Tara. Her sister's desolated emotions came to Brye in waves, enough to warn her not to make any physical contact.

"I want to hate you." Tara's voice was muffled against her knees.

"The feeling is mutual," Brye replied hoarsely.

"I lost everything."

"We both did."

Tara raised her blotchy face. "Don't you dare compare our losses. Gareth is alive, and Aiden is not. He was the only one who could..."

her voice cracked, "who could calm me. Now, what am I to do?" Tara pressed her face into her knees again. "I am alone."

Brye said nothing, for what was there to say? They had barely escaped a senseless massacre of their friends and families, and an explosive bout of magic had just destroyed their island.

They'd lost Lenna.

They'd lost Aiden.

But Tara was right—Brye had Gareth. And while Aiden had been her friend, he had been Tara's mate, and Brye knew Tara would feel that loss until the end of her days.

Just as they would both feel Lenna's. Forever.

Brye rubbed her face and thought of Lenna's final moments. She knew it was her sister in that field. What had she done? What had she sacrificed to give them a few extra moments to escape? How lonely she must have felt. The grief suffocated Brye.

But Tara was also wrong.

"You are not alone," she spoke carefully, gazing over the endless ocean before them. Out of her periphery, she saw Tara shift her face out of her knees once more. "In one night, we lost everything we ever knew—all the people we loved: Enid, Caitlin, and Badar. We lost our island, our home, our safety. Yes, we lost Aiden. And..." Brye swallowed hard. "And Lenna..." She couldn't say the words 'we lost' because somehow, the words made it seem more permanent. "Our *sister*, Tara." Brye turned her face to Tara's, their eyes colliding. The rage and agony in Tara's eyes shattered everything inside Brye.

Another sister she failed. She wanted to take all that hurt away from Tara.

"You are not alone, even if you feel that way right now." Brye touched Tara's face, still round with her youth, a testament to her nineteen years. "Please... I don't want to lose the only one I have left."

Tara's eyes wavered, and her face crumpled as great heaving gasps and sobs came out of her. "I'm so sorry," she managed between rough gasps. "Brye... Brye, everything hurts."

"I know, little sister."

They sat in aching, painful silence for a long few moments, Brye's hand petting Tara's hair.

"Do you remember our bedtime ritual?" Brye asked when Tara's crying slowed down.

"Which of the many?" Tara's voice was rough and reedy.

"*Maither* would tell us the story of the Three Founders."

"Oh," Tara groaned. "I remember almost everything, I think."

"Yes, but do you remember your favorite parts?"

Tara's head came out from her knees. She exhaled shaky. "About the Wolf Shifters and the warriors. It was the only interesting part."

"*Maither* never managed to get the whole story done in one sitting—"

"Because we always interrupted."

"No." Brye waved a finger and gave her a side glance. "You did."

Tara rolled her eyes, a thin ribbon of laughter pulling from her.

"Lenna rarely interrupted," Brye mused, lost in the memory. "She always listened."

"She did mumble as if she was telling the story herself."

"Yes, she did." Brye sighed. "*Maither* told it so many times. We could recite it in our sleep."

"We probably did." Tara finally uncoiled herself, extending her legs and leaning back against her arms. "It was so long ago."

"It was. And so much happened."

Tara was quiet, wiggling her naked toes in the sand. Brye didn't remember when her sister lost her boots. "Will we ever be at peace like that again?" Tara asked, sniffing back tears.

"I don't know," Brye whispered.

They sat silently, watching the waves come in and out until Beltran and Gareth appeared in their line of sight.

"I think both of you should hear this." Gareth rubbed his neck. There was no mistaking the sadness and weariness in his features.

"If you'd sit, we wouldn't have to crane our necks," Tara said, running a hand over her face.

Gareth grunted and sat next to Brye. She immediately leaned into his heavy frame, and his hand settled on her thigh. The touch was comforting, adding a piece of stability to the chaos that was now their lives.

"There is something I should tell you," Beltran said, sitting cross-legged in front of them. "I swore not to mention this unless it was strictly life or death. Considering what we survived, I believe this is that time."

Tara scoffed. "You think?"

Brye narrowed her eyes at Tara before nodding to Beltran. "Continue."

"I am part of the Order, a group of sages that studies magic in the capital of what you call the Shifter Side of the Continent. Before my master died, he gave me a Threaded Book he stole from the Vallerium—"

"Slow down," Brye said. "We can't follow. Vallerium? Threaded?"

"The Vallerium is the Grand Library of the capital city. A Threaded Book is a book created by Clothos, the Bondmaker. They have a mind of their own. Willful and powerful."

"A book with its own mind? Sound dangerous." Tara whistled.

"They are if they wish to be. But this one was tricky. It took me a year to earn its trust. When it was ready, it told me the story of the Three Founders of Avalon and about the Bonding magic on your island."

"And you became curious." Tara raised an eyebrow.

"Yes." Beltran's cheeks colored. "I came to your island to study it. To study you."

"How honest of you," Tara muttered.

"Let him finish," Gareth said. Brye, who had been silent this entire time, rubbed her arms.

"So, yes, I lied. I know my master knew of the book, and was privy to some of the secrets, but he died before the map revealed itself. Once I knew, I decided to come. I did not know how much the magic had waned or that no magical beings were born on the island."

"Until Lenna," Brye said.

"Yes."

"Did you discover everything you wanted to know?" Tara cocked her head to the side.

"No." Beltran exhaled. "And yes. I know that binding magic has been used on the island. But it is not the only thing."

"What do you know about Bondmakers?" Gareth asked them. Brye and Tara exchanged a look.

"Only the story of the Founders and Clothos," Brye answered.

"Bondmaking is ancient magic. The origin is not Shifter or Yuansu. It is said it comes from the original gods. Beings of power who can manipulate the threads that make up all living and non-living things. They are the only beings that can create their magic. Clothos was the last Bondmaker ever to have been registered."

"What are you saying?" Brye asked. "What does this have to do with us?"

"There was another Bondmaker, one almost equal to Clothos."

"You can't mean... Lenna?" Tara asked.

"Yes," Beltran continued. "Lenna was not only a Pure Elemental but also a Bondmaker."

"What? How can you be sure?" Tara's eyes widened.

"We have this." Gareth pointed to Tara's bloody left hand and then his right. "These appeared this morning. We didn't have time to talk about it."

His left hand was covered in small, detailed, lined scars. Brye's right hand was marked as well. She ran her fingers over them, and they sizzled and snapped under her touch.

"Our mating bond," Brye whispered.

"We will never know if Lenna knew about her abilities before she died, but she bound us together." Gareth's gaze hid nothing.

Brye looked away, her brow furrowed. "She knew. I remember some of her memories of the night of the fire lizard. She saw tapestries and threads around her hands, but her thoughts were jumbled. Not only that, I am sure it was her in the field before we left. Probably finishing something that started before we were even born."

"You knew all this," Tara said with a scowl. "When were you planning on telling us?"

Gareth's face fell. "Last night, before I sent Beltran to fetch Lenna. We debated when would be a good time. We had decided to come clean the next morning."

"Then the world ended, and you got distracted." Tara turned away back at the ocean, her shoulders sagged.

Beltran sighed and nodded.

Silence returned between them once again as the waves came in and out.

Brye leaned into Gareth's warmth, and his arm came around her shoulders. She ignored the smell of blood, ash and sweat and concentrated on the feeling of peace and contentment at his side. Even with all the grief that came, like a soft undercurrent. Gareth's warmth held firm. Brye closed her weary eyes for a moment.

A very short moment.

"Now what?" Tara asked.

"You can't let us have one second of peace, can you?" Brye rolled her eyes. Beltran chuckled.

"That didn't answer my question. What do we do now?"

"I think it's obvious, Tara," Gareth stated, giving a sad attempt of a smile that fell flat on his tired face. "We live."

"We make a home." Brye rubbed her knees. "A new one."

"Together?" Gareth asked tentatively. Brye gave him a side glance. She carefully took her hand in his. Relief filtered at the touch, and something more.

The sky and ocean were clear, with seagulls diving to catch their breakfast—the smell of the salty air filled Brye's lungs. There was nothing before them. No island sanctuary. No home to go to. There was no evidence that the bound island had existed.

They only had what was behind them. Behind them lay an unbound continent full of the unknown.

Unknown places and people.

Unexplored cultures and new rules.

A future of their own making.

"So." Tara wiped tears and regarded her sister and companions. "I guess we should get going."

Epilogue

A KNOCK AT THE door in the middle of the night was never a good omen.

Cirian, the Grand Master, knew this more than anyone. How many times in the past few years was he called in the deepest darkest nights to speak to the previous king? To calm his fears and nightmares about the future? To soothe him after the untimely death of the queen and queen mother?

Since the crowning of the new king a few weeks back, he thought he might have a respite from these nocturnal troubles.

He was wrong.

Tonight, he laid down his pen and schooled his features. He ran his hand over the bushy eyebrows that adorned his deep-set dark eyes. He combed his thick, graying hair and set his face in a firm mask.

Not one that scowled as he tended to do when interrupted in the dead of night.

Not one that appeared haggard as he planned the king's three-month progress to the southern edges of the kingdom.

And all it entailed.

The lists he needed to make. The letters were already made and were to be sent at first light. He did not have time for another setback.

The knock came again, more urgent than the last. An unwanted weight settled in the pit of his stomach. Making sure the papers on his desk were hidden away, he sat back and called for the visitor to enter.

The door creaked open, and a young man stuck his head inside. He was no older than fifteen and one of the recruits of the Order. Long and thin, like most adolescent boys, whose bodies grow in different awkward stages. The Grand Master recognized him instantly as the librarian's assistant. What was his name?

Simon.

"Simon, what brings you at this hour?"

"Sorry to interrupt your work, Grand Master, but Raives—"

Cirian raised an eyebrow, and the young boy swallowed, realizing his mistake. "Pardon, the librarian has requested your presence."

"Can't this wait until tomorrow? The king is leaving soon, and I have much to attend to."

"The librarian said it is urgent. He said it has to do with one of the Threaded Books."

It took all of Cirian's self-control not to widen his eyes. Instead, he narrowed his gaze and shifted in his seat. He organized his papers carefully, appearing confident and calm.

"If the librarian believes it is urgent, then we shall go."

He stood, straightened his vest, and carefully placed his notebook and pencil in his pocket. He got his coat, and Simon helped him into the sleeves.

"Lead the way, young man."

The Grand Library, also called the Vallerium, was located in the central government building in the Utrequia palace.

During the day, the Vallerium was filled with scholars from all over the Continent who searched for knowledge and truth in its tomes. At night, the vast corridors and vaults were so silent that conversations that happened on one end could be understood on the other.

After a short walk from his offices, Cirian entered the main hall through one of the massive, carved wooden doors. The door was a work of art, like every part of the Utrequia. It was decorated with symbols and knots representing Clothos, the founder of the Vallerium and the Order. His spells and bindings kept the books, grimoires, and scrolls from aging.

But that was farthest from the Grand Master's mind. As soon as he closed the door, he could hear it. A hum echoed down the walls and raised the hairs on his arms.

"Finally, you're here, Cirian."

Raives' face, always set in a pleasant expression, was drawn, with his lips pinched. He looked ancient in the pale lantern light.

"What is it? Why have you called me?"

Cirian searched around the hall for the origin of the sound but found it empty. As if sensing his arrival, the hum intensified. Straining his ears, he realized it was a song. The melody was sweet and welcoming, like a mother willing her children to sleep.

A bedtime lullaby.

"Thank you, Simon. You may leave," Raives ordered.

Once Simon closed the door, they went down the main hall. The dim lantern light broke the darkness. The corridors were filled with the shadowed shapes of statues that could be confused for monsters. Their steps echoed on the marble floor and down a long corridor to the right.

"Tell me, Raives."

"It began to hum this morning," the librarian explained, picking up his pace as he moved. "Initially, we didn't notice because we had many visitors from the Eastern Lands. By the time evening came and the library was empty, we realized—"

They reached the end of the hall, and the song died away on the last note.

"Has anyone gone inside to see it?"

"Once we knew where it was coming from, I came," Raives said.

"Did you try to read it? To see what it wanted?"

The heavy sensation in the pit of the Grand Master's stomach intensified as he stood outside the room.

"That was the problem, Grand Master. We couldn't read it."

Cirian stiffened at Raives' reply. He unclenched his hands until his knuckles cracked. "What do you mean?"

Raives removed a ring of keys from his belt and chose the one with the emerald stone. He unlocked the door and Cirian stifled a gasp.

The room held Clothos' private books. The books in this section were sentient beings, choosing who and when to share their ideas.

But there was no book more fickle and temperamental than the one placed on the pedestal in the center of the room: *The Book of All Names.*

Made using Bondmaker magic, the book was bound together using the threads of existence and time. It registered the names of all those born on the Continent, including all their abilities and familial ties.

For it to open, a person needed to read the embroidered incantation on the cover. Once the last word left the reader's lips, the book would glow with a color only the person who asked could see. It took years to gain the book's trust and even more to be permitted to read the incantation and ask. Raives was the only one before Cirian to be given the privilege.

Raives raised the lantern. The book hummed ecstatically. Its cover glowed with multicolored threads. Cirian wiped his clammy palms over his pants and came closer.

The cover was blank.

"Leave me." Cirian extended his hand to the librarian. "Leave the keys."

The older man nodded and handed him the emerald key. Cirian escorted him out and locked the door behind him.

When he returned to the book, it floated gently over the pedestal. It's light low but still vibrant.

"All right, my old friend." Cirian stood before it, his hand hovering. "What is it you wish to share?"

The cloth cover changed. Threads moved, and a word formed in the middle.

Welcome.

"Thank you." Cirian's smile barely met his eyes. When his hand touched the words, warmth filtered into his fingertips. It was followed by the excitement that ran like an electric shock up his arm. He waited, and when nothing else happened, he removed his hand and stepped back, rubbing his face.

"Who?" Cirian muttered to himself. "Who is the book welcoming?"

The hum slowly increased in pitch, becoming a song. The melody was pure, and the voice was indistinguishable from a man or woman. The voices melded together perfectly, caressing the Grand Master's ears.

He took out his pocketbook and wrote down the words. He could barely keep up, but once he had them down, the deep weight in his stomach only grew.

"This can't be."

The Book of All Names settled but continued to sing as Cirian rubbed his face and cursed. The Grand Master confirmed what he feared the most.

A knock at the door in the middle of the night was never a good omen.

Oh welcome,
please welcome
Two daughters of the Three,
The Healer whose hands can see souls,
The Shifter whose courage can break bones.

Oh welcome,
Oh welcome,
Two sisters of three,
The third will remain dreaming,
until the realms are in need.

Oh welcome,
please welcome,
Half of the whole.
A prince with no crown
but has more value than gold.

Oh welcome,
please welcome,
Avaloneans three.
To an unbound world
waiting for thee.

The End

Acknowledgements

It took 17 years, and here it is. This little, not-so-little book was published. And I didn't expect my project to become the first of a series, but it did. I didn't do it alone. If anything, I have a lot of people to thank for motivating me, for keeping me sane, and for reminding me how much I really love to write.

The first person I would like to thank is my best friend Diana, who all those years ago took the time and effort (and with terrible handwriting on someone's part) to write stories with me. She reminded me over and over that I just needed to get the words down.

To my husband, a man who always made sure that I followed my dreams. Who loved seeing me happy and always told me that it could be done.

To my dad, that believed in me, even when I truly had no idea what I was going to do. He always said I would "be famous", or a "bestseller".

To my mom, that might not remember reading one of the first drafts and marking it all in red. And being a teacher, that was the color she loved to use to correct me.

To my editor Jess, who became my writing coach and friend. Who clearly understood where I was going, even when I was so undecided, and made sure that I realized I had potential. Who would swoon and curse with every moment between the characters and the person you came up with #bryeth, #tarden along with other hastags that will probably appear in the future.

Finally, thanks to you, my dearest reader. I am humbled that you have read up to here, and I hope that you are ready for the unbound world that comes next.

Hugs,

Nina, also known as G.D

About the
Author

G.D. Roman is a passionate reader and writer. She currently lives with her husband and her Border Collie mix, Misti. During the day, she works as a teacher, but in the evenings, she works on her craft and spends time with her husband. As a child who has moved around, she finds herself more a c of the world than from one particular place. She loves to travel to see her family in Colombia and in Florida.

Books by G.D. Roman

The Bound Island Series
Bound Island (2023)
Book Two (October 2024)

More by
Midnight Tide
Publishing

See the full catalog at www.midnighttidepublishing.com

Of Flames and Curses by Whitney Spralding

Do fairies exist?

This is the question Lainey asks herself after her sister's brutal murder in Central Park. Armed with her sister's diary and the mysterious entries within, Lainey's quest for answers leads her to Phoenix, a surly but handsome fae. The answer to Lainey's question reveals a truth that will change everything she thought she knew about herself and the world she lives in. A sacrifice must be made to break a curse that locked the gate between the human and faerie realms. Leaving the only world she has known, Lainey finds herself surrounded by evil queens, curses, and magical creatures. Together, Lainey and Phoenix must find a way to break the curse that doesn't result in Lainey's death—like her sister's.

Do fairies exist? The answer will change Lainey's life in ways she never imagined.

The Last Daughter by Alexis L. Menard

She's cursed with a dead witch's power over fate, he's a heartless demigod born for revenge and redemption. Once her enemy, now a conflict of interest. The fate of the Nine Realms dangles on a dangerously thin thread. Fate was cruel enough by dealing Ailsa with a fatal illness. But when her father and sisters are killed at war, she becomes the Last Daughter in a long line of shield images. This power comes with a price, however, coincidentally, getting her kidnapped by an elfin she's only heard of through legends.

Vali's realm is dying, inflicted by the black magic, sedir, and the only way to heal his land is by delivering the Tether to Odin, king of the gods. When he finds this power bound inside a mortal woman, he is forced to bring her and her shapeshifting wolven back to his home in Alfheim.

But their journey across the Tree of Life is perilous, and betrayal is imminent. Vali and Ailsa must depend on each other for survival, a mutual dependency that turns into a passionate love affair. With Odin waiting on this promised power, a kindred spirit found in her enemy, and a dark threat neither Ailsa nor Vali intended to find in the bright lands of Alfheim, what started as a simple quest has turned into a fight to save all gods, mortals, and fae alike. Vikings meet magic in this fresh retelling of Norse Mythology.